STRAY MAGIC

STRAY MAGIC

A Strays Novel

KELLY MEDING

HARPER
VOYAGER
IMPULSE

An Imprint of HarperCollins*Publishers*

STRAY MAGIC. Copyright © 2018 by Kelly Meding. All rights reserved. Printed in the United States of America. No part of this book may be used or reproduced in any manner whatsoever without written permission except in the case of brief quotations embodied in critical articles and reviews. For information, address Harper-Collins Publishers, 195 Broadway, New York, NY 10007.

Digital Edition JUNE 2018 ISBN: 978-0-06-284767-6

Print Edition ISBN: 978-0-06-284768-3

Cover Photographs © Jamie Carroll/ iStock /Getty images (Woman) © Straight 8 Photography/ Shutterstock (Badge); © Biker Nut / Shutterstock (Background)

Harper Voyager, the Harper Voyager logo, and Harper Voyager Impulse are trademarks of HarperCollins Publishers.

HarperCollins is a registered trademark of HarperCollins Publishers in the United States of America and other countries.

FIRST EDITION

18 19 20 21 22   HDC   10 9 8 7 6 5 4 3 2 1

STRAY MAGIC

CHAPTER 1

After a four-day stakeout in Arizona that resulted in the arrest of two traveling tooth peddlers and the confiscation of sixteen sets of gremlin teeth—apparently worth a small fortune with the right black magic buyer—there was nothing better than coming home to a hot, naked man in my bed. Specifically, hot, naked Vincent Ortiz, the man I'd been seeing for the last nine months.

And I knew he was naked under the sheets, because when I'd called him two hours ago with my ETA, I told him to be naked. A girl has needs, after all.

I put my gun in the dresser drawer and shut it with a loud enough thud to stir Vincent from his nap. It was after midnight, and he'd arranged to have the day off tomorrow, so we could spend it together. Post-stakeout, I got at least three days off and

I planned to enjoy every second of those seventy-two hours.

"Hey, Shiloh," Vincent said in his lightly accented voice. "Didn't mean to fall asleep."

"No worries." I tugged my shirt off and tossed it carelessly to the floor. "Just don't plan on going back to sleep for a while."

He pulled the sheet back, displaying the excellence of his naked body—chiseled abs and arms from long days working construction, black hair shorn short, lickable caramel skin. My heart pitter-pattered the same way it had the first time I saw him at the diner here in town. And what I'd meant to be a one-night stand had turned into . . . this. Him waiting for me to come home after a long assignment.

Vincent scooted to the edge of the bed. Tugged me closer by my belt loops and kissed my stomach. "Wouldn't dream of going back to sleep, sweetheart. I've missed you."

"Ditto."

"Oh yeah? Show me."

My djinn half responded immediately to that challenge and I tackled him to the mattress. Our first kiss became a bit of a wrestling match, because I was actually stronger than Vincent. He didn't know it, because he thought I was completely human, so it became a game to let him win. For him to get me naked and on my back so he could slide inside.

For me to roll us so I could control the fuck.

Sex with Vincent was always like this. Fast, fun, and just a little bit of a fight. I liked having someone who challenged me, instead of treating me like I was fragile. Someone who touched all the right places, but only after I made him earn it. Someone who always gave me one hell of an orgasm before—

My cell rang with the most annoying ring tone possible in that moment: Work.

"No fucking way," I said as I stopped moving. "I just got home."

Vincent squeezed my hips, his construction-calloused hands somehow the perfect balance of rough and comforting against my skin. I shivered as a thrill shot through me. "Don't answer it, Shi."

I didn't. Whoever it was could leave a blessed message. I was off the clock and way too busy at the moment. I ground against Vincent, and he groaned. The phone finally went silent . . . only to start ringing again five seconds later.

Vincent groaned again, but this time in disappointment, and stilled, his hands falling away from my body. "Just answer the fucking thing."

"I will murder whoever is on the other end of the phone." I very reluctantly climbed off Vincent and retrieved the stupid phone from my jeans. "This had better be good, whoever this is."

"A bunch of vampires are holding a trailer park hostage."

I nearly dropped my phone. While it wasn't the

strangest phone call I've ever gotten in the middle of the night, it certainly ranked in the top five. And if the voice on the other end of the line wasn't from Novak, our team's third-in-command, I'd have accused the caller of playing a sick 2:00 a.m. joke. But as a disgraced incubus, Novak's rare displays of humor leaned toward the bawdy side. Hostage-taking vampires just wasn't his style.

"Which trailer park?" I asked as though the taking of small communities was an everyday occurrence. I padded across the room and yanked open a dresser drawer, knowing without saying that my time off—my time with *Vincent*—was officially revoked.

"Little place called Myrtle's Acres."

"Am I supposed to have heard of it?"

Novak snorted in my ear. "I'm surprised the vamps heard of it. Forty-six trailers, rough population of a hundred and twenty people, in the middle of No-where, Delaware, surrounded by forest and two cornfields of all blessed things."

"And they've got the whole trailer park?"

"Surrounded and locked down. It's blessing unreal."

Years of practice made the act of putting on pant-ies and jeans one-handed relatively easy. The bra was going to be harder. So far, Vincent hadn't com-mented. He accepted my job as a US Marshal in the Paranormal Investigations Unit and the odd hours I kept, and I appreciated him for not asking questions I couldn't answer. Questions about the creatures I encountered on a daily basis, the methods we used to trap the nasties, the lengths we'd go to save the nice ones, and most importantly, why I was part of it.

In the nine months Vincent and I had been together, the whole "my father was an earth djinn and I inherited some of his powers" conversation hadn't been broached. Even though we'd been intimate in both the hold-my-hair-while-I-barf way, and in the much more exciting lick-me-until-I-scream way, I wanted to keep my parentage under wraps as long as possible. It had a nasty habit of being used against me when people found out I could grant wishes.

"Shiloh?"

I snapped back to the phone. Had Novak been talking? "What?"

"I said how long before you can be at the crux?"

"I'm almost dressed, so fifteen minutes. I'll call you when I'm there."

"'Kay."

I hung up, tucked the phone into my jeans pocket, and finished dressing. Green lace camisole under a fitted black jacket. Over the jeans, it seemed a little dressy, but our unit boss Julius Almeida never stood on formality. He cared more about how we did our jobs than what we wore while we did it. Plus the jacket hid my shoulder holster and gun, its clip filled with standard issue silver-jacket bullets.

"Real estate problems?" Vincent asked.

"That's an understatement," I replied, wishing like hell I could jump back into bed and finished what we'd started, but I'd told Novak fifteen minutes.

As though he'd read my mind, a frown turned down the corners of his mouth. "You just got back. Literally. We were supposed to have all day tomorrow, Shi. I took a vacation day and everything."

"I know, babe." I sat on the corner of the bed to zip up my mid-calf boots, taking care to adjust the slim knives tucked into several hidden spots. Done with that, I circled to him and leaned down to plant a kiss on his mouth. "I'll make it up to you when I get back."

"As usual."

I pulled back, surprised by the dismissive tone. "Vincent, I'm sorry."

"I know." His expression and tone remained frustratingly neutral.

Okay, I really didn't have the time nor the inclination to fight. Had I inadvertently released my pheromone last night? It had been years since I'd lost control of the Quarrel—another gift from my djinn father besides wishing. Earth djinn are known for their ability to affect the combative nature of humans, often causing arguments when none should exist. I hadn't realized I could do it until I was ten years old. My parents had taken me to a Phillies game and a small riot broke out over a home run ball I'd really wanted to catch and didn't. Two years of practice with my dad taught me to control the Quarrel and only use it on command. It hadn't stopped me from carrying the guilt of their divorce when I was eleven, though, always wondering if my powers had caused it.

I only lost control when my emotions ran too high on the negative side. Tonight's sexual escapades with Vincent had been a supreme leap from negative (definitely within the realm of lick-me-until-I-scream), so I couldn't have affected him. So why the hell was he so argumentative?

"They wouldn't have called us in early if it wasn't important," I said. As a defense, it was pretty weak. Other government agencies had shadow groups who dealt with paranormal-based problems, but the Marshals' Office had been the public face and official law enforcement of paranormal issues for the last forty years (and handling them quietly long before that).

"I said I know."

"You sound angry."

Vincent scrubbed his hands over his face, accentuating the growth of black beard he needed to shave. "I'm just tired, Shi. Stress at work. Don't mind me."

He hadn't mentioned stress at work, but I hadn't really given him time to chat before I pounced. Our relationship was pretty casual and, even though I found myself missing him while on assignment, I preferred it stayed that way. Except he looked pretty down about our aborted sex-capades. Maybe he'd needed something from me tonight besides a hot fuck.

Or at least in addition to it.

"What's wrong?" I asked.

Thank Iblis, he interpreted that as the rhetorical question it was. "Nothing, baby. Like I said, tired. Go save your town."

He tilted his head. I took it as permission and caught him in another kiss. He returned this one, opening for me and tracing the tip of his tongue along the seam of my lips. I adored the taste of him and the shape of his mouth, and allowed myself a few extra seconds to worship both. I broke the kiss with regret.

"Gotta go, babe," I said.

"Be safe, okay?"

"Always."

I turned and strode to the bedroom door. As I stepped into the hallway, a glance over my shoulder showed he'd curled back up on his side of the bed, back to me. An irrational urge to ignore my summons and curl up next to him lasted the space of three breaths.

Maybe this trailer park hostage crisis would sort itself out quickly and let me get back to him by dawn.

Yeah.

Right.

Ley lines are places where magical energies converge and run in invisible lines. Cruxes occur where these lines intersect. Usually it takes at least three crossing in one crux in order to provide enough magic output for anyone less powerful than a mage or full-blooded demon to sense and use. One of these special places existed half a mile from my apartment, in an alley behind a convenience store. I'd discovered it by accident four and a half years ago during an ill-advised chase of a robbery suspect I happened to catch trying to hold up said store. I had felt its magic the moment I stepped over the crux.

And now it was the only reason I was able to keep my apartment in Denton, Maryland, which was fifty miles north of our unit's headquarters. Even though Novak had been stripped of his incubus duties and banned from Hell, he had retained many of his powers, including teleportation. Not himself anymore—to his eternal consternation—but of others. As long as he had a crux to act as a battery, he could teleport me to his present location.

It wasn't entirely pleasant for me, but it allowed me to live where I wanted to live and still get to emergency situations that didn't allow for the time expense of driving. And as crappy as it was, it was still better than dealing with DC-area traffic.

In a big city, walking half a mile at two in the morning probably would have creeped me out, no matter my abilities. It's why I loved Denton, as I loved most of the smaller towns on the Eastern Shore. The vast majority of the population went to sleep after the evening news, casting the streets in quiet and shadows. The heels of my boots clicked softly on the sidewalk as I quick-strolled toward the convenience store. The few people in town who knew me by name knew I was a federal agent, but I didn't need to draw extra attention from any potential prying eyes by running.

Orange streetlights made the night glow with an ethereal quality I always found calming. More so tonight, with the almost-argument I'd had with Vincent still ringing in my head. I needed to stay focused so I didn't accidentally release the Quarrel and cause more problems. Vampires were immune to djinn powers, but any other local human law enforcement we met there wouldn't be.

The silent convenience store came into view. I turned off the sidewalk, crossed the parking lot and gas pumps, and slipped into the shadows behind the squat building. The rank odors of the garbage container soured my stomach. Couldn't the crux have been created somewhere less stinky, like the middle of a bakery?

Just the thought of warm, gooey chocolate chip cookies reminded me that I hadn't eaten since dinner's grilled steak and salad. Maybe Jaxon would save me with his seemingly ever-present supply of snacks. He was always eating something—a side effect, he said, of skin-walker shifting.

I felt the buzz of the crux the moment I passed the first ley line. I pulled my cell and texted Novak that I was there before I got to the crux—the magic played games with cell reception, even with our hyper-stylized phones—then stepped onto the heart of power. Its strength flared to life inside of me like a current of electricity. The tiny hairs on my arms stood on end. Everything smelled crisper, keener. I closed my eyes and waited.

Novak called to me a second later. I heard his voice in my head, a distant bass as seductive as any fully powered incubus. It caressed my mind, my heart, and my body, and it sent a flare of arousal straight between my thighs—the part of this I hated. Incubi are seducers and their power lies within their ability to arouse and claim you. In order to teleport me to him, I had to want him. It was god-awful embarrassing to arrive on-scene like that, even if no one except my teammates knew.

And you can bet that none of my male teammates liked to be teleported by Novak for that very reason. The first time it happened to Jaxon, I gave him grief for a month. It's the only thing that kept us all sane about it—the fact that we all had to go through it, and we all gave each other shit.

Intense heat surrounded me, followed by the sensation of falling. The trip lasted only a few seconds, and then I was blinking against the bright lights of our headquarters' conference room. I rubbed my eyes, giving myself a moment for the arousal to fade away. It didn't help that I'd already been halfway to an orgasm less than twenty minutes ago.

"Morning, Shi," Jaxon Dearborn said, an unexpected voice somewhere behind me.

I spun around. He was lounging in one of the wheeled, leather chairs that surrounded the long, oak dining table that took up half of the conference room's space. A quarter of the remaining space was K.I.M.'s setup—the very expensive, very unique Knowledge Interface Matrix computer system connecting our headquarters to the West Coast unit's HQ, as well as our phones. Invented for us by a penitent Mammon (demon of greed, for those following along at home) in lieu of banishing him back to Hell, K.I.M. was worth as much as Luxembourg, and she allowed our network to operate as efficiently as it did.

The two Paranormal Investigation Units had officially formed six years ago—thanks to Julius and a few well-placed friends—on the argument that unique abilities were needed to handle other unique abilities. We had practically no oversight from the Department of Justice as long we as kept paranormal-related violence under control and under wraps.

The notoriety of the Para-Marshals gave us an edge over those shadow teams—not in effectiveness, necessarily, but in recruiting and keeping powerful new members of the team. Someone would ask questions if one of us disappeared; same can't be said for the shadow groups. No one in the federal government or human police forces could do what we did with the same efficiency. None of the shadow agencies would get involved in a case so public.

Our units also thrived on secrecy, which was why our headquarters was a renovated, two-story house, set at the end of an otherwise empty cul-de-sac near the very small town of Hebron, Maryland. The Department of Justice had quietly bought out all of the other owners, demolished every house except this one, and added a bunch of security features that kept pretty much everyone from spying on us. It also kept K.I.M. undetectable to computer hackers, telekinetics, and electrically inclined demon infestations.

Bad guys can't attack what they can't find.

The conference room was the dining room and living room areas combined, with only a small jut of wall separating the two. Most of the other downstairs rooms were for storage of weapons and research items, with three bedrooms upstairs sleep-ready, but Jaxon was the only person on the team who lived here full-time. I'd never asked his reasons for moving in here, and he never offered them. They likely had to do with his life prior to being kidnapped and held captive for six months by a magic abuser. Whatever life he'd been taken from, he was in no hurry to return to it.

His rescue from the magic abuser was the event that had sparked the creation of the Para-Marshals. It also brought me, Julius, and Jaxon into each other's orbits. Sometimes I think that was why Jaxon and

I could never make our attempt at a nonbusiness relationship work. I'd seen a very proud man at his lowest point, and he was always trying to prove himself to me. Chemistry and love aside, we became too toxic to each other to stay together.

Working well on our Para-Marshals team was too important to jeopardize by forcing the relationship to work.

Still—it didn't stop the occasional flutter in my chest when I looked at him, and my fading arousal from Vincent and Novak wasn't helping matters.

Jaxon possessed the sort of exuberant personality that attracted people like moths to light and made it impossible to stay angry with him. He wasn't handsome— his eyes were set too close, his nose was a little too long for his short face, and he constantly dyed his hair too blond for his coloring—but his wide, easygoing smile made you forget that right away. Hazel eyes always sparkled with mischief, and his laughter was infectious. His smile and laugh were what had attracted me to him in the first place.

When I'd asked him once what had first attracted him to me, he had gotten very quiet, very serious. Then he said, "You have a fabulous ass."

I'd smacked him upside the head for that.

Looking at Jaxon, no one would ever guess he could turn into a two-hundred-pound, seven-point stag.

"You just roll out of bed?" Jaxon asked. He tossed back a palm full of dry-roasted peanuts from a can in his lap, relaxed like this was a friendly visit and not work related.

"Why, do I have bed-head?" I raked one hand through my thick, brown-black hair, seeking tangles and finding none. It hung a few inches past my shoulders and lived in a strange place between straight and wavy that required little in the way of product management. A brush and a blow-dryer were my only styling tools.

He swallowed his nuts and grinned. "Nope, but you've got a hickey on your neck that looks fresh and you didn't bother covering it with makeup."

I clenched my fingers to keep from touching my throat. This day kept getting worse. I made myself feel better by flipping him off with no real ire in the gesture.

I sensed Novak entering the room before he asked, "You and Vincent must have had quite an evening."

I turned to face him, crossing my arms over my chest, suddenly wishing I'd taken five minutes for a quick shower. The former incubus could smell sex on a person, and judging by the flare of his nostrils and wide eyes, he smelled more on me than just the slight arousal that had teleported me here.

Novak lived close by, although I'd never been invited to his house—okay by me, because I had no desire to invite him into mine. He was an effective teammate, but that's all he was to me. Sure, he was built like a professional linebacker—six-feet-two of thick muscles and smooth ebony skin he liked showing off beneath an ever-changing wardrobe of designer jeans and tight t-shirts. And unlike Jaxon, Novak was hot and he knew it—another incubus bonus feature. Also unlike Jaxon, Novak was scary when he smiled. Everything about Novak exuded sex and intent, even though he no longer hunted souls for Hell.

He may have been changed, but he was still an asshole.

Instead of letting Novak get to me, I tossed him a saucy grin and lied. "We did, actually, several times."

His jaw tightened.

"Are we it?" I asked.

"Kathleen will meet us there," Novak said.

"Julius here yet?" I asked Jaxon. Our leader lived a couple miles away in a bungalow he shared with half a dozen stray cats that he left food for a couple times a week.

"He's not answering his Raspberry," Jaxon replied. He was staring into the open can of peanuts, as if debating the merits of eating more. "I drove by his house, too, but he's not home."

A tiny knot of worry tightened my stomach. "That's not like him." The impromptu nature of our job necessitated keeping our specially-designed-from-stolen-technology cell phones with us at all times. Jaxon was the first one to start calling our phones by fruit names, mostly to annoy Novak, but eventually Raspberry stuck. We all kind of liked the pun.

What I didn't like was that in the six years I'd known Julius, he'd never been out of touch unless required by an assignment.

"No, it isn't," Novak said. "But he knows where the assignment is, and vampires holding humans hostage is too urgent a matter to waste time here." The statement held a small amount of challenge in it.

As second-in-command, I was currently the ranking member of the team. If I said to move out and hope Julius caught up later, they'd do it. I'd run ops before, just not on something quite as grand as this. The idea of heading negotiations with hostage-holding vampires without Julius at my side was daunting.

Daunting and a tiny bit terrifying.

But what choice did I have? A familiar whirring sound crept over the hum of computers and crunch of Jaxon's peanuts. The helicopter was warming up out back on what had once been a private tennis court. One of the nice things about working for the Marshals' Office was technology and transportation. Sometimes they needed us to get places fast. We even had a private jet on retainer at a small airport ten miles away.

"Let's go, then," I said. "And bring the peanuts."

The guys were weaponed-up and ready, so we made our way out the back door without any stops. The rear of the house had a long, white porch that looked out over an expansive lawn that Jaxon mowed once a week, regardless of the weather. Julius and I liked to tease him about grazing.

Fifty yards beyond it was a split-post fence and, just past it, the tennis court and our waiting custom helicopter. Its rotating blades created a gentle breeze that grew steadily louder as we walked across the lawn.

"Do we have details on this standoff?" I asked.

"Not a lot," Novak replied. "Mostly info on the trailer park itself. Whoever's in charge of the vamps hasn't made any demands yet, but they've cut off phone lines, cable, internet, and supposedly confiscated every cell phone and radio in town."

"This was planned." An obvious statement. No one commented. They knew I liked to think out loud. "Vamps don't like drawing attention to themselves, especially negative, so what the hell's got them pulling something like this?"

"Remind me to ask them when we see them."

Vampires have been known—truly known, not just as boogeymen to scare children—to the world at-large for the last sixty or so years, the second species to announce their presence to human beings (werewolves being the first). To say it didn't go over well is an understatement, but tempers and tensions had cooled considerably in the last couple of decades.

When we first learned about werewolves, it was eighty years ago as a publicity stunt during America's early involvement in World War II. They returned from the War among other revered heroes, and many, many myths were dispelled (the hunger for human flesh, for instance), and a few were proven true (such as the need to change under the full moon). In the golden post-War years, few seemed to mind them. Publicly. However, when vampires came out ten years later, things got ugly. The public could handle people who turned into wolves once a month and lived with their Pack, secluded from the bulk of society. They couldn't seem to handle the idea of bloodsuckers living next door, buying blood from willing donors, and generally proving that yes, some things really do go bump in the night. Not even assurances of the control Masters had over their lines, or the care taken in choosing and turning new vampires, seemed to assuage the bulk of folks—especially the religious ones.

Vampires were vilified. Then they were crucified—literally. Humans were killed in retaliation. It all came to a nasty head in Little Rock, Arkansas about forty years ago. Half the city burned down in the riot started by humans, fueled by hatred, and spread by malice. When it was finally over, the news networks took great delight in airing and re-airing footage of two vampires saving a family of six from a burning apartment building.

Seconds after ushering the family to safety, they were dusted by two local cops.

A lot's changed in forty years. Vampires keep to themselves, many returning to a life underground and out of the public eye. Every state with a werewolf Pack was granted several thousand acres of protected land, and many werewolves went to live there. Some stayed in cities, but were still subject to Pack laws and the call of their Alpha. The Para-Marshals were there to deal with the occasional issue stemming from non-Pack werewolves, and to handle the things no one else could explain—the species humans didn't know existed right beneath their noses.

Like me.

After all that, no other magical race I've met will come clean again. If human beings got so lathered up over vampires, discovering the existence of demons would signal the end of days.

Right now, though, I needed to figure out how to end our current predicament with the vampires without bloodshed on either side.

We stopped talking as we neared the fence and the roar of the helicopter took over. After we strapped into our seats, I pulled out my Raspberry and sent K.I.M. a request for the layout of Myrtle's Acres.

One hundred and twenty was our rough hostage

count, give or take folks out of town for whatever reason. It was a stereotypical trailer park, with one road in that split left and right at the entrance. Four rows of trailers at least thirty years old lined the two streets, small parking lots every two trailers, and lots of tall trees and shrubs, which made getting aerial satellite shots difficult. It was a half mile deep, and about a quarter mile wide, with thick forest on all three sides. A cornfield marked the fourth side, opposite the country road leading to Myrtle's Acres. The flat land gave us no tactical advantage. No single trailer in the park was large enough to hold everyone, so the hostages were divided, likely in the two central rows of trailers.

Our only advantage lay in our adversaries. Contrary to popular myth, vampires don't fall "dead" during the day. They are, however, nocturnal creatures and therefore weaker during daylight hours. Not to mention sunlight-adverse. No one had invented an SPF-400 yet, so vamps still had to avoid direct sunlight if they were out and about after sunrise. If the vampire hostage-takers were standing guard in the open, they'd be weaker in roughly three and a half hours.

I snacked on Jaxon's peanuts and tried Julius's cell phone three more times during our thirty-minute flight. Straight to voice mail each time, with no response to my texts or pages. Each attempt raised my anxiety level a notch. We were running close to an hour without word from our leader, which wasn't SOP. Novak and Jaxon reflected my tension in their stiff postures and stony silence.

We had our pilot do a flyover of the trailer park. It was almost perfectly dark, every light source extinguished, individual trailers barely visible in the glow of the crescent moon and reflection of the state patrol's base camp. They had set up roadblocks on the country road, and were set up at the west end. Two patrol cars were parked on the east side, the patrolmen sitting quietly. Nothing moved below. It was . . . peaceful.

Early April in corn country meant the fields were still being turned and fertilized. Instead of landing on a bed of green stalks, the helicopter set down on dark brown earth that reeked of animal shit. The heavy, rotting odor turned my stomach.

"That's just disgusting," Jaxon said. Novak climbed out last and concurred with the assessment by coughing loudly.

We didn't linger, running across the field at a diagonal from the trailer park, leaving the pilot behind to power down the helicopter. He'd stay there until we needed him, like a good little soldier. The state patrol had three cars and an ambulance huddled by the western roadblock, about thirty yards from the entrance. Battery-operated floodlights provided daylight-strength illumination. Six patrolmen and two EMTs were waiting for us, along with a familiar blonde.

Kathleen Allard frowned as we got closer, her wide green eyes narrowing. She looked like an angry ghost beneath those glaring lights, harsh against her pale skin. Even though our resident dhampir looked twenty-one, she was closer to sixty years old. She wasn't immortal like her vampire father had been, but she would live a very long time thanks to his genetic legacy.

"Where's Julius?" she asked. She still carried hints of the French accent she'd acquired during her childhood, but her clothes betrayed a newfound love of everything Seattle-grunge. She didn't seem to mind she'd missed the fashion statement by at least two decades.

"MIA," Novak said. "Shi's got point on this."

"Lovely."

I rolled my eyes. Not my fault I was thirty years younger and still outranked her. "Who's in charge of the locals?" I asked.

"Lieutenant Foster, the one with the handlebar mustache," Kathleen said, pointing.

The patrolman in question was nearly as bear-sized as Novak. His red mustache matched the thick, auburn hair on his head and the smattering of freckles on his nose and cheeks. He approached us with a question in his eyes and disdain on his face. It was a look we received often from law enforcement unhappy to turn control of a situation over to our agency—even if they knew they were out of their league. Lieutenant Foster seemed to be no exception.

"Shiloh Harrison, Para-Marshal's Office," I said, extending my hand.

Foster had a strong grip as he shook. "Lieutenant Abraham Foster. Thanks for coming out, Marshal Harrison."

"How could I resist? It's not every day vampires take a trailer park hostage." I smiled, trying to put him at ease. Being known and semi-common in most states doesn't stop regular folks from fearing vampires.

Foster's expression didn't change, though, so I hunkered down to business. "Any idea what the numbers on our vampires are?" I asked.

"Only three have made themselves visible," he replied, "but they'd need more to watch so many people."

"That depends on the age and abilities of the vampires involved," Kathleen said. "Many Master vampires possess psychic abilities."

Foster's eyes widened. Yeah, this guy was going to be a treat.

"What about communication?" I asked, cutting off whatever the next thing he was going to say. "Our intel says they'd cut all landlines. Have they made contact?"

"Not since the first phone call telling us about the takeover, no," he said. "I've got people in the woods, keeping a perimeter of fifty feet from the property line. They've seen their eyes in the distance, so we know the vampires are watching us, too."

Vampires maintain the same eye color as in their previous life, but when a vamp is angry or hungry, they glow red. A scary, bloodred. I've heard they flash blue and green for other emotions, but my interaction was limited to pissed vamps or calm, colorless vamps. Even as a half vampire, Kathleen could control her color-change and used it to great effect when it suited her.

"They have to know we'd be called in," Novak said.

I was counting on it.

A man's disembodied voice shot through my head like an iron spike, sharp and agonizing. I stumbled under the strength of it. Someone caught my elbow and steadied me.

"Shi? You okay?" Jaxon was in my face, his hazel eyes reflecting silver in the glare of the floodlights. Eyeshine gone wild.

"You didn't hear that?" I asked. With my bearings back, I gently pulled my elbow out of his bruising grip.

"Hear what?"

They only hear me if I wish it. More thunder in my head. Colorful spots danced in front of my eyes. "Stop that!" I shouted. "Get out of my head!"

It pissed me off, being violated like that. And that "if I wish it" line wasn't funny, either.

My teammates stared at me curiously, but Foster

just looked terrified. I shouldered past them and stalked toward the barricade of patrol cars. A pale line of tiki torches and a nauseatingly retro Myrtle's Acres sign loomed in front of me, flanked by a wall of monstrous shadows. From the darkness near the sign, a figure emerged.

He stood in the middle of the road, long hair glinting in the meager moonlight, first white-blond, then black, then auburn. It never seemed to settle on one shade. Shadows cast sharp angles on his pale face, and even from a distance I could tell he was handsome.

Behind me, the sound of leather creaking and snaps popping caught my attention. The patrolmen were reaching for their weapons.

"No one draws on him," I said sharply.

Come halfway so we may speak more comfortably.

If he didn't stop doing that, my brain was going to liquefy and leak out of my ears. I licked dry lips. "Novak, I'm going out to talk to him." I then called his Raspberry, turned it on to speaker, and put it in my pocket. At least they'd be able to listen in.

"Do not turn your back on him," Kathleen said, her voice holding a small amount of awe—not directed at me. "But do not meet his eyes until he gives you his name. To do so before is a challenge. I can sense him from here, Shiloh. He's powerful."

"Yeah, the booming voice in my head sort of clued me in." My sharp retort rolled right off her.

"Be careful, Shi," Jaxon said.

"As careful as I can."

I inhaled deeply, held it, then started walking on the exhale. Tension at my boss's absence was compounded by the sight in front of me. A Master vampire was walking toward me on a dark street, his long cloak swirling around him like a storm cloud. He could be hiding an arsenal beneath that thing. Vampire mind control doesn't work on djinn, and our blood is distasteful to them, but I could still be shot or stabbed if he got twitchy.

Step by step, we drew closer and I began to sense the power Kathleen had already warned me about. It sizzled and popped like water meeting hot grease and made me strangely giddy. I struggled to keep calm when the djinn half of me demanded I turn and flee. Our kinds do not get along. At all. It made me wonder: Was he in my head just to torment me?

As requested, we met halfway, each stopping an arm's reach from the other. He was even more handsome up close, as the sharp lines of his jaw and chin came into focus. His color-changing hair hung perfectly straight to mid-back, further paling his porcelain complexion. Upon closer inspection, I realized his hair wasn't changing color, it actually was multicolored—every imaginable shade of brown, black, red, copper, gold, blond, silver, and white separating the individual strands. If it was a dye job, it had taken days to affect, but something told me it was natural. Or naturally occurring via magic.

The effect was ethereal, mesmerizing.

Kathleen's warning came back, and I halted my appraisal at his straight slash of a nose, careful not to meet his eyes.

"My apologies for causing you such pain," he said. Now that it wasn't blasting through my head, his voice betrayed a pedigree of age and European origin.

"Apology accepted."

We stood in perfect silence for a full minute. I fought against fidgeting. It would be seen as a weakness, as would speaking first. He'd invited me out to this thing. He had to do the talking.

"Thank you for speaking with me," he finally said. "My name is Woodrow Tennyson."

"Shiloh Harrison." I raised my gaze, half expecting to see blazing red eyes staring back at me. All I saw was a pale blue glow that hid his true eye color. At least he wasn't angry . . . or hungry. "You made it difficult to stay away, Mr. Tennyson."

"Of course. The theatrics were regrettable, though necessary to gain your cooperation."

"Is that what this is about? You hold hostages and then what? What do you want?"

"You're direct, Ms. Harrison, I like that. Humans are still so afraid of us. Lieutenant Foster would be pissing his pants if he'd come in your stead."

I couldn't argue with that assessment. "What do you want?" I repeated.

His eyes changed, now glittering red, and with the solemnity of a eulogizing minister, he said, "One million dollars and safe passage to the tropical country of my choice."

I stared.

CHAPTER 2

Tennyson tilted his head back and laughed—a deep, mirthful sound I felt in my bones. His eyes were once again clear blue when he said, "Forgive me, Ms. Harrison, but is that not the stock answer you were expecting?"

"This isn't a movie," I snapped back. "You think this is funny? How many crimes are going unchecked because of this circus you've created here?" First he shouted telepathic messages into my head, then he made fun of me. I was seriously hating this guy, Master or not.

"No, and I do apologize." He sobered immediately, all traces of humor gone. "I require the assistance of you and the Para-Marshals, although I must admit, I was informed that a gentleman led your team."

"He's busy." No sense in telling a vampire that our

leader was, in fact, missing. "You get to deal with me, instead."

"No hardship in that, I assure you."

I rolled my eyes. "If you needed our help, you could have called the office. Taking over a hundred people hostage isn't the best way to endear you to us."

"Securing your assistance was not my only purpose in orchestrating such a dramatic show of strength. You may not be aware that in the last six months, forty-six vampires and twenty-eight werewolves have disappeared."

"Is that unusual?" I asked, knowing full well it was. Vampire and werewolf societies, by sheer force of necessity, have been self-controlling and rigid in their governing laws for centuries. Masters and Alphas rule their respective people with iron fists and swift punishments—and those punishments include crimes against humans. The only exceptions were non-Pack-related werewolf crime, rogue vampires, or large-scale problems like today's little hostage crisis. Then we got called in.

Vampires and werewolves, despite their shared interest in maintaining a positive public image, simply do not get along with each other—understatement, really—so Tennyson bringing this information to me meant something larger was going on within their two species.

The little red sparkles returned to his eyes—interesting. As a Master he should have better control over his emotions. This situation had him truly upset. Unless he was doing it for effect, which was also possible. But the longer I stood there, the less I thought he was faking it.

"What do you know of vampire hierarchy?" he asked.

Less than I should know, if his tone of voice was any indication. Without showing him my obvious disadvantage, I squared my shoulders and said, "Why don't you tell me what you think is relevant to these disappearances?"

He smiled at my elusive response. "New vampires may only be made with permission from the maker's own sire and then, depending on the sire's strength, his sire before him. It prevents weakness in the line, as we are all . . ." He seemed uncertain of the word he needed. "Connected. By the sharing of blood required to turn a new vampire, we are connected to one another on a very basic level. As Master of the line, I am able to sense, however peripherally, the life force of all my vampires. Of the forty-six missing, eleventwelve are mine."

"And you can't sense them anymore?" His admission cemented something I'd long suspected about vampires. I knew permission was needed to create a new member of the line, but I hadn't known about the sensing thing. It had to be crowded in Tennyson's head.

"I cannot." A small amount of grief coated his

words. "I lost my sense of them over a three-day period of time last week. In my anger, I blamed a rival Master and we nearly warred over the dispute. Until I learned that he had also lost people, thirteen of his line."

"Same period of time?"

He shook his head. "Earlier that same week, before mine went missing."

"Any similarities between the missing vamps?"

"Similarities?"

"Yeah, like are they all new vamps? All redheads? All taken from one city? What?"

"Ah, I understand." He gazed at my face as he considered the question, those blue eyes still flecked with furious red. "They were all different in age and experience. Several of mine were turned in the last decade, most within the century. Two had been with me for nearly three hundred years."

Three hundred years. Looking at his sculpted beauty, he could have been thirty-five or forty, max. It was hard to imagine him having lived so long. I'd be super-fucking-pissed if anyone on my team disappeared or was killed, and I'd only been with them six years. I couldn't imagine three centuries of friendship.

"How many Masters have lost vamps?" I asked.

"The question is difficult to answer."

"Explain."

"I am Master of my line. However, once a vampire reaches a certain level of power, he is also a Master."

Oh good God, hierarchies made my head hurt. "Okay, so is there a Master above you? Your sire?"

"No, my own sire died long ago. There are, however, three Masters older than I, of separate lines, two of whom have lost vampires. One other Master, several decades younger than I, has lost as well."

"So four lines have lost vamps."

"Correct."

"What about the wolves?"

"Fourteen each from the Packs of Florida and California."

"Have you gone to the werewolves about this?"

He snorted, an inelegant sound. "My suspicions of a larger conspiracy were met with disdain from their Alphas."

"Doesn't surprise me."

"Does this mean you will assist me?"

I gave him my best intimidation glare. He cared about his people, that much was obvious. But I couldn't simply overlook this hostage stunt and run off to solve his mystery. "Like I said, you should have called the office with this. You still haven't given me a good reason for these theatrics. I should put a silver bullet in your heart and drag you in for threatening so many humans and disturbing the godsdamned peace."

He straightened his back, drawing up taller, more elegant in posture. "It was the only way I could think to protect my people from whoever is hunting us."

Something in his words tickled my instincts and

raised my hackles. I looked past him, at the shadows of the tree-filled trailer park and all of the secrets hiding within the darkness. The overwhelming sense of being watched sent gooseflesh creeping across my neck and chest.

"Mr. Tennyson," I said slowly, "how many vampires are in that trailer park?"

"Five hundred and four."

A strangled wheeze caught in my throat. "Five . . . holy . . . Is that your whole blessed line?"

"Yes, minus the twelve missing, my entire surviving line is now ensconced in your trailer park." With one hundred-plus walking, talking meals. He must have seen something in my face, because he added, "The inhabitants will not be harmed, Ms. Harrison. I give you my word. All of my children were informed to feed well before arrival, and provisions have been provided in case this drags out."

"Where the hell did you put them all?"

His mouth twitched. "Everywhere we could find room. Few are happy about the arrangements, but they agree with the measure. My people are now the hostages of your police officers, as much as the trailer park residents are hostages of mine. Whoever is taking vampires will have no opportunity to take from me again."

The faintest snarl was attached to his final statement, and I found myself sympathizing with Tennyson. The very idea would make my djinn father laugh his head off, right before he verbally smacked me around for it. Earth djinn were mostly harmless compared to other djinn, but he had the temper of his people. Djinn hate vampires. It's that simple.

"So let's make sure I'm understanding your intent," I said. "You want to leave your entire line here, with a hundred innocent human beings, surrounded by local police that will keep anyone from getting in or out of the park, until we figure out who's kidnapping vamps and wolves, and why?"

"Yes."

What would Julius do? It was my go-to question when faced with a situation I didn't know how to solve. Julius was levelheaded. Former Army Ranger. He'd consider the pros and cons of accepting this vampire's terms. He would make sure everyone's cards were on the table. Tennyson had promised no harm would come to the trailer park residents—no harm had a lot of interpretations.

"And if I say no?"

His thin eyebrows rose into almost comical arches. "Are you saying no?"

"I'm asking a question. Can you answer it, please?"

The red sparkles in his eyes coalesced until both orbs gleamed crimson, leaving no trace of the previous blue shade. They glowed like headlights. He drew back pale lips, revealing the tips of his gleaming fangs. Showing off the predator he was and could become at a moment's notice. He couldn't turn me, but those fangs could certainly rip my throat out faster than I could pull my weapon.

I didn't shrink back, didn't flinch, even though my stomach had twisted into painful knots.

"If you say no, Ms. Harrison, we will leave this town tonight. However, we will be taking forty-six with us to hold until those we have lost are returned to their Masters. And we will continue to do so for every further vampire who goes missing afterward. We will start, of course, with your mother."

The world went perfectly still. Voices rose up behind us, and I knew my team was reacting to his words. Probably waiting for me to haul off and shoot Tennyson for making a threat against my family. But I couldn't move. I had to force my lungs to suck in air, expel, suck in again.

"Don't make threats you can't carry out," I said, "or you're going to piss me off."

"I make no threats, Ms. Harrison, only promises." Tennyson's voice was as cold as winter. "I find no joy in this, do you understand that? My people are being taken, not murdered. Taken, and for what purpose I can only guess. You love your mother, I see it in your anger. Imagine if twelve people you loved were taken. Would you not do anything to seek justice?"

"You ask me that while threatening someone I love?"

"Djinn are emotional creatures, and while you are only half-blooded, you do carry that trait. You are more honest in your anger than most humans in their calm."

If my surprise at his statement showed on my face, he didn't react to it. How on earth did he know—

"I can smell your blood, Ms. Harrison," he said, as if reading my mind. Maybe he was. Bastard.

"So you get me mad, get me honest, and then secure my help through blackmail. Good plan."

"I do what I must to protect my own."

"Me, too. And part of my own is all those innocent people in there. So keep that in mind."

"Oh, I do. As I said, nothing will happen to them . . . unless."

"And as I said, that 'unless' is not exactly the assurance I'm looking for."

"Then maybe you should do your job and make sure it never comes to that."

What.

An.

Arrogant.

Jerk.

Yet, even as he said it, I realized what a bind I was in. And the more I thought about his situation, I found myself struggling with the notion of him loving each of his vampires the way a daughter loves her mother. The way a father loves his children.

Crap.

"Look, I'll talk to my team and see what we can arrange."

"Thank you."

"Thank me later." I took a half step forward, hands bunched into fists. "And if you or any vampire you know comes after my family, I *will* make it my business to ensure the Master who ranks below you gets a promotion."

Tennyson threw back his head and bellowed laughter, the same musical sound from our introduction. His eyes lost the red glow and regained their icy blue sheen. "You do not fear me, Shiloh Harrison. This will prove a fascinating partnership."

Frustrating partnership sounded a lot more accurate. "Hang out, I'll be back."

I started to turn around, then remembered what Kathleen said about giving him my back. So I shuffled sideways a good ten feet, until he bowed at the waist. I took it as a dismissal and quick-stepped it back to the barricade.

"You heard everything, right?" I asked as the team, plus Lieutenant Foster, surrounded me.

"This is one for the books," Novak said. "Weirdest blessed situation I've seen in decades."

Kathleen's eyes glittered red as she asked, "Are you seriously going to help him?"

"We *are* helping him, yes," I said.

"But he's taken an entire community hostage. He's a terrorist."

"He's *scared*. And I don't blame him. I admit, his methods are pretty fucked-up, but he's trying to protect his family, widespread and bloodthirsty though it is. That's an awful lot of vampires and werewolves to go missing over a short period of time, which means they're either being hunted or captured." I didn't think they were being hunted, though, and Jaxon agreed.

"There are no bodies," he said, shaking his head. "Capture sounds more likely."

"Capture for what and by whom?" Kathleen asked.

"That's what Tennyson wants us to find out," I said. "Julius would make the deal."

"Should we run this past Weller first?" Jaxon asked.

Adam Weller led the West Coast Para-Marshal unit, and he held the same seniority as Julius. I'd spoken to the man on the phone a handful of times, and met him in person once. Someone higher up than me trusted him enough to put him in charge, but Weller wasn't my unit leader. I didn't know or trust him like I trusted Julius.

"I'm fine with copying him on the decision," I replied, "but as team second, I don't need his permission to act."

Jaxon nodded.

Even after saying that, though, I glanced at Novak and Kathleen. This wasn't a vote, but their support— or lack thereof—would either see this through or stop whatever we did next dead in its tracks. With a small sense of relief, I saw agreement in both their eyes. "Good. We get some marshals out here to back up the state troopers who are watching the town and make sure they understand no one goes in or out.

Tennyson seems to know what's going on with the missing vampires, so we'll need to contact the Florida and California Pack Alphas. See what their wolves had in common."

"Speaking of Julius," Novak said, "we checked with K.I.M. while you were chatting with the vampire. He's not reported in since yesterday, noontime, and the office insists he's not on assignment."

Noontime. Our boss had been off the grid for close to sixteen hours.

"The timing of his disappearance is unsettling," Kathleen said.

"To say the least," I said.

"The vampire threatened your mother," Jaxon said in a tone colder than I'd ever heard. He adored my mom, and she still occasionally fussed at me for our breakup. "Could he be the reason Julius is missing? An ace up his sleeve?"

"It's crossed my mind."

"But?"

I held my hand up for silence and used the other to palm and dial my phone. It rang and rang, so long I felt a cold nugget of worry settle in the pit of my stomach. Then it connected, and a sleep-heavy voice asked, "Yes, hello?"

"Mom?" Instant relief at the sound of her voice released a surge of adrenaline.

"Shi, sweetheart? It's almost four in the morning, what's wrong?"

"Nothing, I just . . . needed to hear your voice." Close enough to the truth without being a lie. "Sorry I woke you."

"Are you working?"

"Yeah, go back to sleep. I'll call you when I can."

"All right. Be careful." Her ability to accept my call and subsequent dismissal without arguing or showing a hint of annoyance was a testament to how normal such a thing had become. Born to gypsies and raised by djinn, my mother has a very unique perspective on "strange."

I hung up and slipped the phone back into my pocket.

Novak fixed me with one of his patented glares. "Feel better now?"

"No, but I'm pretty convinced Tennyson has nothing to do with Julius being MIA. If Tennyson wanted that kind of leverage, he'd have used Julius against us, not threatened to kidnap my mother."

"I agree," Kathleen said. "He is a Master vampire, he has no need to hide his intentions. If he meant to use Julius, we would be aware of his captivity."

"And it's not as though Julius has some sort of useful ability," Jaxon said. Our boss—a man who led a team comprised of a half djinn, a fallen incubus, a skin-walker, and a dhampir—was completely human. He had twenty years of combat experience and full working knowledge of most known paranormals, sure, but still human.

"No, but Tennyson does have enemies," I said, recalling part of my conversation with him. The fellow Master he'd accused of hunting his people was on my list, but not at the top. That Master—I needed to get a name—had lost vampires, too. It had to be someone else who didn't want us helping Tennyson.

"We need to be absolutely certain Julius was taken against his will," Kathleen said. "At present we are merely guessing."

"We've got some pretty damning evidence," Jaxon said.

"But we do need to be certain," I said. "Kathleen and I are going back to check his house. Jaxon and Novak, I want you to collect Tennyson—"

"I do not need to be collected," the vamp in question said. Every one of us jumped and jerked, startled by Tennyson's sudden appearance within the circle. Jaxon had a silver blade out and within inches of Tennyson's neck before I could tell him to stop.

"Do not sneak up on us like that," I said.

"My apologies," Tennyson replied, taking a sideways step away from Jaxon's weapon. He wrinkled his nose at the glinting silver, then gave a half bow to our group. "Thank you for agreeing to this course of action."

I nodded. "You're trusting us with the fate of your entire line, and that's not a small thing. So many disappearing vamps and wolves isn't a coincidence." To Novak, I said, "Debrief him fully and feed the info to

K.I.M. We need names, dates, locations, everything he has on those who've been taken, so she can collate and give us any patterns."

Jaxon snorted softly. "You sure you want to use the word *debrief* around an incubus?"

The joke earned him a sour look from Tennyson, while Novak roared with laughter. "Vamp's got no clean soul to steal," the incubus in question said between guffaws. "Wouldn't be my type on or off the clock, anyway. I like a little tan on my meat."

Now that conjured up all kinds of mental images I didn't need. Not that Novak stole souls through sex anymore. Kicked out of Hell, remember? "Kathleen, let's go," I said. "And if anyone happens to hear from Julius . . . ?"

"We'll call," Jaxon said. "You meeting us back here?"

"Depends on what we find." We couldn't take Tennyson to our headquarters. Even with our security measures in place, he'd have too much access. With any luck, we'd get a lead in the meantime and meet elsewhere.

Kathleen and I broke from the group, heading back toward the helicopter. Halfway there, Tennyson's voice thundered through my head: *Watch your back.*

I had no reason to think he could hear me, but I mustered what I could and shot back a hearty: *Get out of my godsdamned head!*

His distant laughter rose above the strengthening whir of the helicopter's blades.

CHAPTER 3

I fiddled with my phone for the bulk of our return trip, alternately checking for calls I hadn't missed and willing it to ring. I should have been more specific with the willing, because when it finally did ring six minutes from HQ, the caller wasn't the voice I wanted to hear.

"You back yet?" Novak asked, even though he had to hear the roar of the chopper.

"Nearly there. What do you have?"

Kathleen leaned closer to listen, her enhanced senses still probably straining to catch words in the noisy helicopter. I switched it to speaker mode for her benefit.

"Your pal Tennyson is strongly suggesting the other Masters are calling their lines together like he did," Novak said.

I frowned. "Strongly suggesting?"

"Some sort of honor code won't let him tattle on his friends, but he's not being subtle."

"Great, so should we expect a few more hostile trailer park takeovers in the near future?"

"Says he doesn't know their plans and he, in turn, didn't tell anyone what he was doing tonight. His own people only knew to meet in a field half a mile away, tonight at dusk, so it couldn't be leaked."

"Do you believe him?"

"He's a vampire." Novak said the last word as he might invoke a blasphemous curse. "He's built for deception, Shi."

"Yeah, and so are demons."

Silence. It was a familiar jab, part of our regular routine. Jaxon and I were the only people he tolerated making fun of his fallen incubus status, so I couldn't have hurt his feelings. Other voices crackled over his end of the line. The security lights around our HQ glittered to life over the tops of a hundred oaks, maples, and loblolly pines. Almost back.

"Novak?" I asked.

He let out a sharp breath. "The vampire seems sincere."

I could only imagine how much it pained him to admit such a thing. He'd surely prefer rolling naked on broken glass over paying Tennyson any sort of direct compliment. I almost hated not being there to witness the interaction.

"How's K.I.M. doing with our information?" I asked.

"Working through it as we give it to her. She's preparing a global map so we can see where all of the missing vamps and wolves came from, and where they were last seen. I'll send it to you when it's ready."

"Thanks. Look, we're landing. I'll call you if we find anything at Julius's house." I hung up and pocketed the phone.

We landed at HQ, and in under seven minutes, Kathleen was careening into Julius's driveway, slamming her foot down on the brakes of one of our "company cars." Kathleen had claimed this particular silver-blue, and she actually bared her fangs at anyone else who tried driving it. I was more comfortable behind the wheel of an Expedition, so I never objected to her possessiveness over the sports car. I only objected to her driving skills.

Julius lived in a small, quiet suburb, surrounded by identical Cape Cods with identical landscaping, and painted varying shades of tan. Still half an hour from sunrise, the neighborhood was asleep, windows dark of prying eyes. Even Julius's house looked put to bed, the potted plants on his front steps silent sentinels.

I unlocked the front door with the spare key our boss kept under one of his plants. Kathleen stepped into the foyer first, and I followed her in, my gun out and the safety off. Just in case. I gave her room to do her thing. Her eyes glowed faintly red as she drew on her finely tuned senses of smell and hearing.

She took three steps toward the staircase. Paused. Tilted her head a few degrees to the left. Her back was to me, her exact expression turned away. But I could imagine pursed lips, puckered brows—her favored look of intense concentration.

"I hear only our heartbeats within the house," she said after a few moments' pause. "Yours and mine. Jaxon's scent lingers on the porch but he didn't come inside."

Jaxon had mentioned driving by to check on Julius.

"Anyone else's scent?" I asked.

"Julius, of course." She veered to the left, through an archway and into the living room. Three matching leather armchairs and a love seat dominated the space, broken up by a few oak tables and brass floor lamps—typical bachelor furniture. Julius had once bragged about walking into a Furniture Emporium, pointing at one of their showrooms and telling them to wrap it all up. Looking at the watercolor prints on his walls and brown-on-beige color scheme, I believed him.

Through the living room, I trailed Kathleen past a hewn oak dining table and matching sideboard, and into the very modern kitchen. Chrome appliances, faux-marble countertops, and an overfilled hanging pot rack weren't the things that made my stomach quiver—it was the cloying odor of old soy sauce and spoiling spring rolls. Four open takeout cartons, a pair of soiled chopsticks, and a half-drunk bottle of beer decorated the center island.

Nothing else was out of place.

"That's not normal." I wasn't sure why I whispered, since Kathleen had verified we were alone. The house was utterly silent.

Kathleen leaned over the containers, food illuminated by the faint red glow of her eyes, and sniffed. Her nostrils flared. "I detect no toxins or drugging agents, but the food should be tested."

"Julius doesn't waste food like that."

"I know." She straightened, turning her headlights on me. "I still smell no one else in the house recently."

"Let's check upstairs."

We searched the second story—master bedroom and bath, second bath, two bedrooms, and a linen closet. All clean, no other scents. Nothing was broken or seemed missing, no sign of a struggle. The ancient army duffel Julius used on long-term assignments was neatly tucked in the closet.

"Garage," I said as we returned to the stairs. "Let's see if his car is here."

It was. I saw the long, finned shape of his 1956 Chevy in the dim glow of Kathleen's eyes before I flipped on the garage light. It sat right where Julius had last parked it, carefully waxed once a month, the only car he drove while off duty. He never left it in the driveway, choosing instead to keep it ensconced in the garage.

"This is truly puzzling," Kathleen said.

"You think?"

"It's possible Julius was called away on a personal emergency and picked up by someone else."

"An emergency so personal he couldn't bother picking up the phone and telling one of us?" I snorted loudly. "Sure, and it's just as possible monkeys are going to fly out of my butt."

She gave me a withering look. "The only other explanation is someone with practiced mind control compelled him to leave his home and go with them."

"Or do something else." My attention snagged on an object in the far corner of the garage—a freestanding, top-loading freezer. We'd all been to his house at one time or another, famished after a long case, and the first place we always stopped was this freezer. He kept it stocked with steaks, frozen meatballs, and pizzas. Stuff he liked and could keep stored, but still make quickly if the mood hit him. The sight of it sent a chill wiggling down my spine. Bile scorched the back of my throat as old memories clawed toward the surface.

Memories of the first dead body I'd ever seen, stuffed in an old refrigerator. I was eight.

"Shiloh?"

I stopped an arm's length from the freezer, my

hand extended toward the handle. It was irrational, thinking Julius was in the freezer, but I saw it clearly in my mind—the blue, frosted body of my boss folded next to an eight-pack of pork chops.

The body in that old refrigerator hadn't been frozen. He's been half-eaten, preserved in the sealed environment so I could tell he was just a teenager and had died with his eyes wide open. I'd had nightmares for two years.

My fingers found the freezer's handle. Stomach sloshing and hands trembling, I pulled up. The door hissed as I broke the seal. Cold air drifted up in a mist.

A sea of frosty meat products stared back at me, unaffected by the deep sigh I heaved. Or of the relieved tears stinging my eyes. I let the lid drop back down, and it fell with a resounding thud.

"Hungry?" Kathleen asked.

Ducking my head to hide my blush, I brushed past her mumbling "never mind." My refrigerator psychosis was my own, not shared with my team. We all had histories and past traumas, and they weren't things we bonded over with tequila shots.

Our searched concluded in the backyard with only questions to show for our time and trouble.

"Okay," I said as we rounded the east side of the house, heading back toward the driveway. "So who could do what you said? Who could get into a man's head and make him walk out of his house?"

"Human telepaths, obviously," Kathleen said. "A few witches have been known to possess a man's mind for brief periods. A demon—"

"Not a demon. Possession is violent, no matter the rider. We'd have seen signs of it somewhere in the house."

"All right then, not a demon rider. A siren's call?"

I almost laughed at the absurdity of her statement. "Do you see a body of water nearby?"

We rounded to the front of the house. Sunlight was slowly touching the eastern sky with a bright red paintbrush, making me wonder if we were in for rain later.

"There is one obvious choice," she said. With her hands in the pockets of her cargo pants and eyes no longer glowing red, she seemed younger. Uncomfortable. "We just came from someone who could do this."

I stopped in the middle of Julius's sod lawn, gripping my gun in one hand and clenching my other hand into an aching fist. "I thought we ruled out Tennyson."

"Yes, but not any other Master. Only four have lost vampires, and there are rumors of at least eight at a comparable level to the strongest of them. This could be part of a personal agenda. We may not wish to be stuck in the middle."

"Something tells me we're stuck now, no matter what."

"True."

I pinched the bridge of my nose. Another down-side of my strange, mixed heritage—adrenaline surges always ended in headaches. Their longevity depended on the strength of my adrenaline rush. This one had been relatively small. A particularly ter-rifying encounter with a manticore three years ago had ended with a two-day migraine.

"I'll inform Novak," Kathleen said quietly. She palmed her phone as she strode toward the car.

I loitered on the lawn a moment, urging the pres-sure between my eyes to go away and leave me alone. Hard to believe only six hours ago, I'd been in bed with my naked boyfriend, intent on some toe-curling sex. I drifted back to the not-quite-a-fight I'd had with Vincent. I wanted to call and make him tell me what was so stressful at work. I'd never wanted to do that before—call my boyfriend while in the middle of a case.

Keep it casual, Shi, keep it casual.

Kathleen's voice drifted over the lawn. I realized my Raspberry was in my hand, my thumb hovering. Vincent was number six on my speed dial. I could not let our relationship affect me like this at work. It was one of the reasons I rarely dated, and one of the biggest reasons I'd initially avoided Vincent's ad-vances. Relationships complicated things, especially when I couldn't tell him what I really was, or why I disappeared twenty days out of the month. He occasionally mentioned something about his construction work, but I couldn't tell him anything about my work. It left us unbalanced, in a way.

And this time I had disappeared on a bad note, and it bothered me . . . and *that* bothered me. I'd caused an avoidable quarrel with Vincent, and I couldn't blame it on my pheromone. Not this time.

Get it together, Shi.

Vincent later. Job now.

Kathleen waved; I jogged over.

"K.I.M. found no relevant patterns in the vampires taken," she reported, the phone still close to her ear. "However, she may have a pattern in the werewolves. They were not simply fourteen random wolves from each of the two Packs. They were all mated pairs."

I boggled that one for a moment. "Theories on why mated werewolves?"

Kathleen screwed her mouth and forehead into a disgusted face and translated the sounds from the other end of the line. "Novak's theory is reproductive testing, as only mated werewolves reproduce."

My expression mirrored hers. "That could explain the wolves being taken, sure, but the vampires?"

More translating: "The average age of the vampires taken is ninety-one. The youngest was six months turned, the eldest three hundred and eleven years as a vampire. If the interest is research, those forty-six will display a wide range of power and abilities."

Was that really possible? Someone was going around the country kidnapping werewolves and vampires for research subjects? Rumors of such things had floated around for decades. In the six years since the Para-Marshals were formed, our two Paranormal Investigations units had broken up at least a dozen operations—usually small-time criminals who were too dumb for the crimes they were attempting. Nothing on this scale.

Whoever was behind this had managed to mobilize an entire vampire line—out of fear. Fear and the instinct to protect his people.

It took a *lot* to scare a vampire.

And that scared me more than a little bit.

I plucked Kathleen's phone from her hand and barked, "Put Tennyson on the phone," to whomever she'd been speaking with.

The line crackled, then, "Yes, Ms. Harrison?"

His cold fury gave me the willies, even from fifty miles away. "Our boss is missing, just up and plucked out of his house like a phantom. How many vampires could make a man with twenty years of military training leave with them without a fight?"

"More than would make you comfortable," he replied. "Ask me what is truly on your mind."

"Fine—which Masters could do it?"

Kathleen's eyes widened. Tennyson's position and power intimidated her. Hell, it intimidated me, but I would never give a vampire the satisfaction of know-ing it. My dad would never forgive me for showing such a weakness.

If he was angered, though, Tennyson didn't sound it—or, at least, the chill in his voice didn't have an added edge as he said, "Not I, if that eases your mind at all. I could name three Masters with such an abil-ity, but protocol forbids it. Many in their lines, those with the most years, would also possess the ability in a more limited form."

"How do I bypass protocol and get those names from you?"

His laughter turned my willies into full-on chills that rocketed down my spine. Heaven and Hell, he needed to quit laughing. "You have little power to compel me into such a betrayal to my people, young djinn. However, I admire your forthright-ness."

He'd admire it better when I put a silver bullet in his heart. "Okay, try answering another question. Of these three Masters you can't name, would any of them have a reason to kidnap our boss?" Silence so complete I checked the phone display to make sure I hadn't disconnected. "Well?"

"Perhaps," he said slowly, drawing out the word. "I can tell you that of those three, only one has had his people taken."

"So far."

"Yes, so far." Kathleen whispered something to

me, which I repeated. "Of those other two Masters, are either of them your enemy?"

Tennyson made a rude noise. "Both would, I believe, rejoice in my death and the splintering of my line. However, neither possesses the strength to move against so many of us at once. As interesting as this conversation is, your inference that either Master is orchestrating this, or that they have taken your man as insurance against your interference, is unlikely."

"But not impossible."

"No, not impossible. There is, however, one possibility you seem keen on ignoring."

I bristled. "Which is what?"

"Your man could have gone willingly and of his own volition without any duress or control."

"I—" What? I'd considered the idea, and then promptly discarded it. I knew Julius, had worked alongside him for six years. You can't work with someone, in so many life-and-death situations, without developing a sense of their character. Julius was human, yes, but he led our team because he believed in law and order—even among creatures of myth and legend. He wanted to make a difference.

He might be a cliché, but he was no traitor.

Shouting broke out on the other end of the line, punctuated by one of Novak's furious roars. Jaxon shouted something. Tennyson snarled.

Not. Good.

"Cut it out, bless it!" I shouted at the phone, wondering if it would do any good at all. "Novak!" My voice bounced around the quiet suburban street. The last thing I needed was my incubus second-in-command getting into fisticuffs with a Master vampire who had a trailer park full of people under his thumb.

"This is ridiculous," I said to Kathleen. She rolled her eyes dramatically in silent concurrence. "You want to help?"

Finally getting the hint, she took the Raspberry back and held it up. She pressed the forefinger and thumb of her free hand together, then placed both between her lips. I flattened my palms over my ears. Her piercing whistle still made my teeth ache.

The scuffing on the other end of the phone ceased. Movement at the far end of the street caught my eye. We were in the middle of the block, houses on all sides, each end punctuated with a stop sign and fenced tree. A child-sized shadow was hovering near the western stop sign, watching us. As though real-izing I'd seen it, the shadow moved forward, into the circle cast by a streetlight.

"Kathleen," I said, "turn around slowly. There's a hobgoblin with a birthday present walking right toward us."

"Is that the start of some awful joke?" she asked.

"I wish."

She turned, and we both stared as said hobgoblin shuffled down the sidewalk in our direction. Hobgoblins are difficult to describe properly unless you've seen one. They're around four feet tall, but stretched thin and narrow, like they'd been built too short and steamrolled into a larger size. Their skin was grayish yellow, sallow, and hairless, except for the mat of dark green curls that sat like a crown atop their round, too-small heads. Eyes the same dark green glittered in the lamplight.

In its long-fingered hands was, indeed, a birthday present. Sort of. The object was the size of a bowling ball bag and done up in shiny foil wrap, secured with a glittery silver bow. The hobgoblin held it close, as though terrified of dropping it, as it walked straight toward us.

Kathleen lowered her phone hand without ending the call. I drew my gun and held it at waist level, aimed to the side. Our visitor saw it, catalogued it, and kept on coming. Hobgoblins, by nature, prefer the chillier forest climates of the north. I'd never heard of any local to the Mid-Atlantic states, and seeing one here now—at the house of my missing boss—set my internal alarms blaring.

I gazed at the wrapped box, my stomach in knots. The hobgoblin's presence was not a coincidence, and whatever he had in his box was not a gift I wanted. I waited until it reached the edge of Julius's lawn, then pointed my gun at its head. It froze.

"Who sent you?" I asked.

It licked its lips with a forked tongue. "I am told to

bring this box to this home at this hour," it said in a voice as reedy as a dying accordion.

"Told by whom?"

The hobgoblin seemed confused by the question. "I am told to bring this box—"

"Yes, we heard you the first time," Kathleen said. Her eyes flashed red and her fangs had extended half an inch. Enough to terrify most humans and quite a few lower-level demons.

The hobgoblin was unaffected.

I would have been impressed, but all I could think of was Julius right now. "Come forward with the box," I said.

It did, stopping several paces away from us. At my command, it put the box down and retreated to the sidewalk. I half expected it to run. It loitered instead. I couldn't wait for one of the neighbors to look out their window and call the cops, since the hobgoblin wasn't wearing a stitch of clothing.

"Kathleen?"

She took a single step forward and inhaled deeply. Her lips curled back in a sneer. "Blood," she said. "The package reeks of blood, vampire, and hobgoblin stink."

I swallowed against the bile rising in my throat. "Explosives?"

"None that I can detect by odor."

Bending to retrieve a blade from my boot, I knelt in front of the box. It had been professionally wrapped, each fold precise and each cut perfectly straight. My idea of wrapping a gift was tossing it into a dollar-store bag and stuffing some reused tissue paper on top. I hadn't bought a bow in over a decade.

I cut through the paper with precise motions, in case it was rigged. The foil paper slid away from a plain, brown box. I cut the tape sealing the box. The flaps popped open. My heart sped up, sending adrenaline signals to my brain. I fought them. I needed steady hands, needed my wits. Not a blinding headache and the shakes. I folded back the box flaps, screwed up my courage, and peered inside.

A sea of white packing peanuts peered back at me. I poked the blade into the foam pellets. It hit something a few inches down.

"The stench of blood is stronger now," Kathleen said.

I couldn't smell it yet, so I trusted her. I brushed a layer of peanuts aside, then dug down until my fingers found plastic. I pulled out a round, Tupperware layer-cake container. The normally translucent top had been painted black to obscure the contents. The moderately hefty contents. I nudged the box away and put the container down on the grass, bottom facing up. And stared.

"Shiloh?"

I gazed up into Kathleen's face. Her headlight eyes continued to glow, even though her fangs were gone. Her eyebrows were bunched, her mouth open. She looked horrified, which only terrified me further. I forced my expression into something I hoped passed for determined—my insides were quaking so hard I thought my guts would vibrate right through my rib cage—then looked down.

The cake container looked so innocent. My mom had one like it, and had stored many a birthday cake surprise beneath its plastic cover. I knew I'd never be able to eat another Tupperware-stored cake again.

I worked the tip of my blade between the bottom and its lid, then turned it until the seal broke with a sloppy hiss. The thick, cloying stench of blood was immediate. I swallowed back the urge to vomit. Forced my hand to lift the lid until it popped from its groove and flipped to the grass.

Kathleen shrieked, barely a whisper over the roar in my ears. My vision seemed to telescope down, down, until the only thing I saw was the contents of the cake container.

Tucked in a bed of romaine lettuce was Julius's head. His eyes were open, chocolate brown, watchful and warm even in death. My irrational brain told me to close them, like they always did in the movies. He should rest. I reached out, my fingers shaking so badly I didn't think I'd manage. Within an inch of touching him, Julius blinked.

This time I screamed.

And screamed.

CHAPTER 4

The first few minutes post-eyes-blinking passed in a blur. Kathleen must have kept her wits intact and used them proactively, because my next clear memory was gazing around Julius's living room, wondering how the hell I got there. The wrapped box and cake container were on the coffee table, supported by neat stacks of magazines and a telephone directory. The hobgoblin was there, too, tied to one of the leather chairs with a twisted curtain. Its mate still hung on a nearby window.

Kathleen's voice bounced around the living room. I turned and found her pacing back and forth from the living room, through the dining room, and back again, barking into her Raspberry. Cold, angry words I still couldn't register as English. Until I realized it wasn't all English. She'd been raised in France until the age of fifteen, when she started coming into her vampire abilities, and occasionally slipped into French when she lost her temper.

I took a step toward her, then stopped. She hadn't put the lid back on the cake container, and a dark brown crown of hair peeked out over the rim. I shuffled in that direction, intending to cover it. Trying to convince myself I hadn't seen Julius blink. It had been a hallucination, or better still, a nerve firing in his not-quite-done brain. Not the awful, horrifying possibility nudging at the edge of my mind, making itself known.

A few more steps had me within spitting distance. His face was angled forty-five degrees from my direction, eyes still open. Kathleen should have closed them.

Those brown eyes shifted, rolling sideways to look right at me.

The world grayed out. I tottered on my feet, barely able to hold my balance.

"Watch your step, kiddo."

It wasn't Kathleen, and it definitely wasn't the hobgoblin. But it also couldn't be . . .

Severed heads don't talk.

They *can't* talk, not without lungs to force air through vocal cords. Right? I blinked hard, refocusing on the head in the cake container.

Julius was looking right at me. "Shiloh." His lips

moved. Words came out. His voice sounded strained, forced through a broken bellows, not quite his own.

"Not fucking possible," I said.

He blinked. His eyes rolled around, taking in as much as he could from his position on the coffee table. He looked like a sobering drunk who'd woken up with his pants down and didn't remember who he'd gone home with.

"What happened?" he asked.

A couple of garbled words made it past my lips, none of which made any sense to either of us. I'd seen a lot of things in my life, even a couple of zombies out for a Halloween stroll, but never a talking severed head. And not of someone I cared about.

"The others are on their way here," Kathleen said.

I jumped. The backs of my thighs hit the sofa. I fell hard onto the cushion. It would have been funny if the circumstances weren't so bizarre. Julius rolled his eyes up and around in a vain attempt to see who was behind him.

"How is this possible?" I asked her.

"I suspected and Novak confirmed it," she replied. "I believe he is now a revenant."

Warning sirens blared in my head. Necromancy was one of the rare black arts outlawed by . . . well, everyone. Few witches possess the power necessary to pull it off, and the few demons who did rarely stayed off anyone's paranormal radar long enough to manage a spell. Bad necromancy made zombies— mindless, reanimated corpses whose only instinct was to replace their own rotting flesh with the flesh of those still living.

Good necromancy—oxymoron much?—created revenants. Revenants were corporeal ghosts. Their bodies were reanimated, their spirit intact, only they were very much dead and could be controlled by the necromancer who reanimated them. The chosen victim was brought back to life within minutes of their physical death, always occurring in a violent manner so as to bind the spirit to the corporeal world and keep them from crossing over. It's the point where amateur necromancers screw up—they bring back corpses too-long dead, without revenant spirits.

I'd just never heard of a revenant head. It definitely narrowed down his cause of death.

"Who's a revenant?" Julius asked. "Kathleen?"

"Not I," she said. "You."

"I what?"

"You're a revenant," I said.

He gave up trying to see out the back of his own head and swiveled those confused, chocolate-colored eyes back toward me. "I am? I don't . . . is that why I can't feel my legs?"

Understatement of the decade, thy speaker is Julius Almeida, ex-Army Ranger, ex-human being.

I bolted off the sofa and barely made it into the half bathroom across from the front door. Bile and peanuts passed up and out as I clung to the toilet bowl, retching and crying. I sobbed until my throat hurt and my already achy head wanted to explode. He was alert and talking, but there was no coming back from being a revenant.

My boss and friend of six years was dead. My heart ached for the loss.

I fought for control of my grief. Job now, me later. I didn't have a choice, did I? I was still second on this team, still acting leader. Not as though Julius could lead our team from the comfort of his lettuce-lined cake carrier, right? I flushed the toilet, then took a few minutes to wash my face.

The hickey Jaxon noticed earlier stood out darker against my freshly paled skin. I looked stretched, worn, like I'd come off an eight-day bender. Swollen, bloodshot eyes added to the overall image. I hadn't looked this bad since the fairy elixir mishap ten months ago.

Never, ever drink a frothy "cappuccino" out of a teacup shaped like a rose. Ever.

When I came back into the living room, Kathleen was questioning the hobgoblin. It looked utterly miserable, even more so when she threatened it with an iron spike from her hidden arsenal. Half a dozen flat, finger-width burns covered its face and neck where she'd already attempted to get answers. My only objection to her treatment of the little monster was I hadn't been in on it.

"Anything?" I asked.

"The creature is under the influence of another," she replied without looking away from her prey. "It repeats the same line over and over, no matter what I do."

I glanced behind her. "What about him?"

She followed my gaze to the cake container. "I haven't . . . I don't . . . ." As much as she pretended to be aloof and not involved, she cared. Cared enough that she couldn't seem to question our dead boss about how he'd died. Not alone.

I totally understood.

"It's fine," I said, offering a wan smile. I wanted to put the lid on him, raid his fridge for beer, and drown my sorrows until the boys arrived on-scene. Instead, I walked back to the couch and sat down across from the cake carrier.

Kathleen perched next to me, her thin hands clasped in her lap. Her lips were pursed so tightly they disappeared, leaving a dark slash in her face instead of a mouth. With the red sparking in her eyes, the effect was disconcerting.

Not that preparing to question my dead boss was altogether normal.

"Are you okay?" Julius asked me.

The confusion and sincerity in his question, coupled with the papa bear instincts that had made him a good leader, threatened more tears. I blinked them away and drew in a deep breath. Held it a few seconds, then let out a long exhale. It helped. "Julius, what's the last thing you remember?" I asked.

He stared. "I'm not sure, Shi. Have I been missing?"

"Yeah, you have been." Side effect of being a revenant—selective memory loss. Only important things from a revenant's life, often in the form of names and locations, were retained. He remembered us, which was a start. I had to begin slow, give him a focus point. "Julius, do you remember what you had for lunch yesterday?"

He licked his lower lip, as though the flavor of food remained. "I think . . . noodles. Rice. Did I have Chinese food?"

A question, not a memory. "Yeah, you did. What about after the Chinese food? Do you know where you went after?"

"Out?" His eyes became unfocused as he searched his addled memories. "I'm sorry, it's a blur. I can't feel my legs."

"I know."

"If he doesn't remember it," Kathleen said in my ear, her voice barely a whisper, "it's likely he doesn't know who did this to him. Knowledge of personal identity, especially in the case of a violent death, will stick with a revenant spirit. However, the death itself can affect the recollection of specific memories."

"Makes sense," I said.

"What makes sense?" Julius asked.

"Nothing."

"Too true."

"This is a warning," Kathleen said loud enough for Julius to hear.

"From who?" I asked.

She tilted her chin so she could look down her nose at me. Nothing could stop vampires—even half vampires—from acting superior when the mood struck. "Someone who wants us to know what we're facing. Anyone can kill. Anyone can hand deliver a severed head in a box. Only a rare few possess the skill and knowledge to send back a revenant head in a box."

"Okay, fair point."

"The timing of this atrocity with the request from Tennyson is no coincidence."

"Someone knew we'd get involved."

Her look clearly said *duh*. "Given the scale of Tennyson's demonstration and the sheer number of those missing, yes. Someone expected not only the Para-Marshals, but our team in particular, to get involved."

The downside of being a public face to Paranormal law enforcement was the loss of complete anonymity. Allies and enemies alike were more likely to know our faces, possibly our names. I'd changed my last name to protect my mom, and I rotated boyfriends to protect them from my job. We all did our best to protect the people in our lives. But it clearly wasn't foolproof.

"No one could have known," I said, letting my

train of thought run out loud. "No one could have known our team would be the one to get involved in this, unless the kidnapper somehow knew which trailer park Tennyson was targeting."

"Exactly. Which indicates a traitor within his line."

"Or the bastard is playing us himself."

She shook her head. "Unlikely."

"I know." Tennyson wouldn't risk the safety of his entire line by gathering them into one place and then betraying us. Not when a call into the Marshals' Office would bring the full force of the DOJ and the federal government down to wipe them out. Putting the blame on him was just easier. What was the phrase? The devil you know . . .

I just didn't want to be the one to suggest to him someone in his inner circle was a traitor. "Are vampires vulnerable to each others' mind fucks?" I asked.

Kathleen's eyebrows furrowed in a deep vee. "What?"

Sixty-five years old and she still had trouble with slang. "Can one vampire read another's mind?"

"I'm uncertain. The Master of a line can, with permission, access the mind of any he has made."

"Right." Tennyson had mentioned that.

Kathleen continued. "But those powers rarely extend to those outside of his making. What you are thinking?"

"Getting info, is all." Half true, since I was also contemplating the idea that one of Tennyson's enemy was setting us up. A powerful Master could, potentially, poke into the mind of a lesser vamp, thereby getting the location of the takeover. Theory, all of it. Just theory. But with all that was going on and no clear answers, that's the best we had at the moment.

"Who's Tennyson?" Julius asked.

I jumped at the sound of his voice, having forgotten he was there—which is quite a trick, considering his state.

"The vampire Master we are attempting to assist," Kathleen said. "I explained this to you."

Had she? Oh, right, while I was revisiting those peanuts.

"Did you?" Julius screwed up his face, concentrating. "I don't remember."

I asked Kathleen, "Is short-term memory loss a side effect of the revenant thing? Like, he knows who we are, but we have to keep reminding him what's going on right now."

"I am uncertain, as he is my first revenant," she said. "It is possible whatever was done to him to manipulate his memory prior to death or as part of the revenancy spell in order to prevent him from recalling who turned him may have gone awry."

"Awry?" She had such a frustrating way with words, sometimes. "So no matter what we tell him about what's happening, he'll probably just forget."

A curtain of sadness fell across Kathleen's pale face. "Again, it's possible."

I wanted to stamp my foot in childish frustration, but somehow curbed the desire. "All we have are possibilities and no real answers, bless it."

"Yes."

"This really sucks."

"Yes."

"Something bad happened to me, didn't it?" Julius asked. "I can't feel my legs."

I couldn't take it anymore. I grabbed the foil-covered box, flipped it upside down, and placed it over the cake container, effectively obscuring my dead boss's head from view. He didn't protest, and I was glad.

Kathleen's phone beeped. She glanced at the display, reading whatever info K.I.M. had sent. "As of last reporting," she said, "the West Coast unit has not had a member go missing. No one has reported unusual, large-scale paranormal activity within their zone, either."

It didn't really make me feel better. Two teams for the whole US meant huge-ass territories. Ours encompassed the entire East Coast, from Maine to Florida, and as far west as Missouri and Arkansas. Everything else belonged to Weller's West Coast unit, including Alaska—although Alaska's problems were generally limited to were-polar bears running amok—and occasionally bits of Canada. Too much territory for us to be certain that nothing else was going on under our noses. We hadn't even seen the

Myrtle's Acres takeover until it happened, and that was practically in our backyard.

"Does Weller know what's going on here?" I asked.

"Updates have been sent."

I sank deeper against the sofa cushions, the soft leather oddly comforting. I closed my eyes, frustrated and tired. "Should we move back to HQ? The bad guys know where this house is."

Kathleen didn't reply right away. Several long beats preceded her reply. "If this was first warning, they have no need to attack us again so soon. They must have guessed we would be here," she said, nodding her head at the hobgoblin, "so if they were planning something, they would have done so already."

"So we stay?"

"Yes. Also, Tennyson is coming in with Novak and Jaxon."

"Right." We couldn't take Tennyson onto HQ grounds. Here was as good a place as any to figure out our next step. And home base wasn't far if we needed supplies or equipment.

I hadn't intended to fall asleep and woke with an annoyed grunt. Voices were echoing in the foyer, and I bounced to my feet, neck aching from the awkward position. Jaxon stormed into the living room first, his hazel eyes wide as they took me in. He faltered. I sagged a little, not realizing how much I needed him until he was there, and I kind of hated that need. I considered a quip about my appearance, to keep it all balanced, but couldn't find my sense of humor, buried as it was beneath my grief.

I managed a wan smile. He opened his arms, and I fell into his embrace, grateful for the comfort. My fingers bunched in his shirt, and I pressed my face into his neck, drawing on the refreshing, forest smell of him. The familiar hard planes of his chest, the strength in his arms and shoulders. Being this close to him warmed me on the inside, made me feel so protected I wanted to cry all over again.

Jaxon and I had tried, really tried. We'd had fun, made each other laugh, and the sex had been fantastic. Probably the best of my life, even if I'd never tell him so. But the rigorous demands of our working relationship had made a personal one impossible to maintain without knock-down, drag-out fights on a biweekly basis. It hadn't worked, but Jaxon still knew how to hold me the way I liked. The way I needed when I didn't know how to ask, and I loved him for it.

He didn't ask if I was okay. It was a stupid-ass question, anyway. He just held me tight, his lean arms around my waist, hands splayed across my back. Around us, the others came inside. I felt Novak nearby, felt the rage pouring off him. Demon rage, no matter the demon, is like the static on a television screen—get too close and it snaps at your fingertips and sets your hair on end.

An even stronger presence followed him— Tennyson. One of the boys must have invited him inside. I glanced up and met his gaze over Jaxon's shoulder. The Master vampire lingered in the archway between the foyer and living room, his old-fashioned cloak even more out of place among the modern furnishings. He watched me with an unreadable expression, but I didn't miss the tiniest flecks of green in his eyes, natural color still shielded behind the faint blue glow.

Green. Huh.

"Under the box," Kathleen said, somewhere behind me.

"Why'd you cover him up?" Novak asked.

"You'll understand when you see."

I twisted out of Jaxon's embrace, not protesting when he left one arm draped protectively across my shoulders. Kathleen stood near the bound hobgoblin, her arms crossed over her chest. Novak approached the foil box, every muscle in his ripped body coiled and tense enough to burst. He lifted the box.

I didn't think it possible for such a dark-skinned demon to pale, but he did. Few things spooked Novak. He didn't tremble or cry out or drop the box in fright—it was enough that he did a favorable impression of an over-creamed mug of coffee.

"Bless me," he said.

"Novak," said the head in the box, still in that broken bellows voice.

The incubus didn't reply. He put the box back down, and as before, we heard no protest from Julius.

"Fascinating," Tennyson said.

I spun to face the Master vamp, ignoring Jaxon's surprised grunt. "Someone's warning us against helping you," I said to Tennyson, getting back into his personal space. Not a smart move, on my part, but I didn't care. I glared up at his angular face, letting my rage rise to the surface and bubble with power.

"It would seem so," he replied, his voice cold and eerily calm.

"So tell me, then, of those three Masters who have high levels of mind manipulation ability, any of them powerful enough to pull off necromancy? Or should I say stupid enough?"

He flared his nostrils, then wrinkled his nose, as if my close presence offended him. "Necromancy is forbidden," he said.

"Yeah, no kidding. Also, not what I asked."

"I have no other answer for you, Ms. Harrison. Vampires take care to follow the rules of magic and spellcasting, and even then, very, very few are able to manipulate that sort of organic magic. Our magic, which is passed through the blood from Master to child, is not the same. The mixing of the two is dangerous and not tolerated among our people."

Jaxon snorted. "So you're saying even if a Master could pull off necromancy, no one would talk about it?" he asked.

"Yes."

It wasn't what I wanted to hear. I wanted a name, a

face, hell even a geographical location would be better than all of the nothing I had to work with. "Fine," I said. "Do you know of anyone, I don't care what species or inclination, who possesses the knowledge and power to practice necromancy? Successfully, I mean, not the idiots who produce zombies."

Tennyson stilled—not hard to do, since he wasn't moving much in the first place. His pale face seemed carved from stone. "Someone with the skill to do such a thing to your friend, you mean," he said.

"Obviously."

He took another half minute to practice his inner Mona Lisa, then finally nodded. "Yes, I am acquainted with a practitioner of some considerable skill who has been known to dabble in the blackest of the Dark Arts. If she is not involved, she may know who is."

A tiny ray of hope peeked out. "Where does she live?"

"Never in one place very long."

"Which means what?"

Tennyson bent his neck until his forehead was a hair's breadth from mine. His long, multihued hair fell forward in a thin curtain, framing both sides of his face. He released a puff of cool air, more for effect than any need to actually breathe. I kept perfectly still, not backing down, working hard to show no fear in the face of a djinn's mortal enemy.

My dad would be proud.

"Which means you haven't a demon's chance in

heaven of finding her without my help," he said, each word dripping with thirst.

The pulse point in my neck throbbed, and bless it, I shivered. I stepped back, driven by an instinctual need to separate myself from the predator invading my personal space.

"The witch is a traveler, then?" Novak asked, somehow right behind me. Jaxon and Kathleen had circled in tighter, as well, backing me up.

"Indeed," Tennyson said, once more calm and in control.

"I've tracked down travelers before."

"Not of her caliber. Even with your considerable skills, Incubus, only those whom she has invited into her home can sense its location."

Novak made a rude noise. "Let me guess, Vampire. She has invited you into her"—he paused and made air quotes, leaving little doubt as to his innuendo—"home, in the past?"

"Yes, she has. She understands the need for powerful allies."

I reached back and pinched Novak's arm. He stopped before any more arguments or innuendo made it past his lips. It wasn't helping.

"Tennyson," I said, squaring my shoulders, "can you take us to meet her?"

He overlapped my question with his curt reply. "No."

"Why not?"

"She will not welcome the demon, nor is she fond of skin-walkers. The half-blooded she also finds . . . distasteful."

Well, that wiped our entire team off the list, didn't it? "So we're supposed to what? Let you go in and question her alone?"

"Hardly." He allowed a flicker of amusement to enter his eyes, which made me hate him a little bit more. "I take one of you with me under my protection—vouch for you, as is the common vernacular—and she will allow it."

"Why only one of us?" Novak asked.

Tennyson sighed. "He cannot simply be grateful for the existence of a loophole, he must question its constraints."

"He's doing his job," I said. "The last time one of us was out of another's sight, he got turned into a talking head."

"I understand, Ms. Harrison, which is why I give your team my word that I will protect you while you are in my care."

My hand jerked. *Me?* He'd already decided I was the lucky loophole attendee, which made me all kinds of nervous.

"You are this team's de facto leader now, are you not? Or would you prefer I bring your former boss's head along with me in your stead?"

I curled my hand into a fist, tight enough to make the knuckles crack. I had half a mind to crack them again—right across his straight, pointy nose. Maybe it was his perfectly serious manner of speech, or the cold way he spoke about a man who'd died yesterday, I don't know. Something about Woodrow Tennyson, Master Vampire, set my blood boiling.

And not in the "he's so hot, I want to jump him" way.

The tiny part of me that quailed at the idea of being alone with Tennyson for however long it took to track down and question this witch kept hoping one of my team would speak up and insist on taking my place. The rest of me was proud of them for keeping quiet—it spoke to Julius's training and our instilled respect for the chain of command.

I squared my shoulders. "When do we leave?"

"Immediately, if it suits you." He glanced at the living room windows. "Do you have a vehicle suitable for daylight travel?"

"Tinted windows?"

"Yes."

"Maybe. I'll see what I can do." I smiled on the inside, because for the briefest moment, my comment made Tennyson look nervous.

CHAPTER 5

Okay, so I wasn't entirely fair with my vehicle choice. The ten-year-old Element had only a mild tint on the windshield and front windows, with a darker tint in the rear. It forced Tennyson to sit in the backseat with his cloak drawn up and wrapped around him, protecting his delicate skin from the morning sun's glare. Keeping him in the backseat, which was raised up higher than in my preferred Expedition, put him square in my rearview mirror.

Well, put his clothes in the rearview. Vampires may not cast a reflection, but we entertain ourselves by making fun of movies that show their clothes as not casting a reflection, either. Clothes are clothes no matter who's wearing them.

The front passenger seat was occupied by my boss. I was still creeped out by the idea of toting him around in a cake carrier, but I couldn't just leave him behind at HQ, and sending him with Jaxon and the others to see the werewolves was like bringing along an hors d'oeuvre. We also discovered Julius went right to sleep—Zombie Standby Mode, as Jaxon called it, right before I punched him in the chest—when placed in darkness. Revenant Achilles heel, possibly, but at least I knew he wasn't bored closed up inside the carrier.

I'd been driving in silence for forty-five minutes, using his cryptic "north" as my compass, and I couldn't take the quiet any longer. I flicked on the radio. Something modern filled the car with drums and guitar strumming. Much better.

"Must you listen to that?" Tennyson asked.

Habit drew my gaze to the rearview mirror. An empty hood stared back, giving me no expression to match his disdainful tone. "I don't hear you making conversation."

"No, you do not."

Sarcasm detector must be in the off position. "I hate driving in silence, okay? Give me a break."

He immediately disproved my sarcasm theory by zinging me with, "What would you like broken?"

"You know, if I wasn't positive my team would track you down and kill you so painfully your youngest vamp would feel it, I'd think you were serious."

"Do you think so little of me?"

"I don't know you."

After a moment's pause in which I felt him staring at the back of my head, he said, "Complete your thought, please."

I blew out through clenched teeth. "I don't know you, but you're a vampire, so I really wouldn't put it past you. Happy?"

"Not in the least. However, I am pleased you spoke your mind. Djinn are not known for censoring their thoughts or emotions. I imagine you war with your base nature quite often."

"Base nature?" I forced myself to relax my grip on the steering wheel. We were cruising down the highway at eight o'clock in the morning, and I was having a personality discussion with a vampire I couldn't look in the eye. And I hadn't had any coffee.

"You are only half human, Ms. Harrison," he said as though instructing a difficult pupil. "Your djinn half will always be stronger than your human half, just as your friend Kathleen's vampire half will always outweigh her human half. Humans are the weaker species."

"You were human once." As a retort, it was pretty blessed weak. I knew my djinn side was stronger; it's why I struggled so hard to repress my Quarrel and block the magic I felt around me at all times. Ignoring part of yourself is never easy, and I didn't need a freaking vampire Master to reiterate the fact.

"I've not been human for five hundred and forty years."

"Holy shit."

It just came out. I knew he was old. He'd admitted to having a three-hundred-plus underling. I just hadn't expected half a millennium of living experience. Or unliving experience, depending on your point of view.

"My age surprises you?"

"A little." I glanced over my shoulder for no good reason other than needing a look at his face. A reminder of what he looked like, even though he was impossible to forget. My gaze lingered less than a moment, and I took care to avoid eye contact.

The taillights of a silver Cadillac flashed red, warning me of impending contact. I mashed on the brakes with little time to wonder where the car had come from. Tennyson slammed into the back of the passenger seat with a grunt. The Cadillac found its accelerator and zipped forward in the lane. I returned my foot to the gas pedal and pressed until my speed returned to normal, clenching the wheel the entire time.

Adrenaline surged through me—terrific, I needed another headache to make my morning complete. My heart started sinking back into my chest, leaving my poor throat alone so I could find my voice. "You okay?" I asked.

"Yes, fine." His cape fluttered in the rearview as he settled back on the rear bench seat. "Your driving skills are worrisome."

"Blessed car came out of nowhere."

And now that we'd narrowly avoided crashing into it, the Cadillac was quickly leaving us in its wake. It must have merged onto the highway and not realized how fast I was driving. Idiot. The merge lanes on this stretch of highway were long enough for people to gain speed to merge safely into fast-moving traffic.

"We're both fine, Ms. Harrison, please calm down."

"I'm fine."

"I can sense your fear."

"We almost had a traffic accident, give me a br— just let me deal with it, okay?" The adrenaline rush was still working its way through my veins. I inhaled deeply via nose, exhaled hard through my mouth. Several times, until the anxiety faded. The Quarrel— and the headache—stayed put.

And Tennyson stayed quiet. Another half hour passed, filled with the radio station of my choice. Half a dozen times I was tempted to call Novak for an update. He said he'd call me when he knew something, or vice versa. It was our last conversation before I drove away with Tennyson.

"Don't turn your back on him, if you can help it," Novak had said, his usual gruff demeanor tempered with concern. Concern he'd deny, if pressed.

"No kidding," I had said. "Got some advice I don't already know?"

"Powerful witches can be as manipulative as vampires, especially over your human half. The Master knows this, so he won't introduce you. Don't give the witch your full name."

Okay, that was good advice. Most demons will trick you into willingly giving them your full name, which in turn, gives them power over you. Some witches and warlocks possess similar skills, apparently. It was also good to know Tennyson wouldn't give me up—I hoped.

"Well, don't turn your back on the Dame Alpha," I said.

Novak, Jaxon, and Kathleen were flying south to speak with the Dame Alpha of the Florida were-wolves. It was a position she held over a dozen other Alpha males in the state. She also had the distinction of being the only Dame Alpha in the country—a place she hadn't reached with her looks and gentle temperament.

"I'll be fine," Novak said. "Jaxon's the one who'll smell like a venison dinner to the wolves." Sending a fallen incubus, a stag skin-walker, and a dhampir to see the Dame Alpha wasn't the smartest play in our book—a job like that normally fell on Julius (a "helpless" human) and me. Djinn and werewolves get along well, mostly through our shared hatred of vam-pires. But someone had to talk to them, sooner rather than later, and that meant we couldn't wait for me to talk to this witch and *then* talk to the Dame Alpha.

"Just remember, Novak, we need to know what, if anything, is special about the mated pairs who were taken. Specifics of when, from where, how long they've been mates—"

"I know the drill, Shi."

"Yeah, I know you do. Just . . . honey and vinegar, okay?"

"We're questioning them, not catching flies."

"You're catching answers, so the metaphor holds."

"Point. Good luck on your witch hunt."

I had smiled. "Don't go seducing anyone's mate. Werewolves have big teeth, long memories, and are slow on forgiveness."

"Never on the job, kiddo," he had replied with a heart-melting grin.

"At the next stoplight, make a left turn." Tennyson's voice jerked me out of the memory, and I paid closer attention to our whereabouts.

I merged into the next lane, then slowed to a crawl in the turn lane. We were somewhere in northern Delaware, a part of the state with which I was not familiar. Funny, considering I'd lived in Maryland most of my adult life. Funnier still, I was coming here with a vampire, in search of a witch.

My life often felt like a punch line.

"How far on this road?" I asked. We were heading into somewhat hillier, tree-studded country, and seemed far enough north that Pennsylvania had to be around the next bend.

"Ten miles," he replied. "Follow the signs for the University of Delaware."

"Are you kidding? Our witch is in college?"

"No, our witch, as you say, has relocated near the college. She likes the youthful and vibrant."

"Not to mention drunk and disorderly."

Tennyson's warm chuckle caressed the length of my spine. I shivered.

My phone lit up. I checked the screen, surprised to see Weller's name. Even though he was being sent updates, I hadn't spoken to him directly about Julius, Tennyson, or our current situation, and this wasn't the time for a chat. Besides, I'd have more for him after Tennyson and I completed our errand, so I sent the call to voice mail.

The road expanded into a multilane highway, then narrowed again as we came closer to town. A large sports complex stood on the right-hand side, its parking lot filled with cars. We passed a couple of fast-food joints mixed with local restaurants, and then the speed limit dropped.

Given the miniscule size of this state compared to those around it, I half expected its university to be likewise . . . understated. The sprawl of the campus shocked me, as did the hundreds—probably thousands—of students patrolling the sidewalks and lawns spread over several city blocks. We passed dormitories, classroom buildings, fraternity houses, various offices, and onward, into town.

"Pull over a moment, please," Tennyson said.

I wedged my Element into the next available public

parking space. Parallel parking wasn't my specialty, but I managed with little fuss and no fender dings. It was a metered spot. I fished in the cupholder for some quarters while my undead map figured out our next step.

He'd closed his eyes. I saw them moving beneath the lids as he searched—his mind or his other senses, I had no idea. I kept an eye on the sidewalk, armed with a quarter, in case a meter maid came strolling past.

Across the street, an old brick building sported a painted wooden sign: Perk Me Up. The front door opened, spilling four students onto the sidewalk, each armed with a backpack, textbooks, and cups of coffee. Nothing unusual about that so close to a college campus, of course. The attention-grabbing part was the oak fairy flying behind the group, nose in the air, as though leashed to the group by the bitter scent of coffee. Its heavy, brown wings beat the air silently, somehow keeping its toddler-sized body in the air.

Neither the students, nor anyone else on the street could see the oak fairy. Only my djinn blood gave me sight to see the Fair Folk who kept themselves invisible from humans. Apparently oak fairies like coffee—I filed that away under Things I Learned Today.

"Continue on this road," Tennyson said so suddenly I actually jumped.

"How far?"

"Until I tell you to turn or stop."

I cast a poisonous glare at the rearview, then pulled back into traffic. The number of cars buzzing around town surprised me. Newark was a busy, busy place. Foot traffic eventually thinned out as we left the campus behind and moved into a more residential neighborhood. Residential and affluent, if the sizes of the houses and gated driveways were any indication. One of the three-storied, white homes looked straight from the pages of a Southern gothic romance novel, sans the weeping willows and climbing moss.

"No, not here," he said.

"What?" I hazarded another look at him. He was frowning, his lips pressed together, forehead pinched.

"We're going the wrong way."

"You told me to go this way." I pulled over and double-parked as close to the sidewalk as I could get. A passing car blared its horn, so I flipped on the hazard lights, then twisted in the seat to glare at Tennyson. "So what now? Is your vampire radar on the fritz, or is your witch sending mixed signals?"

He huffed. "She isn't at home. Her trail is split."

"Awesome."

"Be silent a moment." He closed his eyes and went statue-still. Enough time passed for me to get an ache in my neck from glaring at him sideways. He looked at me, finally. "Turn around."

I bit back a frustrated retort and did as ordered. We coasted back through the array of fancy homes.

"Left turn here."

Side street, winding toward town again. I recognized several fraternity signs in front of different homes.

"The one with the omega symbol."

I saw it, but had to drive past several homes in order to find a parking spot on the crowded street. Tennyson scooted forward between the front seats and gazed through the windshield at the glaring morning sunshine.

"You're not exactly going to blend in," I said. "Especially if you go running down the sidewalk in a big, black cloak."

"I have little choice," he replied. "Causing heads to turn is a small matter compared to burning flesh."

"Point taken." I glanced at Julius's carrier and debated bringing him along. The notion of terrorizing frat boys with a talking severed head appealed to my quarrelsome djinn side. I was a law enforcement professional, though, so instead, I tucked him onto the floor, out of any direct sunlight.

I climbed out of the Element and into the cool air and sunshine. The faint scents of coffee, frying meat, and alcohol lingered around me—the odors of young men living on their own for the first time. Above it were the sweet scents of earth and trees. The neighborhood was well-maintained.

I opened the rear door and stepped back. Tennyson slid out, his cloak pulled tight around his body.

The hood hung low over his face, obscuring it from view. I had the briefest flash of the Ghost of Christmas Past from some movie I'd watched years ago. Except instead of revealing memories, mine was a ghost who'd suck your lifeblood out of your neck.

"This is your show," I said when he didn't move.

His tall, cloaked form seemed to float down the sidewalk toward his destination. The frat house was one among many, a four-story brick building from a century long forgotten (except by those who'd lived it), with a fraternity banner hung across the front porch. The house seemed quiet—my first clue that something wasn't right.

"What's your witch doing at a frat house?" I asked, keeping pace near his left side.

"Enjoying herself, I would imagine," he replied.

I did not want elaboration, so I stayed quiet. He didn't knock. He simply pushed open the heavy oak door and stepped into a messy foyer. A center table overflowed with stacks of mail, books, and papers. To our left was an enormous living room, equally full of mess—clothes, beer bottles and cans, dirty dishes, pizza boxes, and their accompanying stenches. To our right was a dining room, same décor.

The neat-freak in me wanted to grab a garbage bag and broom.

I closed the door quietly, but it didn't seem to matter. If anyone was in the house, they weren't downstairs. Tennyson loosened his cloak and pulled the hood back, shaking his hair free. He marched toward the wide staircase straight ahead. I barely kept up with his long, two-steps-per-strides. He paused on the second floor and listened. Or sniffed, or whatever the hell he did to sense the witch. The long hallway had at least eight doors, probably bedrooms and at least one bathroom.

He turned abruptly and ascended to the third floor. Similar hallway, this one with five doors, spaced farther apart. I followed him to the second door on the left. Again, he didn't knock, just turned the knob and strode in like he owned the place.

I stepped into the doorway and noticed several things at once. First and foremost was the overpowering, musky odor of sex. A lot of sex. It rolled from the room like invisible fog—thick and tangible without obscuring my view of the activities in the bed. Activities I'd need serious therapy to wipe from my brain. A woman with the thickest mane of spiraled auburn hair I'd ever seen was crouched in the center of a four-poster bed, on all fours, utterly naked. Cantalope-sized breasts hung too perfectly and were being serviced from below by an equally naked young man. A second boy knelt next to her head and was being serviced by her mouth, while a third was behind her—

"Holy crap." It was my squawked protest that finally got the foursome's attention. The three frat boys stared at us with glazed eyes, red faces, mouths

wide with pleasure and exertion. Not one of them
stopped what they were doing.

Only the woman looked at us with a clear expression. She released the boy she was enjoying and licked
her cherry-red lips. Her round, heavily lashed eyes
were the color of spring apples. They drank in Tennyson first, flickering with lust and pleasure, before
landing on me. I didn't meet her gaze; instead, I studied
her face. She was beautiful, with a delicate nose and
strong jaw, each feature perfectly placed. Only not.

The illusion was amazing, because it took me so
long to see it—the left half of her face was covered
by a porcelain mask that blended perfectly with her
natural skin.

"Come to join us, Tenny?" the woman purred, a
touch of Irish in her voice.

"Not today, love," Tennyson replied. Lust made
his voice thick, husky.

My entire body trembled with the need to flee.

"Pity." She flicked her tongue at me. I redirected
my attention to the floor, but couldn't block out the
wet, slapping sounds still coming from the bed. "Give
us ten minutes, Tenny?"

"We'll be downstairs."

At Tennyson's words, I turned and left without
prompting, proud of myself for not running. I made
tracks downstairs, not stopping until I hit the foyer.
My cheeks flamed, and my heart was pounding hard
enough to crack a few ribs. I pressed my hands against

the wall and closed my eyes, gulping in deep breaths of air.

"Does sex frighten you so, Ms. Harrison?"

I whirled around, fingers clenching, to glare at Tennyson. He watched me from the base of the stairs, as composed as if we'd interrupted a Girl Scout meeting instead of an active four-way. "No, sex doesn't frighten me," I said.

His nostrils flared. "You're right, it's not fear. I apologize."

"Will you stop sniffing my mood? It's creepy. And for the record, so is walking in on people having sex."

"Why?"

"Because sex is private, so it should be done in private."

A slow smile crept across his face, curling his lips back over his teeth and fangs. "So it wasn't the sex that bothered you, it was the voyeurism."

"Well, yeah—no! I mean . . . I'm not having this conversation." I didn't talk about my sex life with anyone except my current lover. If I wouldn't discuss it with Novak, who was an incubus for crying out loud, why would I discuss it with a vampire I'd just met?

Pinpricks of green flickered in his eyes. "Have you never had fantasies of being pleasured by several men at once?"

My temper roared to life. "Not. Having. This. Conver. Sation."

He stayed silent, lessening my overwhelming desire

to use garlic spray on him. Ten minutes stretched into fifteen. Neither of us moved in what had to be the strangest unofficial standoff of my life. I wasn't about to show weakness to Tennyson by fidgeting first. Not when I could see the smirk lurking beneath his blank stare.

High upstairs, a door slammed. Moments later, the witch descended the stairs like a queen at a ball. She wore a red-floral sundress, cut low enough to show off her ample cleavage while still being decent. It hugged her curves and flowed in gentle waves to her knees. Thin, freckled legs ended in simple sandal flats. Her thick mane of ringlets was tied back in a loose bundle, making her neck seem longer, her lovely face rounder. Her visible cheek glowed with satisfaction that was reflected in her glittering, pale green eyes.

I admit, I had expected black corsets and spike heels.

"Tennyson, my friend," she chirped, smiling like a woman in love. "It's nowhere near my birthday, but I do love the gift you brought me."

I bristled.

Tennyson laughed. "No, love, she's not for you. She is here under my protection."

"Pity." The witch pouted her lower lip. "Her aura is pure. What sort of protection are you offering her?"

"We've come for your advice on a volatile topic involving the black arts."

She stilled, her seductress routine melting away, leaving behind the persona of a businesswoman. She straightened her shoulders and smoothed her skirt. "A favor, then?"

"My favor, Brighid, not hers."

Brighid heaved a dramatic, put-upon sigh. "Very well, your favor." She extended her hand to Tennyson, who took it in a loose grasp. When she did the same to me, I stared. "I don't bite, girl."

"She's taking us to her home," Tennyson said.

Reluctantly, I took her hand. Her palm was smooth and cool, her grip strong. A shock of power jolted my arm, as though I'd poked a paper clip into an electric outlet. My hand and elbow tingled. Tennyson took my other hand, completing the circle.

The frat house dissolved in bits and pieces, and I watched in utter fascination as the paint dripped from the walls, wood from plaster, layer upon layer, until nothing remained around us, except darkness. Energy slammed through me, a blast of winter air, and I nearly fell. Tennyson's strong grip kept me upright, kept the circle intact. I'd never traveled this way. Unlike full-blooded djinn, I can't teleport on my own, and traveling via Novak Express was nothing like this.

The chill ended abruptly. I blinked once, and we were no longer in blackness. We stood in the middle of a large, circular room decorated in lush shades of purple, red, and hunter green. A bed the size of my apartment's kitchen took up space to one side, bogged down with satins and silks, drapes and pillows. More cushions covered the floor in various formations, all in the same rich colors. The very center of the room held a hexagon-shaped stone fireplace. The fire roared so hot the flames burned blue, but the room remained a comfortable temperature. Scents of herbs, beeswax, and sex mingled in the air.

She had a bookshelf overflowing with books, scrolls, and loose sheets of parchment, as well as a cupboard of . . . well, things. Jars and bowls and baggies and even a couple of Tupperware containers. Dozens of symbols painted the walls, most of which I did not recognize, though they seemed vaguely Gaelic.

Brighid. Like the Irish goddess of wisdom and perfection, a lady of skill in healing and warfare, whose face was lovely on one side, and hideously scarred on the other. This Brighid in front of me wore a mask, too . . .

I pulled away from both of them, moving to stand at a respectable distance. Forcing myself to keep still and not tremble. Tennyson hadn't brought me to see a powerful witch. The bastard brought me to see a goddess.

"Please, make yourself comfortable," our hostess said, her accent coming through more thickly. She indicated the array of floor cushions. I couldn't bring myself to sit and lower myself beneath her. Symbolically, it gave her power in our bargaining.

"I'm comfortable, thank you," I said.

Tennyson quirked an eyebrow at me, but addressed Brighid. "Do you wish your favor now, or after we've had our discussion?"

"After," she replied. "I'm quite satisfied at the moment." She turned to me, her expression mild. "On what business have you come? The djinn are no friends of Ireland, so you risk much in coming to me."

"I don't come for myself or my people," I said. "My needs and Tennyson's are one and the same today, so I come for his people as well as my human side."

The fancy speech seemed to impress Brighid. She smiled, and one delicate hand lifted to her face. She stroked a finger down the curve of her mask, drawing attention to its existence. "You both have questions about the black arts. Should I not then require a favor from you, as well?"

Tennyson took a step toward her, creating a minor barrier between me and the goddess. "Your favor comes from me, Brighid, and me alone. Those terms have been established."

"Spoilsport." She pouted her lip again. "I'd so enjoy putting a stain on that aura of hers."

He growled. Good grief, the vampire was standing up for me. A half-blood djinn. It was the final nail in the—no pun intended—coffin of reality. My dad would never believe this story now. Not that I planned on telling him about it. Ever.

"Perhaps we can discuss the topic now?" I asked.

"Of course," Brighid said, giggling lightly as though the tension had never occurred. "At your leisure." She danced to a grouping of cushions and sat down, curling her legs beneath her.

Tennyson removed his cloak and let it puddle to the floor. Beneath it, he wore black linen pants that looked painted on, showing off tapered legs and a narrow waist. His light gray, button-up shirt was only a fraction looser than the pants. The outfit dared me to point out a single ounce of extra fat anywhere.

As he moved to join Brighid, I snagged his cloak off the floor, folded it, and put it on a nearby cushion. I ignored his amused look as I settled nearby, keeping an attentive posture without looking as nervous as I felt.

"Now," Brighid said, "explain how the path of a half-breed connects to that of a Master?"

Ignoring the labels, I fed her an abbreviated version of last night's events and everything we knew so far about the disappearances. Her eyes lit up when I began describing Julius and his new revenant status, as well as my suspicion that whoever had changed him was also responsible for the kidnappings. She remained silent for several long minutes after I stopped talking.

"Successful necromancy requires talent, precision,

and power," she said, "as well as an understanding of the healing arts."

"Healing?" I asked.

"Healing and harm are opposites, so for one to work at such a level, a knowledge of both is required." Her gaze flickered to Tennyson. "I suspect it's why my friend Tennyson brought you to me, as I am skilled in both healing and warfare."

"Have you ever practiced necromancy yourself?"

Her lips curled back, not quite a smile. "An impudent question."

"We came here for answers. I can't get them if I don't ask questions."

"I see why you've reserved this one for yourself, Tenny. She's a bit of a firecracker and you always did like a challenge."

I bit the inside of my cheek and mentally slapped at the flames of my temper. No sense in correcting her at this point. As long as she believed me under Tennyson's protection—sexual or otherwise—I was safe from her "favors." I just hoped I'd be excused while Tennyson paid up, especially if his owed favor fell along the lines of the frat boys.

"Answer her question, please," Tennyson said.

She glowered at him. "Yes, I have and successfully, but not in the last two centuries. I found the experience distasteful. It is inefficient to kill the same thing twice."

"Have you ever passed your wisdom in necromancy to another?"

"Only once have I spoken of such forbidden knowledge, and in my regret, I sought to kill him soon after."

Crap.

"How soon after?" Tennyson asked.

She lifted one slim shoulder in a shrug. "Four years, give or take."

"Four years?" I repeated. "You waited four years to kill him?"

"Measures of years have little meaning to an immortal, child." She didn't bother hiding her disdain. "I was otherwise occupied, and I did not immediately see his corruption."

"Occupied? Sure. I bet it's hard to see what's happening on the mortal coil when you're flat on your back with your legs in the air."

Her eyes blazed with emerald fury. Energy snap-crackled in the air.

Bad Shiloh, don't piss off the Irish goddess of warfare.

"You understand nothing," she said. "Your entire race is a pestilence to this world and should be destroyed."

I didn't know if she meant human or djinn, but I was past caring. All words of caution given to me by Novak and Tennyson flew out of my head with her insults. What could I do, though? My abilities were fairly static, not really defensive powers. Besides the

Quarrel and a hearty constitution that made me hard to kill with such simple things as bullets and knives, all I could do was walk through solid objects (non-metal, natural material solid objects and with quite a lot of searing pain) and sense power coming at me. My magical abilities to grant wishes were bound by the Rules of Wishing, and it was unlikely Brighid knew the words necessary to bind me to her for three wishes.

I did have a gun, though, which I pulled without thinking. "Look, can the insults, Red," I said, aiming at her uncovered cheek. "Someone I love is dead, people Tennyson cares about are missing, and you're giving us shit? If you want your fucking favor, how about a little cooperation before I put a hole in the pretty side of your face?"

Brighid stared at my gun as though she'd never seen one before. Or she couldn't process the idea of an insignificant half-breed like me drawing on and threatening her. I couldn't believe I'd done it—threatened to shoot a goddess in the face. Fit me for a straitjacket and toss me into the padded room—if I lived that long. I stayed calm, however, even though my insides were pudding, and waited for her to kill me with a snap of her manicured fingers.

CHAPTER 6

She surprised me by throwing her head back and laughing.

Deep belly laughs reserved for truly hysterical jokes and stand-up comedians. I gaped at her as I lowered my gun. I didn't tuck it back into its holster, though. Rather, I held it loosely, my thumb still on the safety. Tennyson seemed caught between amusement at Brighid's reaction and wanting to snap my neck himself.

"Oh my," she said. She fanned her face with her hand as she collected herself. A spot of color darkened her cheek, and her eyes glittered with tears. "I can see why this one interests you, Tennyson, but you will never have her."

"Huh?" It came out as a grunt, part surprise and

part disgust. No kidding, he'd never have me. Gross and ew.

Did I mention yuck?

"You assume much, Goddess," Tennyson replied. Not a hint of emotion.

"No more than you assumed in coming here with your queries."

"And yet you have answered them."

"For you, not her."

"In this matter, we are the same."

She sniffed. "As you wish."

I recognized the gesture—her way of giving in without backing off. I had no desire to show off in front of a goddess. All I wanted were answers. Clearing my throat, I decided to try again. "Goddess, please," I said. "In the four years before you killed that man, could he have passed along the forbidden knowledge?"

"The knowledge, yes, but not the skills." She extended her hand and examined her perfectly manicured fingernails, effectively saying *I'll answer these questions as I see fit.* "Also, I said I *sought* to kill him, not that I had. I discovered he had moved to St. Petersburg, Russia, and died there of influenza. Once I learned of Lord Robert Adelay's death, certain rumors came to my attention. Rumors that he had transcribed the knowledge and hidden it away. No such tome was discovered amongst his considerable estate holdings."

"So this Lord Adelay wrote and hid a how-to manual on necromancy?"

"Such is the rumor, yes."

That book would be worth a fortune on the paranormal black market. "How long ago was this?"

"In a time before this country was claimed by the Old World, when the Ancient World was still free to roam as it wished."

I cast a *help me* look at Tennyson. He said, "Fifteenth century, or thereabouts."

"So the book could be *anywhere*," I said, incredulous.

"Or it could have been destroyed long ago," Brighid said.

A hopeful thought, but one I seriously doubted was the case. "Was Lord Adelay from Ireland?"

"Devonshire. Though his origin does you little good. His descendants have traveled a great deal in the spanning centuries since his death, spreading to many countries, from America to New Zealand to Russia."

"So any one of them, or none of them, could have the book in their possession."

"Precisely."

A technical question occurred to me, and while I doubted she would reveal any specifics of the spell itself, I hoped she would at least answer this one. "How long does it take to successfully create a revenant?"

She arched a slim, auburn eyebrow. "Once death is achieved, the spell takes no longer than one hour.

Death is the variable. Ensuring a revenant spirit remains behind requires a long, agonizing process,
often employing methods of torture."

The second part I knew. The first part shouldn't
have surprised me, but it did. Julius had been missing
for roughly sixteen hours. Take away one hour for
the spell, and a minimum of one hour for torturing
him to death, the spell location could be anywhere
within three hundred miles of his home. Which
meant whoever did it could still be nearby.

Hell, Brighid herself could have done it, only I
fully believed she'd been occupied at the frat house
for quite some time. "Is a specific location necessary for the spell?" I asked, toeing the line here.
"Near water or across a ley line?"

Her eyes narrowed. "Your query requires speaking
of forbidden magic, and I will not. It is too specific."

Bless it. One last question, though, before we
headed home. "Goddess, are there others who may
possess knowledge similar to yours? Knowledge
that could assist them in performing necromancy
successfully?"

Brighid folded her hands neatly in her lap and
tilted her head, pondering the far side of the room.
Her eyes remained still, giving me the impression she
was stalling, rather than thinking. She had the names
in her head. Either she didn't want to give them up, or
she liked seeing me squirm. Probably both. Minutes
passed in silence; I stayed so still that my back ached.

"Brighid!" Tennyson said. "We are immortal, but the girl is not. An answer, please."

She jerked her attention to him, eyes blazing emerald. "I'm sorry. My knowledge of the living is my own, and I will betray the trust of no more dead men. Forgive this rocky ending, Tenny, but I must ask for this audience to end."

"That's it?" I asked. "We get a dead guy and a book we'll probably never find?"

"I have answered your questions, child. Be grateful you are here under Tennyson's protection. The next time we meet, you will regret threatening me with that pitiful weapon." The chill in her accented voice sent ice water down my spine. My poor stomach would develop an ulcer after today.

"Very well," Tennyson replied. He stood gracefully, as though sitting on the floor for so long hadn't affected him in the least. I didn't do as well and stumbled over one of her beaded floor cushions. He caught my arm, and I yanked out of his grip.

Brighid rose and practically danced to the large bed opposite us. She perched on the edge, the skirt of her sundress rising up above her knees, which she then parted suggestively. "My favor, Tenny."

My eyebrows shot up to my hairline. "Please tell me I can wait outside for this."

"It won't take long," Tennyson said.

"What? No stamina?" I regretted the barb the instant I let it loose.

He pivoted to face me, multicolored hair flying. His eyes blazed with annoyance, though curiously devoid of any residual glow, blue, red or otherwise. I wanted to meet him glare for glare, but remembered Kathleen's warning. I knew about vampire gazelocks, and I couldn't give him any chance to manipulate me—not even to see what color his eyes really were.

Still, in the curve of his mouth and set of his jaw, he seemed almost . . . disgusted. "It's not what you assume, child."

Brighid hitched her dress up to her waist, baring shapely thighs and a hint of pink panties, and laid back on the lush bed. Tennyson stalked to her—actually stalked, which surprised me into watching awhile longer—then knelt on the floor between her legs. When he reached up to caress the inside of her left thigh, my brain screeched at me to look away. I didn't need to see him do this to her. Yet . . . I couldn't look away.

The goddess sighed, practically purring at the touch of his hand. My heart jackhammered in my chest, and I knew I was about to witness something intimate.

Tennyson leaned closer to her thigh, until his nose barely brushed her flawless, pale skin. He bared his fangs. My breath hitched. He sank his fangs into her inner thigh, and Brighid let out a wail that rivaled any porn star's climax. Her free leg came up and draped across Tennyson's shoulder, as if to keep him in place.

Her delicate hands gripped the silk sheets, clawing at the fabric, holding herself down. He continued to drink.

I turned away. It was something more intimate than sex, more pleasurable than an orgasm—at least for Brighid. I'd read a magazine article once about tantric sex, and wondered briefly if it had just found its rival in a vampire bite to the thigh.

It continued for several minutes, until Brighid gasped, "Enough! Enough, please," and then muttered something I didn't understand. Gaelic, probably.

The sheets rustled. I felt Tennyson approaching. I didn't turn around. I waited until he collected his cloak and slipped it on.

"Take her hand, Tenny, and I'll send you back." Brighid's voice was low, sultry, a well-satisfied woman. I wanted to slap her. I really didn't want to hold Tennyson's hand again.

His skin was warmer than before; I half expected blazing heat, since he'd just sucked the blood of a Gaelic goddess. I closed my eyes, avoiding all eye contact, until the sense of displacement ended. The heavy odors of sex and herbs were replaced by familiar earth and grass.

I blinked several times, expecting afternoon sunlight and getting only faint streetlights. I pulled away from Tennyson, overwhelmed by the need to wash my hand. And maybe scrub my mind out with brain bleach.

"Why is it nighttime?" I asked.

"Her home is between this world and the next," he replied blandly. "Time—"

"Yeah, is different, I get it." I fished out my Raspberry. Three new missed calls. It hadn't rung once while—oh wait. No cell phone service between worlds. Of course.

One from Novak, one from Kathleen, and one from Vincent, plus the one from Weller. The digital clock said it was after eight o'clock.

"My apologies, Ms. Harrison. I didn't expect her to require the favor immediately, or I would have bargained for the option to return at a later time."

I strode down the sidewalk toward the parked Element, cheeks blazing for no good reason. "Why? Don't like giving sexual favors in front of an audience?"

He was in front of me, an immoveable object in my path before I registered him. I slammed into his chest, then stumbled back. He reached out, as if to grab me, but stopped himself. Red sparks dotted both eyes. "I do not trade sexual favors."

"No? You just gave Brighid a ten-point-oh orgasm by sucking on her thigh. I don't care if your lips never touched hers, it was sexual."

His nostrils flared as the red in his eyes swirled dangerously. "Do you know what the blood of an Ancient World goddess tastes like?"

"No, and I'd really like to keep not kn—"

"Like the sty of a swine in the summer sun."

Okay, he really liked the powerful visuals. My stomach twisted, his open fury and disgust affecting me as much as his description. "Are you lying to me?"

"No."

"You just sucked on someone who tastes like pig shit."

"Yes."

"Why?"

"For your answers."

I felt like the world's biggest bitch. Getting in his face when he'd just done something fairly nasty to help me. I stepped around him and walked to the Element. He followed. Within spitting distance of it, reality set in. He was manipulating me again, the bastard.

I whirled around, nearly clipping him with my elbow. "They were *our* answers, Tennyson. Ours, not mine, so don't try to make me feel guilty because you had to go down on Red."

He snorted laughter, his lips drawing back to show off his gleaming fangs. "You are a fast learner, Ms. Harrison. As a goddess, she requires more than most in order to achieve satisfaction, hence the three boys servicing her. A vampire's bite on the inner thigh achieves a sexual high unparalleled by intercourse. For her."

"Doesn't do much for you, huh?"

"Indeed. The blood of Ancient World beings is repugnant to us. We prefer to feed from humans."

He'd gone in knowing what her favor would entail. It was strangely brave. "So you don't get anything from feeding off her?"

"Indigestion."

His deadpan was so spot-on I actually laughed. "Don't tell me you're developing a sense of humor."

"A man cannot survive as long as I have without one." On that, he walked around and climbed into the front passenger seat of the Element, taking care to tuck the cake carrier between his feet and not kick it. With the sun down, he didn't have to hide in the rear.

"Thank you," I blurted once I was behind the wheel. Where had that come from?

"For what?"

I'd dug the hole, might as well jump in. "Thank you for doing the favor for Brighid and keeping me out of it. I don't even want to ponder what she'd have asked of me."

Danger flashed briefly on his face. "Her favor of you would not have come tonight. Your mixed heritage is unique enough to intrigue her. As it is, you've brought her ire down upon yourself."

"Yeah, I was pretty dumb with the gun."

"You were angry."

"It was still dumb."

"Yes."

She'd threatened me, and I couldn't do anything about it. How do you protect yourself from a friggin' goddess?

"Are we done here?" I asked.

"Yes."

"Great."

I started the engine and pointed us toward home. Once I was back on the highway heading south, I called Kathleen and left it on speaker.

"Where have you been?" she asked. "We called hours ago."

"Between dimensions," I replied, and then filled her in on what little we'd learned from Brighid. I left out the specifics of Tennyson's favor, and she—and he—seemed to appreciate that. I almost wished I had mints to offer him, so he could get rid of the shitty goddess aftertaste. "So we have a tentative radius for the spell's location, but beyond that we're stuck on this end."

"Not entirely," Tennyson said.

"What does that mean?" Kathleen and I asked in tandem.

"Brighid's final answer to our queries," he said, as though the answer was obvious. "*I will betray the trust of no more dead men.* She knows of another vampire who may possess such knowledge and skill."

I nearly rear-ended a slow-moving car in my lane. "She was speaking in code?"

"Yes."

"Did she give you any more so-called codes?" Kathleen asked.

"I believe one more, yes."

"And this is just coming up now?" I said.

He ignored me and continued. *"Forgive this rocky ending.* Unsubtle, but effective."

"It's subtle to me," Kathleen said.

"The Rocky Mountains?" I said. Or was that too obvious?

"Correct," Tennyson said.

Kathleen made a disgusted grunt. "We're looking for a vampire who lives in the Rockies? Good luck narrowing that down."

Tennyson frowned, seeming troubled.

"You know which vampire it is, don't you?" I asked.

"Only a Master with several centuries of experience could possibly perform a necromancy spell. I told you once that eight of us are old enough to attempt it. Only two of those live near or in the Rocky Mountain range."

"Have either of them lost vampires?"

"Only one. He who is the eldest of us all. The other is younger than me by seventy-five years, has had no vampires taken as of last word, and was a well-respected warlock before he was turned."

"Sounds like our suspect."

"Perhaps."

"You don't think he'd do it?"

"Quite the opposite, I believe Piotr fully capable of it. However, if he is involved, he will not make himself easy to track down. And he will be expecting your team. Perhaps even hoping for it."

That was a distressing thought. Yet, I think we had something he might not have planned on. "He won't be expecting you, though."

Even as I said it, my mind raced with information and possibilities. Tennyson had likely suspected Piotr from the start, but that blessed honor code prevented him from narcing on a fellow Master. Getting the info out of Brighid had been a way to circumvent his own rules. Fascinating.

"She's right," Kathleen said, reminding us she was still listening in. "If this Piotr doesn't think we're intelligent enough to find him on our own, he may get cocky. And arrogant people make mistakes."

"Hasn't he already made a big mistake?" I asked. "Using Julius as a warning was pretty ineffective, overall. He couldn't have possibly believed we'd back away from investigating this."

"You may be correct in your theory," Tennyson said. "However, if Piotr has more nefarious goals in mind for those who are missing, he may have used your friend as practice. It is also possible he turned your friend into a revenant as part of a favor or debt owed another, and he has no connection to the disappearances."

"I despise theories," Kathleen said.

"Ditto," I said. "Tennyson, do you know where Piotr lives?"

"Colorado," he replied.

"Could you narrow that down to under five hundred square miles?"

"I could reasonably sense his presence if I was within a few miles."

I banged my palm on the steering wheel, then realized I'd gotten up to twenty miles over the speed limit. I slowed down. Wasting the time of getting pulled over—never mind possibly explaining the vampire and severed head riding shotgun—right now would put a serious dent in my already fractured mood. "Kathleen, how did it go with the Dame Alpha?"

"She didn't eat Jaxon," the dhampir replied.

"Thank Iblis for good news. Got anything else?"

"K.I.M. has been given the relevant data on each of the mated pairs taken. The only similarity between them was the lack of offspring."

"Newly mated then?"

"No, several had been mated for twenty years or more, but were unable to reproduce. The Dame Alpha wouldn't let on, but she was worried about that."

With good reason. There were two types of werewolves in the world: born and forced. Forced wolves were made on purpose (it wasn't possible to accidentally create a werewolf) and without Pack permission, and they were almost always outsiders, living on the fringes because they were sterile, unable to reproduce, and so were considered a burden to the Pack resources.

Born werewolves, like their wildlife counterparts, descended from strong, inter-Pack lines, and they mated for life. If a mated pair was unable to have off-spring, their chances of continuing the line was gone. A Pack with multiple infertile pairs threatened its longevity. And it was pretty friggin' unusual to find an infertile born werewolf. Novak had once made a bunny breeding joke in front of one and lost a pint of blood for it.

"This supports your theory of experimentation," Tennyson said.

"Yeah, it does," I said, wishing it didn't. I couldn't bear the idea of humans testing shampoo on dogs, much less capturing and doing who-knows-what to a bunch of vampires and werewolves, all in the name of science.

Science and the supernatural—not good friends.

"We're staying in a motel here in Florida," Kathleen continued. "We'll travel to California tomorrow to speak with the Homme Alpha out there. And you?"

"As much as I want to fly out to Colorado and start busting some heads, we're heading toward home. If this Piotr was the one who performed the spell, he may still be on the coast. And I have an idea for finding him."

"Do not fall in between worlds again, please. Jaxon was quite overreacting with worry."

"Yeah, I'm sure he was the only one."

"Novak seemed mildly concerned."

"Good-bye, Kathleen." I hung up and debated listening to my voice mail from Vincent. Hearing his voice would make me want to call him, and no way was I calling my boyfriend with Tennyson right next to me. Instead, I listened to the voice mail from Weller. Basic check-in, pledging any assistance they might need and asking for more frequent updates.

Kind of weird, but this was my first experience leading a huge case without Julius to back me up, so I figured it was just standard operating procedure.

"What is this idea?" Tennyson asked.

"For finding Piotr?"

"Yes."

"Who do you call when you want to sniff out a recently cast spell?"

He blinked. "Is that a rhetorical question?"

"Nope." Headlights were coming up fast on my bumper. I nudged into the right lane to allow the speeding asshat to pass me. "Most magic leaves behind a residue of sorts. The simpler the magic, the lighter the residual energy. Necromancy sounds seriously complex and high-energy, so it's reasonable to assume that even twenty-four hours later, the location still has some residue."

"And you know someone who can detect this residual energy."

"Yep."

"May I ask who?"

I hit speed dial on my phone even as I replied, "My mom."

"Mom, hey," I said when her line clicked over.

"Shiloh, sweetheart, what is going on?" She was awake now, her voice less raspy than when we'd last spoken. At four in the morning.

"Um, a lot, actually."

In the seat next to me, Tennyson sniggered. It was a funny sound coming from him. I glared at him sideways, careful to keep one eye on the road at all times.

"Is this about why you called me early this morning?" she asked.

"Yes." I launched into an abbreviated explanation. I choked up a little telling her about Julius. There's something about spilling awful news to your mother that opens up the emotional floodgates all over again. She listened without interrupting, making the occasional grunt to let me know I hadn't lost the connection.

She didn't speak after I finished, and I listened to silence for about two miles. "So you want me to endanger my anonymity again and help you track down the place where your friend was murdered?" she asked finally.

Put like that it sounded dangerous. Put any way, it was dangerous. She knew it. And yet . . .

"Mom, you know I wouldn't ask if it wasn't important. Necromancy is against all of the magical laws, and someone did it to a person I care about. I need you." It was a low blow, tacking *I need you* onto a daughter's plea and appealing to her motherly instincts.

Her sigh hissed across the phone like air from a tire. "Where do you want me to meet you?"

"I'll pick you up." It was all I could do to suppress a triumphant cheer. "We're about an hour away, at most."

"We? Who's with you, Shi? That nice young stud you dated?"

"Stag." I corrected her out of habit. She knew full well what Jaxon was, and to this day, she doesn't understand why we broke up. It's a mother's prerogative to torment her daughter. And had I conveniently forgotten to mention who I was with? "I'll see you in an hour, okay? And Mom? Don't tell Dad about this."

"Why would I tell your father? I haven't spoken to him in a month."

I pondered my surprise at that revelation long after I hung up. Even after their separation my parents kept in contact, usually calling once a week. I know it was mostly for my benefit, but they remained friends even after I grew up and moved away. Wise men say we never really stop loving the great loves of our lives, and I suppose that holds doubly true of us magic folk.

A tremble of fear took root in my heart, and it wouldn't go away. The last time my father had been out of contact for a long period of time, it was because a magic abuser was holding him captive in a cage, on display for the amusement of rich assholes who'd pay twenty-five grand a head to see magical creatures do tricks. Jaxon had been in a cage next to my father, and rescuing them was the mission where I'd first met Julius.

The odds of someone else figuring out how to summon, capture, and hold an earth djinn as powerful as Gaius were infinitely small, but not impossible. And I so did not need that problem on my plate.

Tennyson displayed an amazing amount of restraint. He let twenty minutes pass in silence before he broached the subject. "How exactly can your human mother detect the residual energies of the spellcasting? Is she a witch?"

"Nope, she's the daughter of a Romani and a warlock, raised by water djinn after her parents were killed in a Chicago land dispute between some witches and fairies. By living that close to magic most of her life, she developed an echo sense."

A startled look passed across his sharp features. "You would think I'd have heard of someone around here with that power. Truth?"

"Of course."

Echo sense is a fancy word for sensing magical residue. And her connection to the water djinn is how she met my dad, Gaius, an earth djinn. He's over eight hundred years old, still looks thirty-five, and he'd thumbed his nose at a lot of djinn laws by falling in love with my mother and giving her me. I was a unique birth, and we lived somewhat happily until I was thirteen. Then the aggressive side of his nature— the part that gave me the Quarrel—eventually overshadowed their ability to cohabitate, and Dad went back to his life as a djinn.

"My mother just doesn't advertise what she can do," I continued. "She doesn't like getting involved or taking risks, so she keeps her head down. This is a huge favor she's doing me, Tennyson."

"I understand. You have my word, Ms. Harrison, I will not betray your confidence."

It was my turn to be startled. I hadn't even needed to ask. "Thank you."

"Although I must admit mild surprise."

"At what?"

He shifted in his seat, and I swore I saw him smile as he said, "I did not expect to be meeting your mother so soon in our courtship."

CHAPTER 7

It was easier to let the "courtship" thing slide than try to injure him while driving sixty-five miles an hour. Not that my attempts would produce much in the way of bloody results. He was, after all, a vampire Master. He could snap me in half with two fingers. Besides, he seemed to enjoy saying things that got a reaction out of me. Not reacting was my best course of nonaction for his non-amusement.

My mom lives on the outskirts of a tiny town called Felton, population thirteen hundred, almost smack in the middle of Delaware. You could see a little of it from the highway. Typical, two-lane Main Street town, with new homes built on the perimeter of the historical ones.

Hers was a small rancher, hidden behind a tall hedge, a few blocks from the center of town. She enjoyed the privacy of the hedges and multiple flower beds lining her small lot. Nature's own fencing. She bought the place after I moved out on my own, but I always felt at home there. The guest bedroom was painted in white and lilac, the colors I'd chosen as a child, and I'd stayed there at least a dozen times in the last few years.

It was after nine when we arrived. The house blazed with light, and Mom was at the door waiting before we were halfway up the stone path. Her smile faltered when Tennyson stepped into the glare of the porch light, his pale skin impossibly white beneath it. He held the cake carrier in both hands, like a gentleman caller bringing dessert.

"He's not one of yours, Shiloh," Mom said. She made no move to open the screen door for us.

"No, but he's helping us with this case," I replied. She arched a slender, black eyebrow, not buying it. She could sense his power, much as I had. "Okay, he's the Master of the group of vampires that's holding a trailer park and its residents hostage."

She glared at me as one hand lifted to brush an imaginary strand of hair off her forehead. Her long mane of silver-streaked black hair was tied up in its familiar ponytail, not a bit out of place. "That's not funny, sweetheart."

"Mom, I'm serious."

Her sharp gaze swung back to Tennyson. "She's told you who I am?"

"Yes, ma'am," he replied.

"So you know what she is and who her father is?"

"Yes, ma'am." More cautious this time.

"Good." Mom sniffed. "Because if you hurt her in any way during this investigation, we will bring the might of the earth djinn down on you and your line. Are we understood, Vampire?"

I couldn't help it. I turned my head to look at Tennyson. His face was serious, almost stoic, but I saw the hints of humor around his eyes (blue glow—check) and mouth. Still, he managed a very sincere, "Yes, ma'am, we are understood."

I don't know if my parents could actually raise the ire of all earth djinn for me, but I admired her courage in the face of a very old, very powerful Master vampire.

"Good," Mom said. "He stays outside."

"Mom—"

"I will not invite him in."

"Okay, he can wait in the car. We can't stay long, anyway."

"Come in for a few minutes, Shiloh, please."

I took Julius from Tennyson, then did as she asked. The familiar scents of pine and orange greeted me, and above it, the newer, sweeter scent of freshly baked bread. The living room was done in familiar browns and greens, the furniture tasteful without being expensive. She led me down a short hall, into her Country Apples kitchen, complete with matching curtains, rugs, and teapot.

A fresh loaf of bread sat on her counter cutting board. She headed right for it, picked up a serrated bread knife, and began sawing off thick slices. As soon as the first fell and I saw its green-speckled interior, I smiled. Zucchini bread. My favorite.

"Mom, did you pack an overnight bag?" I asked.

"Yes, it's in the hall, you walked right by it." With three slices hacked off, she wandered to the fridge and withdrew a tub of margarine spread. "Have a snack before we leave, you look pale."

"It's been a long day, that's why I look pale." I put the cake carrier down with a harder thump than I intended.

Mom produced a butter knife from her utensil drawer and smeared margarine on the thickest slice of bread. Silently, she handed it over. I took it, still warm, the spread already melting. She'd made zucchini bread for me right after our phone call. I stared at the slice until my vision blurred, as much from fatigue and frustration as from grief.

"I'm so sorry about Julius, Shi. So sorry."

I swallowed the lump in my throat, then ate the bread. It was warm and sweet, the margarine just melted enough to blend. Heaven. The tears dried up under the medicinal power of comfort food, and I was halfway through a second slice before she asked, "Is that him?"

"Yeah."

She eyed the carrier with a dubious frown. "I have a container like that."

"I know."

"I may have to throw it out now."

I leaned across the counter and curled my hand around hers. She squeezed back, her attention still fixed on the carrier. I studied her as I finished the second piece of bread and realized something—her eyes were puffy. She didn't have allergies.

She reached for the carrier, then paused, hand hovering halfway. She reached again, and her fingers brushed the seal.

"You don't have to," I said. "He sleeps when he's in the dark." I didn't want to tell her that Revenant Julius probably wouldn't remember her, anyway.

Mom had met Julius once, two years ago, when he threw me a surprise birthday party for no other reason than to piss me off. I'd withheld my actual birth date for years—I've always hated big, fussy parties, and yes, it stems from childhood clown trauma—but he found out. And he invited my mother. Seeing her interacting with my team had been amusing, especially her tart way of rebuffing Novak's advances.

"Is he in pain?" she asked.

"I don't think so."

She unsealed it anyway and popped off the lid. I flinched, half expecting a waft of something rotting-sweet. Zombies began to rot after a few days, especially in the heat. I hadn't a clue if revenants rotted. All I got was the scent of warm lettuce and the faded odor of blood. His eyes were closed, his skin sallow and still—like a wax replica of a man's head.

"Julius?" Mom asked.

His eyelids snapped up. Julius gazed at her for several seconds. I waited for confusion.

"Elspeth," he said. His recognition surprised me. His next question shocked the shit out of me. "Did we have plans? Did I forget?"

"No, Jules, no plans." Her voice had softened, taking on the comforting tones of a patient teacher. Or a tolerant lover. I mean, she couldn't have been *that* memorable at my birthday party. Unless—

"Mom!" I stiffened and pulled my hand away. "You and Julius—you were . . . did you date?"

"Last year," she said. Her cheeks reddened, though her tone remained annoyingly nonchalant. "For about six months. He's a charming man, Shiloh."

"He's my *boss*, Mom."

"He was a charming, handsome, single man my age, Shiloh."

Okay, I was being a little bratty. But for crying out loud!

"Did we have plans, Elspeth?" Julius asked. "Is Shi coming with us?" His eyes rolled back and forth between us, lips curled in confusion. Seeing my mom couldn't be doing much for his concentration.

"I wanted to say hi." Mom touched his cheek with

her fingertip. "Shiloh and I are going to spend some mother-daughter time, okay? But I had to say hi first."

He smiled affectionately. "Hi."

Watching your mother making googly eyes at your boss's severed head—nine-point-five on the Creep-Out-Meter.

"Mom," I said. "We need to go."

Julius swiveled his eyes toward me. "You look tired, Shiloh. Get some rest."

"In a while."

"I can't feel my legs," he said.

"I know. Time to sleep again, okay?"

He blinked twice in acquiescence. I replaced the lid and pressed, releasing enough air to create that familiar airtight seal. Closing a head up into a cake carrier, preparing to sniff out magic trails with my mother and a Master vampire—my night could not possibly get any more surreal.

Not that I'd voice such a thing out loud. Murphy's Law, and all.

Mom swapped the margarine for a couple bottles of water, which she tossed into a reusable grocery tote. I rolled the rest of the zucchini bread up in a swath of aluminum foil and shoved it in on top of the water. My little trip between worlds had screwed up my internal clock, and I wasn't going out without some food on hand. Low blood sugar makes me cranky.

"I can't believe you dated him and didn't tell me,"

I said as we headed for the front door with the food and the head.

Mom paused long enough to scoop a blue canvas overnight bag off the floor by the door. "I didn't need your blessing or your permission, sweetheart," she replied coolly. She sounded more amused than annoyed.

"Well, no, but . . ."

She stopped with her hand on the doorknob. "But?"

"He's not just a man I know . . . he's my boss!"

"You already said that he was your boss. He was also a very good lover."

"Okay, I'm *definitely* done talking about this." If my hands had been free, I would have clamped them down over my ears for effect. Yes, my mother brings out my childish side. Whose doesn't?

Tennyson had taken up residence in one of the white plastic patio chairs occupying the left side of the porch. He stood as we exited the house. If he'd been listening to our conversation, he made no indication. He opened the passenger side door for my mother. She gave him a disdainful sniff and climbed in.

I rolled my eyes, put the cake carrier and tote in the backseat, and settled in up front. The back door shut with a bang and the familiar, empty black cloak appeared in my mirror.

"Necromancy is powerful magic," Mom said as I got us back on the road. "Even with my echo sense, powerful magic can be harder to pin down than weak magic. It tends to bounce around like a pinball, instead of staying localized to one place. Normally, what we're trying to do would only get us within a dozen miles of the point of origin."

"Normally," I said. "What's different?"

"Your necromancer made a mistake by sending the revenant back to you," Tennyson said. Apparently he caught on to magical goings-on faster than me.

"Exactly," Mom replied.

I negotiated a turn and angled us back toward the highway. As much as I wanted to puzzle it out on my own, I wanted simple answers. "How's that help?"

"Think of Julius as a magnet, Shi," Mom said, "and the magic as iron filings. The closer we get to the point of origin, the more magic will be drawn to him, and the more I'll sense it."

"Is the reverse also true?"

"What do you mean?"

"The closer we get to the necromancer," I said. "Will he be able to sense Julius and know we're coming?"

"I don't know."

I glanced into the rearview—for all the good it did me. "Tennyson?"

"It's likely."

"But you don't know."

"I'm sorry, no. This is not my area of expertise."

I swore I heard sarcasm. "So Julius could be a warning beacon for his maker, as much as a heat-seeking missile for us."

No one spoke to confirm or deny my statement. It didn't help my nervous stomach. At least my headache had come and gone during the drive to Mom's. Maybe my little cross-dimensional trip had taken the edge off the potential migraine.

Five miles down the highway, it occurred to me I still hadn't returned Vincent's call. I wasn't ignoring him, but my love life was at the very bottom of the priority list. It's why our relationship was casual, instead of serious. And he hadn't left a voice message, so it couldn't have been urgent. Still, I felt irrationally less uneasy talking to him now that I wasn't alone with Tennyson.

I palmed my Raspberry and speed-dialed his number. It rang half a dozen times before switching over to voice mail. His familiar baritone spoke with the noise of rap music in the background—"It's Vince, talk to me after the beep."

"It's me," I said. "I had a missed call from you, and I wanted to say hey. I'll be working for a few days, but I'll . . ." What? I searched for something to say. "We'll talk later. Bye."

Dork, thy name is Shiloh.

"How is Vincent doing?" Mom asked.

I tossed her a sideways glare. "Not talking about him."

"Okay."

A few more miles down the highway, I asked, "So any thoughts on a direction? Or should I just drive?"

"Keep going south," Mom replied. "The echo is extremely faint, but it's definitely south of here."

"South it is."

Three hours south, as it turned out. I stopped once around eleven for a bathroom break and some bad gas station coffee. Mom bought a ginger ale. Tennyson made a phone call to a vampire named Drayden, his second in line and the man in charge of the hostage takeover. It sounded like a status report. The vamps were behaving, the residents were still scared, but quiet. None of the police had made a move against them.

I wasn't shy about eavesdropping on the conversation. For some reason, seeing Tennyson with a cell phone became a source of amusement for me. It seemed way too modern for someone so blessed old. And old-fashioned.

We were back on the road for another hour before Mom started choking.

I was too busy trying to stay awake after twenty-four-plus hours, so I didn't pay attention to the way her hands were gripping her knees. Or her new, tense posture. Those things were discarded by my conscious mind as unimportant details. Then Tennyson shifted forward between the front seats.

"Your mother reeks of fear," he said, speaking for the first time since we left the gas station.

I glanced over at Mom, and all of those peripheral details became crystal clear—death grip on her knees, red cheeks, straight back, open mouth. Tiny little mewling sounds, so faint I thought I imagined them, tore from her constricting throat.

"Mom? Mom!" I slammed on the brakes. We were alone on the highway, so no one saw my crazy swerving onto the shoulder.

Tennyson was out and dragging Mom through her open door before I could properly shift into Park. His arms looped around her waist and he held her close against his chest. Panic set in—distrust and old fears— and I was certain he was going to bite her. I scrambled across the seat and tumbled out the passenger door, fear tangling my limbs. I hit the gravel shoulder hard on my palms, scraping them both raw.

"Mom!"

She whimpered. I reached for my gun.

Tennyson balled his right fist, cupped his left hand around it, and jerked both upward against my mom's stomach. Hand on the grip of my sidearm, I realized what he was doing. He wasn't attacking her while she was vulnerable. He was trying the Heimlich maneuver.

I used the car to stand up, afraid my legs wouldn't support me. Mom's face had turned dark red. Her thick-lashed eyes were as wide as I've ever seen them and rimmed with tears. She locked her gaze with mine, and I saw defeat in her eyes.

"No!" More than ever, I wished for my dad's strength in magic. For the power to save my mother, who was slowly choking to death in front of me.

Tennyson didn't relent. I gathered what will I possessed, each tendril of magic in my body, the strength and solidity of the earth djinn, and cast it at my mom's dying body. It wasn't much.

It was timed with one more pump from Tennyson. She retched up something and it spewed from her mouth in a lump of twisting, writhing black. The walnut-sized thing hit the side of the Element and bounced to the gravel, before trying to skitter away. I slammed my foot down. It crunched like a rice cereal treat.

I lifted my foot, my entire body shaking with adrenaline. Twisted legs stuck out of its smashed body, and a line of greenish goo clung to the bottom of my boot. It looked like a blessed spider.

Mom's choking sobs stole my attention. She was still in Tennyson's arms, and both had crouched to the ground. She shook and sobbed against him, sucking in great lungfuls of air. He stroked her back with his free hand, silent. I went to my knees next to them and touched her shoulder.

She looked up, tears streaking her flaming cheeks, and fell into my arms. I held my mom like she'd held me so many times, through nightmares and skinned knees and childish teasing. As I held her and urged my own pounding heart to calm, I realized something awful—someone had tried to kill her tonight, and it was my fault.

You don't swallow a spider by accident while driving in a car going sixty-five miles an hour. Someone sends it to you. She wouldn't have been targeted if I had left her at home, instead of getting her involved in my work.

"I'm sorry," I whispered. "So sorry."

"This wasn't your fault," Tennyson said.

"I brought her out here. It is my fault."

"No, sweetheart," Mom said, her voice barely a croak. "It was a booby trap. We're close."

"Booby trap?"

She sat up and wiped her eyes with the back of her hands. Her color was almost back to normal, and her breaths came in steady inhales and exhales. "I felt the moment I triggered it. It's like a magical snare, set to snap when a certain kind of counter-magic comes into contact with it. Counter-magic like my echo sense."

I'd never heard of such a thing. "The snare stuffs a magic spider down your throat?"

"As the trapper wishes." She snuffled. A white handkerchief appeared in front of her. She took it from Tennyson with a nod and blew her nose.

"Effective snare," Tennyson said.

"Did you feel it?" I asked him.

"No."

Suddenly my entire knowledge base of magic

seemed grossly inadequate. "Who knows how to lay snares like this?"

Something very close to annoyance peeked through on his face. "The snare itself is not as unusual as you may think. Versions of them occur naturally around homes and sacred places such as churches and holy ground. The sort of snare that befell your mother, however, requires willful desire to injure or destroy."

"Okay, information useful," I said, "but not narrowing down the suspect list. Our necromancer?"

"Likely."

His tone spoke volumes. "But you don't think so?"

"I have not committed myself to a single explanation for recent events. The necromancer may be directly involved in the kidnapping of my people, or he may yet be a pawn in a larger game. This is why we're investigating, no?"

"Yeah, okay." I glanced at the green-and-black mess now smushed into the shoulder of the road. "Will the snare activate again?"

"Unlikely," he replied. "However, the trapper will know his trap has been sprung. We should move quickly now that our presence is known."

"Great."

I stood up and helped Mom to her feet. My adrenaline was waning, leaving my own limbs a bit shaky—no stopping the eventual side effects this time, I felt it all the way through me. Sheer panic born of nearly losing your mother does that.

She tried to look at my scraped palms. I jerked my hands away, loaded her into the front seat, then walked around to get in on my side. Always faster than me, Tennyson was inside and offering Mom a bottle of water before I could get buckled up. She sipped at it, grimacing.

A car sped by in the opposite direction, its head-lights gleaming silver light at us. We were just over the line into Virginia, about an hour and a half from the end of the peninsula and the Bay Bridge Tunnel.

Time to get moving.

We passed through a small town. It didn't consist of much from the highway—a few houses, a church, and a lot of billboards. The kind of place most people drove through on their way elsewhere. A few miles later, Mom grabbed the back of my seat.

"Turn around," she said.

I went up to the next turnaround and switched to the northbound lane. After a few more miles, she said, "Slow down."

I did, down to forty, glad we were still very alone on the road. Half a mile or so ahead was a stoplight intersection, with gas stations on either side, and a restaurant on one corner. A right-pointing sign an-nounced we were close to Chincoteague Island and its wild pony attractions—something I've never bothered investigating. Horses dislike most magical creatures. My djinn half would probably give those ponies fits.

"Turn right."

We were nearly on top of the intersection, so I hung a sharp right down that street, putting the restaurant on my left and gas station on my right. A gas station, diner, video rental combo—definitely a tourist trap disguised as a locals' place. Less than a quarter mile down on the left was a storage unit facility.

It's where Mom pointed as she said, "In there."

I turned and idled in front of the gate. It was the middle of the night. Floodlights cast an awful yellow glow on us from spaced intervals along the ten-foot-high perimeter fence. It was simple chain-link, topped with curling barbed wire. I eyed the office building and the fence itself—no cameras. At least, none that I could see.

"They used a rented storage unit for this?" I asked.

"My echo sense is pointing me here, Shi. This is where Julius was killed."

It didn't seem terribly private, but whatever. "Tennyson? Can you help with the gate?"

He slid out of the vehicle. The gate had a single padlock, which he twisted and snapped with minimal effort. He gave the gate a push, and it trundled sideways on a track until we had just enough room to drive through. He closed it again after us. I parked halfway down the rows of the storage units, far enough from the road to prevent passersby from spotting the Element.

Loose gravel crunched underfoot as Mom and I joined Tennyson by the car's rear. She had the cake carrier tight against her chest, hugging it like a safety blanket, paler than was healthy.

"Mom, you want to wait in the car?" I asked as I slipped my gun from its holster.

"No." It was her *ask me again and I'll brain you* voice, so I left it alone.

Tennyson paused to sniff the night air. "Blood," he said. "This way."

The gravel made it impossible to be silent, and each of our steps sounded like a gunshot in the quiet night. We crunched down to the last of six rows, then right, to the unit farthest from the office and the main highway. It was a skinny end unit, the kind that always seemed useless to me—didn't people rent storage units because they had a lot of stuff?

As with the gate, Tennyson yanked at the padlock. It creaked and broke off in his hand. I snapped my gun's safety off. He rolled up the door, and I swung forward, barrel aimed at the . . . empty unit.

The hell?

The cement floor was bare, the metal walls clean and unmarked. It was barely wide enough to stand in the middle and stretch both of my arms out, and about eight feet deep. The thick, metallic odor of blood wafted out, though, strong enough to make my stomach roil. My neck hairs prickled.

I smelled blood I couldn't see, and residual energy from the revenancy spell had led us here. So why was the unit empty?

Gun first, I stepped inside.

And fell right through the cement floor.

CHAPTER 8

If I had been able to see through the glamour posing as a cement floor, I'd have seen the stairs I was now falling down ass over teakettle. Hard, concrete stairs, half the width of the storage unit above. My elbows and legs scraped the rough walls all the way down. Which was pretty far down.

I finally hit bottom after what felt like an eternity of bumps and tumbles. The world tilted and spun like a carnival ride. My chin smarted, and I felt something wet on my neck. I blinked a few times and realized I was staring back up the dug-and-packed steps I'd introduced my entire body to on the way down. Tennyson and Mom were still at the top, gaping. Probably wondering where I'd disappeared to.

"Shiloh!" Mom's mouth formed the word, but

oddly, I couldn't hear her. She started forward; Tennyson held her back with an arm.

"Stairs," I yelled, unsure if she'd hear me. Her expression change was negative.

I sat up, grateful everything seemed functional, considering the distance fallen. Once again my half djinn side proved useful—hard-to-kill can also be translated into hard-to-poison and hard-to-break-my-bones. So while I'd cut my chin on the way down, and most of my muscles ached, nothing else felt seriously wounded.

Yay me.

Tennyson extended his left foot and felt around. His eyebrows arched when he penetrated the glamour. He said something to my mom, who nodded. The foot came down onto the top step. Then the second followed. Good, he was figuring this out.

Time to see what this dugout tunnel led to. Behind me was a narrow corridor less than six feet long. It ended at a heavy, steel door, the kind that's both fireproof and soundproof.

"Shiloh?" Hearing my first name roll off Tennyson's tongue surprised me. He was nearly to the bottom of the stairs when I looked up at him. His eyes narrowed on my chin. Specifically, on my bloody chin. Dots of green danced in his eyes—was green the color of hunger?

"I'm fine," I said, then again when Mom appeared

behind him. She fussed over my chin, using her borrowed handkerchief to wipe me down. The same one she'd blown her nose into earlier.

Gross.

I jerked away and used the wall to stand. "I'm fine, really."

"You disappeared, Shi," Mom said.

"Yeah, well, the floor kind of gave way."

"An impressive glamour," Tennyson said. He stooped and when he stood, he handed me my gun.

"I don't suppose anyone has a flashlight." Our only current light source was reflecting down from the security poles outside.

Tennyson removed his cell phone and flipped it open. The pale glow helped. I reached for my Raspberry. A strange crackling sound accompanied it out of my pocket. The display screen was smashed and several keys loose.

"Shit." It didn't power up. I relied so much on technology, I wasn't certain I had my teams' numbers memorized. I wasn't even sure I had my own number memorized, now that I thought about it.

Double shit.

A problem for when we were out of here. For now, we approached the door, Mom keeping wisely to the rear. It had a levered handle and no obvious connections to security devices. We'd already tripped the magical snare, and it was possible whoever created the floor glamour knew someone passed through it. No sense in playing it safe now.

I raised my weapon in my right hand, steadying it across the wrist of my left. Tennyson pressed down on the handle and pushed. The door squealed open, heavy and ominous. An assault of smells tumbled out before the door was open more than ten degrees. Metallic blood, peppery sage, charred wood, something sweet like cherries, and other, baser scents I couldn't identify. A tingle of magic wrapped around me like a thousand pinpricks on my skin.

He shoved the door open completely. I spied the familiar shape of a light switch near the door and flipped it. Five florescent floor lamps blazed to life, each spaced at equal intervals around the chamber. Twenty feet or so across, it took me a moment to process the layout.

The room was dug out in the shape of a pentagram, with one lamp anchoring each point, the top point of the star directly across from us. In the center of the room was a wooden table, its surface stained black. The packed-earth floor was likewise stained in pools and splatters of black. Stained chains were still attached to both ends of the wooden table. Small scars on opposite sides made my stomach curl—fingernails could have made those.

Two other objects were in the room. One was a large, mobile tool chest, close enough to have gained its own spackling of dried blood. The other was what looked like a hairdresser's table, with various baskets and drawers. Bottles and sacks of dozens of things— spices, flakes, bones, you name a magical ingredient, it might have been there—filled those baskets and drawers.

Symbols I didn't recognize had been carved into the dirt floor near each lamp, each a twisted reminder that I knew little about the external manipulation of magic by beings not born to it—human witches and warlocks, for example. Warlocks turned vampire, more specifically.

"This is it," Mom said, almost as much to say *something* than for any other reason. She lingered on the threshold, and I didn't blame her. The room rippled with terrible power. If evil could take physical form at that moment, it would be sitting on the table and cackling at us.

"Tennyson," I said, quiet even though we seemed to be alone, "Can you sense if Piotr was here recently?"

"I cannot sense his presence," he said, crushing my hopes. His nostrils flared. "However, Piotr is fond of a particularly unappealing cologne. I believe it's named after a former basketball player. I do detect the faintest hints of its fragrance."

"He can't be the only person who wears it."

"Of course not. The evidence is circumstantial, as you would say."

"Sounds pretty damning to me," Mom said.

"What about all these symbols?" I asked, pointing. "Anyone?"

Tennyson approached the nearest, something that looked like a curly Y. "They appear to be alchemical symbols. Signs of the Zodiac. This one is Aries."

"Do you know the others?"

He walked to each symbol, naming them as he went in a wide circle. "Aries, Taurus, Sagittarius, Scorpio, and Aquarius."

"How in the world are they useful to a necromancer?"

"Alchemical symbols," Mom said from the door. "Alchemy is, at its root, about transformation. The symbols could have been chosen to anchor the spell based on the alchemical properties of each sign."

I gaped at her. "Do you know the properties?"

"No, I'm sorry." She eyed the remains of my phone, which I still held in my left hand. I knew what she was thinking. K.I.M. would know.

"So we have a room shaped like a pentagram, five signs of the Zodiac, a torture table, and a bunch of herbs," I said. "All the ingredients to make a revenant, without exact instructions for doing so."

"The instructions mean little," Tennyson said, "unless you mean to make your own."

"When hell freezes over," I muttered. "Mom, bring Julius here."

She hesitated, then came. "Are you sure this is wise?"

"Not really, but maybe being here will jog his memory." I popped off the lid.

His eyelids popped up, so wide the whites of his eyes showed. He screamed, a high-pitched, tortured sound that made my teeth ache. He screamed and screamed, wild and horrified, a gibbering sound made worse for the lack of lung power. I slammed the lid back down, and the screaming stopped.

Panting a little, I took a step back. "Okay, bad idea."

Mom resealed the carrier, her face pale and drawn.

"His reaction, though, does confirm this as the location of his murder," Tennyson said. "What is your next move?"

"Call the cops."

He stared. "I beg your pardon?"

"We need forensic evidence," I said. "My badge still says US Marshal on it, so they won't ask too many questions. This place needs to be photographed, blood samples tested, and fingerprints lifted. If we're lucky, it'll help us locate this necromancer."

Ten minutes later, two state police cruisers joined our Element outside of the storage unit. Four officers unfolded themselves from their cars, a little sleepy-eyed. I zeroed in on the highest-ranking officer and glanced at his name tag.

"Officer Osborne," I said, flashing him my Marshal badge. "Shiloh Harrison, US Marshals', Para-Marshal

Office." Mom was hiding in the backseat of the Element, a civilian staying out of the way. Tennyson
had chosen to remain below and continued looking
around while I waited for the police.

"Ma'am," Osborne said. He was tall and lanky, with
barely enough muscle not to be considered emaci-
ated. Tanned skin betrayed a love of sunshine and
his angled nose betrayed too many fistfights. "It's not
often we get calls from a Para-Marshal who says she
found a potential crime scene."

The faint sneer with this statement somehow
blamed me for the crime scene existing at all. Not
terribly far from the truth, I supposed.

"Believe me, I was surprised to find it," I said.

"If I may ask, ma'am, *how* did you find it way out
here?"

"Anonymous tip."

His thin lips curled down. He didn't like that
answer, but I had none other for him. Couldn't very
well tell him my mother followed the metaphorical
scent of magic based on the cryptic musings of a
sex-craved goddess. Even though paranormal oc-
currences were fairly commonplace now, folks in
the smaller communities rarely saw it in their quiet
streets. Out here, it was easier to pretend magic was
still fiction.

Osborne slid a long-handled flashlight from his
belt and waved a hand at his companions. The quartet
moved toward the storage unit. Osborne paused in the

entryway, angling the beam up, down, and all around. He turned his head toward me, lips puckered.

"You said there were stairs," he said.

"Just inside," I replied. "The floor is an illusion."

His eyebrows dug down into a deep vee, joining his puckered lips in creating an almost comical expression of disbelief. He shined the flashlight across the floor, as though expecting it to penetrate the glamour. The shortest of the four patrolmen snorted.

Osborne used the doorway for balance and stretched out his right foot. I waited for his toes to sink through. His shiny boot stepped down flat on the cement floor. I sucked in a harsh breath. Osborne took four steps inside, stamping his heels and testing what looked and sounded like a solid floor.

"So, Marshal Harrison," Osborne said as he pivoted on his heel to glare at me. "Pretty solid illusion you have here."

One of the other patrolmen snickered. The short one made no attempt to hide his disgust.

What? The? Hell?

I was escorted off the premises with a stern warning from Osborne, and was informed in no uncertain terms that I was to pay for all locks broken, as well as issue a formal, written apology to the owner within twenty-four hours. I had absolutely nothing to say. I'd been given no chance to explain, no chance to put my own foot through the glamour and prove I wasn't crazy.

One of the patrol cars followed me two miles north on the highway. The instant the car turned off, I pulled over. Mom popped up and I explained what was happening while I climbed out. I couldn't double back. I had no doubts the cops were watching the storage area. I also couldn't leave.

Tennyson was still back there.

No doubt he'd heard the entire exchange above. Possibly he'd even watched from below as Osborne walked about seemingly on nothing.

"It doesn't completely surprise me," Mom said. She joined me on the gravel, both of us looking southward. "Often you must believe in the possibility of magic in order to see through the strongest of glamours. It's how fairies fly around in broad daylight, and why the average person doesn't feel a ley line when they're standing on one."

"I should have known better. Shouldn't have done that. Julius wouldn't have done that."

"You aren't Julius, sweetheart."

"No, but I'm acting leader of this team and I'm making decisions like a fucking rookie."

"Language, Shi."

"Like a darn rookie."

"He'll find his way back."

I angled toward her, hands on hips, and glared. "I'm not worried about Tennyson, Mom—he can take care of himself and then some. I'm talking about procedure. We lost the blessed crime scene. Julius wouldn't have done that."

"You don't know what he would have done, and you need to stop second-guessing yourself. Follow your own instincts."

"I did, which is why we're standing by the side of the road right now."

"Yes, and you also have something you didn't have an hour ago, Shiloh. You have the location of the crime scene, as well as more information on how the spell was performed. You also have circumstantial evidence that places this Piotr at the crime scene. All because you followed your instincts and asked me to help you."

She was trying to make me feel better, and it was working. I didn't want to feel better.

"We need to know who was renting that particular unit," I said. "But I can't get back there on foot fast enough, and I can't drive back without being seen. The sun will be up in an hour or so." Two cars had already passed us heading south in the opposite lane. Even if I had a working cell, I didn't know Tennyson's number. I kicked the gravel in petulant frustration. Mom put her hand on my shoulder.

"So we wait until sunrise."

What else could we do?

The minutes ticked by, traffic along the highway increased, and each time I spotted what looked like a cop car, my anxiety skyrocketed. While the locals could throw every charge in the book at me without any possibly sticking, I didn't have the time to waste. We were working on twenty-four hours and change on the trailer park crisis, and I imagined Lieutenant Foster and his men were getting antsy.

Thirty minutes later, just as the first faint throbs of a migraine were tickling me behind the eyes, a familiar black cloak broke from the brush, and then Tennyson was standing on the shoulder. Grass and twigs clung to the fabric and his hair was wind-mussed, but even for the exertion and the mileage, he wasn't out of breath. Not that vampires breathed, but still.

My relief at his appearance surprised me, but I think I managed to keep it off my face.

"Well," he said, "that did not go quite as expected, did it?"

"Understatement of the year," I said. "Sorry about leaving you."

"No need, it gave me time to continue searching the room. I used my cellular to take photographs, as well as catalogue herbs and ingredients I recognized. I was uncertain when or if we'd manage to return, so I was thorough."

"Thank you." Next to him saying *I was smart enough to stop at the office and pull some paperwork,* it was the best news I'd had all day.

"I also stopped at the main office on my way out." My mouth fell open, which made him smile. "I liberated the file on that particular unit, and I hope you find it of use."

Most girls get weak-kneed when a boy brings her flowers. Apparently I get excited when a guy brings me rental agreements.

I flipped open the manila folder and scanned until I found the renter's name. A cold fist grabbed my heart and squeezed. I searched lower, spotting the familiar, doctor's-scrawl signature, and the fist closed tighter. I think I even forgot to breathe for a minute, because the paper blurred. My vision grayed out. A rush of air from a passing vehicle blew the pages out of my hand.

Mom was saying my name. Tennyson scooped up the loose pages and looked at them. His eyes locked on to me, genuine surprise on his face. Then confusion. I concentrated on not passing out. My eye-throb grew more intense.

"Doesn't make sense," I stuttered, once I discovered my lungs still worked.

"Will one of you talk to me, please?" Mom asked.

Tennyson cocked his head, a silent question for me. "It's his signature," was all I could force out.

"I'm very sorry, Ms. Juno," Tennyson said, not addressing me this time. He held the papers out to Mom. "But it appears the unit was rented out by Julius Almeida."

CHAPTER 9

Tennyson took charge, and for a little while, I allowed it. He ushered Mom and me back into the Element, took the keys, and got us on the road again. Ten minutes later, he pulled into a gas station advertising hot coffee, cheap gas, and lotto tickets. He parked near the rear of the lot and turned off the engine. I was riding shotgun with the file, trying to keep my brain from throbbing out of my skull. Mom was folded into the rear as far from the cake carrier as she could physically get without climbing through the door.

"You are positive the signature is his?" Tennyson asked again.

"I've seen him sign hundreds of documents," I replied. My voice sounded funny, almost hollow. I scanned the pages again, checking all of the vital information. The cold fist hadn't released my heart.

"Birth date, address, home phone which he does not give out to anyone—it's all correct. Not impossible to find under the right circumstances, but . . ."

"Maybe he didn't know," Mom said. "Maybe he rented it for someone and he didn't know."

I snorted. "That's lame."

"You'd rather believe Julius capable of conspiring with a necromancer?"

"No, but Julius wasn't an idiot, Mom. He wouldn't blindly rent a storage unit for someone else, and then not know what was going on with it. He just wouldn't."

"How were his financial circumstances?" Tennyson asked.

"He never complained about money," I replied, certain of where his train of thought was leading. "We all get salaries. If he needed money, he could have asked any of us."

"A man who leads a team of warriors," Tennyson said. "A man who came up through the military ranks and understands country above self. Do you truly see this man asking charity of anyone?"

"Before he sides with this kind of evil? Yes."

"And if the debt was larger than money? Of a grander scale?"

I slammed my palm against the dashboard. Little lights winked behind my eyes. "Bless it, I don't need conspiracy theories, I need answers."

"So ask him."

Three simple words. They didn't compute. Not at first. Then I remembered how Julius had screamed when he saw the crime scene. Those agonized shrieks still echoed in my mind. Had he screamed like that while being tortured to death? Did he walk down those steps on his own steam? Could he have possibly known his fate?

"Not here," I said. "Not in the car. We need to go back to headquarters and regroup. I have to call Novak and tell him what's happened."

"Can you not use my phone?"

I forced a breath through clenched teeth. "No, because I'm such a friggin' techno-brat that I can't remember any of their actual phone numbers."

"'Techno-brat?'"

I almost told him to bite me, then thought better of it. "Switch with me."

We ended up playing musical chairs, with me landing in the driver's seat, Mom up next to me, and Tennyson back in the rear. My entire skull hurt—I swore my hair even hurt—but with the sun touching on the horizon, he'd need the extra protection. We had a little over an hour's drive ahead of us.

Tennyson's phone rang forty minutes into the return trip.

"Drayden," he said, before answering. "Yes?"

Habit had me checking his nonexistent reflection in the rearview. Mom stared straight ahead, lost in her own thoughts. If her sense of betrayal was half of my own, then she was in some serious emotional pain.

"Of course," Tennyson said. "Thank you, Drayden." He shifted forward and held his phone out to me. "It seems your incubus is quite clever. He hasn't been able to reach you, so he sent a police officer to track down one of my people in order to seek me out. He now has this number and will be calling momentarily."

"Thank Iblis," I said, and took the phone. Sure enough, it rang again less than a minute later. "Harrison."

"There you are," Kathleen said. "Where have you been, between dimensions again?" That was as close to a joke as I'd ever heard from her.

"I fell down some stairs and broke my Raspberry."

Pause. "To someone else that might sound strange."

"Oh, no, that's not the worst part of my night, trust me." I didn't want to elaborate over Tennyson's phone, though. Not about this. "Look, where are you?"

"San Diego. We're meeting the Homme Alpha in the morning."

It is morning perched on the tip of my tongue, until I remembered the time difference. "Look, I have a lot to tell you, but it needs to wait until I'm at HQ and back on a secure line. Can I call you guys back in about an hour and a half?"

"Yeah, the three of us are resting at a hotel until our eight o'clock appointment. The Homme Alpha is much stricter about schedules than the Dame Alpha."

"Well, even werewolves need their beauty sleep, I guess."

Behind me, Tennyson snickered.

"But you're all right?" Kathleen asked. "Jaxon wants to know."

No. "Yeah, I'm fine. Any other reports of massive vampire activity?"

"K.I.M. has collated contact information on over a thousand known vampire employees who failed to show up for their legitimate employment yesterday. Since they cannot be identified on sight by their lineage, she cannot tell which vamps belong to which Masters."

Getting together in large groups was worrisome, but given the circumstances, not altogether unexpected. The good news? No more blatant displays of aggression. "Thanks, Kathleen. I'll call you soon."

She said good-bye. I handed the phone over my shoulder. Tennyson slipped it from my fingers with a gentle brush of cool skin. I was grateful for the call. I felt less isolated from my friends, less like I was floundering alone in the dark.

It wasn't until I had turned down the road of our cul-de-sac that I realized I was about to commit a serious breach of security by taking a vampire into our headquarters. Something I'd have never considered doing twenty-four hours ago. Funny how your perspective can change so radically in a day.

I entered my security code at the outer gate—a twelve-foot-tall, iron job that ran the perimeter of our ten acres of land, all the way to the back of the helicopter pad. Heat sensors scanned the Element and verified two hot spots (me and Mom) and one cool spot (Tennyson). The revenant didn't even register on the scan. I tucked that information away, then accepted the scan as correct. The outer gate swung inward. I drove through and it closed automatically behind us.

The second gate was fifteen feet inside the first, only this was one was invisible. Like those underground dog fences, the interior perimeter was set to electrify if anyone or anything got through the first gate without the correct authorization codes. The setting was high enough to knock even the strongest vampire for a serious loop.

We passed without incident. I parked on the street, at the top of the cul-de-sac. Each of us had something to carry. Mom took her overnight bag from the rear. I snatched her bread-and-water-bearing tote. Tennyson was stuck with the cake carrier. He tucked it beneath his cloak, which he'd pulled tight around his body. The hood was up, tugged low to protect his face.

He waited until we ladies were in the foyer and then made a dash from the car at the still-open door.

He stopped at the threshold and gave me an expectant look.

Here we go. "Come in," I said.

He did. I shut the door. The downstairs had quite a few windows, especially on the east side. Almost instinctively, I walked around pulling drapes and shutting blinds. They stared at me from the hall until I realized they were waiting to be told where to go. Neither of them had been here before. I could count on one hand the number of non-team members who had. Ever.

"Mom, there are some spare rooms upstairs if you want to put your bag down," I said. "First on the left and second on the right. Don't go into the one that smells like popcorn, that's Jaxon's room."

To Tennyson: "Put the revenant, um . . ." I cast about for a good holding place, only it didn't seem to matter much. Julius wasn't walking off on his own, and when the hell had I started thinking of him as "the revenant?" "Put him anywhere. Just don't go around messing with stuff, okay?"

"I will not meddle in your private affairs," he replied stiffly. "I would not insult my host in such a manner."

Had I just insulted him by insinuating he'd insulted me first? Or maybe that was a dig at how I'd acted at Brighid's home. I *had* acted foolishly and lost my temper.

Mom had disappeared upstairs. I ached to follow

her. I wanted a long shower, a good meal, and at least twelve hours of sleep. Instead, I had an unpleasant phone call to make.

Tennyson deposited the cake carrier on the kitchen counter—for some reason this made my sleep-deprived self snort giggles—and followed me into the conference room. I stalked over to K.I.M. and turned on the audio interface.

"Recognize Harrison, Shiloh," I said.

"Recognized," replied K.I.M.'s digital voice. Not unlike an automated telephone service line. "Query."

She had a query? "Proceed."

"Perimeter sensors indicated a cool source in an approaching vehicle. Source is likely vampire. Is a vampire on the premises?"

"Affirmative."

"Security protocols restrict—"

"I know security protocols, but circumstances are a little abnormal right now."

"Query. I did not understand. Please rephrase."

I sighed. The audio interface with our supersmart and supercomplex computer system was pretty sweet—most of the time. K.I.M.'s programming required specific phrasing of questions and answers for her to process information and form coherent replies. "Disable security protocols surrounding vampires." I gave the computer my code clearance.

"Processing," K.I.M. said. "Security protocols disabled."

Good. The last thing I needed was for one of K.I.M.'s sensors to decide Tennyson was a threat and spray him with silver dust—only one of many fun, built-in security features of the house, and why it was our safest location right now.

"Query," I said.

"Proceed."

"Display United States map overlaid with known addresses of all missing vampires."

"Working." Next to the audio gear, a twenty-four-inch computer monitor flashed to life. The map appeared first, with Hawaii and Alaska off-set on the left-hand side of the screen. Tiny red dots sprouted like fast-growing fungus all across the country. "Task complete."

Kathleen was right—not much of a pattern.

"What does this tell you?" Tennyson asked.

"Nothing useful," I replied. "Just that whoever was taking vampires did it from all over. I guess to try to hide what they were doing for as long as possible. Six vampires missing from one town is more suspicious than one from six towns."

"Until Masters begin missing their children."

"Right."

K.I.M.'s desk was a huge old thing, strong enough to hold her massive setup, without losing its antique aesthetic. I tugged open the bottom drawer—it tends to stick—and retrieved a brand-new Raspberry. "Activate communication device A-S-54," I said.

"Command accepted," K.I.M. said. "Device activated."

"Identification Harrison, Shiloh. Transfer all necessary data."

Her system whirred. "Transfer complete."

"Remarkable," Tennyson said. "Your technological advancements are astonishing for a small group on the government's payroll."

"K.I.M. was a gift."

"And the computer's upkeep? These grounds? Your security measures?"

I knew what he was getting at, but I wasn't in the right headspace to entertain the theory that maybe some of our fund came from less-than-savory sources. I powered up the new Raspberry while I stalked into the kitchen. Dialed Novak's number. Hungry as I was, nothing in the fridge or cupboards was appealing. Maybe I'd hack off another hunk of zucchini bread.

"Novak," he barked over the phone.

I set it to speaker, placed the phone on the counter, and hopped up onto a stool. "Hey, is everyone with you?" I asked.

"They're here. What's going on, Shi?"

I started with my mom and why I dragged her into things, detailed the magical snare and my tumble through an imaginary floor, the symbols we'd discovered in the pentagram room, and the cops kicking us off the premises. They let me talk for the better part of fifteen minutes without interruption, until I told them about the rental agreement.

We rehashed the same explanations I'd debated with Tennyson.

"He never talked about money problems with any of you?" I asked. "Mentioned it casually, commented on even having a storage unit?"

"No," Kathleen said. "He rarely spoke of money in any capacity in my presence." To which Jaxon added, "Ditto."

"Putting aside the issue of money," Novak said, "what other possible reason could Julius have had for cooperating?"

No one had an answer.

"Have you asked him?" Kathleen asked. "He is still with you?"

"He's here," I replied, eyeing the container on the counter less than an arm's reach away. The screaming in my head began again, which only made my ebbing migraine roar back to colorful life. I'd told them about his reaction to the pentagram room, but had no words to truly describe those shrieks.

"Well?"

"All right, hold on."

Tennyson handed the carrier over to me, and I smiled my thanks. He'd stayed silent throughout, well aware I hadn't told my team he was inside. Novak was likely to blow his stack. I pulled the lid off and put it down on the counter.

Julius woke up immediately, his brown eyes rolling wildly, taking in his surroundings. He fixated on me, and I allowed him to focus. No screaming, thank Iblis. "Shiloh," he wheezed. "I had the worst dream."

"What did you dream about?" I asked.

"A star. Fire."

My stomach twisted. "What do you remember about the star?"

"Fire."

"Was the star on fire?"

"Yes."

Okay, he could mean the five lamps lighting the room, or he could mean literal fire. I'd smelled charred wood, but saw no evidence of it. Metaphorical fire? "Julius, I need to ask you about something real, okay? Not about your nightmare."

"Sure, kiddo. Why can't I feel my legs?"

I closed my eyes briefly, drawing on every ounce of calm left in me before opening them again. "Do you remember renting a storage unit last winter, down south in Virginia?"

He stared at me like a stone drunk who'd just been asked to spell his entire name backward. "Last winter . . . I . . . no. Why did I rent a storage unit?"

"That's what we're trying to find out."

"Everything's so fuzzy, Shi. Wasn't your mom here?"

"She's upstairs." The lettuce around his head was wilting, giving the entire presentation a truly macabre look. If I didn't quit having conversations like this, I was going to lose it. "He doesn't remember."

"Are you certain?" Novak asked.

"Yes, I'm certain." I snapped without meaning to, and couldn't bring myself to care. I needed answers, bless it. I replaced the lid and sealed it tight, then shoved the thing across the counter. Away from me.

Tennyson showed me the screen of his phone, where he'd been typing out a message: *check his house for records.*

I nodded. "Look, Novak, I'm going back to Julius's house to look around. See if he keeps any financial records in his desk or in a safe somewhere. I'm not getting anything by sitting around questioning his head."

"All right," Novak replied. "Keep your eyes open— our enemies know where he lives."

"I will."

"Hey, Shiloh?" Jaxon spoke up. "Where's the vampire?"

I flinched. Oh, well. No sense in lying now that he'd asked. "Sitting about three feet to my left, why?"

"You took him *inside*?" Novak roared, at the same time Jaxon said, "What?"

"What did you want me to do with him? Hand him an umbrella and leave him outside the gate to get third-degree burns while I regrouped?"

Novak growled softly—the only further disagreement we had on the matter.

"Look, call me when you've spoken to the Homme Alpha," I said. "Or I'll let you know if we find anything at Julius's house."

"Understood."

I don't set out to piss off our incubus. It just sort of happens. Occasionally, it seemed like taking orders from a female impugned on his manhood, which was a very serious thing for an incubus. Most demons, actually—a breed heavy on the male-side. *Understood* was his grumpy way of protesting my decision to allow Tennyson access.

I just hoped I didn't come to regret it, myself.

"Shall I accompany you?" Tennyson asked.

"Huh?" I was staring at my phone and looked up at his question. "Where?"

He canted his head at the cake carrier. "His home."

"Yeah, okay. I'll tell my mom where we're going—"

K.I.M.'s perimeter alarm sounded. The squeal was constant, like a stuck microwave timer. Tennyson beat me back to the computer interface, a reminder of just how fast he was. K.I.M.'s main screen flashed to a shot of the outer gate. A single figure stood next to the code box.

"K.I.M., magnify central image."

The security camera angled in on the figure. He or she wore a long trench coat that brushed the asphalt, buttoned all the way up to their throat. Gloves covered both hands. It looked like a scarf had been wound around the person's neck and chest, and further protection came in the form of a floppy-brimmed hat.

"Vampire," I said. No one else needed that much protection from the rising sun.

For a moment, nothing happened. Then the vampire raised their right hand and waved at the camera.

"K.I.M., scan intruder."

"Command accepted. Scanning." The screen split in half. The left remained the recorded image, while the right shifted into a heat-signature scan. The image ran cool, just like Tennyson's. "Nonhuman signature detected. No weaponry detected."

"Open external audio."

"Command accepted. Audio activated."

I picked up a small microphone attached to one side of the computer system. "This is private property," I said in my best *who the hell do you think you are?* voice. "State your business."

The vampire angled their head toward the lockbox, attention never diverting from the camera. They had good enough eyesight to see the cameras we'd hidden around the property. "Is this Para-Marshal Shiloh Harrison?" he asked. His muddled accent, sharper on the *S* and growling the *R*s, put a big sign on his head that said PIOTR.

CHAPTER 10

Tennyson growled, cementing my theory. I glanced at him and mouthed the word "Piotr." He nodded.

"It is," I said to the vampire outside. I expected seething rage, but all I felt was utter shock at seeing Piotr show up on my doorstep. Caution and curiosity nipped right at the heels of shock.

"May we have a word in private, Marshal Harrison?"

"We're speaking aren't we?"

"I would prefer a face-to-face chat, if you don't mind." He paused; I couldn't see his face clearly to gauge his expression. "You don't trust me."

I couldn't stop a snort of disbelief. "Fuck no, I don't trust you, if you've done what I think you've done."

"I don't suppose it would help my case if I admitted to you that I am the necromancer you are seeking?"

Okay, first of all, suspects don't march up to your front door and announce their crimes. Second, vampires don't willingly admit to crimes in broad daylight, when they are physically weakest. Third . . . I didn't have a third, just a gut-deep feeling this wasn't as open-book as it sounded. Vampires always had ulterior motives. Always.

"The only way it helps your case, Piotr, is to guarantee I won't kill you until you've answered all of my questions. Maybe I'll even let my incubus friend have a go at you."

Piotr laughed, high-pitched and jovial. "I admit, Marshal, this is the first time I've been threatened with torture-by-incubus. You Americans are so clever."

The laughter was helping rage get a head start on curiosity.

"The gossip tree has my old friend Woodrow Tennyson at your side," Piotr continued. "Is this rumor true?"

"Shouldn't someone as old as you know better than to trust rumors?"

"You know my name, as well as my age and strength, which is proof enough of his assistance."

Crap. "Look, you said you wanted to talk."

"Face-to-face."

Tennyson made a slashing gesture across his throat. I muted the microphone.

"Are you considering this?" he asked.

"He's got answers I need, Tennyson, and I'm not bringing him inside the perimeter fence. Not with only the three of us here and no immediate backup."

"What's to stop him from breaking your neck the moment you step outside of the gate?"

"Not a blessed thing." The certainty of the statement sent quakes of fear through my stomach. Going outside was as close to suicide as any move I'd made in my career, but I needed answers. I needed to look Piotr in the face and find out why he'd turned Julius into a revenant. I needed to know if he had any connection to the disappearing wolves and vamps. I needed to know if Julius had betrayed us.

Tennyson gazed at me, his thoughts guarded behind a stony expression. "I cannot decide if you are brave, or merely foolish and young."

"Gee, thanks." I cut off another remark with a slash of my hand, then unmuted the microphone. "I'll be outside in five minutes. Don't crisp before I get there." I cut off the sound on the edge of Piotr's chuckling.

The hall closet wasn't for coats. Inside was an arsenal of weapons, both legal and illegally modified. I still had my sidearm loaded with silver-jacketed bullets. The closet offered a variety of other anti-vampire items from which to choose. Many of the basic items—cross, holy water—wouldn't work unless the target was from a Christian faith background. Not likely, given this one was originally from Russia. So I stuck with garlic spray and plenty of silver. A silver knife went into my front hip pocket, and a thin band of silver—a flexible, herringbone weave, not unlike a bracelet—went around my neck like a choker.

Tennyson eyed my new items from a distance as I went back to K.I.M. and made a few adjustments.

"You'll be able to listen in," I said, finished. "This side is muted. It's also recording, just in case." I didn't need to elaborate the point.

"Don't look him in the eye."

"I know—"

"No, you don't." A startling vehemence had entered his voice. "Necromancers have power over the soul, Ms. Harrison, more powerful than a simple gazelock. Don't let him have a taste of yours."

Eyes. Windows to the soul. Don't look. Got it.

I tiptoed upstairs to check on my mom before I left. She'd sprawled on a bed in one of the spare rooms and fallen asleep. Her silver-streaked hair was out of its tie and fell across her face, hiding most of it from sight. Her chest rose and fell steadily. I hoped she was having good dreams. No spiders allowed in those dreams.

Tennyson was waiting at the front door. He held it open as I slipped out, and I felt his intense gaze on my back as I walked. A cool breeze blew across the yard and cul-de-sac, rustling early spring leaves and bringing the damp promise of rain. April around here felt like Seattle was reported to be—rainy, chilly, and very gray. Our streak of sunny spring days seemed on the verge of ending.

Our street was roughly a quarter-mile long, and the outer gate came into view long before I reached it. Piotr stood on the other side, a perfect, jacketed statue. I strode up to the fence, gun in my right hand, safety off.

"You wanted face-to-face," I said. "You going to show me yours?"

He lifted the brim of his hat and tugged the scarf down, angling his body away from the sunshine. His pale skin stood out starkly against the black of his costume. He was of average height, his build impossible to determine, but his face was narrow, almost sunken. He might have been handsome before being turned, but time and external stress left him fierce-looking, predatory.

I swallowed, careful to look him straight in the nose. "So you're the big bad?" I said.

"Big bad," Piotr repeated. "Your colloquialisms are amusing, Marshal. No, I am merely another chess piece on this board set by others, much like yourself. That is why I came."

"Oh really? Then who set the board?"

"I apologize, I cannot tell you. I am bound to silence by a blood oath. Breaking it would cause . . . harm."

"Seeing harm come to you is kind of an incentive right now, not a deterrent."

"You misunderstand. Harm to the one to whom I betray my oath. You."

The news just kept getting better and better. I took a deep, steadying breath, unnerved by the steady ripples of power flowing off him like a lover's caress. It was similar to the power I'd sensed in the pentagram room, though more immediate and concentrated. He could kill me without breaking a sweat.

"If you can't tell me anything, why did you come here?" I asked. "To gloat? To prove how badass you are and tell me to keep my nose out of your business, or you'll do to me what you did to my friend?"

"I doubt I could do to you what was done to your friend," he said, speaking slowly, choosing his words. "I sense power in you. It protects your soul from necrotic magic."

Necrotic—magic that destroys, rots from the inside out. Djinn aren't inherently good or evil. Like humans, we make conscious choices with our magic and how we use it. Some are affected more strongly by their base—being of earth, water, fire, air, or ice determines many characteristics—but all are free to choose. Unlike demons, who are evil, or vampires, who trend in that direction.

Unless said djinn was bound to a wisher—then our choice was taken away. Had Piotr's comment about my power protecting me from necrotic magic been a dig or a hint? I needed to find out more about his past so I could put together the puzzle in my present.

"You were a warlock in Russia before you turned," I said.

He nodded. "Rasputin himself was one of my greatest students. It is unfortunate his reach far exceeded his grasp."

"So you moved to the States and took up Necromancy for Beginners?"

"The weather here is much more pleasant."

"You live in Colorado where it snows in April."

"Po-tay-toe, po-tah-toe." It came across oddly, with his accent.

"You didn't answer my question. Why am I here?"

"To receive an apology."

I looked away, focusing on a link in the fence, wrestling with my anger. My clenched fist ached. Nails dug into my left palm. I forced myself to look up again, at the tip of his pointed nose. "Did you honestly expect forgiveness?"

"No. However, one must attempt atonement for the worst of wrongs."

"Isn't it a little late in your career to worry about your immortal soul? Not that you have one anymore."

He flinched.

Interesting.

"No, Marshal Harrison, it is not my soul I battle for. It is for the right of my children to exist once I'm gone. I fight for their survival."

Hell. I'd had a similar conversation with Tennyson yesterday. Him protecting his line by hiding them in a trailer park, surrounded by police protection. His goal had been the same—their survival. Had Piotr been forced to use his knowledge of necromancy in return for the lives of his people? And if so, who was manipulating the vampire Masters so skillfully? The scope of this issue was expanding by the hour.

"You're being blackmailed?" I asked.

"I cannot answer that question."

"Are your people in immediate danger?"

"I cannot answer that question."

Tennyson's voice roared into my head at the same time I scowled, which covered up the overt agony of it. *Do not ask direct questions that he cannot answer. Be indirect.*

"Julius was killed and turned into a revenant," I said slowly, carefully this time, migraine be blessed. "He was returned to us as a warning to not interfere, and as a sign of the power we stand against."

"The intentions are almost entirely correct."

There was another reason, then. Asking Piotr directly was an exercise in futility, but knowing it existed made me nervous. So I kept with the more obtuse questions.

"Julius rented the facility in which the spell was performed, that was easy enough for us to discover on our own. He'd been renting it for over a year. Is your knowledge of this the same as mine?"

Piotr cocked his head, considering my phrasing. "My knowledge concurs."

It didn't mean he knew Julius last year, just that he knew of the rental—strongly hinting they knew each other. This had been in the works for a frightening length of time. I knew Piotr had the knowledge and skills as a necromancer, but not how long he'd been practicing the dark magic.

"Was Julius your first revenant?"

Indirect! I flinched.

"I cannot answer that question."

Irritation on the rise, I was less inclined to care what "harm" befell me if he broke his blood oath and just gave me some straight answers. Dancing around the truth was fueling my headache. "One revenant came out of the pentagram room below the storage facility," I said. He seemed to do better with statements, instead of questions.

"To my knowledge." A "yes" dangled off the end of Piotr's answer, which was as good as saying Julius was the only one so far. Unless . . .

"You are the only necromancer capable of such a feat."

He hesitated, mouth opening and shutting several times. "Uncertain."

Okay, badly phrased on my part. "Your employer has employed no other capable of necromancy."

"I cannot respond to that."

A shiver raced down my spine, sending goose bumps across my shoulders and lower back. The clues started falling into place. Piotr had the knowledge and skill to perform the spell. His line was threatened to ensure his assistance. He specifically mentioned mentoring Rasputin, apprenticing him. Crap.

"You trained a new necromancer who's loyal to this mystery employer," I said, as much for Tennyson's benefit as mine. "Julius was practice."

Piotr's jaw tightened. It was as good as a yes.

"And you know who it is."

More confirming silence.

"Piotr, what exactly is this harm that will befall me if you break your oath?"

Shiloh, don't—

Shut up, Tennyson!

"I am uncertain," Piotr replied. "Blood oaths between vampires, if broken, result in the sanctioned death of the one breaking it. My oath was not with a fellow vampire. The consequences shall befall you, and I do not know what they may be."

"And I bet you can't tell me what you made the oath with? Sidhe? Witch?"

"I cannot."

"But it could potentially bring this person down on my doorstep demanding penance for breaking your oath?"

"Possibly. However the price may be extracted remotely via magic."

"The more likely scenario."

"Yes."

This is ill-advised. You have no idea what will happen. You could die.

I didn't know you cared.

The fate of my people is still in your hands.

I would have laughed if the exchange wasn't making my head throb like an unpopped zit.

It's a trick, Tennyson boomed. *If the oath maker knows Piotr has broken his promise, what is to stop the oath maker from slaughtering Piotr's people? Nothing. Piotr has everything to lose by cooperating.*

He was right, and I was a fool for not seeing it sooner. One question answered to break his oath, and Piotr's puppeteer would have me over a barrel. Had Piotr been sent here to trick me into opening myself up for such an attack? Or was his employer testing me?

"You know, you almost had me," I said. "Bravo, that was well-done."

"I beg your pardon?" Piotr asked.

"Beg all you want, pal, now go tell your boss she didn't fall for it."

The air around Piotr seemed to shift, electrify somehow. He was getting angry. "You are as big a fool as he said."

"He who?" dangled on the tip of my tongue, but I pulled it back. It was the opening Piotr needed to say he'd broken his oath. Blessed, lying, manipulating vampire bastard. "I've been called worse."

"Undoubtedly, half-breed bitch."

I bristled. "Say that again."

He did, with gusto. I raised my right hand and fired, counting on his speedy reflexes. I didn't want to kill him, so my heart-aimed shot tore a bit of meat from his right shoulder as he jerked out of the way. Blood splatters on the black coat sizzled in the sunlight, then shriveled into pale ash.

Piotr snarled, fangs gleaming. "You will regret this day, djinn."

"Like I haven't heard that one before."

"You will die screaming after you witness the deaths of your comrades."

"Blah, blah, blah." Bravado in the face of furious Master vampire screaming death threats—check.

Piotr's lips drew back in a smile so sinister and full of malice my knees wobbled. Deadly intent was radiating off him. He'd lost and didn't seem keen on going back to his employer and telling him or her so. Could you get any lower in the vampire world than being outsmarted by a djinn? Probably not. I took a step back from the fence. Our defenses would hold. Even if he got pissed enough to climb the outer fence, he'd be fried into unconsciousness at the inner perimeter. He could try to jump the fence— I've seen vampires leap as high as three stories with a good running head start—but our sensors would fry his ass before he hit the ground. We'd sacrificed a lot of robins and seagulls in testing those settings.

The vampire started laughing. Not hysterical, the-bad-guy's-lost-it laughter, but maniacal, this-is-too-good-not-to-share chuckles. The kind that liquefied my insides and made me want to sit down. Preferably far, far away from him. I couldn't ask what was so funny. I didn't dare ask him any more questions.

Ms. Harrison, come back inside, Tennyson said.

Sick of the mental pokes, I thoughtfully retorted, *So it's Ms. Harrison again?*

"He's communicating with you," Piotr said, that awful laughter still in his voice. "I should have expected it. You don't hide the agony of his intrusions very well, girl."

"Yeah, well, it's like a jackhammer to the brain, so you'll have to forgive me the faces."

"Of course. I am eager to see the faces your friend Vincent makes under similar circumstances."

Everything slowed down. A chill settled over me, and I began to pant. He was lying. Vincent was safe. No one outside of the team knew where I lived, or who I was dating, including Julius. No. No, no, no, this wasn't possible.

But he said his *name*.

My mouth was dry, too dry. I couldn't seem to find words over the roar in my head.

"You're lying," I said, barely above a whisper.

"Am I? Call him."

My left hand went for my phone and found an empty pocket. I'd left it inside.

"Better yet." Piotr produced a digital camera, turned it on, then spun it around so the display screen faced me.

I took a step closer to the fence, my hands trembling harder with each passing second. The image mocked me, laughed at me—Vincent strapped to a table not unlike the one we'd found in the pentagram room, naked, eyes wide and staring. Drugged. The digital numbers on the bottom had today's date, 12:04 a.m.

"You son of a bitch," I said.

Vincent Ortiz and I had only been dating nine months. The sex was great. He brought me nacho chips and mango salsa instead of roses, because I loved junk food more than flowers. Our dates often consisted of dinner, a DVD, and bed gymnastics, which was the perfect way to relax after long days or weeks of work. We got along well, made each other laugh, and our jobs kept us apart enough to keep the sparks alive.

It wasn't serious. But I cared about him. He was innocent, and now Piotr had dragged him into my secret life to be used against me. The second person I cared about to be used against me in two days.

Strike that, third person. Tennyson had briefly threatened my mother when we first met. It counted.

"How would you like his head?" Piotr asked. "I was thinking in one of those Iceman coolers, the ones with the reversible lids."

My gun hand twitched. A silver bullet in the heart

wouldn't kill him, but it would weaken him enough for capture. He'd stay weak until it was removed. Or until I cut off his head. I needed to know where Vincent was. I couldn't leave him to those monsters. And I couldn't learn any of that until I got Piotr to break his oath.

Shiloh, what are you doing?

Get out here, I thought back. *Now!*

I raised my gaze and let my eyes meet Piotr's. He blinked, not expecting me to do it, and it made him hesitate. I fired at his heart, three bullets, and each one hit. Piotr shrieked and collapsed, breaking the start of our gazelock. I entered my code in the lockbox on my side of the gate and stepped back so it could open.

"Who's going to turn Vincent now that you've fucked up and gotten yourself caught?" I asked.

Piotr's head twisted toward me, his face still shadowed by the hat and scarf, features twisted in agony. "The one I taught, in order to save the lives of my people. My debt is now complete. You are his, and they are safe."

Something in the air changed, became keener, crisper. I looked at the sky, half expecting a lightning strike. Wind rushed at me, and then Tennyson was there, his own cloak thrown hastily over his head and shoulders and tugged close. His expression was thunderous.

"What you did was foolish," he said.

"So far so good," I replied. Maybe the oath thing was just a bunch of bull—

The sting startled me into dropping my gun, and it clattered to the asphalt. I turned my throbbing hand fast enough to see the black, eight-legged thing just before it leapt to the ground. Tennyson was faster, and his boot smashed it into a familiar puddle of spiky legs and green goo.

White fire shot through my right hand, up my elbow, all the way to my shoulder. The tiny, twin puncture wounds, perfectly centered on the top of my hand, oozed clear liquid. Redness erupted around them as the site began to swell. All I could do was stare.

"We need to—" Tennyson started.

"Get Piotr secured and inside," I replied. My lungs felt cold—not good. "I knew what I was doing. If he gets away, it's for nothing."

At least he didn't argue. And Piotr didn't struggle much while Tennyson manhandled him to his feet and toward the house. Probably didn't want to risk those bullets shifting and doing even more damage. Potentially irreparable damage. A vampire with a shredded heart won't die right away. He'll slowly succumb to thirst and hunger, no matter how much he eats.

I couldn't seem to recall why . . . .

My arm went numb. Not the tingly pins and needles numb. The I-don't-know-if-my-arm-is-still-attached-to-my-body kind of numb. I stumbled to the lockbox and hit the big blue button that shut the gate. Then I turned and face-planted on the asphalt. The jostle lanced agony up my numb arm, into a flame that fanned across my chest, neck, and abdomen. I tasted blood.

Blessed spider.

My head seemed to weight fifty pounds and was impossible to lift off the ground. Lying there felt nice. It hurt when I moved. I'd stay there until the numbness spread all over and nothing hurt anymore.

No, I couldn't do that. I had something else to do, something important. I got bit for a reason, bless it all. If I stayed here to die, it would be for nothing. Can't lie here and let the bad guys win. Will not.

Footsteps beat the pavement toward me. Someone strong and smelling faintly of blood and sage rolled me onto my back. I shrieked as fingers of pain raced through my body, tiny daggers slicing across muscle and organs and bone. He gathered me up. I had no strength to protest, no sense of coordination to hold on tighter. The fizzle-pop of power told me it was Tennyson.

I let him carry me back to the house, up the stairs, and into one of the bedrooms.

That's when the real torture began.

CHAPTER 11

"Shiloh! My God, what happened to her?"

"She's been bitten."

"By what? Her arm—"

"A spider, as penance for breaking a blood oath."

Mom and Tennyson's dialogue faded a bit beneath the haze of heat and wet cotton balls invading my brain. I'd closed my eyes and left them closed. Opening them hurt. Moving anything hurt, so I did nothing as my traitorous body succumbed to the spider's venom.

"Magic," Mom said.

"Yes. Draining the wound will do little good at this point. The venom is in her blood."

"She's half djinn, she's strong. Spiders can't—"

"It was more than a simple spider, Ms. Juno."

I wanted to comfort my mom, to tell her it was

okay. Tell her how glad I was the spider she choked on hadn't bitten her, too. Apologize for dragging her into this mess in the first place. I wanted to tell Vincent the same thing. God, Vincent . . . .

The whimper must have come from me, because both of them said my name.

"We have to do something," Mom said. Was she crying? On the verge? I couldn't tell, could only hear the grief in her voice. A gradually thickening voice, as the wet cotton in my head pressed down harder. Smushing my feverish brain into the sides of my skull.

"Her djinn half may be strong enough to combat the venom," Tennyson said. "However, her human half weakens her."

"Her father might know how to save her."

Oh please, no, don't call my dad. The last thing I needed was to have both of my parents mixed up in this mess. It's my own mess. Only I couldn't get the breath to protest. My tongue felt thick, heavy, my lungs too cold.

"Her phone is downstairs by the computer."

Mom's shoes clattered out of the room. *Tennyson has a phone. Is he worried about roaming charges or something?* A weak giggle worked its way loose.

Something swished, then clicked. The bed settled a bit on one side, and the tiny movement sent agony signals to my sizzling brain.

"Can you hear me, Shiloh?" Tennyson asked. His

voice was quiet, his tone gentle. Eerie, from such a terrifying vampire.

The giggle worked once, so I tried it again. It came out more like a sob. Hot tears leaked from the corners of my eyes.

"You're dying."

No kidding, you think?

"I believe your human blood is making you weak, and I have a theory on how you may yet beat this."

Then what the hell are you waiting for?

"Your permission."

I forced my eyelids to open. My eyeballs felt like balloons filled with scalding water, ready to burst at any moment. The dim light in the room cut into my head like a blade. Through the pain, I saw Tennyson's face looming over mine, framed by swaths of painter's palette hair. His eyes sparkled with red and his mouth was set. Determination rolled off him stronger than his aged power.

Even through the fever of the spider bite, the telepathy worked. And he was sensible enough to not shout his thoughts into my overtaxed brain.

Holding his gaze, I asked, *What do you need to do?*

"It is widely known that vampire blood heals the wounds of other vampires. It is a guarded secret that drinking from a willing vampire donor can also heal the wounds of humans."

I had to think that one through several times for it to make sense. It hurt to think. My chest had gone numb, as well as my left arm. My father wouldn't get here in time to save me, even if he knew how. I couldn't die yet. Vincent had been kidnapped. Vampires and werewolves were being stolen off the streets, and we had a restrained vampire who was mixed up in all of it.

Too much else to do; dying was off the list.

Will I change?

"No, there will be no blood exchange. However . . ." He looked troubled.

What?

"I have heard of instances of djinn reacting to vampire blood as a human to illegal narcotics. It can become addictive."

Gross.

He raised a slender eyebrow. "There is little time, Shiloh. Your body is already taxed beyond its limits—"

Do it. Let me drink.

"You are certain?"

I'm not ready to die, Tennyson. Please.

He shifted to kneel next to my head, each jostle another stroke of fire in my body. He cut through the underside of his wrist with his fangs, then pressed the bleeding wound to my mouth. My rational brain protested the very idea of drinking his blood (or anyone's blood), and the warmth trickled down my chin.

"Please, Shiloh."

The way he said it—a respectable distance from begging, but more than a simple request—parted my lips. Hot, thick, and unbearably bitter, his blood spilled into my mouth, across my tongue, scorching its way down my throat. I lost it somewhere below my neck, as my lower body was already numbed beyond sensation. I closed my eyes and drank deeply, sucking hard on the wound, thirstier than I'd ever been in my life. And hating myself for every single drop.

The pulsing started in my toes—one of the last bits of my body I still felt—and spread upward. I felt it behind my eyes, a softer pulse that cooled the fever, only to replace it with rage. Unfiltered, undirected rage. It rippled through my sensitizing chest, flowed out to my extremities, then ran back to pool in my heart in a fist of hate as black as pitch and boundless as the heavens.

Tennyson yanked his wrist away, and I shrieked out my rage. How dare he? With energy born of anger, I clawed at his face, scrambling for the wrist he'd offered and then taken away. Nothing mattered except getting it back. I fought and snapped, but he was stronger. Bless it, why was he stronger than me?

He shoved me down and climbed aboard, straddling my thighs. His hands clamped around my wrists and pressed them down on either side of my head. I gnashed my teeth at his arms, at the sweet blood flowing beneath them. At the wrist still oozing down his hand, onto mine, teasing me with its heat. Bastard!

"Shiloh, stop!"

I laughed. How dare he command me? I wasn't one of his children, one of his chosen. He'd done this to me, given me this terrible thirst, and he deigned to tell me to stop. I arched my back and nearly dislodged my captor. His legs clamped down tighter around mine. I kicked my feet, using the bed as leverage, reveling in this strange new strength.

He slid his body down the length of mine, covering me completely, raised up only by his straight-armed grip of my wrists. Our bellies pressed together, our hips, our legs—so perfectly. Too bad he was a filthy vampire.

"Get off me!" I was more surprised than him when I screamed those words at the top of my lungs. Fists pounded on the door, and a voice shouted my name. Demanded entry. "Mom!"

Harder banging, then Mom: "If you hurt her, Vampire, I will kill you myself!"

"Mommy!" Tears strangled my voice, stung my eyes and nose. Terror sharper than any blade cut through me like a winter wind. Something was very wrong.

My right hand was on fire, being charred to a crisp. Tennyson didn't care, the bastard, he just held me down. I yanked and bucked, pleading for him to let me go, let my hand go. He held fast.

Something heavy was hammering at the door. El-speth Ann Juno to the rescue.

"Ride it out, Shiloh, you can beat it," Tennyson said. "Ride it out."

I wriggled and wrenched. "Just let me go, it hurts."

"You will beat this."

"Hurts."

"I know."

I was crying in earnest. Taxed from no sleep, the spider bite, the blood, the agony of it all in such a brief space of time. Confused by wanting his blood and despising myself for something so disgusting. The pain of the bite was back in my right hand, which felt sixty-times its normal size, ready to explode if introduced to the tiniest prick. The rest of my body was alive with pins and needles—or, more precisely, knives and nails. Everything ached, smarted, felt like it was being ripped apart and stitched back together.

"More blood," I said, hating myself for asking. Stupid, idiotic, moronic—worst of all, weak. Weakness in front of a vampire is a good way to get yourself killed.

"No more blood tonight, Shiloh, you've had enough."

The door pounding continued. Wood cracked.

"Hurts so much."

"I know. It's working. My blood is healing you."

Crack.

I whimpered.

Crash!

My mother launched herself at Tennyson, all flailing fists and screeches of threats to his body. Her initial attack did little. He remained above me, an immovable object. I saw her palm the pencil. He didn't.

She stabbed him in the back.

Adrenaline had her discombobulated enough to stab him on the right side, opposite his heart. He roared and reached back for the offending object, setting my arms free. I sat up and shoved him with feral glee. He toppled sideways and rolled off the bed, still grabbing backward for the pencil.

Mom reached for me, arms open, face painted with worry and helpless tears.

I shoved her away, too, just as hard. She stumbled and hit the nightstand with a pained shout. I bolted past her, for the door, every tortured muscle shrieking as I forced them to move faster than they wanted. I had to get away from them both; I had to find someone to slake the thirst in me. Someone to make the thirst and the ever-present pain go away.

Tennyson tackled me in the hallway, his long, lithe limbs tangling around me like a fisherman's net. I howled, cursing and punching and wriggling like a fish. He held fast, my back to his chest, his arms across mine to hold them down, legs looped and twisted at the ankle.

He wheezed air, which struck me as strange, even through the haze of my fight-or-flight instinct gone haywire. Mom must have punctured a lung with that pencil.

"Shiloh, baby?" Speak of the devil.

A hand got within biting distance, so I snapped at my mom's manicure. She gave a startled yelp and jumped back.

"Stay back, woman!" Tennyson's roar forced her to retreat several steps. She hit the hallway wall and stopped with a thunk.

I glared at her ankles, unable to lift my head. Moving took too much energy. Energy I didn't have, because I was too busy crying. Crying in front of the vampire. Bless it! Again, fury at showing weakness fueled my body. I lurched and nearly broke free. I jerked my head back and heard a satisfying crunch, followed by a streak of swearing. The back of my head ached from breaking his nose.

Something hot and wet flowed from my right hand and soaked into my jeans. I couldn't see it. Didn't care. Tennyson hadn't loosened his hold. I snapped my head again, hoping for a second blow. He jerked to the side and forward, effectively trapping me between his chin and shoulder. Breath from his wounded lung hissed across my cheek.

A strange, keening sob ripped from my throat. Confusion muddled my world. Up, down, left, right, everything I knew was wrong. Backward. Nothing made sense, would never make sense again.

"You need rest," Tennyson said. "Forgive me this trespass."

"What are you doing?" Mom asked.

Tennyson bent his head lower, changing the angle to press his lips to my neck. Mom let out a startled squawk. I trembled and whimpered, but did not protest. His fangs broke skin in twin bursts of pain that quickly melted into a pleasant tingle. Then numbing pleasure spread from my neck, down to my groin, and I groaned.

A lovely sleepiness came over me, melting away the rage and shame and agony of the last few minutes. Cocooning me in warmth and safety, and I fell. Fell down, down, into the darkness below.

And I didn't dream at all.

Sensations and scents sneaked through the haze of unconsciousness long before I clawed my way up and out. The damp pillow beneath my head, soft sheets over my body, pleasant warmth without fever. The sharp odor of sweat lingered over the residual scents of emotions—fear, anger, confusion. Not mine.

Other people were afraid, angry, and confused. Why?

I shoved the question away and concentrated on the pillow—this wonderful little invention aiding in my restful slumber. Sleeping felt amazing, as though I hadn't done it in quite a long time. Why mess with a good thing?

Two new sensations stole through the veil of sleep and poked me in the mental eye. The first was my right hand. It ached like I'd been clenching it for hours, stiff and unyielding. The second was my neck. It ached as well, but in a different way. Tiny, twin tingles, more sore than painful. Why was—?

A vampire bit you, you idiot.

Why did a vampire bite me, though? I didn't really want to know. If I fell back to sleep, I wouldn't have to think about it.

Eventually I'd have to wake up, though. Putting off the inevitable didn't make it go away. It just delayed the . . . ah, inevitable.

I clawed against the heavy veil of darkness swaddling my mind and body, yanking and tearing until it gave. With it came nauseating clarity. My entire body ached like I'd been smashed with a steamroller. My right hand wasn't just stiff, it was also bandaged and swollen. The twin tingles in my neck remained the only soft pain, barely there over the agony of the other injuries.

Spider. Blood. Running.

Crap.

My tongue was thick, dry, and stuck to the roof of my mouth. I worked it off and ran the tip over my fuzzy teeth. No fangs. A shudder of relief wracked my body, and I started working on my eyes. They felt crusty, sealed shut. So gross.

"Shiloh?" His was not the voice I wanted to hear.

I mumbled something intended to come out as, "Go away," but managed only garbled nonsense.

Bastard took it as permission to sit next to me, his pop-sizzle of power stronger than ever. It felt like the gentle burst of carbonated soda off the top of a freshly poured, frosty glass of the stuff—cold and sparkling. I didn't want him near me.

He stood up and moved away with a whispered, "I'm sorry."

The unexpectedness of it gave my left hand the energy to creep up and wipe the crusties off my eyes. I blinked them open, immediately grateful for the dim lighting. Tennyson stood a few feet away, close to the wall, hands clasped behind his back. His face was stony, his thoughts impossible to read from expression alone. And I say that, because I un-expectedly felt a wave of regret from him—a chill I couldn't explain any other way, coated with a repeti-tion of his spoken words.

I licked my lips, working up enough moisture to speak. "You bit me."

"I felt I had no choice," he said, and again, that re-gretful chill rolled off him. "You needed to rest and allow my blood to heal you."

"Did it work?" My right arm was tucked beneath the sheet and comforter, and felt too blessed heavy to withdraw.

"It did. The venom was forced back through the bite, although the actual wound is taking longer. It should be gone within a day or so."

Good news. I felt around on my throat and found

only sensitive skin. No punctures, no puckered skin or scabs.

"It healed as well," he said. More regret. He really needed to turn that off.

I glanced at the blue comforter, then the ivory walls. I was in the room I used when spending the night at HQ. How had he known?

"Your scent is concentrated here. I thought you would like a familiar place to continue your recovery."

I grunted. "Quit reading my mind."

He blinked and seemed . . . startled. As if it hadn't occurred to him that I had thought the question and not asked it out loud. My stomach churned. Was this a side effect of being bitten? Or biting him in return? We'd shared blood. Not enough to turn me, and not in the right order, but enough to do something. Alter *something* between us.

The energy wafting from him changed from a chill to something cold and spicy, like chipotle ice cream. What was that? Anxiety? Distress?

"Yes," he said.

"Personal space!" I coughed, desperate for a glass of water.

"I am not intentionally reading your thoughts, Shiloh. They are merely . . . open to me, as are the thoughts of my line when in close proximity. It is an ability forged through shared blood. The strength of our connection may dissipate over time."

"May?"

More cold and spicy. "I have never shared blood with someone whom I did not turn. I am uncertain as to the end results, and your djinn blood makes guesswork impossible. I'm sorry."

"Awesome." The fact that he was the only person in the bedroom finally caught up to me. "Where's my mom?"

"Downstairs arguing with your father."

I groaned, wanting to sink deeper into the bed and never get out. This was so not good news.

"He seems pleasant enough for a djinn," Tennyson said blandly. "When he wasn't threatening to cut out my heart and serve it in a stew for lunch."

The idea that my dad—an unimposing figure, even though he ranked somewhat high on the djinn-power totem pole—had physically threatened a vampire Master made me smile. He was nothing if not protective of his only half-human child. If he was protective of my three full-blooded half siblings, I'd never know it. I didn't even know them. Partly because they were all seventy-five years older than me, and partly because his relationship with my mother and me was something of a rarity among djinn. Most djinn preferred to ignore our existence, which worked for me. I was raised as human, among humans, and identified with humans—except on the rare occasions I embraced my djinn powers.

"Only lunchtime?" I asked. Felt like way lon—

"Lunchtime Friday," he said. "Your teammates

have returned, as well, and have been studiously avoiding contact with your parents."

"They're scary when they argue." It still didn't explain why Tennyson was here, in my room, instead of Jaxon or Novak.

"I convinced them I was the safest choice to watch over you. I was uncertain as to your reaction when you woke. They agreed that if you had changed, my guidance would be required to calm you."

My stomach churned. "There was a chance I could have turned?"

"I led them to believe there was."

"You lied?"

"Misled."

"Why?"

A cacophony of scents and heat levels bounced off him too fast to catalogue or even attempt to identify. He crossed back to the bed, but didn't sit. Instead, he crouched to eye level. His eyes burned with flecks of burgundy, darker than any shade of red I'd previously seen. I met his intense gaze without fear.

"Not since my early years have I taken blood from someone without their permission," he said. "I vowed long ago to never do such a thing, and yesterday I broke that vow. I stole without asking, and I needed to ask your forgiveness before the chance was lost." He spoke with such anguish that tears actually prickled my eyes. A gentle warmth tinged with the subtle scent of cloves enveloped me. He truly was tied in knots over this.

"You saved my life," I said.

"I could have as easily destroyed you."

"You didn't."

"You are as uncertain as I am as to the extent of damage I have caused you. Certainly your involvement with me has brought you no end of grief. Your leader is dead, your lover has been kidnapped, and your mother attacked."

I tried to sit up and failed to even get my head off the pillow. So I settled on glaring at him sideways. "My involvement with the Para-Marshals has brought me no end of grief, Tennyson, not you. Julius was involved in this long before you held Myrtle's Acres hostage, so don't you try shouldering all the blame. There's enough to go around."

Surprise softened his features, making him seem less fierce. "You contradict your species, Ms. Harrison. A djinn would be more than eager to lay all blame at the feet of a vampire."

"I'm not my species," I retorted hotly. "And will you please call me Shiloh?"

"As you wish. Do forgive me my trespass?"

"Your what? The biting thing?" He really needed to quit being so formal. "Yes, I forgive you. Just . . ." I couldn't forget the unquenchable thirst I'd felt after drinking his blood, the fierce desire to have more. He'd warned me beforehand, sure, but I hadn't expected it to drive me into attacking him. And my mother.

"What is it?"

"The blood thirst. It was temporary, right?"

He cocked his head, contemplating the question, his emotions strangely guarded. He raised his left hand to his mouth and sliced the tip of his thumb on his fang. Blood welled. I scented it right away—warm and sweet and metallic. Coins and honey. He held out his thumb, stopping a few inches from my face. I stared at the shiny redness, and realized too late that I was licking my bottom lip. He withdrew his hand, taking with him the tantalizing scent.

"Bless it all," I said. I shivered, horrified by my reaction, and the endless teasing it would extract from Novak. The disgust from my father.

"I'm sorry."

There was that word again. This time, though, I wasn't feeling quite as magnanimous—it was a little late for sorry. But on the bright side . . .

"I'm alive, Tennyson, that's what's important. Magic has side effects, and so does using vampire blood to heal from a venomous magical spider. I'll deal."

He nodded. "Then shall I fetch your parents? Your friends?"

"My mom," I said. "I need to apologize for trying to eat her."

"She understands."

"So she says. Mothers hold grudges. It's part of the job description."

"As you like."

He opened the bedroom door and left. I struggled to sit up higher on the pillows. Energy was slowly coming back and would only improve once I had some food and liquid nourishment. The image of a nice, medium-rare burger with all the fixings and an icy cold beer made my empty tummy sit up and beg. It wanted something besides the zucchini bread and blood it had been fed in the last twenty-four hours.

Ugh.

Footsteps thundered on the stairs—more than just two feet. Mom breezed into the room, pale-faced and red-cheeked, and was trailed instantly by my dad. Gaius Oakenjin was of average height and slim build, with taut muscles and a gymnast's lean frame constantly hidden beneath baggy khakis and too-large coats. He was also stunningly handsome, his looks rivaling cover models with his dusky brown hair, wide, heavily lashed eyes, and an aw-shucks grin. He looked exactly the same way my entire life—and my mom's life, and her mom's, and her . . . .

Except right now, rage and worry darkened his features, and his magic radiated off him in waves of static electricity. As an earth djinn, he embodied strength and stability. The loss of either one brought out his aggressive side, and my little episode had done that in spades. We spoke maybe once a month, but I was still his daughter. Seeing him so angry and helpless broke something inside of me, and I started to cry.

"Shi, baby, you're okay," he said in a voice as strong as the earth itself. He sat on the bed and pulled me into his arms. I let him hold me, lacking the strength to hug him back, and cried against his black polo. Mom situated herself behind me, and I was in a parent sandwich, all hugs and warmth and love.

They let me cry it out, my sobs punctuated by the occasional coo or whispered word of support. I hadn't cried so much since my Nana (Mom's adopted mother) died three years ago of old age. Since djinn don't react normally to human medicine, doctors could do nothing for her, not even ease her agony as her millennia-old body failed. Mom and I had been there at the end, holding her frail hands as Nana freed her spirit and went to rest.

Eventually, Mom handed me some tissues, then a glass of water. Snot-free and semi-hydrated, they let me settle back against the headboard, finally able to sit up straight. I got a good look at my right hand, which was wrapped tight in white gauze. The bandages over the top of my hand were stained with something yellowish-green, and each finger was swollen. The five tiny sausages barely moved when I flexed them. My fingernails were shiny red and looked ready to pop off at a moment's notice.

Gross.

I almost laughed at the thought, but instead, I just

settled back, too tired to give in to amusement at the moment.

"What you did was foolish," Dad said finally. He'd kept his spot, forcing Mom to shift over to the opposite side of the bed. His tone dripped with disapproval, though his expression remained conciliatory.

"Which part?" I asked.

He frowned.

"Leave her be, Gaius," Mom said. "Shiloh made a calculated risk and it paid off. She's fine."

Fine was relative and remained to be seen, and I didn't know how calculated my decision to break the blood oath had been. I'd made it in the space of five seconds or less, fueled by anger and the instinctive need to protect what was mine. Protect Vincent from the bastards prepared to hurt him.

Not that I'd say any of that out loud in front of my parents.

"The vampire has tasted her blood," he said, not to me. "Do you think he'll stop now that he's had her? Vampires take what they've claimed, Elspeth."

I made a startled noise. *"Claimed?"*

"She's protected herself against worse and without our help," Mom replied.

"There is little worse than a Master vampire who has focused on a new toy."

"'Toy?" Neither of them seemed to hear me, so caught up in their argument.

"Djinn taste bad to vampires, and you know it, Gaius, having been bitten a few times yourself."

I stared, shocked by that little tidbit. Was I still in the room?

"It's our magic that tastes awful to them," Dad retorted. Fury blazed a black light in his brown eyes. His temper was up and, with it, his magic. It blazed around him like a tiny thundercloud. "She's also half human, which is their vintage of choice, so there's no telling how the vampire reacted."

"So you're assuming he enjoyed it."

"Assuming otherwise is foolish."

"You weren't there, Gaius. You were never there for her."

The final statement hit my father like a slap in the face. He jerked, his lips parting. Mom looked so smug I wanted to slap her for real.

"Shut up!" My volume surprised even me. "Please, shut up and stop fighting, for fuck's sake." I rarely swore in front of my parents, so the tirade had its desired effect—silence from both parties. No hints of embarrassment for their behavior, but I'd work with what I had.

"Maybe breaking Piotr's oath wasn't the smartest thing I've ever done," I said, "but at the time I saw no alternative. So unless Piotr got away and any chances I had of questioning him are out the window, I have no regrets. None."

"He's under restraints," Dad said. "Your large friend Novak is questioning him, I believe."

I quirked an eyebrow. Novak's favorite method of extracting information from a suspect was seduction. It was his best skill, he said, as well as the most fun for the fallen incubus. I'd witnessed it a few times, but always left feeling like a dirty voyeur, and for good reason.

It was usually pretty effective, though.

"Good, problem solved," I said. "I want to be perfectly clear: *I* made the choice to drink Tennyson's blood. He didn't force it on me." I reached out and grabbed my dad's hand. "He saved my life, Dad."

"I know, Shi." He squeezed back, mayhem in his eyes. "That's the only reason why I haven't killed him yet."

I didn't miss the way he emphasized *yet*. I shivered at the intent—it wasn't a statement, it was a promise.

CHAPTER 12

It took a little help from my mom to get me out of bed, down the hall to the bathroom, and out of my underwear and tank top—who'd gotten me out of my jeans and jacket was a topic for later discussion—and then into the shower. She tried insisting on filling the tub and letting me soak, but I didn't want to risk sitting. We'd need extra hands getting me back up, and I was embarrassed enough to be naked in front of my mom. I wasn't dragging anyone else into it.

She unbraided my hair while I sat on the toilet in a towel. She brushed it like she had when I was ten and prone to massive tangles—gently and with care to never pull or cause pain. I let her mother me. She was scared and she needed the distraction, to feel useful. I don't know if she'd seen her own mortality in the spider that bit me and could have bitten her instead of merely choking. I couldn't ask.

"I'm sorry," I said.

"For what, Shi?"

"Trying to bite you."

The brush paused in a downstroke, then continued to the ends of my hair. Up to the scalp, down again. "You weren't yourself."

"I know, but I wanted to say it."

"Okay."

She squeezed my shoulder and put the brush down on the sink. She turned on the water, adjusted the temperature to just below scorching—that's where I liked it—then helped me stand and step into the tub. My body still felt ten times too heavy and we'd taped a plastic grocery bag around my bandaged wrist. She shut the curtain and left me to it.

I got what I could one-handed with a bar of soap. My hair was harder and I didn't do a good job of it. Not that it mattered, since I planned on having Mom braid it up again. No muss, no fuss. Long hair was often more trouble than it was worth, but I treasured the times I could wear it down in thick layers and feel like an attractive woman. Vincent liked running his fingers through it while he—Vincent. I swallowed hard.

At the end of my patience with the bathing process, I checked that all the soap had rinsed away, then turned off the faucet. I coiled my hair around my left hand and squeezed. An avalanche of water spilled to the bottom of the tub and swirled away.

The corner of a red towel peeked through the shower curtain. I grinned, a little surprised Mom had hung around. The bathroom had to be a sauna by now.

"Thanks," I said as I took the towel. "You may want to step out, though. I'll probably need the full width of the bathroom in order to manage drying off."

No answer.

I tossed the towel over one shoulder and yanked back the curtain with, "Seriously, Mom—"

Only it wasn't my mother leaning against the sink, it was Jaxon. The only reason I didn't immediately sic the Quarrel on him and send him downstairs to pick an ill-advised fight with Novak was because he met my gaze and held it. His eyes didn't wander, even though everything except a brief swath across my left breast was on full display.

"Do you want me to hurt you?" I asked.

"I wanted to make sure you were okay," he said. The tension in his jaw and brow, old clues I'd picked up a long time ago, bore witness to his sincerity and concern.

"I'm fine, and you could have seen for yourself after I was dressed."

He quirked an eyebrow. "I've seen you naked before."

"Yeah, when we were having sex. You know, back when we were dating. Two things of which we are doing neither right now."

"Would you rather your mother towel you down?"

An acid retort died on my tongue. Drying off had seemed like a tedious chore a minute ago. Letting Jaxon do it wasn't my first choice; however, he won out over anyone else currently occupying our HQ. A gentle, no-strings-attached male touch won't go amiss right about now—especially one I'd once enjoyed and found to be quite skilled.

I tossed the towel at him. He stood up and helped me out onto the fuzzy green floor mat. He made a spinning motion with his forefinger, so I turned around. A flutter of nerves erupted in my stomach. With a gentle touch he used the towel to squeeze water out of my hair, then worked the soft terry across my shoulders and down each arm and all along my back. He used the taut towel and no hands on my backside, and equal gentleness on my legs. As much as dry me off, the light caresses also woke me up, teasing and warming my skin. Kind of like when—

No. No sexual thoughts about Jaxon. Bad Shiloh!

Spinning again to face him gave my insides another nervous flutter, and I watched him as he dried my front. Around my breasts, soft on my belly, avoiding anything lower altogether, which produce a gentle pang of regret. After all the emotions and physical exertion of the last few days, a release from a skilled lover—and for all our differences, Jaxon has always been terrific in bed, intently focused on giving me as much pleasure as possible out of each encounter—was something that would be amazingly welcome.

But we weren't together—couldn't be together, as both of us knew only too well. He was an excellent partner, but it was strictly business. And usually that was easy to deal with.

Until little moments like this, when I remembered how many intimate secrets we knew about each others' bodies. Secrets most coworkers never learn. A pang of longing hit me square in the chest, along with a sense of missing him, even though he was right there.

I didn't notice the stack of neatly folded clothes on the back of the toilet until Jaxon knelt to finish drying my feet. Someone had dug them out for me. As much as I wanted to salvage a little dignity, I let Jaxon help me dress. Underwear and bra, jeans and a t-shirt, and a pair of fuzzy socks.

He untied the plastic bag and rewrapped my bandages, giving me a brief look at the spider bite. The twin punctures were wider than I remembered, open sores still oozing clear, greenish liquid. Magic venom took a long time to go away, apparently, vampire blood or not. My fingers seemed less swollen, though, a little more flexible.

Jaxon really won points by brushing my damp hair

and then securing it in a ponytail. It wasn't a braid, but it was up and out of my face.

"I draw the line at doing your makeup," he said.

I laughed. "Me, too, actually. I don't need you poking me in the eye with a mascara wand." Not that I wore mascara. Maybe it was me, but even the expensive waterproof stuff ran and gave me raccoon eyes.

His smile disappeared behind a pensive frown. A tiny glimmer of fear flashed in his hazel eyes. "You really did scare the hell out of me."

"I scared the hell out of myself." I couldn't believe I'd admitted that out loud.

"You mean so much to me, Shi. I don't know what I'd do if I lost you."

I failed to control the burst of warm fuzzies that buzzed around my heart. "I'm fine."

"You almost weren't."

"I know."

Something shifted between us, invisible but no less powerful. An acknowledgement of old feelings. An admission of how close to dying I really had come today. Jaxon still meant a great deal to me, too, but I'd never say it out loud. Not even when the words were perched on the tip of my traitorous tongue, ready to leap off and be spoken.

To cover, I asked, "So you get anything useful from the Homme Alpha of California?"

He opened the bathroom door, allowing some of the moist air to escape and be replaced by a whoosh of coolness. It evaporated the residual moisture on my skin. "Same basic info we got from the Dame," he replied as I followed him into the hallway. "All of the mated pairs were infertile. The only oddity was one of the pairs had reproduced, but their three children all died young for no apparent reason. And I don't mean SIDS young, I mean two-and four-year-olds who died in their sleep."

"That's strange, right?"

"More than strange, and the Pack code forbids autopsies, so no one could figure out what killed them."

"Did we get names?"

"Yeah, K.I.M.'s got all of the relevant info. We've got her digging up anything she can find on those three kids who died. Where they were born, who the parents knew, the doctor who signed the death certificates."

"Did the Homme Alpha think foul play was involved?"

"For the kids? He said no, only that the deaths were tragic and puzzling, as were the disappearances of all of his wolves."

"In other words, butt out of Pack business."

"Yeah."

We'd wandered slowly down the hall and reached the top of the stairs. I grimaced. Jaxon looped an arm around my waist without asking, and we descended the stairs together, one at a time. Instead of tiring me, each foot forward woke up my inner reserves of strength. My hand ached less. Maybe I was coming out of this.

We reached bottom and he let go. I didn't want him to, but he did. The enticing fragrance of cooking meat greeted me. Lunchtime. I walked into the living room on my own steam and was greeted by four sets of eyeballs, all swiveling in my direction. Novak and Kathleen lounged on the sofa, both munching away on hamburgers and potato chips. Dad was just beyond them, poring over papers spread out on the conference table. Tennyson stood stiffly somewhere in between, back against the wall, arms crossed over his chest like a sentry.

Someone banged a pot in the kitchen, and I finally placed Mom.

I met Novak's gaze first. He held it a moment, then nodded. "Jaxon bring you up to speed?" he asked.

"I gave her the overview," Jaxon replied.

"K.I.M. have anything on the werewolf pair whose children all died?" I asked.

"Working on it," Novak said. "Hungry? Your mom makes killer burgers."

"She gets soup!" Mom shouted from the kitchen.

Jaxon snickered. I went the childish route and rolled my eyes.

"Anything from Piotr?" I asked Novak.

"Guess I'm not his type," the incubus drawled. "Vamp's got a good vocabulary of insults, though. Didn't say much else."

"He has not been questioned further," Tennyson said. "I thought you'd like the next opportunity."

How sweet. "Where is he?"

"In the holding cell you installed in your basement, secured to the bars with several silver chains. He is quite uncomfortable."

"Good."

Mom strode into the living room with a bamboo tray in her hands, delicately balancing a soup bowl, a glass of orange juice, and a glass of ice water. "Sit down and eat something, Shiloh," she said. "Get your strength back before you go torture the vampire."

She said it the way a normal person's mother might mention carbing up before a big track meet. And she was wearing her Mom Face, so I dutifully sat in the room's only unoccupied chair. She put the tray down on my lap, gave me a critical look, then retreated to the kitchen. I sniffed the steaming bowl. Nothing like reheated condensed chicken and stars soup.

"So I'm guessing Tennyson filled you guys in," I said.

"Yeah," Novak replied. He put his empty plate on the coffee table and picked up a sheet of printed paper. "Did some research on those alchemical symbols." He passed the paper to me via Kathleen.

I read it while I gulped down some of the orange juice, its cold, pulpy goodness settling nicely in my empty stomach. Aries stood for decomposition through calcination. Taurus for modification through coagulation, and Sagittarius for modification through ceration (a word I didn't know). Scorpio was separation through filtration, and Aquarius union through multiplication. For the most part, their relation to necromancy made sense.

"What does ceration mean?" I asked.

Novak plucked another sheet of paper off the table. "Adding a liquid to something while heating it, usually resulting in giving the finished product a waxy appearance," he read off the notes.

"It's part of the modification process of the spell," Tennyson said. "Add it to coagulation, and you have a recipe for preserving dead tissue."

"What about those herbs we found in the pentagram room?" I asked. "Anything on those?"

"Sage, witch hazel, henbane, angelica, tulsi, sweet violets, and the dried powder of several organic compounds."

"Such as?"

"The samples will have to be tested, if we cannot encourage Piotr to tell us."

I nodded, then asked Novak, "Any new vamp activity reported?"

"Atlanta PD has gotten several reports of suspicious lights at an old plantation outside of the city," he said. "Looks like one of the Masters has brought his linc together and is trying to keep a low profile."

"A New Orleans plantation would have fit the stereotype better."

Kathleen snorted laughter.

I used my fingers to fish a few ice cubes out of the water glass, then dumped them into the still-steaming soup. I stirred them in while staring at Kathleen's half-eaten, medium-rare burger. The idea of tiny pasta stars in reconstituted grease-broth was not as appealing as that pink, juicy meat. My stomach gurgled.

"I don't suppose we have any way of using the rest of that spider for anything, do we?" I asked. Sipped a spoonful of hot soup.

"Very little," Dad said. He gave Tennyson a glare and a wide berth as he joined us in the living room. "My tracking skills are a tad rusty, but I managed enough to know it wasn't conjured by the vampire you've got trussed up downstairs. And I received serious magical feedback when I tried to trace it to its source. Whoever is pulling these strings, Shi, he's a powerful puppeteer."

I swallowed more soup before retorting, "Yeah, thanks, I kind of got that."

"The question more important than who is why," Kathleen said. "Why blackmail a vampire into teaching necrotic magic to an apprentice? Why kidnap forty-six vampires and twenty-eight werewolves of specific lines or reproductive abilities? Why now? Why here?"

So many questions and so few answers. Time to get some, bless it. I forced down a few more spoonfuls of soup, but even with the tiny bits of chicken, it wasn't what my stomach wanted. I drank the rest of the juice, then put the tray on a nearby end table.

"Let's go see if Piotr can shed some light on those questions," I said, standing.

And then I'm getting a blessed burger.

The basement wasn't finished when we took over the house. A rickety set of wood steps had led down into a dirt pit that reeked of soil and mildew. With a little time and elbow grease, we put down a concrete floor, as well as protective wards in all four corners, and replaced the wood stairs with a sturdy aluminum set. The cement block walls were treated and reinforced with the wards. Basements were uncommon this close to sea level, because of flooding dangers, so we lucked into this one. It gave us somewhere to erect a cage of alternating silver and iron bars—guaranteed to trap and hold almost anything—human or otherwise.

Piotr was secured to the cage's interior bars by a length of silver chain. His fangs were bared and he was sweating pink. The gagging-sweet odor of seared flesh tickled my nose the closer I drew to the cage. Anywhere the silver touched bare skin it burned.

Silver chains. Silver bars. All of our specialized silver bullets and knives. The garlic spray only our team used. K.I.M. A high-tech, coded and thumb-printed security system. Had the Marshals' Office really wrestled this sort of money from the Federal budget? I'd never questioned our house or our gear before; not until I found out Julius had rented a storage unit for a necromancer. Possibly unknowingly, but if he'd known? Had he been paid to keep silent? Had that money gone into this house? Our equipment.

I truly hoped not.

Tennyson flanked me closely on my right side, Kathleen on my left. Dad had followed us down, but stayed back near the stairs. Between Piotr and Tennyson, and Kathleen's vampire half, Dad had to be on revulsion overload.

I pressed my thumb to the cage's locking mechanism. It popped open. Piotr finally lifted his head and looked at me. His hooded eyes swam with red sparks and a brief flare of surprise. I stepped inside, taking care to avoid his gaze directly. He was bound physically, but he still had power.

"I heard you didn't die," Piotr said, the disappointment in his voice a living thing. He'd failed big-time, and he knew it.

"I'm tricky like that," I replied. "I heard you didn't feel like talking."

"I have nothing to say."

"I think you've got plenty to say, and there's no blood oath keeping you from spilling your guts to me. So I'm guessing there's something else."

Silence.

"When you broke the oath, you said your debt was fulfilled and your people safe," I said. "What did you mean?"

"Exactly as I said."

"When Julius rented that storage unit last year, did he know its intended use?"

Piotr wheezed laughter. "Your incubus attempted to retrieve answers to those questions an hour ago, djinn. What makes you think I'll tell you?"

"An hour ago, you weren't certain I was alive. Your puppeteer is going to be pretty pissed that his plan to kill me didn't work. Your people may not be as safe as you believe they are."

Snaps of green light played in his eyes, combining with the red to create a queer holiday glow. "I cannot stop what is being done to them," he said so quietly I strained to hear. "As I could not stop it before."

"How many have been killed?" Tennyson asked.

Piotr swung his gaze past me. "My six strongest are dead. I felt them all die."

"If you can't protect them, then what's stopping you from cooperating?" I asked.

"I negate their sacrifice by assisting you."

"You could save the rest of them."

"Unlikely."

"But not impossible," Tennyson said. He appeared on my left side. If he was ill at ease so close to all that silver, he made no indication in his rigid stance and clenched jaw. "Yours are not the only vampires being threatened, Piotr. Other Masters have lost children and their abductor must be stopped."

"It is too late," Piotr said. "The new necromancer will rise, and then it will matter little what you and I try, my brother."

"What matters most is that we *do* try. I will not be manipulated into inaction, not while I have the strength to protect my people. Help us and we may yet save yours."

"No."

"You're a coward," I said.

The green in Piotr's eyes drowned beneath a gale of red. "And you are a half-breed, neither human nor djinn. You are of two worlds, and have tasted the blood of a third. I smell his power in you."

"Nothing a good laxative won't cure," I quipped. "Look, you stay here and work on your grill marks until we solve this thing on our own—which we will, by the way—or you can agree to help us, we'll let you go, *and* we'll try to save your people."

"No."

"Great Iblis." I gave Tennyson a frustrated glare. "Are all Masters this stubborn?"

"He has something yet to lose," Tennyson said.

"Like what? A home in Maui?" I reached behind me and Kathleen pressed the handle of a silver blade into my palm. I moved to stand an arm's length from Piotr, whose gaze was fixed on the gleaming metal. It was the size of a paring knife, its custom blade infused with pure silver, and I held it level with his eyes. "Tell me what I need to know, or we'll see if your eyeballs regenerate as quickly as other tissue."

Most men quail at the idea of having their eyes cleaved from their skulls. Piotr threw back his head—which made a loud, painful crack against the bars—and laughed. Deep, piteous laughter that was equally horrifying and terrifying. "Open my shirt, half-breed," he snorted. "There is little torture you can devise that will come within half a mile of what I've already suffered. Your threats mean nothing."

Curiosity drew my blade hand down. I cut through the fabric easily with its sharp tip, exposing Piotr's sunken chest and belly. It looked like the moon's surface, pale and pockmarked, as though chunks of flesh had been carved away and the skin healed over before the tissue could reassert itself. My stomach sloshed, rebelling against its liquid contents.

A low growl filled the basement, and it took me a few seconds to assign its source to Tennyson. "Who did this?" Danger lurked in his voice and his face, anger sharpening every angled feature.

"The same man who is murdering my people," Piotr said. "The same man who had me teach his chosen one how to control necrotic magic."

"The same man who is kidnapping vampires and werewolves across the country."

"Yes."

I blinked, shocked Piotr had offered up even that

small tidbit. Then I realized Piotr had made the mistake of looking Tennyson directly in the eyes. The two were battling in a silent gazelock, and as the stronger, Tennyson was winning. He was forcing Piotr to answer.

"Why?" Tennyson asked.

"I do not know."

"Who is this apprentice you taught?"

More pink sweat popped out on Piotr's forehead. He lurched against the chains holding him. He ground out, "No one."

"Did Julius Almeida know that rental unit was to be used for necrotic magic?"

"He was paid handsomely to rent it for us."

I flinched at that, but we'd finally gotten something useful out of him. Tennyson latched on to it and asked, "Paid by whom?"

"No one."

"He was paid to rent the storage unit under his own name, and not told why, so that if it was discovered, it would lead his team to doubt his loyalty to them and tear them apart," Tennyson said, summarizing perfectly my own thoughts.

"Yes."

"This was Julius Almeida's only role in recent events, and his death and revenancy were merely additional tools to break apart his team."

"He was practice for the apprentice."

"So you said. Was my previous statement correct?"

"No."

A ripple of tension swept the room. Behind me, Kathleen shifted as though to strike. I stared at Piotr, while Tennyson merely seemed puzzled. Magic filled the room, so powerful my lungs hitched and threatened to make me cough. Piotr had gathered energy to fight back against Tennyson's gazelock, and the feedback was stunning. The air snap-crackled, keen and crisp with electricity.

Julius had been chosen as practice, because he had rented the storage unit, and its discovery would send us running in circles. It would make us suspect him as complicit in the necrotic magic. His death would hurt us. Something else, though, was missing from the list.

I twisted my head to look behind me. Dad still hung back by the stairs, his face twisted in disgust, practically green from the force of the vampire magic. He caught me staring, saw the question in my eyes. He tapped his forefinger against his temple.

Think? I was thinking, and blessed hard, too. He repeated the gesture, working too hard against being sick to offer more. Not think. Mind. Sight.

Crap.

"Tennyson," I said. "Ask him about the link created between necromancer and revenant. What sort of control does he have over the revenants he creates?"

"Answer the lady," Tennyson said tersely. A fine sheen of pink perspiration had formed on his face, giving his usually ghostly skin an almost normal glow of color. "Can you control the revenant?"

Piotr roared, a beastly sound that set my teeth on edge. He said something in Russian, then switched to English. "Yes, when it's awake."

"Have you controlled it since its return?"

The lack of response made my chest ache—it was as good as a yes. I remembered how Tennyson had described his link to all of his vampire children. They were connected by the mind and emotions. Since revenant spirits were all about emotional turmoil, it stood to reason the necromancer had a similar sort of link. And since Julius was only awake when he took off his lid and interacted . . .

"He's spying on us," I said. Piotr's left eye twitched. "He used his connection to Julius and has been spying on us. Son of a bitch."

Piotr hit the chains like a wolverine, snarling and snapping. I took a step backward, propelled by the wave of energy slamming my way, flavored with fury and hatred. Tennyson took a sideways step that put his body between me and Piotr. Neither of us had to ask if my assumption was true.

"Release me!" Piotr roared in a voice so guttural it seemed torn from the belly of the earth. The monster was defeating the man. I'd seen it happen once and barely survived with my life.

Vampirism isn't a disease. Science will never understand it, cure it, or replicate it. It's a dual existence, on a level that can only be explained by magic, occurring at the point of death through blood exchange. No longer fully human, infused with the instincts of a predator to hunt and drink and mate, vampires must learn to control their monster side early on in order to survive amongst humans. It's why those chosen to be turned must be approved by the line's Master— weak, irrational vampires weaken the line and bring unwanted attention.

It's rumored among the djinn that the first vampires were former djinn, cast out for using their magic selfishly and cursed with bloodlust. Funny enough, no one knows for sure, and the vampires . . . ah, dislike being referred to as fallen djinn. Really dislike it. In the same way djinn despise being referred to as fallen angels (even though they are, technically).

In our first year together, our Para-Marshal unit was dispatched to hunt a rogue vampire who'd lost control of his monster. He'd gone on a killing rampage in the Philadelphia Zoo one night, devastating the animals and at least six caretakers before being cornered by a helpful troll. The carnage had looked like a scene from a slasher movie—guts and muscle and stringy red bits all over the ground and in trees. The vampire had been animalistic in its fury, eyes glowing red and fangs extended to over two inches. It had taken eighteen silver bullets to slow it down. I took a slice to my femoral artery when I moved in to decapitate the blessed thing.

Red-eyed and fangs growing longer by the second, Piotr looked much like that feral vamp had six years ago. And unlike that feral vamp, Piotr was both very old and a necromancer. If he lost control, I doubted very much the cage would hold him.

Tennyson backed up. I did, too, to avoid being stepped on, and then we were outside of the cage. I slammed the door into place. Tennyson hadn't broken his gazelock, but judging by the sweat curling down his clenched jaw and the blazing red of his eyes, he was on the verge of losing Piotr. Letting the monster out.

"Kill it, Shiloh," Dad said. "Before your vampire loses control and the beast is free."

My vampire?

"Release me!" Piotr's second demand was more guttural than the first, harder to understand.

Kathleen circled the cage and stopped behind Piotr's straining back. She plucked a silver blade from her belt.

"Wait," I said. "Wait, will killing Piotr also kill Julius?"

"He is already dead," she replied.

"I mean with the spell. Does killing the necromancer destroy the revenant's ability to function?"

"There is but one way to find out."

"He was using the revenant to spy on you," Dad said. "You don't want to keep it around, anyway, no matter who it used to be, Shiloh."

I held his gaze a moment, but saw nothing useful there. Dad saw a monster that needed putting down. Kathleen saw the same thing. I saw a link to the remains of an old friend, but I also saw a potential opportunity. We'd used Julius to track down the pentagram room. We may yet use him to find the apprentice—an apprentice Piotr could still identify.

"Give me the blade," I said, moving to stand next to the Kathleen.

She handed it over without question. I tested its weight in my palm, its perfect balance and shape. The cage's bars were spaced far enough apart to thrust my hand through while fisted.

"Do something," Tennyson said through clenched teeth, the strain obvious in his tone.

I eyed my target and drove the blade home.

CHAPTER 13

I shoved the knife into Piotr's spine, directly between his shoulder blades. He didn't scream. His entire body sagged against the chains as everything below his chest went slack. His fingers still twitched, so he hadn't lost complete control of his arms, but the fight had gone out of him. As long as the blade stayed in place, he couldn't heal and regain mobility.

It also had to hurt like hell, but I didn't care.

"That wasn't what I had in mind," Kathleen said.

"He still has information we need," I said. "If we dust him now, we'll never get it."

Tennyson was sitting cross-legged on the floor, head down and cradled in his palms. I approached slowly, scuffling my feet on the concrete floor to announce myself.

"I need a moment," he said as I reached out to touch his shoulder.

The announcement stayed my hand. I hazarded a look at Piotr, instead. His face was bloodless, his eyes downcast. Some internal war continued raging inside of his mind, but his damaged body could no longer seethe against its captivity. We'd be lucky to get any more answers from him. I just couldn't sever the final link to Julius—not yet.

Dad's color was better now that the levels of vampire magic had reduced to a faint buzz. He was watching me like I was a particularly interesting bug specimen. Was that . . . surely that wasn't disappointment? Over me not killing Piotr? Okay, so I understood the deep-seated hatred between the two species, but I was confident I'd made the right—

His gaze dropped to Tennyson, then flickered back to me. Oh.

Oh!

I gave Dad my very best petulant teenager face, then squatted next to Tennyson. It made my entire body ache. Dad made a rude noise, punctuated by his feet stomping up the stairs. Kathleen followed him.

"Thank you," I said.

Tennyson looked up. His face was a strange, mottled color where the sweat had stained his skin. No hint of color remained in his eyes. A waft of tepid, clove-scented energy hit me. Coupled with the taut lines around his eyes and mouth, I categorized that one as pretty close to pain. "You're welcome," he said. "Thank you for not killing him."

"I didn't do it for you."

"I realize that. However, the death of a Master can throw the line into turmoil when there is no clear leader to replace him or her."

"Clear leader?"

He studied my nose—in pain but polite enough to avoid my eyes. "It is considered bad form to openly challenge another Master without cause, and it has happened only twice to my knowledge. In both instances, the victor is awarded all possessions of the slain Master, including control of his line."

I blinked, surprised by the information. "What happens if I kill Piotr?"

"Nothing. You are not a vampire, therefore cannot be expected to control the line. Either a potential Master would emerge from the line and petition for leadership, or the line would fracture and scatter into smaller groups. Those individual nests are not unheard of, but they exist outside of the protection of our laws. If they are killed by law enforcement or other means, as Masters we are under no obligation to punish the culprits or demand recompense for their losses."

"Wow," I said.

He frowned—which was pretty impressive, given his already tense expression. "You are not aware of internal vampire politics." It wasn't a question.

"Not much of it, no." I hated admitting to ignorance. "I suppose it never occurred to me that a Master could be killed."

"We can, of course, but it is extremely difficult. Piotr would never have been captured today without my assistance. As such, I could successfully petition for claim over his line in the event of his death at a non-vampire's hands."

My heart pitter-patted. "Giving you control of how many vampires?"

"Several hundred, unless they are all murdered by this mysterious figure Piotr spoke of." He must have understood something in my expression, because he offered a tentative smile. "It is my experience that adopting the vampires of another's line is extremely taxing, both mentally and physically. Establishing a link with one you have not sired is difficult and time-consuming."

It is my experience. Those words haunted me. He knew of instances where such a thing occurred. Was he one of the two that had killed a fellow Master and assumed their line?

"That is a story for another day," he said. I glared, and he added, "I apologize, but your proximity makes it difficult to ignore your thoughts completely. You are an emotional thing, and you tend to project."

I stood up fast enough to make myself woozy, and then stalked toward the stairs. Show a little compassion and get insulted—check. At least I'd gotten a little more information out of him and knew enough to not kill Piotr if it could be helped. The last thing I needed was to be blamed for Tennyson gaining control of more—

"Shiloh."

His hand wrapped around my left wrist and tugged. I spun into the motion, in no mood to be grabbed, and drove my knee into his groin. An approximation of it, anyway, since he was a bit taller and faster, and he managed to swing his body far enough to the side to avoid full-package contact. My knee pummeled the spot where his left leg met his hip, which threw me off balance. He kept me spinning, until I stopped with my back to his chest, my arms pinned over my stomach.

I had a momentary déjà vu to the upstairs hallway and bit back an instinctual shriek. Bringing my teammates—or my dad for that matter—back down for this would only end badly. I didn't need rescuing from Tennyson.

"Let. Me. Go."

He did and stepped back to a respectable distance. As much as the Master vampire terrified me, he also infuriated me like no one I'd ever met. Power and arrogance far outweighed any positive qualities I'd observed in the few days we'd known each other.

"I have no desire to acquire Piotr's line," he said in a voice cold enough to challenge an icebox. "None at all. My only desire is to ensure the safety of my existing line and to reclaim that which has been stolen from me."

"Which I've already promised to help you do." I couldn't quite match his glacial tone. "And now we know the same man who took your people is pulling all the strings, and he wants a necromancer under his thumb. Missing vampires, mated werewolf pairs, and necrotic magic—how does all of this fit?"

The creation of vampires and forced werewolves were similar. Each needed the victim near death for the transformation to take place. Vampires had an eighty-twenty success rate. Werewolf transformation was closer to forty-sixty, because blood was not given back to the victim in the same manner as vampirism, and the physical effect was far more violent. Necrotic magic had similarities to both, in that the magic worked best with the brutally tortured. It was control of the dead.

Or the undead. Vampires were not exactly dead, but they also were no longer alive.

Tennyson made a surprised noise, as though he'd been following my train of thought and had come to the same conclusion. I was so thrown by my answer that I looked into his red-tinged eyes. My skin crawled as I felt the start of a gazelock; surprisingly, he blinked and averted first.

"Could a necromancer alter the revenant spell in order to establish control over a vampire?" I asked. Just saying it made my stomach squirm.

"Theoretically, it is possible. However, I know little of necrotic magic, and even less of altering spells to create a different end result than what is intended. It is not an efficient method—"

"It is if you can control a Master."

He chewed on that for a minute. "Control of a Master means control of the line."

"Bingo. And right now, this big bad has forty-six vampires he can let his necromancer experiment on to get it right."

"The other Masters must be warned."

"Can you trust them?"

His dark look said it all. "You saw what was done to Piotr. He was cooperating under coercion. No Master would willingly align him or herself with someone whose end goal is to dominate our race."

It sounded melodramatic said like that. He wasn't wrong, though. If whatever we were facing could capture a Master and successfully put him under his thumb, the other lines would be in serious danger. Hunted by their own kind. Not to mention the fact that human authorities would be forced to intervene. It would be chaos for vampires. I could only imagine the anger and betrayal I'd feel if someone had told me this about the djinn. Tennyson was living it.

"We're getting all of the whys and whats figured out," I said. "Now we need the whos and the wheres." I cast a look at Piotr's limp form; he didn't seem conscious.

"We will learn little else from Piotr now. Even through the gazelock, his thoughts were protected from me. We must seek further answers elsewhere."

I started toward the stairs again.

"You have a plan?" Tennyson asked, tailing me up.

"Yep. A little old-fashioned detective work."

The assortment of people collected around K.I.M.'s widest monitor looked normal enough from the outside. As I waited for the computer to bring up my requested information, I mused on the assortment of supernatural entities standing in a semicircle in the converted dining room. Six hundred-year-old Master vampire and his mortal enemy, an earth djinn; myself, a half djinn; and my mother, the half Romani daughter of a warlock; a fallen incubus who wore sex on his sleeve and could seduce male or female with a smile; a dhampir who hated her vampire half as much as she hated the weakness of being half human; and a skin-walker as comfortable running the woods as a seven-point stag as he was chasing a suspect through alleys with bullets raining down around him.

Yeah, we were an odd bunch, hanging around a supercomputer invented by a demon, waiting to get a look at the cell phone records for Julius at the time he signed the storage unit lease. I gave K.I.M. a four-week window, asked her to separate any calls made to other Raspberries, and only show calls made more than once.

Dozens of lines of data still streamed across the screen. Checking up on those frequent calls was our best lead, and after revealing our suspicions to the rest of the group, everyone seemed to agree that finding this big bad was urgent. Seriously urgent.

Multiple names came up more than four times. Adam Weller, the leader of the West Coast Para-Marshal Unit (not a shocker there). Linus Parker, an old Army Rangers buddy of Julius's of whom I'd heard dozens of stories, mostly good, mostly involving alcohol and bar fights. Catherine Gibbons, someone Novak identified as Julius's shrink from the VA hospital (I hadn't even known Julius saw a shrink). And three more names no one in the room knew offhand, which made them the likeliest of suspects.

However, to further shed darkness on this thing, none of them spoke with Julius on the actual day of rental. The least likely suspect on the list was also the only one who called Julius's phone the day he disappeared—Adam Weller. Judging by the records, the pair spoke every week, sometimes more than once. Given their rather solitary roles as lead Para-Marshals, the communication was expected.

"Has anyone spoken directly to Weller recently?" I asked, unsure what had been done during my convalescence. "Not just emailed updates? He left me a voice mail yesterday, but didn't ask me to call him back."

"Yeah, yesterday while you were visiting another dimension with Tennyson," Novak said. He was standing behind me and to my left. "Said he talked to Julius around lunchtime, was reporting some unusual vampire movement near Sacramento, and asking if we'd noticed anything out here. Said Julius was waiting on Chinese food delivery, and they hung up when the food got there. Last he heard from him."

The computer logs confirmed the call had lasted sixteen minutes, beginning at 12:14 that afternoon.

I gave K.I.M. new commands—bring up personal information on Parker, Gibbons, and the other three names. "So we've got five potential suspects," I said, also commanding the information to be printed. "And five of us."

"Five?" Jaxon repeated, then jacked his thumb at Tennyson. "When did Fangs join the team?"

"When he saved my life," I replied, in no mood to argue Tennyson's inclusion. Jaxon could go from sweet and charming to complete ass in point-two seconds.

"Four suspects," Novak said as he skimmed the computer screen. "Something tells me this Louisa Malcolm isn't our bad guy."

"Why?" I turned to look at one of the names I hadn't recognized.

"She's his grandmother."

"He has a grandmother?"

"According to this, yes. Has he spoken of her to you?"

I shook my head. "Anyone?"

More nos. Funny the things you never really get to know about your coworkers.

"That simplifies things," I said. "We split up, take two names each."

"Let me guess," Jaxon said. "You go with the vampire."

I spun to face him, temper rising. I aimed the full force of my glare at him. "Anyone in this room who would rather be partnered up with the vampire, please raise your hand." No one did. Tennyson actually looked amused. "Well, guess what, Jaxon? Now you're coming with us, too. Novak and Kathleen can handle themselves."

Jaxon started to protest, then clamped his mouth shut. I might have been slightly woozy, and still lacking in the full-range-of-motion department, but he recognized my position. Julius had trained us well.

My parents stood apart from the rest of us, close enough to touch and not arguing, which was a nice change. "Mom, I'm sorry, but I think you should stay here," I said. "If Piotr really did use Julius to spy on us, then whoever we're hunting could know where you live. We can't risk you going home."

Mom, bless her, seemed more resigned than angry. She also appeared on the verge of ordering me back to bed. Which she didn't, which was a relief.

Less of a relief was when Dad broke apart from her and crooked his finger at me. I trailed him into the living room, away from the cluster of people.

"I know a sidhe who is sensitive to black magic," he said softly. "If she has sensed anything, she won't give it up lightly."

A sidhe—worse than a djinn when it came to collecting owed debts. "How does she bargain?"

"As many do, for what is most valuable."

Memories. The sidhe care little for money, and even less for sex. They traded in precious goods, and for most sentient creatures, that meant memories and magic. Djinn magic was almost as distasteful to the sidhe as to vampires, so it would be memories. Or a favor at a later date, which was also possible, though less likely.

"If she has information that leads us to the necromancer," I said, choosing my words carefully, "then I will bargain the cost once the necro is killed."

He shook his head. "Shiloh, I didn't intend—"

"Yeah, I know, but this is my case, my team, my problem. I'm glad to see you, but Mom really shouldn't have called you."

"You're facing someone of unknown power here."

"Exactly why I don't want you and Mom involved any further than you have been. Please, Dad, do this for me. I'll bargain with the sidhe if, and only if, the information helps us."

He pressed his lips into a thin line and for the briefest moment, he looked old. Not just older than his outward thirty-five, but ancient. A flicker of the weight he carried from his eight hundred years of existence—everything he'd seen, everyone he'd known, and all of the magic he had cast. He knew the power of memories. As an earth djinn, his were one-hundred-fifty proof compared to my own wine cooler-level memories.

"I'll take it to her," he finally said. "She may not agree."

"She'll agree. I know how rare half djinns are."

My self-awareness was not making him any happier. "You are as stubborn as your mother."

"I'll take that as a compliment."

"It wasn't meant as one. And you are overlooking another obvious clue."

I stared, waiting for more. He didn't give it, and I realized it was for the same reason he'd tapped his head in the basement. As a djinn, he was required to offer assistance only to those who bound him to the Rules of Wishing, or with whom he'd struck a bargain. Djinn didn't work for free, and they couldn't interfere in human affairs without such a bargain— even if it was their daughter. He could hint, infer, and make gestures, but he couldn't tell me point-blank what I needed to know.

As I ran through everything I knew about the case so far, he grew impatient and lifted my right arm by the elbow. I stared at my bandaged hand. The fingers were almost back to normal size and color, and the poison hadn't oozed through this layer of—oh. Oh!

"The spider," I said. It was so obvious I wanted to slap myself. "It was used twice, once as a snare and once as a curse for breaking a blood oath. We need to know who has dark power over spiders."

Dad grinned. "That's my girl. Watch your back."

"I will."

He closed his eyes, tilted his head upward, and concentrated. The air shimmered, and then he was gone in a thunderclap of sound and faint odor of dried leaves. I envied him the ability to teleport, and often wished I'd inherited the gift.

I turned and nearly plowed into Jaxon.

"I think this is the first time I've seen your dad since that day in Denver," he said.

"He doesn't have a lot of time to stop over for dinner. And he may have a lead."

"You and your dad look the same age."

"Gee, I didn't know I look like I'm eight centuries old."

His eyebrows rose to his hairline. "Wow. That's old."

"He's a djinn, Jaxon. They aren't immortal, but they usually live for a millennium or so."

"So he's up there among the powerful."

"Yeah, I guess."

I understood my dad's status, and I totally got the reverence with which the oldest, most powerful of magical creatures were discussed. Especially coming from a skin-walker, whose ability to shift into his spirit animal is dependent upon inherited power and execution of the walker's chant. It isn't an ability they are born with. A skin-walker is chosen by their spirit animal during a ritual performed on the child's tenth birthday. In order to shift, the child must kill the spirit animal, drink its blood, and carve out a piece of its skin or feathers. Once upon a time, the piece of the animal was worn in a pouch around the neck. Nowadays it's surgically grafted to the child so it can never be stolen.

Jaxon's patch of deer skin is on his neck, barely hidden by his hair. He used to love it when I rubbed it during sex. Made him blow like an atomic bomb . . .

Okay, not going there.

No sexy thoughts about Jaxon, because the jerk had just reminded me how weak my human side made me. I'd never be a quarter as powerful as my father and didn't like having it rubbed in my face, unintentionally or not. I had enough neuroses.

"What do you know about spiders?" I asked.

"Uh, they eat mosquitoes and make sticky webs?"

I thumped him on the chest. "Magical spiders, dumb ass."

"Outside of Arachne, not much. Last rumor had her sunny side up in the Riviera."

Yes, *the* Arachne. Greek weaver of great designs cursed by the goddess Athena, because Arachne's fabrics always won the Pantheon's equivalent of the State Fair blue ribbon. Whoever first coined the phrase "Hell hath no fury like a woman scorned" likely based it on those early Greek goddesses. They were petty as hell about everything, especially beauty.

Arachne's curse was lifted about three thousand years ago, when Athena went batshit over Zeus's latest fling with Helen of Troy (yes that Helen, and no, some men never change) and was imprisoned in Hades for a few dozen millennia until she cooled off. As the mother of all spiders, Arachne maintains a sort-of control over her children. She views death-via-spider-venom as a worthy offering to her greatness and is rumored to honor those sacrifices by gifting artistic ability to children. I don't know if it's true, but the notion that da Vinci's paintings exist because some other Italian croaked from a spider bite makes me giggle.

She was also so full of her own self-importance, I doubted she'd lift a perfectly polished fingernail to help anyone else.

"I can research that," Mom said. I hadn't seen her creep up behind Jaxon, and now she stepped out from behind him. "If you teach me how to use your computer, I can look up spiders while you, um, go question people."

There are reasons my mother is awesome, and moments like this are among them. "That's a great idea," I said.

"I'll get you set up, Elspeth," Jaxon said. "Everything's voice activated . . ." He continued explaining as he led her back into the dining room.

Novak and Kathleen were poring over several printed sheets of paper, hopefully comparing the suspects by relative location and ease of travel. Judging only by the area codes, the two unknown suspects were semi-local. I'd likely score those two, since it was too risky trying to take Tennyson on an airplane, and our helicopter didn't have solar shielding.

Speaking of Tennyson . . .

I didn't see him, not in the living room, kitchen, or conference room. Had he wandered back upstairs? Downstairs? Certainly not outdoors. It was mid-afternoon and high-crisp time for vamps. I closed my eyes and tried something new—I felt for him. Sought those odd waves of temperature and scent I'd experienced ever since we'd shared blood. I didn't expect it to work.

It did.

A sense of frigid spice lured me toward the stairs, not unlike what I imagined a frozen chili pepper might taste like. Cold always came with emotions like anxiety and pain, but this was colder than either of those and coupled with the heat of a terrible peppery bite. The whole thing was giving me a headache.

I found Tennyson sitting at the top of the stairs, feet braced on the first step down so his knees were drawn up close to his chest. His long arms hugged those legs, hands clenched so tightly around his forearms that his knuckles were white. He stared at nothing in particular, his eyes glowing red with faint specks of blue, mouth drawn tight. He didn't move as I approached, and the cold pepper sensation grew stronger. Even without our connection, I could sense his distress.

I sat next to him on the top step, leaving a few inches of air between us. He didn't move or acknowledge me. "Tennyson?" I asked softly.

His red eyes flared brightly a moment, then settled back to an intense crimson. He didn't blink.

I licked my lips. "Tell me what's happening."

"He's torturing them." Tennyson's voice cut like a scalpel, white-hot with fury, although barely audible.

My stomach quaked; I didn't have to ask who was being tortured. He could sense his missing vampires again. Someone was allowing it. I kept my voice steady, firm. "Can you tell who's doing it?"

"Silver nails have been driven through their eyes. They cannot see, only feel. I cannot hear a voice, only vicious laughter and screams of anguish. Four are gone. The others will follow."

Tears sprang unbidden to my eyes. Crying over vampires I didn't know. My dad would be thrilled. But no, I wasn't crying for them. I cried for Tennyson, a vampire I *did* know, and for the undisguised suffering in his voice and body language. I cried for a man who felt his children dying.

Saying I was sorry sounded stupid—a generic platitude he wouldn't have appreciated under the best of circumstances. "Can you, um, use this connection to locate them?"

His head turned a few degrees in my direction. A pink tear squeezed from his visible eye, marking a flesh-colored path down his pale cheek. "The emotions are overwhelming. Their fear and agony is . . . difficult to overcome."

No kidding. If what I felt was only a fraction of his experience, I didn't know how he was so calm. Then again, vampire. If he could focus past the suffering of his people, maybe he could hear or sense a clue. Something to help us identify the location, or even the person torturing them. Only I couldn't use my magic to productively assist Tennyson unless he made a wish. Wishing, unfortunately, tied me to him by the Rules of Wishing.

Djinn can be summoned via specific spells, and most djinn will only respond to them. Because of their more volatile nature ice djinn have been known to appear when the right emotional cocktail is applied to a verbalized wish. The emotional cocktail usually consists of equal parts vengeance and rage.

Being half djinn, I can't be summoned by those spells. However, if someone knows what I am and knows the words to bind me to the Rules of Wishing, I must obey them. It's happened four times in my life—three because I allowed it in order to help someone. The fourth . . . not so much.

Current problem staring me in the face: I can't speak the binding words out loud. No djinn can. If Tennyson didn't know them, then the plan failed. Downside to this plan succeeding: being bound to Tennyson for two more wishes. Not only magically, but I'd also need to maintain a level of physical proximity to him or I'd experience literal, physical pain by stretching our magical tether too far.

Hellfire. I rubbed my forehead with my fingertips. The binding wouldn't even work with a vampire. The same cosmic rules that prevented me from speaking the words also prevented our cousin race from doing the same. Sort of a universal tit for tat, since our little quirks (my Quarrel, for instance) don't work on vamps. Unless . . . .

Can you hear my thoughts, Tennyson?

He blinked and turned his head a few more degrees, still not attempting to look directly at me. Red light from his eyes washed over my skin. *Yes, I can.*

I flinched. This was going to give me another migraine. *I think I can help you off-load some of the emotion you're feeling so you can dig deeper and seek clues as to your vampires' whereabouts.*

How?

I need you to wish me to do so.

Vampires cannot—

Yeah, I know, you can't speak the binding words out loud. Try speaking them like this, telepathically.

He quieted. The thunder of his voice coalesced into a steady hammering behind my eyes. I pinched the bridge of my nose, grateful for the brief respite.

Why would you bind yourself to me, Shiloh?

Because whoever has your vampires has Vincent. They killed Julius. They're responsible for this entire mess. We need every lead we can get.

The red glow flickered as he blinked again. *Are you certain you want me to do this?*

Yes. My lack of hesitation must have cemented his decision.

Shiloh Harrison, child of Iblis, I bind thy magic as my servant three times over, and bind myself according to thy terms.

A tremor raced down my spine from neck to butt, spreading goose bumps across my shoulders and ribs. Warmth filled my chest as though I'd just sucked down hot tea. Magic tingled between us like bolts of static electricity. The faint odor of ozone tingled my nostrils and was soon overpowered by the taste of blood. My entire body shuddered, as though attempting to repel its magical connection to a vampire. Then it was over.

The impression of a rope, thick as my pinkie finger and made of glimmering gold, ran from my mind to Tennyson's. Not a physical rope, and it wasn't one I could actually see. Rather, I sensed it. The tether binding my magic to his wishes.

A splash of fear chilled me. We'd gotten around the limits of vampire/djinn magic. What if he used this loophole to circumvent the Rules of Magic?

Rule number one: we cannot alter a person's heart or existing physical condition. Or, in simpler words, I can't cast a love spell or heal someone who's dying. I can't cure cancer, I can't mend a broken bone, and I can't prevent a heroic fireman with third-degree burns over eighty percent of his body from succumbing to an agonizing death. We can only change the condition of inanimate objects, or affect the mind of a person, like what I did with Tennyson.

Rule number two: the magical expenditure of the second wish cannot exceed the first wish. It prevented wishers from going overboard on subsequent wishes once they realized just how powerful a djinn's magic is. It comes in handy when one of us is accidentally summoned. The wisher wants to test our abilities, so he asks for something small, unobtrusive, like turning his coffee table from oak to granite (true story). It means the rest of the wishes can't be any more complicated than that. Pisses people off royally, but it's really their own stupidity, no?

Rule number three is one I rarely get to see the effects of in person. It states that the magic will return to the wisher threefold. So if some joker makes a selfish wish—I've heard stories of people wishing coworkers would lose their jobs, or wishing an ex-spouse into bad financial luck—it'll come back to bite them in the ass. Three times as badly.

"Why are you so afraid, Shiloh? Did it work?" Tennyson's strained voice was less intrusive than his telepathic one, but it still cut into my headache and left my temples throbbing. He shifted to face me. The single tear had dried into a dark track, and lines of stress and strain bracketed his mouth. Those red headlights fixed on me.

"It worked, and I'm fine." Hopefully he was out of my head for a while, too. "Okay, make your first wish."

"Wish?" Novak's voice boomed up the stairs. "What under heaven are you doing to her, Vampire?"

CHAPTER 14

Bless it all. "Novak, go away a minute," I said.

He thundered toward us. "Not a chance. What do you mean 'wish'?"

I stood up and descended until I ran into Novak. Three steps down, the huge incubus was still at eye level with me. He snorted like a raging bull. I spread my hands out, doing what I could to block his path. "Novak, go back downstairs and give me a minute."

"Forget it." Fury blazed in his dark eyes and his wide nostrils flared. "You djinn never say the word *wish* out loud, so this isn't nothing, Shi. What did he make you do?"

"He didn't make me do anything. This could get us some answers."

"By binding yourself to that bloodsucker? Did you forget what happened with Kress?"

My fist ached and his head had jerked sideways before I registered punching Novak in the mouth. Dark blood flowed from his split lip, down over bared teeth. I was shaking head to toe, far beyond anger now. "Use that against me again," I said, "and I'll find a way to banish you back to Hell where you can't hide from the unfallen incubi."

He snarled again, but kept silent. I didn't know if I could actually manage my threat, but it shut him up and made him back off. I'd never threatened Novak in such a way, but my experience with Kress had been traumatizing for any number of reasons, and he knew better than to throw it back in my face.

"Just . . ." I took a deep breath. Exhaled. "Give me a few minutes, okay? Tennyson can sense his missing vampires again, and we may be able to get some indication of who's holding them."

Novak glared. "If you get killed, I'm not paying for your funeral." Coming from him, it was as good as a solicitation of luck.

"Please keep everyone downstairs."

"Will there be screaming involved?"

"I hope not."

"Good, 'cuz if Jaxon finds out he'll drive those antlers of his right through the vampire's heart."

"Do not tell Jaxon what's going on. Please." Because Jaxon probably would do exactly what Novak said.

He continued glowering, but he did nod once, so

I took that as the end of our argument and turned around. Tennyson was gone. Again.

I took the stairs two at a time and followed the pull of our bond to my bedroom. He hadn't shut the door. I did after I stepped inside. He stood near the window, heavy curtains drawn shut against the afternoon sun, his head bowed. Both hands were clenched in tight fists. The room was absolutely frigid with his grief.

He looked up, his headlights alternating red to blue, washing the dark bedroom in an ethereal glow. More tears streaked his cheeks. "They killed Ambrosius," he said. "Two hundred and seventy-eight years had he been mine. A lover in life and death, he shared my bed for forty years before our attentions turned elsewhere. He was beautiful."

"I'm sorry." The dreaded platitude slipped out before I could stop it.

"Six are gone. Please, Shiloh."

I'd ponder the revelation of Tennyson's male lover another time. I crossed the bedroom and stopped an arm's reach away, strengthening the grip of our wish tether with proximity. I ignored the bone-deep chill and head-aching spice of his emotional output, and I focused on him. Braced myself for was about to happen. "Make a wish, Tennyson," I said. "Be specific."

"I wish . . ." He grimaced, as though the words tasted like shit on his tongue. "I wish for you to bear the burden of my emotions for the next quarter hour."

Our tether shimmered and glowed red, an intangible bond he couldn't see or feel. The power of his request settled bone-deep, and the magic of the djinn was forced to comply to the wish of he who held me in his grip. I licked my lips, mouth suddenly dry, needing to speak the final words aloud and seal the wish.

"Granted," I said hoarsely.

The tether pulsed as my magic fed toward him, and then reversed course to send the weight of his emotions right back at me like a heat-seeking missile. I stumbled backward from the blow, until my knees hit the bed and I dropped into a sitting position. My vision blurred. My stomach twisted and churned. I sobbed out loud, tears falling, as the memories began.

A nimble blond man in breeches and a waistcoat, rosy-cheeked and delicate-boned, smiles at me with devotion in his eyes. Bluest eyes open wide and he takes me into his body as no one else has—as I have never wanted before. Then he shrieks in agony and fright—I feel the silver in his flesh, taste the blood welling in his mouth, know his certainty of death. I am heartbroken by it. Ambrosius, we have loved each other.

A raven-haired man in a World War I uniform bares his fangs and then winks in greeting. He's a free spirit, left to die on the German front by his retreating platoon, and I can't bear to let this gentle soul die.

He accepts my gift willingly. We are good friends, Leonardo and me. He feels every draw of the saw's blade as chunks of flesh are removed over a matter of minutes. Silver floods his body, and I mourn another death I cannot prevent.

Three woman, another man. Four more faces, four more histories. Four more gruesome, painful deaths that rend my soul with their losses.

I curled into a ball, hugging my knees to my chest, sobbing hard enough to choke on my own snot. Head throbbing, I gasped for breath, trying hard to push the grief away. No use. My chest ached, as though someone had reached in and crushed my heart into a bloody pulp, then filled the void with boiling oil. Empty. Used. Destroyed.

And then, when I thought it was over, two more deaths came one after the other. The first was a girl with a crooked smile, turned at the time of the Spanish Civil War, and love for her rivaled only what I felt for Ambrosius. The second was a strapping young man of twenty, turned a mere six months ago. Both losses left another empty hole in my heart, a mark on my soul. My people were dying, being ripped away, and I was helpless to stop it.

The last were murdered as horribly as the first, each death a white-hot spike to my psyche, a physical loss that fueled my wracking sobs. I'd failed them. Let them die. A mournful wail bubbled up, and then arms were around me. Someone tugged me close, cradled me in his arms, and I pressed my face into a cool neck. Sobbed onto equally cool skin, so familiar, but uncomforting.

"Let them go, Shiloh," Tennyson whispered, his breath puffing near my ear. "It's over. They're gone. Give them back."

"Can't." Why couldn't I? I struggled to remember through the gauze of grief weighing down my brain. This was important. Hadn't he wished for something? "Can't undo a wish."

His embrace tightened. I fisted his shirt in my hands and held on, allowing someone I barely trusted and disliked on principle to hold me. I couldn't seem to remember why I was crying. The memories were distanced from the grief, until the grief was a sentient thing. It beat me down and tore at me until I thought I might shatter.

The bubble of loss I'd existed in for what seemed like days finally shrank and coalesced into a manageable nugget, pulling out of me and into itself. It shot away from me, across the tether, leaving me exhausted. Physically wrung out. Sniffling away errant tears.

Tennyson groaned. Instead of letting go, he held me impossibly tighter. If I'd been fully human, his strength may have broken a few ribs. The spicy-cold sensation of his grief returned, surrounding me from the outside, rather than from within.

"It's over," I said. The fifteen minutes was up. My voice was hoarse, my throat sore.

His arms withdrew immediately, and my ribs thanked him. I sat up. His eyes were closed, his head tilted up. I didn't move, and he didn't shove me out of his lap. Sitting there felt strange, but I didn't want to startle him. Not with his fangs peeking down from beneath his upper lip.

He lowered his chin and opened his eyes. I expected the red glow, and instead, got his unhidden eyes and saw the color for the first time—brilliant coppery brown, like two shiny pennies. The whites of his eyes were tinged pink. Gratitude and determination flickered in those expressive orbs.

"Thank you," he said.

"Your wish is my command." The quip fell flatter than intended, but he didn't seem to notice. I also realized I was looking him right in the eye and shifted my gaze to the bridge of his nose.

"I was able to focus beyond the emotion. I'm uncertain as to the benefits of this information."

"What did you sense?"

"I smelled many things, among them those herbs we found in Virginia. I smelled blood and sweat and tears, as well as something else. Farm smells, such as straw and baling rope and motor oil. I was uncertain, at first, but I also believe I smelled cow manure."

"Cow manure? How do you know?"

"When you've lived many years in many different places, you come to learn the subtle differences in excrement. It is, after all, merely the product of what is ingested."

He had a point. "I don't know how well that narrows down our choices, though. The Eastern Shore itself has dozens of bovine farms."

"Yes." His gaze darted away a moment as he thought. "I heard a bell. Not quite a church bell, but large and rung in a similar fashion. I was able to get into Luisa's head before she passed, and she distinctly recalled the face of one of her captors."

"Could you see him through her eyes?"

"No. I have an impression of him through her senses, though. He is physically large, golden-skinned, midnight hair, with a scar above his left eyebrow in the shape of a sickle."

I tried hard to place such a description. "Doesn't sound like anyone I know."

"I did not assume you would."

I resisted the urge to roll my eyes. Doing so would just make my headache worse. "Be a nice coincidence, though, at this point."

"Yes." He brought his gaze back to me, and I met his copper-penny eyes without fear. "Are you all right?"

"Oh sure. My eyes are bloodshot, my nose is swollen, and I feel like my head is stuffed with wet sand. I'm great."

"Your sarcasm is not entertaining."

Oh, well, it entertained me quite a bit. "Look, I

haven't cried that hard in a long time. I wasn't really expecting it to hit me like it did."

"I apologize for not properly preparing you."

"You're a vampire with several centuries of emotional memories, Tennyson. I should have expected it."

A sharp knock on the door preceded it opening. I tumbled out of Tennyson's lap and hit my knees. Okay, so my balance wasn't quite back. Novak filled the doorway, thick arms crossed, silent anger radiating.

Tennyson stood and offered me his hand. I let him pull me to my feet. The tether flickered on the edges of my vision—two more wishes.

"Well, you aren't dead," Novak said to me. "You get anything useful?"

I made use of the dresser's box of tissues while Tennyson repeated what he'd learned. By the time I could breathe properly through my nose, Novak seemed at least partially convinced my decision had been a good one. Not that he'd ever admit it. But he looked less ready to rip Tennyson's head off with his bare hands, and that was something, at least.

"I'll get K.I.M. working on a list of cow farms and slaughterhouses on the—you get any sense of distance from here?" Novak asked.

Tennyson tilted his head to the side, thinking. "Distance is difficult to judge based on a telepathic link. However, I would place them within five hundred miles." It didn't narrow our search grid down by a whole lot.

"If they were practicing locally with Piotr," I said, "it stands to reason they'd be in the area. And there are plenty of cow farms to pick from in Maryland, Virginia, and Delaware."

"Yeah." Novak gave me a critical stare. "Speaking of nearby, once you guys are ready, Kathleen assigned you to interrogate the two semi-locals on our list."

"Semi-locals?"

"Nathan Fowler is a security systems specialist out of Baltimore, and James Caine is a building contractor in Bowie. Julius used both of them to get this house up to snuff."

"So calling them isn't exactly out of the ordinary." Unless Julius put them into contact with the person who'd paid him off. Now I wanted to talk to them both very, very much.

"Maybe, maybe not. I don't recall any new installations last June, so why so many phone calls?"

"Good point. Does everyone know?"

Novak frowned. "About these two? Yeah."

"About the wishes, Novak," I said, glaring.

"No. I said the vampire needed to meditate because he could feel his people." He gave me a dry look. "If I'd said the word *wish* if front of your mother, she'd have come up here screaming like a banshee."

And likely armed with a solid weapon.

"So no—I didn't tell anyone. But I am curious: how come he could suddenly feel them again?" Novak asked.

"Whoever had them wanted me to feel them die," Tennyson replied steadily. He'd completely regained his composure, though his face remained paler than usual. "I was lost in their agony, too lost to concentrate. It was the reason Shiloh offered the wish. I was able to concentrate through the pain and grief and glean what little I did."

A fraction more of Novak's loathing melted away. The large incubus looked at me with something very close to respect in his dark face. "Big risk."

"It paid off," I said. So far, so good. And no one had to remind anyone else that I still owed the vampire Master two wishes.

"I must contact my other people," Tennyson said. "Drayden needs to know the status of our missing. One of them was his."

"Tennyson, do you have a way to contact the other Masters and find out if their missing have been killed, too?" I needed to know if this was going on across the board, or if Tennyson alone had been targeted. Instincts said the latter, but I couldn't yet discount the former.

"Perhaps."

"Bless it, yes or no!"

Okay, so the stress was getting to me. But I needed some friggin' straight answers, not this stupid vampires-versus-humans crap.

His copper eyes fixed on me, glittering sparks of red. Good, I'd gotten his dander up. "Am I guaranteed that no devices in this compound will attempt to trace the telephone numbers I call?"

"Yes." We had equipment set up to handle that sort of spying, but I didn't tell him so. He was a guest in our compound. He didn't need a pencil drawing of our security precautions, and I'd just given him my word we wouldn't betray his secrecy. "Make your calls. We've got travel plans to finalize. Come downstairs when you're ready."

I shooed Novak out the door. Downstairs was about as far from Tennyson as I could physically get with our magic wish tether in place. I could definitely do without any more pain today, thank you very much. No more for the rest of the year would be ideal.

Novak went into the hall. I reached back to pull the door shut behind me and looked up long enough to catch Tennyson's gaze. His carefully schooled control had fractured, allowing hints of grief to peek through. I didn't fully understand vampires, or the bonds they forged with those they turned. I never thought of them as having feelings. Emotions, sure—rage and lust and conceit and passion—but not feelings. Feelings that could be crushed when one of their own died.

I never imaged a vampire could grieve.

"Shiloh," he said, his voice barely a whisper. "I will not abuse your trust by taking advantage of my other wishes. You have my word."

I hadn't expected such a promise.

In some ways, Tennyson's wish had been self-ish, but the fact that he made a wish at all broke all known theories about how djinn magic works. He shouldn't have managed it. Perhaps the rules did not apply. It wasn't as though the wish had been against my will.

"Thank you," I said. "Hold on to them, though. Might come in handy before this mess is completely cleaned up."

"Indeed." A muscle below his left eye twitched. "May I ask you a question?"

"Sure, but I reserve the right not to answer it."

He listed his head in that annoying way of his. "Who is Kress?"

A flush of shame and anger rose from deep in my guts. I'd so break Novak's nose for saying that name out loud. In some traditions of magic, a name meant power over a person. In the realm of past mistakes and idiotic failures, a name held that same power. Only it turned us into weak emotional blobs we'd otherwise not be reduced to. Kress was one of those names for me.

"A mistake I paid dearly for," I choked out. "Years ago, and I'm not airing that laundry today. No, make that ever."

"He hurt you."

"What part of 'not talking about it' didn't connect for you? Now make your goddamned calls."

I stepped out and slammed the door shut. My

shaking knees carried me down the hall to the stairs, where I leaned on the banister for a moment, urging my body to stop trembling. No use. The adrenaline was going. Could he feel it the way I felt his emotional spikes? I hoped so. I hope he choked on my shame and fear.

Bastard.

His voice whispered through my head so softly I thought I'd imagined it. Had he learned to stop shouting in my brain? Did it matter? I wanted to be angry with him. I didn't want him to tell me he was sorry.

CHAPTER 15

Two hours later, Jaxon was driving us over the Chesapeake Bay Bridge toward sunset. We were twenty minutes or so from Bowie, Maryland, and the home of James Caine. Tennyson was stuffed in the far rear compartment of the Element, safe from the lowering sun's golden rays. The russet orb nearly touched the horizon. It should set completely by the time we found Caine's residence.

I glared ahead at the sun and its mocking brightness. We needed a little brightness on our side, maybe even a tiny bit of good luck.

While Tennyson's phone calls told us none of the other missing vampires had been killed—at least, we assumed, since their Masters hadn't felt them die—Drayden's were growing increasingly restless. The line was going on their fourth night in Myrtle's

Acres, stuffed into trailers like undead sardines, and local authorities had been stretched to their breaking point. A snapping twig could set off a massacre.

My half-baked suggestion that Tennyson consider moving his people was met with a glower and a growl. He knew the fragility of the situation. Time was short.

On the heels of that exchange, Kathleen brought up a just-filed coroner's report for Baltimore County. Nathan Fowler had been found dead in his home, the victim of a poisonous spider bite. The venom was unknown at the time of the report. I could guess how painfully the man had died.

Scratch one more potential suspect off the list. It also made locating the others much more urgent. So we split up as planned and left Mom at home to research cow farms and spider spells.

And to think her life two days ago consisted of reading mystery novels and playing bridge once a week.

Jaxon impressed me for the entire drive west by keeping his mouth shut. He hadn't asked about what went on upstairs, even though he had to be champing at the bit for dirt. He knew Novak was in on the secret, which had to rankle. Jaxon and I kept few secrets from each other.

"Why are we moving so slowly on a multilane highway?" Tennyson asked from the rear.

"Rush hour," I replied. Our westbound lanes

weren't as congested as the eastbound traffic heading home from work in the nearby cities, but we still couldn't manage much above forty miles an hour. Maybe twenty minutes to Bowie was overstating it a little.

My cell rang. It was the HQ line. "Harrison," I said.

"It's me." Mom. "Your computer produced something you may find interesting."

"You could have had K.I.M. send it to my phone."

"Well, yes, if I knew how to do that, I would have. Jaxon only gave me a handful of rudimentary commands." She had a point. "Anyway, it's about the werewolf couple who had three children."

"Hold on a second." I set the Raspberry to speaker and turned up the volume a notch. "Okay, go ahead."

"As I was saying," she continued with a hint of put-upon-ness in her tone, "the werewolf pair from Sacramento, Raymond and Alice Anderson, had three children under the age of four who died. The official police report stated carbon monoxide poisoning, even though both parents were home at the time and suffered no ill effects. And as you know, Pack law forbids autopsies."

"Okay." I was following her so far, waiting for the punch line.

"Well, two months later the cemetery received a court order to exhume the body of the eldest and perform an autopsy. It was carried out before the Homme Alpha could intervene, and the autopsy report disappeared. There's no official indication of what it might have said."

"Who got the court order?" Jaxon asked.

"Raymond Anderson," Mom said.

Jaxon and I shared a brief look, the same question in both of our frowns. A werewolf had willingly gone against Pack law in order to find out why his child died. He didn't believe the carbon monoxide had killed him or her. Something else had potentially caused the death.

"Well, that adds a new wrinkle to matters," I said.

"To a werewolf, Pack law overrides human law," Tennyson added from the rear. "Raymond Anderson had a very important reason for ordering the autopsy."

I didn't bother telling the vampire I already knew that, instead replying, "He doesn't believe his children's deaths were accidental."

"Quite likely."

"Mom," I said, "find out everything you can about the Andersons. Any enemies they might have, threats against them, even unpaid parking tickets."

"On it, sweetheart," she replied.

"If the Pack believed the deaths to be foul play," Tennyson said, "it's likely an internal investigation was launched. You should contact the Homme Alpha again."

Jaxon snorted. "Yeah, he wasn't too crazy about talking to us the first time. No way he'll offer up confidential information about a murder investigation that may or may not exist."

"True, but there's no rule that says we can't talk to the detectives involved," I said.

"Who were probably paid well by the Alpha for their silence."

"Maybe, but it's a lead." I glared sideways at Jaxon. "Mom, can you—"

"I'll put together everything I can and then make a few calls on your behalf," Mom replied, all business. On my behalf? What was she now, my secretary? "How do I send things from the computer to your phone?"

I explained the proper commands and heard a pencil scratching across paper as she wrote them down. We were nearing our exit by the time I got her off the phone. The new information tumbled around my head while Jaxon navigated into Bowie, which has one of the strangest residential layouts I've ever seen. Each section is lettered, and all street names begin with that letter. We were headed toward *P*.

An inquiry to Caine's office told us he'd taken a half day in order to watch his son's school play in the afternoon. A call to the school put the play ending with the regular school day, so after Caine did the prerequisite, divorced parent "take my son out for ice cream before handing him back over to his mother for dinner" pattern, he'd head home. If he wasn't home already.

Cars were slowly filling driveways of older ranch homes and a few newer prefabs. Most of the houses here were at least fifty years old, and many hadn't seemed too modernize on the exterior yet. Old aluminum siding, pale colors, even a few flamingos on lawns. It was an amusing mix of eclectic and retro.

Caine's house was a brown bungalow tucked between several large oak trees. The driveway was cracking, each line choked with dandelions and grass, his wild lawn barely kept in check with a waist-high linked fence. An oversized Ford pickup truck was parked in the driveway and lights blazed behind curtained windows.

Jaxon parked on the road, purposely blocking the driveway. The sun had dipped below the horizon, leaving the sky burning with golds and reds, without direct sunlight. It was safe to let Tennyson out of the car, but . . .

"Maybe you should wait here," I said, leaning over the seat to face him.

The vampire cocked his head, his face impassive. "Am I intimidating?"

I swallowed laughter. "No, but you really do scream vampire, with the hair and the pale skin. He may not invite you in." And by "you" I meant "us," and he knew it.

"A wise assessment. I shall remain here."

"Thank you."

I stretched as I got out, exercising muscles that

had atrophied during the two-hour drive. I still felt achy all over, like I was stuck with the remnants of a pesky flu. And that blessed tether to Tennyson followed me everywhere, in my peripheral vision like watery yarn, there then gone again when I tried to look directly at it. Good thing I wasn't going far.

I did, however, wish I'd worn different clothes. Even with my black suit jacket on, my jeans and t-shirt were a little casual for a business call. At least Jaxon had on his customary khakis and a dark green polo that set off his blond hair nicely. Made his eyes a little less hazel, more blue. I always loved them like that.

Gah! I was so not doing that. No warm fuzzies for Jaxon.

He pulled the screen door so I could knock.

Note: when searching for a suspect, it's generally a bad sign when a door that should be secured falls open after slight pressure from your knuckles.

Our guns were out and pointed to the ground, and I stepped inside first. Slowly. A very short foyer led into an open living area, decorated in Divorce Chic—worn leather sofa, mismatched tables and lamps, takeout boxes and beer bottles decorating all available surfaces. No immediately weird smells. The house was completely silent, save the gentle swishing of our clothes as we split up. Jaxon darted left, toward a kitchen and dining room area.

I picked the hallway to the right. The first door

was a bathroom—empty and a bit ripe. The next door was shut, its painted surface covered in artwork produced by a well-meaning child and taped up by a loving parent. I bypassed it for now and scooted to the open door at the end of the hall, each step as silent as I could manage.

The vaguest scent of urine and waste stung my nose. Not a good sign. I peeked around the door frame, into the dimly lit room, annoyed that Mr. Caine hadn't opened his curtains to allow more light.

At first, I didn't see him. All I saw was the queen-size bed in the center of the room and what looked like a white canopy—which was stupid. Adult men didn't string gauzy canopies over their beds. Especially a canopy speckled with dozens of dime-sized black dots.

My guts twisted, and I nearly dropped my gun. Not dots and not a canopy.

James Caine was dead. It was obvious when I finally noticed his body curled on the center of the bed. He'd hugged his knees close to his chest and died in the fetal position. His skin had turned a greenish color and was pocked with more bites than I could count. He'd been dead long enough for his bowels to empty.

Someone was tying up their loose ends.

With fucking spiders.

The spiders began moving all at once, as though suddenly aware of a fresh meal nearby. They skittered down their long, intricate threads. My hand throbbed, and I backpedaled right into Jaxon.

"What?" he asked.

"Go. Now!" I shoved him back down the hall.

He stopped short at the front door, and I slammed into him for the second time in half a minute. Two garish, fuzzy-legged spiders the size of a half-dollar were racing back and forth across the front door, weaving a web over its surface. Trapping us. They didn't attack, just kept at their task.

"You have got to be shitting me," I said.

"Shiloh, get out of here."

"I'm not leaving you in here." Sure, I could get through the walls of Caine's house and avoid more spider bites, but no way in the real, true Hell was I leaving Jaxon inside.

"Come on," I said, grabbing his wrist and yanking him back the other way. The opposite side of the living room had glass patio doors that appeared to be spider-free. Halfway there, though, a cloud of spiders no larger than honey bees scurried out of the air vent above the patio doors. They swarmed over the glass, leaving trails of milky white string as they went.

The spiders currently doing their best to block our exits hadn't attacked directly, but I had no doubt it was coming. Memories of my own bite, of the agony and white fire that had raced up my arm, soured my stomach and left me short of breath.

Shiloh, you are distressed, Tennyson said.

I was actually glad to hear his voice in my head, oddly less migraine-inducing than usual. Maybe the wish tether had a few perks, after all. *There are spiders in here, and they're blocking the doors.*

You require an exit.

Yeah, preferably not facing the street.

"From the look on your face," Jaxon said, "is it a fair guess your vampire is coming to our rescue?"

"Don't sound so happy about it. Unless you want to be spider food . . ."

Also: why did everyone keep calling him *my* vampire?

Jaxon and I retreated to the center of the living room, back-to-back. The spider army had sent small platoons to each of the windows, as well, and their engineers were busy constructing measures to keep us contained. They still didn't seem interested in biting, which was hopefully giving Tennyson time to do whatever he was about to do. I'd never had a full-blown panic attack before, but standing in that small house, with every available exit being sealed shut by magically controlled spiders—spiders that had nearly killed me once this week, thank you—the panic was building. My insides felt like mush, my palms were sweating so hard I had trouble keeping a grip on my gun, and I had a very real urge to pee.

My bitten hand was also throbbing, as though being close to those spiders and their magic was enough to cause me pain again. And their weaving was drastically reducing the amount of light in the house, as the sun had set and we hadn't flipped on any lamps. I did not want to be trapped in the dark with these things. I also couldn't bring myself to move.

"What's taking him so—" Jaxon started, only to be cut off by a crackling thud against the dining room wall.

The light fixture tinkled and swayed, and the thud repeated itself. A long, jagged crack appeared in the center of the drywall, and then a third thud sent it exploding toward us in a spray of gray powder, paint chips, and stud splinters. Tennyson burst through with a tire iron in his hands, his dark clothes smothered in debris bits.

I gaped.

Jaxon didn't hesitate, though, grabbing my hand and hauling me into the dining room. Spiders were already scuttling toward the new hole, moving like cockroaches on the scent of food. We burst through the jagged exit and into the cool evening and Caine's freakishly overgrown backyard. I didn't have the wits to comment on his need to own a lawn mower. It took everything I had to run around the side of the house, back toward our parked Element.

The spiders didn't follow us past the house itself. A cloud of them came over the roof and stopped above the rain gutters. They looked like an oil stain on the old shingles—a venomous, sentient oil stain.

Once we were safely back inside the car, I sucked in several long, deep breaths to calm my racing heart.

"Were either of you bitten?" Tennyson asked from the backseat.

"Not me," Jaxon said. He was so pale I thought he'd pass out at any moment.

"No." I loosened my death grip on my gun and carefully slid it back into its holster. "No, I'm fine."

"That was the freakiest . . ." Jaxon trailed off as he lost the words to describe the experience. He didn't need to, though. I'd shared his terror, and I was certain Tennyson sensed mine.

"Someone knew we were coming," I said, trying not to look at the mass of arachnids on the roof of Caine's house. "Police reports on Fowler's death would have mentioned a house full of cobwebs and spiders, but it said one bite."

"No one but us knew we were coming here," Jaxon said. "We three at least have been in each others' sight since we found out about Fowler. Julius is boxed up and in sleep mode."

I swallowed, desperate for some moisture in my mouth, and fished out my phone. I hated having doubts about my team members, so I had to put a kibosh on this right now.

Novak picked up on the second ring. "Yeah?"

"Where are you?" I asked.

"In a helicopter somewhere over Pennsylvania, why?"

"Kathleen's with you?"

"Yeah."

"Has she been with you since you left the house?"

"Yeah . . ." He drew that one out slowly, his way of asking what the hell I was getting at.

"Just checking."

"You're checking for a blessed reason, Shiloh, what's going on?"

"I'll tell you later, just be careful." He snorted and hung up. I shifted in my seat to more directly face Jaxon as he navigated us away from the house. "Okay, let's think about this. Fowler and Caine died within hours of each other, so how did this spider wrangler know we'd end up at Caine's house first?"

It was the question of the night. Even if I believed one of us was a traitor, we hadn't been apart long enough to pass such information along to the head honcho.

"It is possible he or she used the process of elimination," Tennyson said. "He or she sent the spiders after Fowler first, knew he would be found first, and waited for us to investigate the one not reported dead."

"Maybe," Jaxon said. "That's also assuming this big bad knows who we're researching, and that we were even looking for Caine and Fowler."

"Which no one else can know," I said. "K.I.M.'s protected from any sort of outside network hacks and . . ."

My entire body went cold, and all thought processes seemed to shut down. Except for the name blaring in my head like a neon sign. It was impossible. I was wrong and my suspicions were completely off base, but I had to entertain it. We had so few options right now, I'd rather have a theory shot down than never discussed.

He had access to K.I.M. and her records on our searches. He'd been kept informed of our investigation. He knew Tennyson was working with us.

"Shiloh, what is it?" Tennyson asked. He touched my forearm, and his palm was actually warmer than my own skin.

"Weller," I said. "Marshal Adam Weller knew."

The Element swerved sharply. Jaxon gripped the wheel so hard the leather covering creaked. "That's a huge leap, Shi," he said.

"Is it? He's on the phone sheet. He was the last person Julius spoke to the day he disappeared. He knows every move we're making, everything we are researching on K.I.M.'s system. He has resources and access and knowledge."

"Motivation?"

"How should I know?"

It was Tennyson who answered: "An army of vampires under one's control makes your jobs as Para-Marshals much simpler. No other agency in the world, shadow or otherwise, could challenge you."

I twisted around in my seat to stare at him and

saw only sincerity in his eyes. He wasn't being sarcastic or flip. He was dead—no pun intended—serious. "That is absolutely . . ." I wanted to say insane.

"Brilliant," Jaxon said. "Really brilliant, actually, and also kind of nuts."

"Yeah, if we're right. But it doesn't explain the werewolves." They were still the wild card in all of this. I understood the uses of a necromancer-controlled vampire Master. I couldn't fathom the usefulness of infertile, mated pairs of—

Wait a minute.

"What are you thinking, Shiloh?" Tennyson asked.

"I'm thinking about the Andersons, the only werewolves taken who had children."

"Their children died."

"Yeah, but the dad didn't seem to buy the carbon monoxide thing. Why else go against Pack law and order your kid's body exhumed and autopsied?" I followed this train of thought to its logical conclusion. "Could those children have been murdered?"

"Possibly, but for what purpose?"

"I don't know, but it really makes me want to talk to the people involved in the investigation. I can't imagine going to the Homme Alpha with our questions will do any good."

"Especially if he's involved in covering up the murders," Jaxon said.

"He could also be investigating it privately within the Pack."

"Your theories hinge upon circumstances that lack proof," Tennyson said.

I scowled. "Yeah, well, we're working on the proof part." I started dialing the HQ phone, then stopped. "Crap. We can't use the Raspberries anymore, not if Weller is involved." My phone, of course, chose that moment to ring. It was from the house. "Mom?"

"Yes, it's me. Shi, are you all right?"

I had to get my voice under control a little better. "Yeah, I'm fine." How to tell her what was potentially happening without announcing it for anyone who was spying on us to hear? "I'm glad you called. Do you remember the story you told me about your djinn sister Frieda and the stolen locket?"

"My sister . . . yes?"

Good. She got the code. Frieda was actually the name of a summoner who'd bound herself to my father a few years ago. She'd misplaced a family heirloom and been so utterly convinced that her conniving neighbor had turned against her and stolen it, she'd wished for her neighbor to always tell the truth. It hadn't worked out well for either of them, and it turned out Frieda's husband had pawned it for gambling money. The moral of the story, as my father had told it, was that sometimes the person who's stabbing you in the back is the one closest to you.

"Remember the end of the story?" I asked.

"Yes."

"Good. Sit tight, and we'll be home in two hours."

"All right, hon. See you soon."

So it wasn't the most casual of conversations, but we hadn't broadcasted anything, and that was useful. I hated that we were two hours away—more if traffic was still bad. Mom was resourceful, though, and she didn't have the gate lock code to let anyone in, even if Weller was ballsy enough to go after her there.

"We should swing by Walmart on the way home," Jaxon said.

"What for?" I asked.

"We're going to need phones. They have prepaids."

I eyed my Raspberry and all of its applications sadly—until we figured out whether or not we could trust Weller, it was being replaced by a cheap wannabe. Worth it, of course, to keep my mom safe.

It didn't stop me from working on my ulcer.

Buying and activating the new cell phones didn't help us much, since the house line still ran off of K.I.M.'s network. The only person we could safely call was Tennyson, and he was sitting three feet away from me. I hated radio silence, and I had already ignored one phone call from Novak. I texted that we were chasing a lead, I'd call him soon. He texted back a couple of swear words.

Ten minutes from home, right before I turned off my Raspberry for the duration, the new message light flashed. I hesitated, then checked the origin. Vincent's phone, two nights ago. My frustration piqued. Why in the name of Iblis was I getting the message now?

Oh yeah, Weller could hack into K.I.M.'s system and delay my messages until they'd hurt me the most. Summoning up some courage, I ignored a curious look from Jaxon. I didn't want to hear the message, not really, too afraid of my own reaction to his words and to hearing his voice, knowing he could be suffering unimaginable torture right now.

I played it, lowering the volume as far as I could for privacy. "Hey, babe, it's me. Look, I'm sorry about last night, I just . . . work is going well, and I guess I was jealous of your job. You see it more than you see me, and I . . . I want to see more of you." My pulse raced. "More than this casual thing we've had, and I hope you do, too. Anyway, we'll talk about it when you're off assignment. Take care, baby."

I listened two more times, memorizing Vincent's voice and hoping—praying—he'd called before he was taken. That the words in his message weren't some cruel joke, words he was forced to say by the people holding him captive. I wanted to believe he wanted me. For all of my absences and sudden trips and secrets, he wanted to have more than a casual relationship. I'd never had a boyfriend offer such a thing, not until Vincent. I didn't know if I wanted things to get serious—with him or anyone else—but he came to me with it. No matter my answer, I had to save him.

The men in the car wisely kept quiet, even though Tennyson could have easily listened in. I wasn't in the mood for commentary.

The outskirts of town came into familiar view, and then we were coasting down the empty neighborhood street toward the gate. Halfway there, Jaxon slowed the Element to a crawl.

"What's—?" I started to ask, then saw the answer for myself. Fifty yards ahead of us loomed the front gate to the compound. Six figures swarmed the street, moving around each other with predatory ease.

"Vampires," Tennyson said. He scooted between the front seats, his eyes blazing red.

"Friends of yours?" Jaxon asked.

"No."

"Friends of Piotr's?"

"Possibly."

"Tennyson," I said, "there's a trunk of weapons in the rear."

"I've seen it."

He shuffled around behind us. My gaze never left the street. We were still moving forward at a snail's pace, headlights glaring down the road not quite far enough to slash across their faces. They didn't scatter. They closed ranks, forming a tight line across the road. Waiting.

Tennyson settled the smooth, metal storage locker on the floor of the backseat and popped the lock. I took my seat belt off and twisted around. The mini-armory had clips of silver-jacketed bullets, silver knives of various lengths and shapes, a couple extra pistols, a shotgun, and a machete. The supersecret, magic-based stuff was in the false bottom Tennyson didn't seem keen on discovering. Not that we'd need to dive down there tonight.

I grabbed silver-bullet clips for myself and Jaxon, as well as a pair of knives each. My hand still wasn't one hundred percent, but it would hold out if we had to fight. "Help yourself, if there's something you want," I told Tennyson.

He turned those red headlights on me. "What is your plan of action?"

"We'll try to negotiate first. See who they are and what the hell they're doing loitering in the street at ten p.m. But I'm not going out there unarmed against six vampires I don't know."

Jaxon put the Element into Park fifty feet from the defensive line, headlights giving us the full effect. Two females, four males, each vampire dressed in simple jeans and t-shirt combinations, which made them look like college students milling around the quad, waiting for class to start. Only these college students had glowing red eyes, protruding fangs, and an "I want to rip your throat out" vibe coming off in waves.

Tennyson's emotions wafted around me like heated sweetness—hot cocoa minus the chocolate. What the hell was he feeling? Curiosity? Amusement? I wasn't sure, and his face told me nothing. As usual.

I handed Jaxon his weapons. He ejected his old clip and replaced it with the silver-jackets, as did I. I pocketed the knives, palmed my badge, and climbed out. The others followed, Jaxon on my left flank and Tennyson on my right. All I could think about was my mom. Our standard perimeter defenses were still up, but the vampire safeties inside the house were not. If they somehow got inside . . . got to her . . .

My badge dug into my good hand, and I wondered if something could make me upset enough to crush it.

If they hurt Mom, I might just find out.

The vampires didn't move. I stopped, leaving a respectable ten feet of space between us, and flipped them my badge, gun very obvious in my right hand. Might as well start this out somewhat by the book, even though it had even odds of going south pretty fast. Six vamps didn't show up at your doorstep unless they wanted to rumble.

"United States Para-Marshal," I said, giving my voice as much commanding bark as I could muster. "You folks lost?"

The vamp in the red t-shirt stepped forward, out of line, hands shoved nonchalantly in his jeans pockets. He ignored Tennyson, gave Jaxon a cursory glance, then settled his matching red eyes on me. I stared right at his nose, but even in my peripheral vision, I caught the odd, black ring around the red.

"You Marshal Harrison?" he asked in a voice betraying Eastern European roots. Huh.

"Who wants to know?" I asked.

"We're here for Piotr."

Should have guessed. His companions stayed quiet, deferring action to his signal. "Piotr is currently being held for questioning in relation to a recent crime. He's not allowed visitors at this time."

"We don't want to visit." Red kept canting his head, trying to get me to meet his eyes. Sneaky bastard.

"Okay, good. Now that we've established that, you want to get out of the street and let us pass?"

"We're here for Piotr."

Someone's repeat button was stuck. "You. Can't. Have. Him."

What are you doing? Do not taunt them. Tennyson's voice in my head was less freight train than it was station wagon, but it was still darn intrusive.

I ignored him. "Who sent you?" I asked Red.

He bared his fangs in a wicked smile. "He who is Master of us."

The necromancer.

No kidding! I snapped back, putting as much mental oomph into it as I could muster. "What's your Master want with Piotr?"

Red's eyes burned. The black ring seemed to widen, dwarfing the red. My gun hand twitched. Tennyson shifted to my side and clamped a hand firmly on my wrist.

"We must speak," he whispered.

I angled slightly away from the vamps, trusting Jaxon to keep both eyes on them for me. "So speak."

If you must fight them, I cannot help you.

My jaw unhinged. I couldn't help it. "Why the hell not?"

These vampires belong to Azuriah, one of the eldest of us all. They will likely not attack me, and to directly attack his people without provocation is an act of aggression. By our laws, I would be declaring war on his line.

"They don't—" Off his look, I switched over to yelling at him with my brain. *They don't belong to this Azuriah anymore, they belong to the necromancer.*

A vampire belongs to his Master until permanent death. Our law stands.

And if they attack you first?

His eyes glowed crimson. *Then I will delight in the battle. I have . . . aggression, which needs to be expended.*

I bet he had aggression. If they didn't attack Tennyson, we had a problem. Jaxon and I were good, we were weapons trained, and he was vicious in his stag form, but it was still two to six. All one of the vamps had to do was take a bite out of our carotids and it was game over.

Jaxon cleared his throat, and I turned my attention back to the vamps. The line had moved forward, closing half the distance. Red gazed at me with unbridled contempt. All of them seemed to vibrate with tension—the instincts of a vampire at war with the control of an off-site necromancer. Unless . . .

Tennyson, could the necro be nearby? Watching us?

It is possible.

Then go hunt around. We'll deal with crowd control.

Are you certain?

Yes.

He melted into the shadows of the nearby lots and was gone, as swiftly as a puff of smoke in a windstorm.

"Where is he off to?" Red asked.

"Coffee run," I replied. "If we're going to stand here yakking at each other for a while, I'm going to need some caffeine."

"Give us what we want—"

"And you'll go away? Yeah, I've heard that line. Tell me why you want him, and maybe I won't have you all detained for trespassing on federal property."

"We will get what we came for, Marshal. Even if we have to drain you, turn you, and then make you open the gate." His tone left little doubt that he'd do exactly as he threatened.

I flicked the safety off my gun with my thumb. "I'm guessing your Master didn't tell you my little secret. Turning me is going to be a lot harder than you think."

Red smirked. "It will be my pleasure to try."

They were on us faster than we could fire. I caught one of the females in the thigh and she stumbled. Jaxon fired in a wide arc even as magic shimmered all around him and he shouted his spell to change.

Red charged me, clumsy, and I sidestepped his lunge. I slammed my knee into his gut, aiming for a painful spot rather than his lungs. Being out of breath wasn't exactly a problem for vampires. He doubled forward far enough for me to drive my elbow into his spine and down he went.

A shadow darted to my right. I fired. Heard the bullet strike flesh. Someone slammed into me from behind, and I went flying to the ground with a writhing, clawing body on my back. My arms scraped pavement, but I didn't let go of my gun. Claws dug into my shoulder, trying to bare my neck.

As if.

I angled the gun behind me and fired. The roar blasted my eardrum and made my head swimmy. Something moist splashed my neck and cheek.

A meaty hand grabbed my wrist and twisted. I yelped, numb fingers releasing the gun. Crap. A matching hand wrapped around my throat and hauled me to my feet. Blazing red eyes rimmed with midnight. I kicked at his nuts, and the linebacker vamp gave me a mighty shake, hard enough to send my brain rattling like marbles in a drawer.

Thundering hooves preceded the crash. Stag Jaxon and his mighty antlers skewered the vamp and drove him backward. The vamp hollered. I fell to my knees, gasping, searching for my lost gun. It had been kicked out of reach, near another prone vampire. I palmed the knives. Three bodies were sprawled close by, and Jaxon was still grappling with Linebacker.

Where was—?

For the second time in three minutes I hit the blacktop. Whoever had me rolled at the last minute, so they landed on their back with me on their chest. Wire-strong arms crossed over mine, legs came up to loop and capture, and she squeezed—her breasts against my back were a dead giveaway. Squeezed so hard I gasped. I drove my head backward, hoping to break a nose, and nearly cracked my own skull off the ground. Bitch was fast.

Real fear hit me for the first time, chilling me all over.

Jaxon bellowed somewhere out of sight. Then cried out, a painful sound I didn't recognize and that hurt my heart. No! They didn't get to hurt Jaxon, godsdamnit.

Red loomed over me, fangs protruding, eyes a demonic swirl of red and black. He was laughing, and I swore I heard two voices in one throat—his own and the man controlling him. He knelt, and the female vamp held me tighter. My lungs and ribs ached from being slowly crushed—if I'd been fully human, a few would have been broken by now. Red brushed hair away from my throat. I snapped my teeth at his fingers.

He hit me in the temple, and fireworks exploded behind my eyes. He grasped my chin, yanked my shirt collar sideways, and his head descended.

CHAPTER 16

I tensed for the pain of fangs breaking skin.

Only nothing happened.

"What are you waiting for?" the female vampire hissed. My question, too. Not that I was complaining about the temporary reprieve.

"She's been marked."

I've been . . . what?

"Do your job!" a male voice roared from the woman behind me. Not Weller's voice, as I almost hoped (make my job a lot easier), but someone else, angry and with the vaguest accent. *"Obey me and feed!"*

Cold lips brushed my throat. Crap.

A primal shriek of rage—not mine and not Jaxon's—was punctuated by a whip of air, and then Red was gone. My vampire-prison was so startled she loosened her hold. I wrenched my hands free and plunged the silver blades down in sweeping arcs, burying them in both sides of her ribs. She practically threw me off her, and I tucked into a roll, one blade still mine.

I barely had time to come up to my wobbly knees before she charged, bloody knife in hand. We hit the ground hard, slicing and clawing at each other. It wasn't elegant, it wasn't controlled. It was a battle for survival. Pain seared my left bicep, and she snapped at my face with bared fangs. A cold, black light flared in her eyes—the necromancer's control. Was he actively engaged in this little brawl, instead of simply observing from parts unknown?

I sank my knife into the vamp's back. She twisted up, sideways, shrieking at the pain of the silver in her. I grabbed her head with my hands, one on each cheek, and yanked her down toward me. Surprise and fury flared in those inky black depths, and I hazarded a peek into them.

"Fuck you, Necro!" I screamed, and sank both thumbs into her eyes. Eyeballs popped like overcooked eggs. Fluid and blood ran down my hands. She shrieked long and loud. I pushed her off and rolled to my knees. Found her abandoned blade on the ground and drove it into her heart.

Ash billowed seconds later. I sneezed.

The world blurred and tilted. I fell to my hands, nauseated beyond reason, ribs aching, my temple throbbing. Holy hell, Red hit hard.

A dark cloak swirled, and then Tennyson had crouched in front of me, hands on his knees. I looked at his chin, the red glow of his eyes enough to insinuate his mood, even if wafts of boiling vinegar weren't drifting off him like cologne. I sneezed again, sending my head into Def Con Three. Blessed vampire ash.

"Did we get them all?" I asked.

"Yes."

"Thank you." He'd saved my—wait. "Jaxon!"

I lurched to my feet as I shouted his name, somehow alert over the roar in my head. I was vaguely aware of something warm and wet coating my left arm, but ignored it in favor of locating my best friend. His earlier scream echoed in my mind, taunting me. Where was he?

The oddest animal cry drew my attention behind me. The mighty stag lay on his side, the dark hide on his back streaked with blood from shoulder to tail. One of his antlers lay a few feet away, forlorn, ripped from his head, which lolled to one side. He made the strange cry again—some foreign, female scream choked with a lamb's bleat. The wrenching noise settled in my chest and released a cry of fury, followed by a splash of hot tears.

I stumbled toward him, desperate to help him. He thrashed suddenly. Tennyson yanked me back by my good arm. Jaxon's muscled hind legs would have broken my ankle. He was terrified, in pain, and probably allowing the beast to take over. Rationalizing the situation with two-hundred pounds of deer was not happening.

Sweet Iblis, please don't let him die.

"We need to get him inside the gate," I said. "More vampires could be on the way. Did you find—?"

"The necromancer is not within a one-mile radius of this location," Tennyson said.

No, because that would be too blessed easy, wouldn't it?

"If I get behind him," he continued, "perhaps I can drag him through the gate."

I huffed. "That will only injure him more."

"Would you prefer we leave him here for the time being?"

My silence was his answer. He strode in a wide circle until he was behind the stag, whose big brown eye followed the vampire's every move. The stag only saw enemies and knew he was injured. He would fight us. I took a step forward, hoping to distract him. He thrashed again, coming within inches of crippling me with one fierce kick.

Tennyson was a blur, using his strength and reflexes to wrap his arms around the stag's back just below his powerful shoulders and drag. I came to my senses a split second later and was at the gate first, punching in the security code with shaking fingers. I ran back for the Element and got it inside the gate with inches to spare. It shut with a clang.

For another dozen yards, the stag continued to

fight and scream that awful sound. The front door of the house opened and Mom raced toward us, probably alerted by the noise. One more agonized noise belched from the stag, and then he went limp. Tennyson staggered under the sudden change and nearly fell over. Whatever magic allowed skin-walkers to maintain beast form crashed with a shudder and spark, and then Tennyson was holding a human Jaxon in his arms.

Blood coated one side of Jaxon's face and a chunk of hair and skin was missing from his scalp. Tennyson swung him more easily into a fireman's hold, and I saw the torn clothes and bleeding gashes on Jaxon's back. Mom looked on the verge of hysterics when she met us, but wisely stayed silent until we were inside.

Tennyson went straight upstairs with his burden.

"You're bleeding," she said.

"I'll live. Jaxon's worse."

She went off to fetch the medical kit. I stood dumbly in the foyer for a while, even after Mom went upstairs. My brain hadn't really caught up to the shock of the fight. Adrenaline was cutting off, leaving my entire body with a used-up, watery feeling, like I'd burst if someone poked me too hard. My head throbbed (again), my arm stung, my knees were sore, and both palms were rubbed raw (another again).

I hated feeling so helpless to move, so overcome by my second near-death experience in as many days that I wanted to curl up and sob. Preferably in my mother's arms. I was twenty-eight years old, and I wanted to be five again, so I could believe in my parent's ability to make the boogeyman go away. Only I wasn't five anymore, my best friend was critically injured, a supposed ally was my number one suspect for the big bad, and I couldn't even call my other teammates for an update, because our godsdamned phones were likely tapped.

This is why I'm the second-in-command and not the leader. Give me an order and I have no trouble following it. Put me in a situation without a clear path and make me the order-giver and nothing. I fall apart.

I fail.

No.

I shook myself from head to toe, as if I could shrug off the doubt like a dog shakes off water. If I failed now, my friends could die. Dozens of vampires and werewolves could die. The already strained relationship between the human world and the vampires could snap with one man's itchy trigger finger and a bad temper (or to be fair, one hungry vampire's need to feed). If we didn't do something about Myrtle's Acres, Tennyson could lose everything.

My father, of course, chose that moment to poof into existence in the living room.

"By the elements, Shiloh, are you all right?" he asked, closing in on me with a grace possessed only of the full-blood djinn. His rugged face twisted into a mask of anger and concern, and a swirl of colors sparkled in his eyes as he reached for my arm. "Why are you standing here bleeding all over the rug?"

"Waiting my turn," I said dumbly. Why is it my dad's mere presence has the power to turn me into a cowering child? Oh, yeah, because he's one of the oldest, most powerful djinn on the planet. Duh.

"You're—" His eyes widened as he picked up on my emotional state. He knew I was teetering on a meltdown, and he knew a gentle push in the wrong direction could release my Quarrel. Not that it would immediately affect anyone except Mom and Jaxon, but so not the point. I had lost control of it only once in the last decade, and that had been a special circumstance not to be repeated.

He framed my face with his palms and got into my personal space—a favorite maneuver of his since I was a child. It forced me to look at him, forced me to listen and really hear him.

I pressed into his touch. How could someone so old have hands so smooth and steady? It didn't seem fair.

"Focus, baby girl," he said. Though quiet, his voice was commanding and not to be ignored.

I did focus—right on the kindness of his eyes and the warmth of his love. "We've got serious problems, Dad," I blurted, then told him everything. From the moment he disappeared—excluding the binding words with Tennyson and his wishes, because I was

still half-sane—through the trip to Bowie, our suspicions about Weller, right up to his reappearance
here.

He listened without judgment, holding me still
the entire time, and it wasn't until I finished that I
felt the coolness of my cheeks, the way my entire
body was drained and energized all at once. He'd
been misusing his magic to calm me down and keep
me that way. Had he done it before when I wasn't
old enough to realize it?

Did it really matter at this point in time?

"Jaxon is hearty and strong," Dad said. "He'll
pull through. But you must tend to yourself, as well
as your team." He disappeared and popped back a
moment later with a dish towel.

I clenched my teeth and swallowed a lot of swear
words when he tied the towel tight around my
wounded arm. I wasn't sure it was still bleeding, but
it gave him a moment to be paternal. He hadn't had
a lot of those kinds of moments, being djinn and not
often home. He ushered me into the living room. I
perched on the corner of the sofa as he slunk into a
leather chair across from me.

"What did the sidhe have to say?" I asked.

"She is willing to bargain for her information."
From the vehemence in my dad's tone, he could have
been telling me a convicted serial rapist was about to
get clemency.

"Isn't that what we wanted? What information?"

Dad hesitated. "She has sensed the black magic, even from her chosen lair in Mongolia—"

"Mongolia?" I boggled for a moment, then remembered the teleportation thing. Kind of made air miles pointless.

"She says she can give you the necromancer's ritual chamber within one half mile of accuracy."

I shot to my feet, suppressing a whoop of joy. "This is great news, Dad, you couldn't have led with this? If we can get that close to this bastard, Tennyson's memories of how his people died can help us sniff them out the rest of the way. We can finally end this."

So why did Dad look like he'd just sucked on a lemon?

"The information is costly, Shiloh."

Oh. Right. My joy deflated like a pricked balloon. I asked a question to which I really did not want to know the answer. "What sort of memory is she asking for?"

"I don't know. She may ask for a month of no specified time period. She may ask for a specific event and all things related. She may ask for your memory of one person. She said it was for her and the bargainer to discuss." He stood up, his expression sympathetic without crossing into pity. "You are not bound to accept her help, Shiloh. It's a steep cost—"

"Set up the meeting." I had to say it before I changed my mind. As it was, I was beating back fear with a mental stick, desperate again not to dissolve into tears. It was our best means to find the necromancer. We had to take it.

"Our memories make us who we are," Dad said. "Once it is lost, it cannot be restored. It is gone. Do you understand?"

I understood. In order to see this through and solve this perplexing puzzle something had to be sacrificed. It wasn't as though I was giving her my magic, or a limb or something. I could live without a memory or two if it meant stopping this necromancer and getting our answers. Getting justice for Julius and for Tennyson's lost people, and making sure no one else practiced this forbidden necrotic magic.

"Set it up," I said. My voice was more *I just signed my own execution order* and less *See how confident I am?* But Dad nodded.

He brushed my cheek with the back of his knuckles, a kind of pride gleaming in his eyes. "I'll return shortly. Get that arm checked." And with that he poofed away.

The stairs creaked. Tennyson stood at the bottom of them. Had he done that on purpose so he didn't scare the crap out of me? His mouth was drawn tight, and I still felt ghosts of his anger.

It took a few tries to get my mouth working. "How's Jaxon?"

"Resting. Your mother is quite skilled with a needle

and thread. The wounds on his back were deep, but no major arteries were severed, and the bleeding is under control."

"What about his head?" On any other day, I'd have added a sarcastic note to such a question and turned it into a joke. But I had no idea how a skin-walker was affected—physically, emotionally, or magically—by losing a part of their animal shape. His antler had been ripped off, for Iblis's sake.

"He is in a great deal of pain from the wound, which continues oozing blood. Your mother says she senses an echo of magic around the wound, which could attribute to its inability to heal."

Frozen claws of fear grasped my heart and squeezed. Jaxon had charged the vampire and saved my life, and now he was suffering for it. What right had I to be so scared of giving up a memory in exchange for locating the necromancer? None.

"Your loyalty continues to surprise me, Shiloh."

"What?"

"I apologize if it was meant to be private, but I overheard the sidhe bargain you wish to strike." He strolled toward me, his body rigid while his expression remained as soft as I'd ever seen it. Fluffy clouds carved in stone looked softer, though, so it wasn't saying much. "You will sacrifice part of yourself to see this finished, and I admire that. In my long existence, I have never admired a djinn."

I found his words oddly touching, although not

even a little comforting. "We don't have a choice. This information could get us right up the necro's ass, and we will not get a better shot at taking him down. Those six vamps we killed were a test."

"The necromancer is growing stronger."

"Yes. If he can choreograph six at once today, there's no telling how many he can control tomorrow. And if he gets a Master under his thumb, all he has to do is control one. The Master will do all the work."

"His gamble to reacquire Piotr failed. But he won't stop. He will come at us again."

"If Piotr's the one he wants."

Tennyson tilted his head in a silent question.

"Think about it," I said. "This necro and the guy pulling his strings have been pretty careful so far with their plays. Even if I bought him being confident in Piotr's ability to trick and therefore kill me, I don't buy him risking his king in such an uncertain move. Another piece on the board, maybe, but not the king."

Two things struck me at once. The first being an observation my shock-fritzed mind had carefully filed away under Think About Later: Tennyson had saved my life when he attacked and killed one of Azuriah's vampires, something he said was considered an act of aggression toward the entire line. Bad. Very, very bad. And I hadn't even thanked him for it.

The second thing was how perfectly so many jagged pieces had fallen into place and created a much clearer picture of Piotr's part in the game. He wasn't the king in play, he was just another piece on the board, a bishop perhaps, moving other pawns toward the ultimate goal—the apprehension of a more powerful Master, whose entire line was firmly ensconced in one place like a quartered Army regiment. And challenging Azuriah via those controlled vampires gave the necro an excuse for a vampire war.

"Shiloh? You paled. Perhaps you should sit."

"It's you."

"Pardon me?"

I grabbed his shirt, curling my fingers into fabric stained black with drying vampire blood, more to stay upright than with any notion of shaking sense into him. His lips slanted in a frown, but he made no move to untangle me. Once I'd recovered from the latest shocking realization—let's face it, I'd had some stunners recently—I explained my somewhat wobbly thought processes. He terrified me by not immediately providing an alternate theory, or laughing it off as absurd.

Crap.

His hand covered mine in a cool grip. "Your theory is sound," he said softly. "Attempting to capture me directly is foolish, and this big bad, as you call him, is no fool. Torturing my people and allowing me to feel their deaths was a brilliant maneuver on his part. It ensures my desire for personal vengeance and will deliver me directly to his doorstep in order to acquire it."

Something in his use of the present tense jarred my internal alarms. "Only if this is his plan. And now that we know we can, you know, not do that."

"I see no alternative to the path on which we have been placed. All of the pieces have been put into position for a checkmate."

"Then opened your blessed eyes and look harder." My grip on his shirt tightened, and I very nearly did shake him. He squeezed my hand harder. I let go and stormed across the room, stopped near the dining room, and glared at K.I.M. sitting quietly on her table.

"The necromancer must be stopped at any cost," Tennyson said, still on the other side of the living room. "You said so yourself, Shiloh. I have absolutely no desire to succumb to the whims of a madman, and I will do everything in my power to prevent such a thing from happening, including ending my own existence. However, my people deserve justice. Piotr's people, Azuriah's people, Craddock, Raoul, all of us deserve vengeance for our losses. Confrontation is our only option."

He'd commit suicide before allowing the necromancer to perform the spell. I admired that. In his position, would I be strong enough to do the same? To take my own life, rather than risk others suffering greatly for my weakness and failures? I didn't know. It seemed an impossible question to answer.

"What if he does capture you?" I asked, whirling to face him. Furious. "What if you can't pull off a noble suicide and the necro takes control of you and your line? He'll use you and your people to murder every human in Myrtle's Acres, and then Iblis knows what else, up to and including open war with Azuriah's line. Can you risk that?"

He was in front of me, so fast it felt like someone had cut the frames of film showing his progress across the living room. There and then here. The iridescent tether binding us magically pulsed. What was he—?

"It is no risk," he said. "Because you will be bound to kill me should such a loss of control occur."

I took a step back, heart hammering. "Don't."

"It is a simple wish, Shiloh, less powerful than your taking the burden of my emotions."

"Not yet." If he didn't make the wish now, I had a chance to talk him out of it later. "Wait on it until I speak with the sidhe. Her information might be bogus"—though I seriously doubted it—"which makes our confronting the necro and his puppeteer a moot point."

"We will confront them both sooner or later."

"Yeah, and right now we're bound by the Rules of Wishing. You can make your wish in Indonesia and I'll be summoned to grant it."

"I may not have the words. Why are you resisting this?" He seemed genuinely puzzled, which made me want to slap him.

"Because you're not a rabid dog to be put down,

Tennyson, and I make it a personal rule not to execute people who've saved my life twice in as many days."

"It would not be an execution."

"Bullshit."

"It would be a mercy."

His eyes shifted to a brilliant emerald glow, and I hazarded a look. The intensity of his stare sent frozen fingers skating down my spine and turned my resistance to jelly.

"I prefer existence, as does any creature," he continued, a cold edge to his voice that screeched his mind was made up, no matter what arguments I made. "However, I am old and I have lived many lifetimes over. I no longer fear permanent death. If it prevents a greater tragedy, it is a small sacrifice to make."

"But your line—"

"Drayden is a powerful Master in his own right. He will be a successful Master of the line." He paused. Not a muscle twitched, while I was having trouble standing upright. "Why do you resist this course of action?"

"Because it isn't something that can be undone, Tennyson. What if there's a chance of rescue or of winning, but because of the way the wish is worded, it's too late and you've already been sacrificed?"

"So be it."

"Yeah, well, you aren't the one who'll be living with the guilt, pal."

He blinked. "Guilt?"

"Yes, guilt. A sense of responsibility for having done something wrong. You've heard of it, yes?"

He seemed truly perplexed by me, and I had to say the feeling was mutual. He shifted his footing, as if a change of posture would help him understand better. "You would be fulfilling the bonds of a wish, nothing more."

"Nothing more?" I must have been out of my mind with pain and worry, because I grabbed the nearest object—which happened to be the handset for one our cordless landlines—and hit him in the chest with it. Hard. He let me hit him three times before he grabbed my wrist and hit a pressure point. The phone fell from nerveless fingers.

Still furious, I tried to deck him with my left hand, which only rose to waist height before a slash of agony rolled up my forearm and into my shoulder. Tennyson tugged and spun me around, and I fell back against his chest. Both of his arms went around my waist in a loose, restraining hold.

When under heaven had I started crying again? Every part of me that was djinn rebelled at his touch, at showing such open weakness to a despised vampire. Loathed the very idea of receiving aid and comfort from him. The rest of me was exhausted— mentally and physically—and in dire need of a vacation from the vortex of crazy that my life had become. I wanted a month away from everything except a bright sun, a sandy beach, fruity drinks with umbrellas in them, and Vincent.

Hot, sexy Vincent who looked like a Sugar Daddy pop when he took his shirt off—oh sweet Iblis. I had to rescue Vincent. I had to release Julius. I had to find out what happened to twenty-eight missing werewolves. I had to bargain with a sidhe for a part of myself.

I also had to break down into a puddle and sob until my head exploded like a blister, but that wasn't happening until I cleared the rest of my To Do List.

"I do not understand your anger, Shiloh." His voice was in my ear, so soft I thought he'd spoken via telepathy.

"I'm a half-breed," I said, using the forced words to refocus and calm my hysteria.

"Yes."

I cleared my throat to remove the rough edge. "Earth djinn are totems of solidarity and strength, and my human half makes me weak when I should be strong. I experience the emotions associated with wishing differently, in that I experience emotion at all. Djinn grant the promised wishes and go about their business. They don't obsess about the ice patch a man in a yellow Camaro hit, which spun him into a guardrail and life in a wheelchair, because a hateful man wished it so. They don't fall to pieces when a wisher circumvents a rule with clever language, and the result is a broken, battered woman who didn't deserve her fate. They don't feel sick at the idea of causing the death of a man, even if he is a vampire, because it feels like friggin' assisted suicide.

"They don't, Tennyson, but I do."

He didn't say he was sorry or offer other platitudes. He must have understood, because he said nothing at all. A comfortable silence filled the downstairs, interrupted by the occasional fan burst from K.I.M.'s mainframe. I stood there, letting his sinuous arms bear the bulk of my weight, and concentrated on calming down.

The meltdown had to wait for another day. Maybe early next week.

I shored up my courage and stood a little straighter. Tennyson relaxed his hold and gently spun me around to face him. I looked up and focused on his nose, not interested in a gazelock. The rigid stone of his face had softened, and his eyes had reverted to their natural coppery brown.

"Do not bear the weight of your emotions as a burden, Shiloh," he said. "Embrace them as part of yourself, for it is a gift enjoyed by humans and few others. As vampires, we must control ourselves at all times, lest we revert to our monstrous natures." His hand brushed mine. "I would give anything to feel the freedom of true human emotion once more."

I blinked. Had he just stated intention to make a wish? No, the tether hadn't changed or sparked; it was merely a statement of fact. But it was something

I could grant him, if he so desired. Besides, human emotions aren't all they're cracked up to be.

"Shi?"

I angled my head to look over Tennyson's shoulder. Mom stood just inside the living room. Blood stained her blouse, and she was worrying a hand towel between her fingers. My half smile seemed to signal her that it was okay to approach, and she did, her face carefully schooled into neutrality. I could only imagine what she thought of her only daughter standing so close, speaking so quietly, with a vampire a hundred times her age.

"Let me take a look at your arm," she said.

"Jaxon?

"Resting as best he can. I wish I could do more for him, but I'm afraid anything I try will make it worse. I know so little about skin-walkers . . ."

"It's okay." I took her elbow with my good hand and squeezed. "For all the scrapes we get into, this is the first time I've seen this sort of injury in his animal form. I don't know how to help, either. He's never talked about it. Is he coherent?"

"Babbling, mostly, from the pain I think."

So much for asking him how to help. We could probably get the information we needed off K.I.M., and if Weller was involved in the attack, he'd know we'd been hurt by the vampire tag team. Did I have a choice?

"I'll see if K.I.M. knows—"

Mom made a noise somewhere between a grunt and a gasp. "You will not, young lady. Tennyson is quite capable of doing a computer search for you. That arm needs to be taken care of before it gets infected."

Young lady? Tennyson smirked the word at me.

Shut up. "Can you?" I asked him out loud, for Mom's benefit. "See what we have on skin-walker injuries? And then have K.I.M. call Novak. They need to come home ASAP." It was the first time since the attack I'd even thought of Novak and Kathleen. They had to be worried sick if they'd tried to call my shut-off phone and gotten no answer for the last few hours.

"Of course I can," he replied.

I followed Mom upstairs to the bathroom and sat down on the toilet seat. She left for a moment, then returned with the medical kit. I managed to stay relatively silent, head turned away and eyes shut, while she unknotted the towel and swabbed away the drying blood with alcohol wipes. The wound blazed. My shoulder felt like someone had cleaved it from the bone and poured lemon juice across the meaty ruins.

"Shiloh, what cut you?"

"Silver knife."

"Poisoned?"

My heart stuttered. "No, one of mine." I thought back to the fight. The female vamp had cut me with the knife I'd used to stab her first. "It had vampire blood on it."

Her sharp intake of breath set my internal alarm ringing. Too many seconds passed in silence, so I hazarded a look at my wound. The skin on my upper forearm was inflamed without being swollen, and likely feverish to the touch. The slice was five inches long, a lateral cut from front to back, just below my tricep. It was deep, which didn't surprise me. It was also jagged on the edges and turning black, which did.

Okay, it didn't surprise me so much as made me want to vomit. The words *necrotic tissue* flew through my mind. Something told me peroxide wasn't going to clean this. I looked away from it, struck by the overwhelming need to cry again.

"Honey—"

"Get Tennyson." He'd told me vampire blood given willingly could heal a human. What happened when we came into contact with vampire blood forced on us in the heat of battle?

I listened to her footsteps, first in the hall, and then on the stairs. *Don't panic, don't panic, don't panic . . .*

"Sweet Mary." The surprise in his voice didn't help quell my anxiety. In fact, it pretty much skyrocketed.

"The blade had vampire blood on it," I said.

"Your mother told me as much." His clothing whispered, and then he was crouched by my side, examining the wound. Cool fingers touched my heated flesh, and I winced.

"Magic's a funny bitch, isn't she?"

"How so?"

I shrugged my good shoulder. "So much depends upon force of will. You willingly offer your blood and it heals. You get blood on you during a drag-down fight and it tries to rot your arm off."

He was so quiet that I turned to look at him. His eyebrows were knotted in worry, but the rest of his face was . . . calm? Contemplative? Something. The fever in my shoulder was messing with the emotional back-draft I usually got from him. Or his blood booster had worn off enough to make that particular connection dissipate.

"I have never considered it in such a way," he said. "You are correct. Magic is a funny bitch."

Hearing him speak my own words back at me forced my mouth into a smile. He rummaged in the medical kit and produced a pair of shears, their well-kept blades gleaming. He pressed their sharpest edge to his palm. "My blood healed you once before. May I?"

It was why I'd asked for him. Another dose of vamp blood and its resulting bloodlust was a minor price to pay if it meant I avoided losing my arm to the encroaching necrotic tissue. "Yes, do it."

CHAPTER 17

Tennyson sliced his palm neatly. Blood welled in a straight line, gathering in his hand, and then he pressed it against my wound. I started to shriek. Clamped my mouth shut instead, as fire raced up my shoulder and across my chest, down my arm to my fingertips. I clutched at my leg with my right hand, then found myself squeezing Tennyson's. Hard enough to snap a few fingers if he had been human. My heart thudded wildly, and my stomach churned with barely contained nausea.

The fire ceased as suddenly as it began. A caressing throb remained when he drew his hand away, his own cut already half-healed. I hazarded a look at my wound. All signs of dying flesh were gone. A narrow, partially healed slice remained, the skin pink and healthy. It might scar, but it would mend without stitches.

I realized I was still squeezing the hell out of his hand and relaxed my hold. "You know something?" I said, blinking away the tears that had pooled without actually spilling. "I think I've cried more times in the four days I've known you than in the last four years."

He pulled his hand completely out of mine. "I apologize."

"Sorry, not saying it's your fault. Just an observation. This partnership is hazardous to my mental health." I tapped his leg, and he looked at me. "Thank you. You saved my life outside by attacking Azuriah's vampire, and you didn't have to."

His eyebrows arched a fraction, barely perceptible but enough to indicate his surprise. "It was a rash decision. However, I do not regret it, and I will face its consequences. You are important . . . to this investigation."

"Thanks." It was all I could think to say.

He bandaged the wound so it would stay clean while it finished healing naturally. The scent of blood in the house struck me suddenly, like a bad wind had shifted upstairs. Warm and metallic, but also spicy and enticing. I licked my lips, then chided myself. Ugh. Gross. It was probably Jaxon's blood, too. He'd never let me live it down if he found out I was craving his blood for a late-night snack.

Jaxon. I had to see him.

We met Mom in the hallway. She eyed my bandaged arm.

"It's fine now," I said.

"There's not much in your computer about skin-walkers," she said, and I nearly fell over from shock that she hadn't asked for details on how my arm was "fine now." She continued: "Mostly history and explanations of the skins they use and how the incantations help them shift shape. One or two articles on how to reverse the incantations if you're battling one, which mentioned rendering them unconscious as an alternative method."

I'd seen that in person—Jaxon shifting back to human form when the pain had plunged him into unconsciousness. "Nothing at all about wounded skin-walkers?" I asked.

Mom pursed her lips. "K.I.M. said the system had recently purged six files related to skin-walkers."

My skin crawled. "How recently?"

"Within the last ten minutes."

"Crap." It all but verified what I'd suspected about Weller. Only someone with top clearance—which meant him or Julius—had access to the programs that purged K.I.M.'s files. Purging was only done in case of extreme emergency, or if ordered by the DOJ in relation to a sensitive case.

Weller knew Jaxon was wounded. Weller was hiding information that could help us save his life. Bastard.

"Shiloh?" Mom asked. "What's that mean?"

I filled her in on everything she didn't know, and watched a marathon of emotions track across her face—shock, disbelief, anger, disgust. "It's all starting to make a sick kind of sense," I said when I'd brought us full circle to now. "The only thing I can't make fit is the werewolves."

"Maybe it doesn't fit," she said. "Maybe the timing is coincidence."

"Maybe, but I doubt it." My doubt didn't discount the possibility, though. I hated the idea of it being unrelated, because it meant a whole other mystery to solve once the necromancer was stopped. And I didn't want another mystery. I wanted a vacation. Drinks with umbrellas in them.

"Oh, and your other friends will be back within the hour."

At least that was somewhere in the realm of good news. With any luck, Dad would return soon with information from the sidhe, and we'd be able to start formulating an attack plan against the necro's compound.

"What about him?" Mom asked, pointing at Tennyson.

"What about him?"

"He's healed you twice. Jaxon is mostly human. Can't he heal him, too?"

"His wounds are magically inflicted," Tennyson replied. "I cannot guarantee my interference will not make it worse."

"Shiloh's spider bite was magical."

Tennyson's eyebrows drew together and his mouth flattened into a thin line. I watched him, unwilling to ask such a favor on Jaxon's behalf. He'd despise the idea of vampire blood healing him. But he'd probably despise dying even more.

"Do you wish me to do this?" Tennyson asked me.

I thought of sweet Jaxon, always ready with a smile and a joke. Snack food readily within reach. Great in bed, and funny to boot. Smart and strong, a former lover, and one of my very best friends for almost six years. I didn't know what I'd do without him giving me grief on a daily basis, and hugs exactly when I needed them.

I needed Jaxon to live. If it worked, I'd gladly suffer through him being pissed at me for the method. "Yes," I said. "Please try."

He nodded and strode down the hall toward the strong scent of blood. I followed him to my room. The sight of Jaxon on the bed made me want to scream. He lay propped on his right side, bare-chested except for the swaths of bandages criss-crossing him front to back. Pillows behind his legs and shoulders kept him sideways. Blood had soaked through the bandages on his back, and the cloths on his head wound were similarly stained. He was paler than white, his skin papery-thin.

For a moment, I didn't think he was breathing. Then the subtle rise and fall of his chest struck away an icicle of fear. Seeing him like that hurt my heart. The sudden grumble of my stomach and desire to taste his blood made me sick. He could barely stand violence in movies. He'd be disgusted by any residual bloodlust this may cause.

"Shiloh, please hold his head back and open his mouth," Tennyson said.

I carefully crawled onto the bed behind Jaxon. As gently as I could, I turned his head and worked his jaw open. No eye flutter, no sign of waking. Tennyson punctured his own wrist with his fangs, then pressed the oozing wound to Jaxon's mouth. The small holes dripped blood slowly enough to prevent choking. I rubbed his neck with my free hand, coaxing it down, and it worked instinctively to swallow.

Tennyson had to reopen his punctures three times to get what he deemed to be enough blood down Jaxon's throat, who had amazingly remained asleep through the entire production. I was salivating by the time Tennyson finished, which only fueled my anger. Blessed bloodlust. I was officially the worst djinn ever.

"Shiloh?" Dad's voice was in the hallway, preceding his appearance in the doorway by a half beat.

Mom pivoted toward the door. "Gaius?"

He took in the scene, his face settling into unveiled disgust. Whatever. I was so not up to his anti-vampire crap right now.

"May we speak in private?" he asked.

"One sec," I replied. I wiped errant drips of blood

from Jaxon's lips, then carefully turned his head back into its previous position. His color was a little better. Nothing else seemed to have changed. I pressed a kiss to his temple before standing.

I followed Dad into the hall, all the way to the back stairs leading up to the unfinished attic. We didn't keep anything up there—plenty of rooms existed downstairs for storage—so it held the musty odor of disuse and abandonment. Wood planks made the floor, and bare studs and exposed insulation the walls. He closed the door behind us.

A flash of white light seared my eyes and I squeezed them shut. The sweet fragrance of flowers and fresh-cut grass filled the attic, so out of place my eyelids popped back up. A woman stood in front of us. Her skin was a dusky gray color, almost corpse-like. Long blond hair flowed nearly to the floor. A green dress and cloak matched the sparkling emerald shade of her eyes, accentuating her radiating beauty.

Dad bowed politely. I just stared. She stared right back a moment, then her ruby lips curled into a creepy smile.

"You must be the offspring of Gaius Oakenjin," she said. Her voice sounded like a brook babbling over pebbles, snarled with a faintly Scottish brogue.

"I am," I said, feeling stupid for no good reason. "Shiloh Harrison."

"Such trust to offer your name so quickly."

Crap.

Her smile only widened. "Shiloh Harrison, it has come to my attention that you require knowledge I possess and are willing to trade for such knowledge. Is this correct?"

"It is."

She took a step forward, her shoe clunking heavily on the wood floor. No, not shoe. Her skirt had shifted back, revealing a shiny black split-toe hoof. Oh-kay.

"I have sensed the black magic being wielded by a man dabbling in the necrotic arts. It is a forbidden practice among magic users, avoided even by the abusers. It taints this world with its unnaturalness. My way is not to track this magic to its source, but I can give you a location that is accurate to within one kilometer of its origin. Is this what you were told?"

I swallowed. The attic felt ten degrees warmer. "Yes."

"I trade only in what has value, and to mortals, memory is a most cherished possession. I will require such a trade from you. Is this also what you were told?"

"Yes."

"Excellent."

"What memory?"

She frowned—even creepier than her smile—and stared at me as though I'd just asked why the sky was up. "My price is the memory of the person in your life whom you love the most."

Cold dread squeezed my heart. The person I loved

the most. I wanted to flee the attic and never look back at the Green Lady and pretend she'd never suggested such a thing. How could I agree to pay such a staggering cost? And how on earth would I know who I loved most? Mom? Dad? Vincent? Who?

Dad's hand gripped my elbow. "You don't have to agree to this, Shiloh."

He knew I did. We needed this location. Without it we could never hope to strike at the heart of the necromancer. He would just keep attacking us until no one was left.

"How do I decide who I love the most?" I asked.

"I will know."

"Even if I don't?"

"Yes."

I didn't know if I believed her, but I had no choice. Or did I? "May I add a term of my own to this agreement?"

"I will hear the term first."

Oh, gods, oh, gods, don't screw this one up, Shi.

"My term is this: I keep all of my memories intact until after the necromancer we seek is successfully incapacitated or killed, and no longer in a position to continue his forbidden magic."

Her face didn't so much as twitch, and I had no idea if that was good or bad.

I continued. "My reasoning for such a term is this: until the necromancer is successfully incapacitated or killed, I am gaining nothing of value in this bargain.

For the bargain we make to be fair and free, value should be traded at the same time."

She smiled that gut-liquefying smile. "You trade for the value of my information, daughter of Gaius Oakenjin."

"The information has no value to me unless it leads to such an end as I have described. I will not trade a memory of such value for information that, simply imparted here, has none."

Her silent contemplation stretched out for such a length I almost started tapping my foot. She was in no hurry, but I was. Every passing moment gave the necromancer more strength.

"You are a clever girl, Shiloh Harrison," the Green Lady said. "I agree to your term. Payment to me will be rendered at such a time as my imparted information leads to the successful capture or death of the necromancer you hunt. Are we in agreement?"

I swallowed, mouth suddenly full of cotton. "Yes, we are in agreement."

She extended an elegant, gray-skinned hand. Her fingernails were long, carefully shaped, and the same thick, dark brown as her hooves. I forced myself to shake her hand and not shudder at the cold, tree-bark rough texture of her skin. Hey, I had to feel just as foreign to her touch. I even managed to not wipe my hand on my jeans when she released me. A flare of magic sparked between us, a miniature firework of green and brown and silver lights, sealing the pact we'd made.

The Green Lady stepped back until several feet distanced us. She held her right hand out, palm down. Mint-colored light glowed from her palm, and an outline etched itself on the rough wood floorboards of the attic. It wasn't quite a pentagon—only two sides were completely straight lines. The other straight line had a jagged chunk missing. The top lines were mountain-rough, the point flattened. Her light seared the image into the wood with the familiar scent of scorching. A single dot burned itself near the peak.

Her light ceased. I crouched down to study the image. It was familiar, I just couldn't place it. A flash of white light removed the scents of flowers and grass, and then she was gone.

"Perfect," I muttered.

Dad peered over my shoulder. He pointed to the right side of the pentagon, where the jagged chunk was missing. "This is familiar to me. If it is a map, this is likely a body of water."

"Delaware," I said. It had to be Delaware. "That's the Rehoboth and Indian River Bays. We need a map so we can figure out what town she's showing us."

We simplified the plan by using a large sheet of paper to trace the map, then took it downstairs to scan on K.I.M. I set her security settings as high as I could on the search, which ought to alert us if anyone accessed the information—let me know how on top of things Weller really was. Mom and Tennyson had joined us in the conference room by the time K.I.M. spit out her findings: Route 16 outside of Milton, Delaware.

"Bovine farms?" Tennyson asked.

"Several," I replied. "Which works with the images you saw this morning of farms and the odor of cow manure. As evil lairs go, it's certainly an inconspicuous location. No one goes looking for necromancing chambers on a cow farm."

"Indeed."

"With such a close location," Mom said, "I'd have no trouble echoing the magic back to its source."

"No way," I said, in the same moment Dad said, "What?"

Mom tilted her chin, adopting the Determined Mother look she used to get when I refused to eat my string beans at dinnertime. "I helped you source the first one, Shiloh—"

"And it almost got you killed."

"I know how the magic feels now. I can track it faster than you or your friends, and you know it."

"What almost got her killed?" Dad asked, indignation in his tone. Oops. Had I forgotten to tell that part of the story?

"It was a magical snare, it could have happened to

anyone." Mom waved her hand in the air as if to erase the question.

"But it didn't happen to anyone," I said. "It happened to you. I can't put you in that kind of danger again, Mom." I couldn't risk it, not if she was the one I'd lose my memory of—dying and then being erased. I'd lose everything about her if that happened. "As a United States Para-Marshal, I am ordering you—"

"Sweetheart, you can't order me to stay behind." Radiating calm, she touched the bandage on my arm, then met my gaze. "This necromancer attacked me and he attacked my family. I may be a civilian, but I am still your mother. You can't keep me out of this."

"I won't be there to protect you, Elspeth," Dad said.

Mom smiled patiently. "As I recall, our separation forfeited your right to try to protect me from anything, Gaius, including my own stubbornness. Djinn law may prevent you from coming with us and actively engaging, but I'm bound by no such limitation. She's my daughter."

Dad flinched. "She is my daughter as well, and I have done what is within the limits of my powers to do."

"As always."

"Enough!" I stomped my foot, once again reduced to childish gestures by my squabbling parents. "Dad, thank you for your help with the sidhe. Without her, we'd have no location. Mom, I will tie you to a chair and gag you, if it keeps you from coming with me and getting yourself killed or kidnapped. I've got one hostage situation ongoing in Myrtle's Acres, the necro already has Vincent to use against me, and I don't need to negotiate for you, too. Do you understand?"

"Shiloh—"

"Do. You. Under. Stand?"

She held my stare for several seconds, and I watched a reel of emotions play across her face. She looked away first, slipping back into a mask of resignation. "I hate that you do this job," she said.

"I know. But right now no one else can do it. Please stay here with Jaxon."

"All right."

Okay, good, progress.

K.I.M. beeped and without waiting for a command, switched her main display to a streaming news feed. The sound was off, giving no voice to the close-up of a male reporter. Fire trucks and distant licks of flame were visible over his shoulder. The ticker at the bottom of the screen made my stomach heave: Helicopter Crash Near 404.

I couldn't seem to kick-start my brain. All I could do was stare at the screen and the distant flames.

"Shiloh, you don't know—" Mom started.

"Yes, she does," Dad said.

"K.I.M. wouldn't have come on without a command," I said. Was that really my voice? So hollow and deep? Everything around me felt cold, far away. Blood roared in my ears. "It's my fault. I wanted K.I.M. to call Novak. It gave away their location."

Mom touched my elbow. "They probably got out—"

"They would have called." A haze of rage edged my vision. I'd assumed Weller wouldn't attack us directly so soon, without assuming he'd use a method other than controlled vampires. I should have shut down our connection to K.I.M. entirely when I first suspected Weller and never used her for anything related to this hunt.

All.

My.

Fault.

I dropped to my knees and crawled beneath the table housing the majority of K.I.M.'s hardware. Julius had shown all of us how to disconnect her systems from the line networking her to Weller's half of the Knowledge Interface Matrix. It was a safety measure in case of exterior hacking—chances: next-to-zero—or internal malfunction—not quite what was happening, but close enough.

This was basically a combination of the two, and it made me sick.

The orange cable stared at me from a small cluster of wires varying in size from pipe cleaner thin to hot dog thick. This one was the size of my thumb, with a splitter connecting it to another of similar length. I yanked the cord out of the splitter. The tip sparked once.

Above me, K.I.M. blared a warning that she was off-line. *Yeah, no kidding, you bundle of chips and parts.*

I crawled back out to three concerned faces. I brushed off my knees as I stood, working hard to keep my expression blank. If they expected me to have a breakdown over the helicopter crash, they had a long wait. I didn't have any more tears. I definitely didn't have the time to sit around and wait for them find me.

"If Novak and Kathleen are alive they'll find a way to contact us," I said. "We can't—"

Dad disappeared.

I blinked at the empty spot on the carpet where he'd stood just a moment ago. Surely he wasn't . . . .

"We need to get to Delaware," I said to Tennyson. "The two of us against who knows how many wasn't how I wanted to play this, but I don't see a choice." It wasn't as if I had a SWAT team in my back pocket, or a squad of federal marshals on standby. The trouble with being only one of a two-team, specialty branch of a government agency was lack of backup. I could request a marshal unit, but any local they could spare was already at Myrtle's Acres. We couldn't afford the time it would take to get someone from outside. Besides, I had no idea how far Weller's reach had spread—was anyone else in the Marshals' Office supporting his agenda?

Were we to play the part of the fool in this little production?

Tennyson held up his cell phone. "We have my people."

I blinked. "Even if I could call off the marshals watching the trailer park's perimeter, which is highly unlikely given the circumstances, you put them there for a reason—to keep them safe."

"Your Para-Marshal Weller knows where they are. They are no longer safe in Myrtle's Acres, and they can certainly be of assistance to us. A dozen marshals and as many sheriff's deputies are nothing. They do not keep my people in check within the town. I do. We will rain down upon that bovine farm like Hell's own fire."

If that statement had come from anyone else, I'd have demanded a sobriety test. "Once you pull your people, Weller will know. He'll have to heighten security. He may even abandon the location."

"Perhaps. However, going in alone guarantees failure. We are strong, you and I, but we cannot defeat these men by ourselves. Of this I am certain." He started to dial, then paused. His eyebrows slanted a fraction. "Peculiar."

"Good grief, what?"

"A thought." He met my gaze, his copper eyes blazing with confusion. "Yesterday your incubus friend used Drayden to relay a message when he could not contact you directly."

Yesterday, two days ago, the day we found the storage unit. Time was bleeding together. "I remember," I said.

"This evening you were unreachable for several hours."

Ding, ding, ding! "And he didn't try to call via Drayden. Bless it."

"Shiloh, what's going on?" Mom asked, comfortably oblivious.

I conjured up a mental image of Novak—strong, muscular enough to give a bodybuilder wet dreams, and handsome as a cover model. He had a deep-timbre laugh you felt in your bones, a temper the size of a big rig, and a loyalty streak as long as the San Andreas Fault. Julius brought him into the Para-Marshals to protect him from Hell and keep him off the demonic radar. Novak had spent the last eight years hiding and surviving. He wasn't dumb enough to risk it all to help Weller.

Was he?

Everything he knew about this case . . . every time he'd fought against keeping Tennyson around. Was any of it more than just Novak being Novak?

"I don't know," I finally replied. "We could just be paranoid and seeing conspirators everywhere."

Tennyson grunted. "It's hardly a conspiracy if—"

"If everyone's really out to get you. Yeah, I know the line."

He gave my shoulder a gentle squeeze, his hand lingering. And of course, Dad chose that moment to poof back into the room.

CHAPTER 18

Tennyson removed his hand from my shoulder slowly, deliberately—not taunting, but refusing to acknowledge he'd done anything wrong by offering a physical gesture of comfort. Not that Dad cared. He bristled at the sight of it, and I wasn't sure what bothered him more: that I was close with a vampire, or that I was close with a man.

Dads!

I was very proud of myself for not rolling my eyes.

With Dad came the faint odor of smoke and gasoline, and his skin looked a tad sooty. Surely he hadn't—"Where did you go?" I asked.

"To the crash site."

My heart hammered against my ribs. "Really?"

"Yes, Shiloh."

"And?"

"The helicopter is burning hot and fast, and on-site investigators are unable to determine how many bodies may or may not be inside."

"Okay . . . but were *you* able to tell?"

He didn't restrain himself from rolling his eyes. "Yes, I was able to get closer to the heat of blaze than those humans. Close enough to see only one body in the pilot seat."

I admit it: I whooped for joy. Literally and loudly. Tennyson took a step backward. Dad smiled. My elation was short-lived, though, as explanations began rolling through my head. Had someone removed Novak and Kathleen from the helicopter, and then orchestrated the crash and burn to throw us off track? To make me believe the rest of my team was lost? Had it happened recently? Hours ago? If the latter was true, there went my earlier assumptions of Novak's possible involvement. If not—

"This means your teammates are likely now hostages," Tennyson said.

Hooray for Captain Obvious. "I know," I said, "but at least it means they're alive somewhere. And alive somewhere is a hell of a lot better than dead there." I threw my arms around Dad's neck and hugged him tight, not caring that he smelled worse this close. "Thank you."

His hand came up to pat the center of my back. "You're welcome. Unfortunately, it's all the magic I can expend here before someone notices."

"I know." I drew back and kissed his cheek. "Luck?"

"Luck is for leprechauns."

"And half djinn up against impossible odds."

"You are a half djinn, Shiloh, a heritage you never asked for and yet have embraced, despite the obstacles of belonging to two worlds. And if you can overcome those obstacles, then nothing else against you is impossible." On the scale of strange compliments from my father, it certainly rated high on the meter. He stepped back and gave Tennyson a scathing look. "If you get her killed, I will drain every drop of your blood and spread your ashes over the Chesapeake Bay."

Tennyson inclined his head as though acknowledging a friendly wager.

Dad gave Mom a curt nod. "Elspeth."

"Gaius," she replied.

He poofed.

Tennyson closed his eyes and tilted his head to the left, brow furrowing. I started to ask what was wrong, and then realized he was listening. Hard. Something out of my hearing range, because strain as I might, I couldn't figure out what he heard. His eyes popped open, blazing red.

"Piotr," he said, and ran.

The moment the basement door opened, agonized wails echoed up the stairs. I followed Tennyson down. Piotr was as we'd left him, suspended from the bars on legs paralyzed by a silver knife in his back. Contact with the silver bars had burned away the flesh on his back and arms, and scented the room with charred meat and ash. His eyes blazed red and blue, and the light glistened off elongated fangs. His skin was sallow, stretched like rice paper over his bones, more monster now than man.

He muttered to himself, words I didn't understand at first. His voice had adopted a much thicker accent as he lost himself in the past, of a Russia long gone. Tennyson and I approached slowly, even though the bars would stop Piotr cold if he somehow managed to lunge. Something about a mad vampire would make even the bravest person cautious. Words continued to drip from his lips, and I started to recognize names: Ivanya, Eketarina, Vasiliy, Tanya, Leonid, Pascha. Old friends? His vampires?

"Piotr," Tennyson said.

He didn't seem to hear. He kept muttering, crying, screeching—rinse, repeat.

"Piotr!"

Nothing.

"Could the necromancer be doing this to him?" I asked.

"Unlikely. The silver is slowly poisoning him. Unless he feeds soon, he will go feral and need to be put down."

"I thought we couldn't kill him without causing a line inheritance problem."

His red headlights flashed at me, a hint of green in their centers. "He is suffering."

I bit back a tart *so what?* and managed a more polite, "I can see that, but you're the one who lectured me on why—"

"I know." A flash of sympathy was there and gone again. "However, if I am correct in my guess, most of his line is gone already."

My stomach churned. "They're being killed off, even though Piotr did what was asked of him."

"I believe so."

"Bastards." I make no bones about my general hatred of vampires, but mass slaughter out of spite is beyond any sane, reasonable person's level of tolerance. Still, Piotr was complicit in the recent goings-on, and I hated the idea of giving him death as an easy out.

I plucked a key from a hook on the wall and strode to the cage. Piotr thrashed at my nearness, but didn't directly acknowledge me. I grasped the handle of the knife in my left hand. The silver was blazing hot, reacting to the vampire. The flesh around the wound was little more than a scorched crater the size of an apple. I swallowed hard, forcing away a pang of nausea, and pulled. The blade slid out with a squelching sound. No blood, just a bit of brackish fluid.

Gross.

I dropped the blade with a clatter and quickly unlocked the chains. Piotr crashed to the floor of the cage like a sack of wet laundry. He didn't cry out, just huddled there as he'd fallen, still muttering in Russian. Bits of ash clung to the silver bars. Vampire or not, mortal enemy or not, he'd been tortured enough by us.

"Will you kill him?" Tennyson asked.

"No." I kicked the silver blade to within arm's reach of the cage. "But I won't stop him if he wants to end his own suffering."

"He may do so. I have lost twelve and each death is a burden. I cannot imagine the agony of losing so many at once."

"Me, either." For the fifteen minutes that I'd born the weight of Tennyson's grief, I had suffered in a wholly unique and horrifying fashion. I never wanted to feel like that again, and it was beyond my imagination to apply it to hundreds of losses. Could anyone return from such a thing with their sanity intact?

Piotr screeched, a piteous sound that set my teeth on edge. He flopped onto his back like a beached fish. His spine would take a long time to heal, if it ever did. The silver poisoning could have cauterized the spinal cord at both ends. Had I paralyzed him?

Did it matter at this point?

More Russian words tumbled out and, based solely on his inflections and attempts at eye contact, they were curse words aimed at me. He swallowed several times, his Adam's apple working hard. "End. This."

The two English words were guttural, demanding action.

Tennyson stepped closer to the cage. "Who is the necromancer?" he asked.

Piotr growled.

"Tell us," Tennyson said, "and we will end your suffering, old friend. Remain silent, and we will leave you here."

He didn't growl this time. Maybe he was considering the offer. A vampire Master with no vampires is a sad thing, indeed, especially considering his injuries. He'd already been tortured for a year and a half. I'd probably paralyzed him. His line was being murdered. How did someone start over after enduring so much?

"He tortured you," I said, not certain to whom I was referring, but it didn't really matter. "He kidnapped your people and abused you into cooperating. Took you piece by piece. He is murdering your children."

"You owe him nothing, and he has nothing left with which to compel your silence," Tennyson added.

Piotr licked cracked lips with a swollen tongue.

Going for broke, I asked, "Is Para-Marshal Adam Weller the person orchestrating this?"

He hissed at the air above him. Sounded blessed close to a yes.

I needed more than blessed close. "Is he?"

A guttural, "Yes," finally cemented my fears. I closed my eyes against a sudden attack of vertigo. Suspecting something and hearing a confirmation were two entirely different things. My former ally really was my enemy. But why? What the hell was he up to?

"Is Weller also the necromancer we seek?" Tennyson asked.

Piotr answered that with a clipped, "No."

"Then who?"

The half-feral vamp struggled with several different syllables and sound combinations, none making any sense to me. He hadn't fed in days. He needed blood, but no way was I offering him a vein, even if it cleared his head long enough to help us. One vampire feeding per lifetime was enough for me, thanks, and Tennyson had filled the quota saving my life.

Tennyson seemed to catch on to Piotr's word attempts faster. "Adelay," he said.

Piotr grunted.

It took me a moment to identify the name. "Wait, Brighid's Adelay? She said she killed him."

"Book," Piotr hissed out.

"Adelay's book on necromancy," Tennyson said. "So it wasn't just a rumor. It exists."

"Found it. Hid it. Stolen."

"Stolen by whom?"

Piotr grunted and thrashed. His head twitched side to side in some vampire version of a seizure. Blessed silver.

To Tennyson, I said, "So Piotr found and hid the Adelay book. As a practicing warlock before he turned,

I bet he guarded that thing with his life. He wouldn't tell just anybody he had it, but someone found out. They wanted information on necromancy, so they tortured him, stole his people, got the book, and got to experimenting."

"That is a sufficient summary of events," Tennyson said. "The question is still who has the book. The answer will lead us to the necromancer."

I glanced at the convulsing figure on the cage floor. "We know where to find the necromancer. Maybe his identity will have to wait until we get there and start beating the crap out of him."

"A good point." He tilted his head. "Is it wise to leave your mother here with him?"

"Why, think she'll hurt him?"

"You know that was not my meaning."

I shrugged. Okay, so he wasn't in the mood for sarcasm. Really, I wasn't, either. It just slipped out when I was this frustrated and angry. "Unless Piotr learns how to squash his body into a four-inch thin pancake, he's not getting through those bars. She'll be fine."

Halfway up the basement stairs, he stopped. I nearly rammed my face into the middle of his back. He pivoted and looked down at me, his brow furrowed, contemplating something. When he didn't share right away, I heaved a dramatic sigh and planted both hands on my hips.

"Okay, the thought bubble above your head is on

the fritz, so do you mind spilling verbally?" I asked.
"What?"

"The Rules of Wishing," he said softly, his voice
a whisper even though Piotr was not likely listening
to us.

"What about them?" He wasn't going to wish me
to kill him, was he? I'd knock him unconscious first,
so he couldn't think it into my head.

"What are the limitations on wishes that request
information from outside parties?"

I considered his question. "It depends on the
wording of the wish. I can compel information
magically, but the information has to exist within
the mind of the person I'm compelling. And I can
only get what they believe is true, so if they overheard a conversation in which Sally tells her friend
that Aunt Mary killed the cook, that's what I get.
Even if it turns out Sally really said Aunt Mary was
so pissed about the chewy steak she only threatened
to kill the cook. Make sense?"

"Yes."

"But I can't compel vampires, so don't waste your
wish on Piotr."

"Doing so was not my intention. And the limitations of transportation?"

"Huh?" I shooed him the rest of the way up the
stairs. Standing like that, gazing straight up, was putting a crick in my neck. Once we were back in the hall

with the basement door firmly locked and Mom nowhere within earshot, I said, "Run that by me again."

"If I was to wish us into the middle of the necromancer's lair, would you be able to take us there?"

"Am I able to perform such a task? Yes." I shook my head. "Unfortunately, I'm pretty sure the power expenditure of that one is higher than your first wish. Rule number two."

"Unfortunate, indeed."

Yeah. Teleportation was not a casual talent, but I could use it to fulfill a wish. I've only done it once, though, and it hurt like hell. Body pulled apart into a bazillion atoms, sucked to the location of choice, and then reassembled on the other side. I half expected my fingers to reappear as toes. My back ached for a week afterward. Just thinking about it made me once again covet the ease with which Dad poofed in and out of existence.

Tennyson was gazing at a point just over my shoulder, seeming lost in his thoughts. I could practically see the hamster wheel spinning. My own hamster had given up and died a little bit ago, depriving me of clever ways to help us win the day.

"Can you teleport someone else to us?" he asked.

"Potentially, although I think I'd be limited by my knowledge of the person's actual, physical location. And there's still rule number two about the power expenditure."

He nodded. "In that case, I believe we have no choice."

"No choice in what?" Blue flecked his eyes and I remembered. "No way, not that. I do not want to be responsible—"

"Your wants are irrelevant, Djinn." His words carried an edge as sharp as frozen steel, and as much as I hated to admit it, they stung.

I crossed my arms and cocked one hip, giving as much attitude as my bruised ego could muster. "Fine, Vampire."

The stairs creaked. "Everything all right?" Mom called down.

"Peachy," I said. "How's Jaxon?"

"Groggy, but waking up. And I think he's starting to heal."

"I'll be right up." To Tennyson, I said, "Look, there are weapons stored in one of the upstairs bedrooms. The Element is too obvious, so stock up the Expedition. We're pulling out in five minutes." He raised his eyebrow. "Please."

"Very well."

He followed me upstairs and turned to the room I pointed at. I was glad the wish conversation was temporarily over. Even if he blindsided me with it later, it gave me time. A few extra minutes before I became responsible for potentially killing a Master vampire.

Mom waited at the door to Jaxon's room. I sidled

past her, and she pulled the door partway shut. Jaxon was propped up a bit higher on the pillows, still awkwardly angled on his side. Twin spots of fever colored his cheeks, but his eyes were open and aware. Mom must have changed his dressings, because the bandage on his head was white. The bleeding had stopped.

I perched on the edge of the bed, relief slamming home hard. I squeezed his hand, then kissed his knuckles. He squeezed back and blinked sleepily.

"You look terrible," he rasped.

"I'm not the one with a hole in my head."

"Need it like a hole in the head." Okay, so maybe he was still a little delirious. "Tastes bad."

"We'll get you a mint." I knew full well what he meant. Vampire blood liked to leave a refreshingly ashy aftertaste. "Thank you."

"What for?"

"You saved my life out there."

Something flashed in his hazel eyes, so dark they were almost stormy gray. It passed and he winked. "Wouldn't have if I knew I'd lose an antler."

"Yes you would. Anyway, we'll get some payback for you."

"Going now?"

"Yeah."

"Wish I could help."

"Me, too." More than he knew, with both Novak and Kathleen out of the game. My allies had dwindled to exactly one, and he still scared the pee out of me sometimes.

I brushed my lips across his forehead, feeling the heated skin and fine sheen of sweat there. I found a tiny spark of hope in the constant that was Jaxon Dearborn. Knowing he was safely out of this fight gave me a small measure of comfort. He'd be here when—if?—I came home.

"Good luck," he said. Had his breath become more ragged than before, or was my imagination creating the illusion?

"Luck is for leprechauns," I said, winking.

"What does a djinn ask for?"

"Tomorrow."

His eyes widened a fraction. "Then I'll see you to-morrow."

I gave his hand another squeeze and stood with some effort. "See you tomorrow."

Tennyson was in the midst of organizing an arsenal in the Expedition when I came downstairs. I met Mom in the foyer and pulled her into a fierce hug. She didn't know about my deal with the Green Lady. She didn't know I could lose every single memory I had of her, if the sidhe decided my mother was the person I loved most.

"Be careful, Shi," she said, hugging me back with

the fierceness only displayed by mothers of threat-ened cubs.

"I promise, Mom." I inhaled her flowery perfume, the citrus of her shampoo, the tang of her sweat and tears. "I love you."

"I love you back, kiddo."

I pulled away before she could sense my fear and hesitation, before she could feel the chill spreading goose bumps across my shoulders and back. I drank her in. Wavy brown hair threaded with silver, dark brown eyes, high cheekbones, full lips. The idea that I could no longer remember her tomorrow was unfathomable. She was my mother. She'd bandaged my scraped knees and taught me to color inside the lines. She eased me through the awkwardness of adolescence and gave me the confidence to embrace my duel nature.

My stomach froze into a tiny knot, and my lungs stopped working right. I had to force an inhale. Exhale.

"Shiloh?" Not Mom, but Tennyson from the door-way behind me.

I swallowed hard and pivoted to face him. He radiated calm, and I soaked it in. He'd sensed my impending panic attack. I offered a half smile in thanks, and he nodded.

"The car is full," he said. "Are you ready?"

Not a chance. "Yes."

"We'll hold down the fort," Mom said.

"Thanks. I—"

A telephone rang, and it took me a long moment before I realized it wasn't a cell phone. It rang so rarely I almost didn't recognize the tone. Only a handful of people knew the number.

I bolted into the living room and snatched up the nearest landline handset. The caller ID set my nerves jangling, and I nearly dropped the phone.

Weller, A.

CHAPTER 19

Tennyson made a strange sound. Something like a hiss, not quite a growl. He could hear the conversation easily, and I didn't want Mom any more involved than she was, so I did not put the phone on speaker when I answered.

"Harrison," I said, impressing myself with the iron in my voice.

"It's good to hear your voice, Marshal Harrison," Weller said. His tone was well laced with genuine concern, which made me want to reach through the phone and smack him. "You've been unreachable for several hours and I was starting to worry."

"That's sweet."

"Are you any closer to resolving the situation in Myrtle's Acres?"

Screw it. I was not going to stand there and pretend I didn't know what I knew. "Fuck you, Weller, I know what you are."

Silence. It stretched into five, ten seconds. Fifteen. "You know what I am? I assume you don't mean my mixed-Norwegian descent."

"No, I'm talking about your extracurricular activities involving kidnapping, murder, and necrotic magic."

"Ah, that." When he spoke again, his voice was cold and clipped. Businesslike. "You're a smart woman, Marshal Harrison. You figured me out faster than I would have hoped. Bravo."

The open admission threw me. He wasn't even denying it, or trying to pretend it was all my imagination. Um, good, then. Maybe. "What do you want?"

"Not even going to ask me if Novak and Kathleen are all right? Ask me what I'm willing to trade for their lives?"

"Nope. You'd just find a way to double-cross me and kill them anyway." He didn't know how close we were to finding his lair. He thought he held all the cards. Let him keep thinking it, the bastard.

"How about your friend Vincent? He doesn't seem to be enjoying his accommodations."

I clenched the phone and forced my voice to remain steady. "You're a coward, Weller. Kidnapping a civilian and using him as a shield? That's beyond weak."

"In your mind, I'm certain that's true. However, my goals far exceed the cost of one man's life."

"Nothing exceeds the cost of one man's life."

"We'll soon see, won't we? Don't worry, he's still alive. A lover is of more value than a coworker."

His yammering was starting to grate. "What do you want?"

"Well, now that I've discovered how much you know, I want to make you an offer."

"I'm not on the market."

He chuckled, and oh, boy, it was creepy. "Don't be so sure, child. We both want the same things, after all."

"We both want you arrested? Good to know."

Another chuckle set the hairs on my neck standing on end. "Your sarcasm is refreshing, but no. We both want order, within the known and unknown paranormal races, and we want a means to ensure order is maintained."

"That's what the Para-Marshals are for, Brain Trust," I said.

"The effectiveness of the Para-Marshals is neutered by the oversight of the Department of Justice, you must see that. Twelve people against thousands of creatures who continue to defy us at every turn."

"We have all kinds of freedom to act without DOJ oversight. You want more? So you what? Create a regiment of vampires you can control to act as your foot soldiers? That's your grand plan to maintain order?"

"Of course not. My grand plan, as you call it, is far more complicated and has farther-reaching implications than you can imagine. And I want you to join me."

I burst out laughing. "Dude, I don't know who put the psychedelics in your oatmeal this morning, but I want what you're having. The delusions must be awesome."

"I'll only make this offer once."

"Good, because I hate reruns."

He belted out a weary sigh. "Very well. Is that a firm no, then?"

"It's a firm *hell* no. I will not join your crazy little army brigade, and I will continue doing everything in my power to stop you."

"So we're clear."

Something scuffled on his end of the line. Metal rattled, and I heard the distinct sound of flesh striking flesh. My heart skipped. A woman moaned, then hissed. Another thud. Kathleen's distinct voice uttered a harsh curse, first in English and then in French. My stomach plummeted at the confirmation of my friend's location.

The first gunshot made me jump out of my skin. Kathleen shrieked. The second shot silenced her. The third sent a wave of nausea through me that nearly brought me to my knees. I clutched the phone. If Tennyson hadn't stepped up behind me and put his hands on my waist, I probably would have fallen over.

"Bring the Master vampire to me. You have half an hour to decide before I kill the incubus."

It took every ounce of concentration I possessed to force out my response. "He won't come willingly."

"I believe I've found a way to convince him. Turn your Raspberry on. I'll call back in thirty minutes." He hung up.

I dropped the phone, uncaring that I hadn't even ended the call. Weller had killed Kathleen to prove his point, and he'd kill Novak unless I played along. I continued leaning on Tennyson, willing my heart to stop beating so fast. Urging what little I'd eaten in the last twenty-four hours to stay down and not revisit me.

"My condolences," he said softly.

I grunted, gathered my tattered courage, and stood up straight. Picked up the phone, put it back in its cradle, then turned to face Tennyson. "He's overconfident, counting on the fact that I have no idea where he is or where to start looking. But that doesn't really help us, because we can't get there in half an hour."

"We will get as far as we can and play this by ear. No matter Weller's instructions, he will not be expecting our early arrival."

"He said he found a way to convince you." I circled

back to Weller's chilling statement. "What do you think he meant?"

Tennyson's eyes flashed crimson. "Any threats he makes to me or mine will be revisited upon him tenfold before he dies."

I swallowed. "Let's go, then."

At the front door, I paused once to look back at the stairs. Mom sat on the landing, watching us with her hands clasped between her knees. She smiled. I summoned up my confidence and smiled back, winked, knowing full well I may not remember her tomorrow.

Dear Iblis, please let the sacrifice be worth it.

At three in the morning, we made good time on the mostly deserted highway and were halfway to our destination before the cell phone rang. I'd already disabled the GPS on my Raspberry, so Weller couldn't track us. Tennyson and I hadn't spoken for the entire trip—he lost in his thoughts and me in mine—so the call broke the silence like a thunderclap. More surprising than the sound was the source: Tennyson's phone.

He frowned at the display screen, then answered it. "Drayden?" I couldn't hear the other vampire's voice, but the sudden spackle of red across the dash clued me in that this wasn't good news. I sneaked glances at Tennyson's profile as I drove. The frozen chipotle scent of his emotions returned, chilling me bone-deep.

"You're certain it's them?" His voice was horrifyingly flat, cold. The red flecks coalesced into twin headlights as the emotion blared like beacons of fury and anxiety. Weller was apparently keeping his promise to secure Tennyson's cooperation.

"Do not engage them, Drayden. Remain inside of the park's perimeter. Do not give the humans an excuse to end us all." He listened. "Soon, my friend. Very soon." He said something in a language I didn't know—Latin, maybe?—and in a soft tone that surprised me. It was a calming tone usually reserved for frightened children or worried lovers.

I stayed quiet after he hung up, even though I ached to know what was happening. Tennyson needed a moment. That much was frighteningly clear in the way he clenched and unclenched his fingers. The line of his jaw was so tight I thought he might snap a few teeth.

"My twelve," he finally said. "They are . . . I never imagined . . ." He couldn't even say what was happening, but in a flash of clarity and horror, I understood.

"Sweet Iblis. He used the revenant spell on your vampires."

"Yes." Never had a single word carried the weight of so much disgust.

And if Drayden called—

"They're in the trailer park, aren't they?"

Tennyson breathed sharply through his nose, nostrils flaring, and I desperately wanted out of the car. "They have wounded or killed all of the law enforcement personnel surrounding the town, have taken the gaggle of reporters hostage, and are now taunting my people, goading them to emerge from the safety of their hiding places. And the human residents are becoming more vocal.

"It's falling apart, Shiloh."

I reached out, overcoming my fear of him, and squeezed his arm. "This is Weller's move. He'll threaten to have the revenants murder the reporters and the wounded, then he'll threaten to turn them loose on the park residents."

"The scent of so much fresh blood will be maddening to my people."

"Couldn't Drayden take some of your people out to dispatch the revenants?" It was such a simple question, but I knew it couldn't have a simple answer.

"It's far too risky. My people obey my commands as best they can, but they must also be true to their base nature. It is going on four days that they have been cooped up so close to humans without fresh blood to sustain their needs. They will be on edge, hungry, frustrated. Even believing the revenants are no longer their kin, I fear they will not stop with only killing those twelve. Once they taste blood, I fear they will slaughter the residents."

Frozen fingertips skated down my spine. Definitely

not a simple answer. If Tennyson's people acted first, the humans could die. If Weller's revenant-vamps acted first, Tennyson's people would be forced to act . . . and the residents could die. And I didn't have any forces hiding up my sleeve capable of dispatching the revenant-vamps.

As for our grand plan of killing the necromancer? It would stop him from ordering the revenant-vamps around—which came with a plus and minus.

Plus: no slaughter of reporters or residents.

Minus: no one controlling a dozen vampire zombies left to roam the countryside.

Allowing Tennyson to house his line in Myrtle's Acres was ranking at the top of my Stupidest Decisions Ever list.

I glanced at the clock radio. Weller's call was due any moment.

"Shiloh." Tennyson's voice was calmer now, almost contemplative. I wanted to give him my full attention, but even though the highway remained mostly deserted, I also didn't want to crash us. "Vampires have long been enemies with both humans and djinn. No matter how this night ends, thank you for all that you have done for me. It will not be forgotten."

My heart swelled at the unexpected thanks. "I wish I could have done more."

"You have done enough. You have fought for me, and you nearly died in service to myself and my kin."

Ding! It came to me like a bolt of lightning, sudden

and jolting and a little bit awful. Something that had seemed vaguely familiar and my subconscious mind needed to place on its own. Something to do with the spiders. "Fuck me," I said.

"Beg your pardon?"

I was vibrating between excitement at connecting the dots and feeling like a complete moron for not doing it sooner. "When your missing kin were tortured and killed, do you remember the impression you got from one of them? Of her captor?"

"Luisa, yes."

"Large man, golden skin, black hair, right?"

"Yes, and a scar."

My hands tightened on the steering wheel hard enough to make my knuckles ache. "I can't swear to the scar, because I never saw him up close, but I think I know him. Knew him. It could be a man named Lars Patterson. He's a spinner. Was. He was a Para-Marshal on Weller's team, and he supposedly died two years ago."

"A spinner?"

"A warlock who specializes in manifesting from our subconscious. He manifested fear in the creepy-crawling way, and if he's been dabbling out of the picture for the last two years, it's possible he's refined his magic."

"Refined the manifestation into poisonous, controllable spiders."

"Yeah." Recalling the deliberate army of spiders in

Caine's house, I shuddered. "Bless it all, I should have figured it out faster."

"You figured it out now."

"Fat lot of good it does us at this point."

"Knowledge is power."

The nugget of wisdom tugged the corners of my mouth up. "You sound like a PSA."

"Is that an insult or a compliment?" He sounded genuinely confused.

"Dunno." I glanced at the clock again. Thirty-four minutes had passed. What was Weller waiting for? My stomach churned. He said he'd kill Novak in half an—

"I feel I must apologize to you," Tennyson said.

I blinked and gave him a sideways glance. The first car I'd seen in ten minutes passed us in the south-bound lane. "For what?"

"My decisions to hide my people in Myrtle's Acres and to involve your team have caused only suffering and loss. For that I am sorry."

"You were doing what you thought best for your people, Tennyson. No father would do any less for his children."

"My desire to protect them has only placed them in graver danger." He didn't seem to notice his unintentional pun. "I fear many more lives will be lost before the morning sun rises."

In just over three hours. If Weller meant to have the revenant-vamps move against the trailer park, it would happen soon. Intent on getting this the hell over with, I grabbed my Raspberry from the cup holder. It chimed in my hand.

"Lose your watch?" I asked by way of salutation.

"A problem arose that demanded my attention." Something in Weller's voice told me his wordplay was completely intentional.

"Yeah, well, jerk off on your own time."

Weller chuckled. "My, my, the stress of the situation has certainly given your vocabulary an edge."

"You don't know me, so don't pretend to know my fucking vocabulary. We got your message, by the way. What's the move?"

"The vampire is with you?"

Tennyson leaned across the seat, close enough to speak clearly and be heard without shouting. "He is," he said.

"Then I don't suppose I need bother explaining the precarious nature of events unfolding in Myrtle's Acres. How it ends is up to you both."

"We're listening."

I concentrated on driving, easing onto an eastbound back road that would take us closer to our destination. It was darker here, without the interspersed random gas stations and small towns. The moon was waning, too low on the horizon to provide much light.

"I will offer you this, Woodrow Tennyson," Weller said, as if making a grand gesture Tennyson was sure to accept. "Your people need not die, nor do they need to undergo revenancy. As you have no doubt deduced, it's a quite painful procedure, and too many individual minds at once are difficult for my necromancer to control."

"So far you have offered me nothing," Tennyson said.

"A war is coming, and I am in need of soldiers."

"There is no war. This war only exists in your own paranoid mind, fueled by your desire to accumulate power and strength. Since coming out in public sixty years ago, we have strived to live peacefully among humans. It is you who seek to undo the balance of things."

"You're deluding yourself, Vampire, if you think the balance has only recently been upset. I didn't create this storm, but I am trying to weather it."

"Oh, for Iblis's sake," I said, sick of the bantering and blame-throwing. "What's your offer, Weller?"

"The vampire surrenders himself to my necromancer and undergoes the revenancy," Weller said. "With him under our control, there is no need to torture his children to death."

"Instead, I condemn them to never-ending slavery," Tennyson said.

"The alternative is that I set my revenants loose on the trailer park, and the bloodlust turns your children into the monsters they are. Anyone who isn't killed will be hunted by law enforcement and executed as an example to other vampires who can't control themselves. The line of Master Tennyson will be forever stained in the eyes of his kind. No survivors will be given refuge."

Weller had the connections to follow through with the threat. He had Tennyson bent over a barrel and was just waiting for him to say "go ahead and fuck me." Getting Tennyson's coerced cooperation probably made Weller feel like less of a monster.

Made him an even bigger one in my book.

"In exchange for my cooperation, I would ask for one guarantee," Tennyson said.

I gave him a sharp glare, which he promptly ignored. His eyes showed swirling flecks of red, green, and blue all at once, unable to keep up with his conflicting emotional state. He stared at the dash, his face stony.

"Ask, then," Weller said.

"Immunity from harm for Shiloh Harrison, her mother, Jaxon Dearborn, and the incubus Novak."

My hand jerked the wheel and I struggled to keep control. My throat tightened. I wanted to punch Tennyson in the head. Or kiss him. Maybe both at the same time. His noble streak was going to get him killed in the very permanent way.

"As long as they stay out of my way, I won't seek them out," Weller replied.

Tennyson growled low and deep. "Not good enough. Immunity. They are left alone."

Silence stretched out into a full minute. I strained to hear hints of whispers, any signs of Weller conferring on his end of the line. Finally, he said, "All right, immunity. I will release the incubus once you have submitted to the procedure."

Procedure. Weller made it sound like a hernia operation. I loosened my grip on the steering wheel, wincing at the ache in my knuckles. I wanted to say no and couldn't bring myself to do it. It saved me. It saved my surviving friends. And we still had one last trick up our sleeves to prevent Weller from winning. A trick I'd have to find a way to live with, just as I'd found a way to live with what Kress had made me do.

"Agreed," Tennyson said. "Where?"

"Where are you now?"

He didn't know we had a head start, so I lied, "Just over the state line, heading into Delaware." We were, in fact, thirty miles farther north. Surprise was the only advantage we had left.

Weller made an indeterminate noise. "Switch over to Route 1, keep going north. Call back at this number when you're north of Lewes."

He hung up.

Route 1, also known as Coastal Highway, ran the entire length of the state. We were coming at the small town of Milton from the west, so we didn't need to get on that particular stretch of road. I knew enough about the area to fake it if Weller asked for landmarks. He'd expect our call in another half hour or so, which gave us more than enough time to find him first.

The invisible tether binding me to Tennyson by the Rules of Wishing flared suddenly, glowing brighter in my periphery, a phantom warmth all around me. Oh, no.

"What are you—?"

Shiloh Harrison, my second wish is this.

I winced at the volume of his telepathic voice and braced myself to once again be forced into something I didn't want to do.

In the event the necromancer we seek successfully completes the revenancy spell on me and takes control of my mind, I wish that—

Don't say you want to die, because you're technically already dead and after the revenancy, you'll really be dead, so the wish won't—

—my body be engulfed in flames such that cannot be doused until I am utterly destroyed, so that I cannot be used for another's whim.

The idea of purposely causing Tennyson to spontaneously combust sickened me. I swallowed against rising bile, battling the tether and my blessed djinn instinct to immediately grant the wish. I'd hoped any wish binding me to kill him would be of greater power than his first wish, thereby preventing me from granting it. Either the magic wasn't stronger, or the Rules did not apply to us as they did to others. We'd already circumvented the little fact that vampires can't bind djinn to the Rules. Did they apply at all? What if other vampires found out about this little loophole?

Shiloh?

"Granted," I choked out.

Magic flared hot and fast. A thread of orange flame danced across the tether, me to him, and he winced.

All things considered, it was a well-thought-out wish. I destroyed his body with fire, which left nothing for the necromancer to control. The time and effort would be for nothing. My friends and I would be safe from reprisals (unless Weller went back on his words, which was an entirely possible scenario). There was just one thing—

"What about your line?" I asked. "If I'm the one who causes your death, what happens to the line?"

Tennyson cleared his throat. Some of the tension he'd been wrapped in had loosened its hold, giving his harsh features a softer edge. So nice that he felt better about this, the jerk. "Technically speaking, as my murderer, you would take control of the line. However, as you are not a vampire, I would ask that you verbally relay my wishes that control pass to Drayden."

"And if something goes wrong in Myrtle's Acres and he's killed?"

"Seek out a woman named Jade Tsang."

"All right." I negotiated a wide curve in the road, tapped the brakes, then revved back up to speed. "So what's our actual plan? Other than letting you waltz in and turn yourself over to Weller, I mean."

"We did bring an arsenal. I assumed an assault—"

Something large and vaguely human-shaped darted into the road. My headlights flashed on copper skin and opalescent eyes, and I yanked the wheel. We swerved the roadblock, only to hit a log on the opposite lane. I didn't have time to wonder why a log was in the middle of the road. The Expedition bounced and tilted. Adrenaline surged through me as I fought for control of the wheel, but something else hit us from behind.

We careened off the road, wobbled, then flipped, landing upside down in a ditch. My head slammed against the steering wheel. I dimly heard glass cracking, Tennyson shouting my name, and then nothing at all.

CHAPTER 20

Cow manure.

The first thing I smelled as I struggled to wake up and collect my bearings. It was immediately obvious I was no longer suspended via seat belt from the upside-down Expedition. I was on a cot in a room the size of a broom closet, with a single barred window casting a faint glow of light on the bare wood walls and floor. Testing limbs and extremities, I found nothing broken. Just lots of aches and pains, plus a headache crushing my skull into mush.

I was alive, though, so bonus points for not killing myself in the crash. But why was I here—wherever in heaven here was—instead of a hospital? And why was I surrounded by the faint odor of cow manure?

It wasn't an accident.

The understanding catapulted me into a sitting

position. A maneuver my head immediately protested by beginning a bass line behind my eyes. My vision blurred and my stomach rebelled. I leaned over the edge of the cot and retched, managing to eject only a small amount of liquid from my relatively empty stomach. I didn't remember the last time I'd eaten. Was it even still the same night?

I didn't have to search to know my phone and weapons were gone, but I did anyway. Even the slim blades in my boots were missing. A cut on my fore-head was bandaged and in the near-dark, I found a few scratches and scrapes that were also recently cleaned. Not quite scabbed over, so it had to be the same night. Maybe an hour or two since the accident.

Accident. Yeah, right.

Fear crashed over me like a wave of cold water. They had Tennyson. The necromancer could be turn-ing him right now, and at any moment the tether could flare and demand I send the killing fire.

My legs wobbled on my way to the window. The bars were solid, the frame sealed shut. My room was on the second floor, facing a yard right out of a tractor advertisement. Tall oak trees bordered one side and a red barn the opposite. A clothesline bisected the left edge of the property. A pickup truck was parked near it, its bed loaded with what looked like scrap metal. Random bits of farm equipment littered the rest of the yard, and beyond the barn, I saw the cow pasture.

Was the pentagram inside of the barn? In the house? Somewhere else entirely I couldn't see from here? Where the hell was Novak?

I didn't need the window to get out of here. I jiggled the doorknob. Locked. Not a shocker. Fortunately that didn't matter, either—as long as no one thought to reinforce my room with metal bars. Like teleporting, moving through solid objects was a talent that hurt more than it helped, unless faced with a situation leaving no other choice. Kind of like right now.

In order to pass through something, I had to vibrate my body at an atomic level, fast enough to match the vibrations of the other material and allow our atoms to mingle. Ever the handicap, my human half makes it feel as though my body is on fire, consuming itself from the inside out by white flame and agony. Full djinn did it with a smile on their faces.

I pressed my ear to the door and listened. No footsteps, no breathing, no voices. Bracing for the inevitable agony, I placed both palms flat against the door and closed my eyes. Felt around for the spark of djinn power I usually ignored—the spark that fueled my Quarrel, my wish magic, and my ability to walk through walls.

Found it.

Lava flooded my veins. I was on fire, being ripped apart as I began moving through the wood door. Some tiny, rational part of my brain insisted I'd be foiled by an exterior cage door. But either Weller didn't know this fun fact about djinn, or he assumed I couldn't do it.

I came out on the other side in a haze of agony and fell to my knees. Everything tilted sideways and spun in circles, both clockwise and counterclockwise, fast enough to make me dizzy. I held on until it stopped, fingers digging into the smooth wood floor beneath my hands. Sweat trickled down my nose and cheeks.

And then it was over. The world righted itself, and the consuming pain fled with my dizziness. I swallowed. Rubbed the bridge of my nose. The headache remained a dull thud behind my eyes, a constant reminder of how lucky I was to have survived the car crash at all.

No alarms sounded. No one came running. The hallway was deserted, its plain, ivory walls devoid of personal artifacts. No rug on the old floorboards, which squeaked beneath my feet. I checked four other doors as quietly as I could. One was a bathroom, dirty and in need of an updated tub. Three bedroom doors stood open, displaying their dusty, unused rooms. One had a cot like mine. The other two boasted a couple of spiderwebs.

If the farmhouse had an attic or third floor, I found no evidence or stairway. I reached the top of the stairs and paused to listen. I caught the faint odors of fried food. Someone had cooked recently. The stairs opened to the room below halfway down and would expose me to anyone watching. With a careful breath, I descended as far as I dared, then bent at the waist and with a hand on the banister, peeked.

An empty living room presented itself. The furniture was somewhat dated, but clean. The fireplace had a fresh stack of logs next to it. Attached, off to my right, was a dining room, complete with matching table and chairs, its flat surface covered in used paper plates and plastic cups. Whoever was staying here didn't like doing dishes . . . or cleaning up after themselves.

The kitchen seemed to be off to the left somewhere. My means of escape—the front door!—presented itself directly ahead of me. I tiptoed to the bottom of the stairs. Listened. Halfway to the door I stopped. The house didn't seem to have more upper floors, but that didn't preclude a basement. We were at sea level, so basements weren't common, but they did exist in old homes. Ancient root cellars, mostly.

I tested the front door and found it, not surprisingly, locked. It had a metal plate on the bottom half, probably storm reinforcement or something, but it blocked me from going through. I turned around and spotted another door nearby, hidden in the corner of the living room like a dirty secret. Probably a coat closet, but I checked it anyway. The knob surprised me by turning beneath my grip.

It squealed softly, and before I had the door open more than a few inches, the thick odor of waste wafted out on a gust of hot air. I swallowed back the need to cough and retch, then pulled the door open completely. And stared.

Coat closet, sans coats. Its only decoration was Vincent, curled haphazardly on the floor like a sack of dropped laundry. His ankles and wrists were hand-cuffed, and a length of cloth was tied over his mouth and eyes. He was pale, bare-chested, dressed only in a pair of white boxers stained with filth.

I couldn't find any tears for him. Only a cool splash of directed rage. Directed right at Adam Weller and his pals. I crouched next to Vincent and, even though I saw the soft rise and fall of his chest, pressed two shaking fingertips to his throat. Felt a thready pulse.

"Thank Iblis," I whispered. "Vincent?"

Nothing. He was out cold, either from drugs, magic, or a serious concussion. Then I felt the wetness coating the side of his neck I couldn't see. My fingertips came back stained with blood, and I swallowed a scream. Turned his head a little to the side and saw the twin puncture marks. He'd been drained to the point of unconsciousness. My rage quadrupled.

I kissed his forehead, wanting to promise all sorts of things to him. I just didn't have the time.

I hated myself for closing the door on him, but I couldn't risk someone entering the house and realiz-ing I was moving around. I had to stop the necroman-cer first. Then I'd call an ambulance and finally, I'd beat the shit out of Weller for every one of my friends he'd hurt.

I tiptoed across the living room, moving into the kitchen. It was the only somewhat updated room in the house, with new appliances and paper sacks of groceries littering the counter. Dirty pots and pans filled the sink. Their combined stink of bacon grease, old soup broth, and scorched cheese turned my stomach. Gross.

I hazarded a peek out the back door. Still facing the backyard, I saw nothing I hadn't noticed from the upstairs—strike that. I had a decent view of a small shed perpendicular to the barn that had probably been hidden from above by one of those massive oak trees. Inside of the shed was the twisted, damaged shell of the Expedition. My weapons were there, unless they'd been seized, and the vehicle's appearance only cemented the notion that Weller had caused the accident. But how had he known where we'd be on the road?

Yet another mystery that would need to wait.

A quick check of the pantry located my prize—cellar door. I pulled back the dead bolt and opened it. The hinges squealed. I winced. Down below, someone grunted. I knew that grunt.

Hope lit a flare in my belly. I flipped a switch by the basement door. A single bulb brightened the dirt-dug room below and the rickety wooden stairs descending to a hard-packed earth floor. The grunt repeated itself, closer to a growl this time. The old stairs were impossible to take quietly, so I settled on quickly. I hit the bottom and turned to my right.

Novak was chained to the dirt wall, naked except for his black boxers. His legs were immobilized, as were his chest and shoulders. His hands, though, were clamped into twin containers of brackish liquid that fizzed like peroxide. Sweat drizzled down his ebony skin, and his mouth was twisted in pain. His dark eyes stared at me as if he'd never seen me before.

"You're alive," I said as utter relief hit me square in the gut. The weight of it made my knees wobble.

He didn't speak. The bulging muscles in his throat and neck spoke to his imminent loss of control. I let my gaze drop to the vats of liquid, and it finally hit me—they were torturing him. I doubted it was acid. That lacked finesse. It's a little known fact that demons are allergic to salt. They can't ingest salty foods, and the ocean is a huge problem, which made Novak hiding on a peninsula surrounded by salt water rather ingenious. Likely it's what they'd stuck his hands into.

The chains were secured with simple padlocks. I raced back upstairs and rummaged in the drawers, haste making me a little stupid. No keys, of course, so I found a kitchen knife with a narrow point and some kind of skewer thingie. I wasn't much of a lockpick, but I had to try something. I'd seen Jaxon do it a dozen times.

"Hold on, pal," I said to Novak as I grabbed the lock near his right arm. He merely grunted, then closed his eyes. I swallowed hard. After a minute or so of wiggling and turning, the lock popped open. I unwounded the chains and pulled his right hand free of the vat. The skin was completely blistered, individual fingers looking as though they'd been created from dozens of tiny brown marbles instead of skin over bone. Some of the blisters burst and wept.

The same length of chain wound around his neck and down his left arm. A moment later, I had his second hand out. I didn't have to examine it to know how it looked, and the deep release of air from Novak sent a surge of fury through me. Someone had hurt my friend badly.

He sagged away from the wall and somehow remained on his own two feet. I didn't try to prop him up or offer my arm. He was a demon and too proud to accept my help as long as he could manage alone. It didn't stop me from planting a kiss on his chin, as close as I could get to his face without him stooping.

"Sorry I took so long," I said.

He shook his head, dismissing my apology. With a sweaty forearm, he wiped his equally sweaty brow and flinched. "Kathleen?"

My chest ached. I gave him the highlights of the last few hours while he gathered his strength. His thoughts were impossible to guess from the stone-cold glare on his face. I finished with the crash, waking up here, and finding Vincent alive and still (as far as I could tell) human.

Novak flared his nostrils. "Don't remember much after the crash," he said. "Weller tried to make me talk, tell him what I knew about what you were up to." He snorted like a furious bull. "Waste of his time. I'll rip his blessed heart out through his throat for Kathleen," he said.

And Jaxon. For all of us.

"We need to find the pentagram," I said, starting toward the stairs. "They've had Tennyson long enough to start the revenancy spell."

"Thought they had to torture him a while before it could work."

I glared over my shoulder. He frowned, but didn't argue further. His bulky body made silence on the stairs impossible. I darted to the top and kept lookout as he ascended. The house remained silent. Weller obviously hadn't expected me to walk through walls, or he'd have had a guard or two on the place. Score one for the good guys.

"They towed our vehicle here, so with any luck we've got weapons," I said quietly once Novak joined me in the kitchen.

He raided the drawers with hands that looked ready to shrivel up and fall off, and produced a handful of knives—steak, chopping, chef, and one little paring knife. Lacking pockets in his boxers, he palmed what he could manage, then handed three over to me. Better safe than sorry, his intent frown said to me. I agreed. We still had to get across the yard, and lights from the farm and half-moon gave us few shadows.

I slipped out the back door and onto a small porch. Two faded wicker armchairs kept company with a rusty, potbellied barbecue grill. Faint odors of charred meat mixed with the faraway tang of cow manure. I'd never understand how people lived so close to such a nauseating stink.

The barn was directly across from us and the likeliest place to find the pentagram. More than fifty feet of empty yard lay between us and the shed sheltering our weapon stash. Another twenty or so from the shed to the barn. Watchful eyes could be anywhere: the trees, the upper level of the barn, hiding in the shed itself.

A tremor tore down my spine, spreading chills along my back and shoulders. The cool scent of cloves came out of nowhere, and I recognized it immediately. Tennyson was in pain. I sought the tether. It was so faint as to almost not exist anymore, tapering off only a few feet from me, as though dissolved by stronger magic.

Stronger magic. That horrified me on so many levels. If Tennyson was projecting pain this far and through so much magic, then the spell had begun.

"Shi?" Novak hissed.

I swallowed and then pointed at the shed. "There. Weapons."

He lumbered across the yard, not quite at full

steam, and I followed. I expected warning shouts, maybe even a few bullets to rip through me. Weller apparently had something more elegant planned, because a few steps from the shed doors, six figures emerged from the shadows. Novak pulled up short, and I nearly slammed into his back.

The vampires—more from Azuriah's line?—bared their fangs, eyes swirling a familiar red-black. Impossible. How could the necromancer control these six, plus the twelve at Myrtle's Acres, and still perform the spell to change Tennyson? They didn't give me a chance to truly ponder it. The six attacked without hesitation, swarming us like vermin.

I slashed with my knives and ducked blows, letting adrenaline work away the last of my headache— promising a new, stronger one later—and propelled my body into the fray. Novak roared. Blood spurted. The vamps hissed as they darted in and out, slashing with their claws and snapping with their jaws. I lunged at one's throat, but it pulled away before my butcher knife made contact and I realized that they weren't trying to kill us.

They were distracting us.

Novak seemed to get this, too, and bellowed his frustration. No sense in being quiet about it now. Sick of the dancing, I tackled the nearest vamp and sliced her throat as we fell. Hot blood poured over my hands, and I rolled away. She floundered in the grass. I took another swing, hoping to sever her head from her neck and truly end her, but another vamp hit me from behind.

We went rolling. I held the blade away from my body, in no mood to cut myself and get another infection. The vamp on my back slammed my forehead into the ground. Bright lights burst behind my eyes. I snapped my head backward and connected with cartilage. Blood flowed down my back.

Behind me somewhere, Novak made a terrible sound—something close to agonized ecstasy, and I knew the demon in him was rejoicing in the slaughter. He was also projecting a lot of pheromones, because the muscles in my abdomen clenched of their own volition. Dear Iblis, I did not need this right now. Ignoring my sudden arousal, I shook off the broken-nose vamp and rolled to my knees. He lunged, and I buried the blade in his throat hard enough to protrude from the back of his neck. He fell.

Novak dropped someone's severed arm and snorted long and loud. Pieces of four vampires littered the ground around him, and his dark skin was coated with shiny crimson. It dripped from his bald head, his ears and nose, down his arms and blistered fingers. He bared his teeth at me, chest heaving, a deadly fire in his eyes. He also had a massive hard-on that his boxers were having a hard time hiding.

So rarely have I ever seen our incubus lose control. His body shook with small tremors, head to toe, as he fought an internal battle to remain calm. Meanwhile,

I fought his infernal pheromones—ice, ocean, cold, frozen tundra, unsexy things—and battled against their power. If he caught scent of me in a half-aroused state . . . oh, boy, he'd lose it completely. And a bloodlust-crazed incubus was not gentle—whether or not it killed me, he'd never forgive himself for it.

Still kneeling on the ground, I remained still. Focused. Calm. Even though my insides quivered like jelly. I didn't want to hurt him, but I wouldn't let him—

He released a massive breath, and the fire in his eyes died. Then they widened. I felt the whoosh of air behind me, but I couldn't move fast enough. The barrel of a gun pressed between my shoulder blades. Novak screamed something indecipherable. The ground by his feet burst twice, gunshots cracking off to my left. Another figure circled into my peripheral vision, armed with a shiny new SIG Sauer.

Lars Patterson held his weapon on Novak. The golden-skinned man's face was impassive, almost bored. Novak ignored him, though, his intense glare focused on the person behind me.

"My, my, you've been busy." The familiar voice sent icy daggers through my guts. It couldn't be.

Novak bared his teeth, the furious snarl only proving what I didn't want to be true. A hand bunched in my hair and hauled me to my feet, the gun never leaving my back. Kathleen leaned over my shoulder, her cool breath fanning my face.

"So glad you could join us for the finale," she said.

CHAPTER 21

In the face of discovering one of my supposed allies was a lying traitorous bitch, I thought I'd be angrier. I expected to be furious, disgusted, maybe even feel idiotic for not seeing it sooner. Instead, all I felt was sad. Sad for how she'd fooled us all, sad for Julius, sad for everyone who'd been hurt because of her and Weller.

Okay, and a little stupid for not seeing through her in the first place.

"You do realize what this means?" I asked, amazed at my calm tone.

"And what's that, Shiloh?" Her breath was still in my ear, cool and ticklish. "You must now swear to kill me for my traitorous ways?"

"No—it means no Christmas bonus for you." I jammed my elbow back, striking the hard planes of her abdomen. She grunted. The butt of her gun came down between my shoulder blades, and a bolt of lightning slammed through my head. I dropped to my knees, stunned by the blow, my brain once again throbbing inside my skull.

"Behave yourself," Kathleen spat.

"Why, so you can kill me later, instead of sooner?"

"Do not tempt me."

Before my fuzzy brain could puzzle that statement, a phone buzzed behind me. I glanced at Novak. His glare hadn't shifted from Kathleen, even though Lars was bearing down on him with a loaded weapon. Kathleen answered her phone with a clipped, "Yes?" Pause. "I'll bring them down."

Uh-oh.

She grabbed my arm and yanked me up. I stumbled. Even my djinn half could only withstand so many blows to the head in one hour. Novak came to my side. We allowed our captors to guide us forward, toward the wide double doors of the barn. It was a traditional shape and size, painted the usual red with white trim. Upper doors and a pulley hinted at a hay loft above.

"Go on through," Kathleen said.

I reached for the door. She sighed and gave me a mighty shove. I raised my shoulder, expecting to slam into wood. Instead, I stumbled through the illusion of barn doors and came to a knee-scraping stop just inside. Much like the floor of the storage unit, the barn was an illusion to hide something more insidious.

The metal structure was built in the shape of a pentagram, and it rose up like a menacing silver circus tent. The wall was only a few feet shy of the barn's illusion, and a metal door was a few steps away, closed. Power thrummed through the metal—not silver, but something powerful and able to conduct energy. It must have been constructed to amplify the necromancer's powers.

Novak touched my shoulder with his blistered hand. I stood up. Dirt mixed with the blood on my hands to create a thick paste, which I wiped on the seat of my jeans. More yuck. Lovely.

Kathleen circled around us and yanked open the metal door. Sage, rosemary, and half a dozen other herbs wafted out, carried on the sound of an agonized scream. My heart hammered against my ribs. Tennyson. I jerked forward. Kathleen raised her gun, a SIG Sauer that matched Lars's, and sneered at me.

"Behave yourself inside, or I will have to restrain you," she said.

The moment I crossed the door's threshold, unholy magic hit me like a hammer and whooshed the air from my lungs. My scalp tingled and itched, and I balled my hands into tight fists. My tether flared and flickered, struggling to maintain its connection through the haze of power between me and my wisher, who lay strapped to a table in the center of the five-sided room.

Like the dugout we'd found, symbols were set in

the earth in all five corners. These symbols, though, were made of metal poured into the etched ground and left to harden. A garden of dried herbs hung from ropes dangling from the ceiling. A tray of instruments stood next to the head of the table, as well as a clay bowl the size of a watermelon on its own freestanding pedestal. Red smoke coiled up from its interior, the odor vaguely sulfuric.

Tennyson had been stripped and secured with silver manacles around his wrists, ankles, waist, and throat. Blood dripped to the floor from the dozen or more wounds carved into his bare chest and torso. He turned his head and crimson headlights stared at me. His mouth was pursed tight, lips already pierced by his own fangs.

I'm sorry, I thought at him as loudly as I could.

He closed his eyes and tilted his head away. I choked on my own breath. Next to me, Novak growled again.

I paid attention to the other people in the room. Adam Weller stood at the foot of the table, dressed in a black robe that made him look like a cult reject. I'd only met him in person a handful of times—same salt-and-pepper hair, same wide blue eyes and round face, same dark beard. But this man was a stranger, an enemy of the worst caliber, and I was hit with sudden, all-consuming hatred for him. He, on the other hand, seemed mildly annoyed.

Two strangers stood in flanking positions on the

far side of the room—a tall, thin man with black hair and an unfriendly sneer, and a female werewolf in half form, fur thick on her naked, semi-humanoid body, teeth elongated and eyes wild. The man was one of Weller's, I was sure. The she-wolf I didn't know.

A fourth figure was the necromancer himself. He stood at the head of the table, near the smoking bowl and arrangement of weapons, with what looked like a silver melon baller in his hand and a wad of smoking herbs in the other. He wore a black robe identical to Weller's, a gold amulet with an embedded red jewel the size of an apricot, and a look of intense, closed-eyed concentration. Long, wild white hair was pulled back to the nape of his neck. He was old, craggy-skinned and sunken-cheeked, evidence of a hard life and the physical destruction of black magic. Abuse magic and it abused you right back.

I didn't recognize him, but attention zeroed in on his left hand, which bore a gold triskelion ring. A Celtic symbol that didn't fit with the rest of his ensemble.

"You'd have been smart to stay where I put you," Weller said. His voice had a faint Southern twang.

"I don't like being locked up while my friends are tortured," I shot back.

"I told you I'd release you."

"Yeah, well, after you crashed my car, I didn't have a lot of faith in you keeping your fucking word."

Weller made a face that said my suspicions were

correct. He would have recruited us or killed us. Probably turned us over to become revenants ourselves—if revenancy even worked on djinn or demons.

The necromancer spoke angry words I didn't understand. The inflection was familiar, though. Some mad mix of Russian and . . . something else. Eyes still closed, he reached across Tennyson with the melon baller and dug it into the vampire Master's chest. Tennyson screamed, his agony shattering my heart. I caught a shriek of my own and forced it back. Hatred burned in my chest as the necromancer scooped the flesh and dropped it into the smoldering bowl. It popped and sizzled. The wound sent more blood dripping to the packed-earth floor.

My stomach twisted and bile rose up. I swallowed hard, nails digging into my palms, my fists so tight I thought my knuckles would split from the pressure.

Weller retreated to our side of the room so as not to disturb the precious ritual playing out in front of us. Novak shook from head to toe, and I could imagine the strain of remaining in command of his faculties. The blood and agony had to be seriously screwing with his control.

Bless my own magical limitations. I couldn't use my magic to harm anyone, and I couldn't manipulate the situation without a wish. I had no weapons. The she-wolf seemed ready to attack at any moment, as though the blood was getting to her, too. The tall man just looked bored. Lars was still somewhere behind me, and Kathleen wore a pensive expression I couldn't quite decipher.

Maybe if I tried launching myself at the necromancer . . . if I could somehow interrupt the spell, it could buy us all time.

Kathleen was just as likely to shoot me in the back as soon as I started moving. Traitorous bitch.

As if needing those simple words, my fury bubbled to the surface and I whipped around to glare at her. She blinked. "Did you stand here like this while they tortured Julius to death, you coldhearted half-breed?" I said. "You gonna stand there when they do this to me, too? And Novak? Huh?"

Her cold eyes narrowed, and she drew back her upper lip, exposing protruding fangs. "Remember yourself, child," she spat back. "You've not seen the reach of my temper."

I punched her in the mouth. Her fang cut my knuckles, and it hurt like a son of a bitch, but I didn't care. Watching her stumble backward, lip split and oozing blood, gave me such a wonderful sense of satisfaction I didn't see Weller move until he hit me. I fell to my knees, ears ringing, positive my aching skull would start oozing brain matter out of my ears.

"Don't do that again," Weller said. "You won't have to wait much longer to see real magic in action."

"Black magic," I said. All voices sounded underwater. Gray fuzzed the edges of my vision. Not good. He'd hit me with something solid. The butt of a gun, maybe. I wouldn't be feeling it so awful if it had been his fist. Warmth trickled down the back of my neck. The back of my skull felt strange.

Crap.

"And there is nothing more powerful, is there? It's for the greater good, Ms. Harrison."

If my head didn't hurt so much, I'd have snorted. Maybe laughed. All I really wanted to do was lie down in the dirt and sleep until my skull fracture went away.

Shiloh.

I jerked my head up, which released another wave of dizziness. Tennyson's eyes were still closed, every muscle in his body tense, but it had been his voice. *I hear you*, I thought back.

My final wish . . . The tether hummed and fritzed, struggling to maintain a connection as he invoked its power.

The necromancer made a strange noise, then said something in a mash-up of Russian and . . . was that Gaelic? It hit me suddenly, as conversations with both Piotr and Brighid rolled back. Brighid hadn't actually seen Adelay's dead body, and Piotr said the book had been stolen from him. By its rightful owner, perhaps? Someone already incredibly versed in the black arts, so he'd have the power to control so many revenants at once.

The necromancer was Lord Robert Fucking Adelay himself.

"Adelay," I said, mostly to be sure.

The necromancer's lips twitched but it was enough of a confirmation for me.

Tennyson's head listed toward me and his eyes opened. Blue battled the red for dominance. Perspiration bathed his face, pinking the skin. Weller was talking to Adelay, but I ignored them both.

I wish—

Tennyson's words were lost to a blur of motion. With a furious glare, Adelay hurled the thing I'd called a melon baller at my chest. White-hot agony exploded below my left breast and that lung stopped working. I don't think I screamed. Someone else did. Chaotic movement on all sides made no sense as I fell.

Slamming into the dirt onto my shoulder didn't hurt like it probably should have. The fire in my chest blocked out everything else, even the intense pain in my head. I thought I saw Novak and the she-wolf clash mid-air in a flurry of claws and snarls. Possible. Then I thought I saw Kathleen tackle Weller from behind. Not as possible—weren't they working together?

The magic in the room roared in my ears, and the tether between Tennyson and me sparked and demanded attention. I had no idea what he'd wished for, but it didn't matter to the magic in me screaming to obey. I lolled my head, barely able to see the outline of Tennyson's body on top of the table.

"Granted," I hissed. Warm, metallic liquid bubbled

into my mouth, and I fought hard against the over-whelming need to cough. Maybe I'd vomit a little, instead. I really wanted to sleep.

Tennyson launched himself off the table, the bands holding him down tearing as if they were made of paper (and just maybe they were now). He pivoted with amazing grace and speed, considering his chest looked like it had been chewed on by rats, and caught Adelay by surprise.

Someone kicked my foot. Behind me came the squishy sound of a fist striking wet flesh. Novak's fa-miliar roar of triumph bellowed through the metal tent. So much happening, and I was transfixed by the sight of Tennyson with his arms around Adelay's chest and waist. The way the naked Master vampire's red eyes glowed like hot coals and his fangs glis-tened before he sank them into Adelay's neck.

Tennyson didn't drink. He ravaged. He ripped and tore and soon blood flowed freely from both men. One grew stronger as the other faded. Red light changed to blue as fury was overcome by the influx of power.

Then Lars was crouching in front of me, and I didn't have the strength to tell him to move. That I wanted to see. He was a bad guy anyway.

Novak, his ebony skin streaked with fresh blood, sank to his knees next to Lars. A tuft of gray fur was stuck to Novak's cheek. I tried to raise my hand to brush it off and failed. Neither hand worked. I couldn't do anything, except lie there and gasp. More blood rose into my throat, choking me. The magic around me shifted, tightening and then bursting like a fireworks display, breaking gossamer threads in front of my eyes. Bright swirls of red and green and yellow and all colors in between. No one else seemed to see them.

No one else sensed magic like I did.

Up I went, lifted suddenly into strong arms and whisked away. Frozen spice surrounded me. Laid me down on something hard and flat. Tennyson's face hovered over mine, his eyes bright blue. Normally pale skin was flushed with blood and the aura of power—more power than from a normal feeding.

Of course, he'd fed off someone tapped into black magic. That had to have been a rush.

"Let me heal you, Shiloh, please." Oh, right, he was talking. I tried to focus past the gray blur in front of my eyes. My good lung had stopped compensating for the loss of the other, and then neither worked.

I couldn't seem to nod my head or form words. I mustered my last tendrils of strength as my heartbeat slowed, and I sent a single thought at him: *Yes*.

He sliced his arm with his fangs, flaying flesh from wrist to elbow. Hands held me down as blood dripped into my mouth. Pressure pulled away from my chest, then exploded in blinding flashes of agony. Heat followed and on its heels came the gentle caress of magic.

I stopped fighting.

CHAPTER 22

Shhh, Shiloh, it's all right. You're safe now.

Am I dead?

No, you're resting.

How come I can hear you if I'm resting?

I'm uncertain. Perhaps it is the massive dose of blood we shared. The necromancer's power was still fresh. It may be enhancing our bond.

Bond? You shout in my head.

Am I shouting now?

No. You're kind of quiet. It's almost relaxing.

Then continue to relax. You have much healing to do.

How do I shut this off?

Simply stop thinking. Embrace the darkness for a while. I will be here when you wake.

Okay.

I blinked awake, pushing away the last threads of sleep still fogging up my mind. I was flat on my back on something soft and covered with a blanket. The rough, crossbeam ceiling was unfamiliar, and faint odors of grease and cow manure rolled my stomach. I pitched sideways and vomited over the side of the sofa, spewing a bit of red liquid onto a faded, floral print carpet.

Why was I vomiting blood?

Oh yeah, I'd swallowed some. Again.

"You're awake," a smooth voice said.

I flopped back against the sofa's under-stuffed pillow, too tired to give Tennyson anything other than a flat, "Duh. Alive, too."

He squatted next to me, bringing us to almost eye level. Brilliant copper-penny eyes smiled at me, though his mouth remained in a straight line. He'd found a t-shirt and jeans somewhere and the informal outfit, combined with his long, red-stained hair, made him look like an aging hippie. His skin was still mildly flushed, almost a natural shade of ivory. Foreign power rippled inside of him—was this new magic a friendly guest or a cancerous invader?

"You stopped breathing, and your heart nearly failed," he said. "I feared you were too far gone for me to help."

"I'm unpredictable."

"You are that. As are your friends."

I cast around the room, but saw no one else. "Where's Novak?"

"With Lars and Kathleen, tearing down the structure."

"Huh?"

"Once the necromancer died, the barn illusion fell. We felt it foolish to leave such a thing standing."

Was he playing stupid, because I really wasn't in the mood. "With who?"

Understanding dawned. "Ah, yes. My apologies. It seems Kathleen Allard is—what's the term? A double agent. Or, rather, a double-double agent. It's—never mind that for now. Just know she works for a shadow agency whose purpose is to hunt and destroy practitioners of black magic. She went undercover against Weller a few months before he supposedly planted her into your Para-Marshal team."

My brain bounced that around for a little while. It'd be easier if I came at it when I felt less like I'd been hit repeatedly with a baseball bat. "And Lars?"

"In collusion with Kathleen. His death was fabricated for the reasons we assumed. He was meant to grow in his role as a spinner and use his abilities to further Weller's agenda."

"Guess he furthered his other boss's agenda more."

"Perhaps."

"Do we know who they work for?"

"Neither will disclose the information at this time."

Which meant a big fat no, and very likely not in the future, either. Kathleen didn't want to tell us, fine. I'd figure out how to throw some formal charges her way. See how her shadow boss liked that. If I even had a job with the Marshals' Office. One Para-Marshal team leader was a revenant without a Master. The other one was a turncoat who'd used our resources to further his own agenda, not to mention a laundry list of kidnappings and attempted murders as long as my arm. Kidnappings . . . hostages . . . .

"Your people!" I sat up so fast I almost clipped him in the jaw with my elbow. My chest throbbed with the effort, and I flopped back down flat with a pained gasp. The couch wheezed, ancient springs protesting my weight. "Sweet Iblis, that hurt."

"Then do not sit up," Tennyson said with a wry smile. "And my people are fine. I was . . . I am unable to explain it."

I clasped his arm gently, an automatic gesture that didn't really register until he looked down at my hand. I didn't pull away. His skin was still warm, almost alive.

"For one brief moment," he said, struggling for the words, "I felt my lost twelve again. I felt them through the power of the necromancer's blood, and I was able to free them of their chains to him. They are truly gone now and, I hope, at peace." His free hand rested on mine, a gentle touch. "I am glad to have given them that."

"I'm sorry you had to lose them."

"As am I. But no more have been lost. And . . . I was also able to use what power I had to free your friend Julius."

The news relieved me more than upset me. No one should have to spend the rest of their after-life as a confused, bodiless head. Especially not a man who'd been so strong and helped so many—a memory tarnished by his willingness to take money for renting a storage locker and not ask why. I still had so many questions that needed answering in the days ahead, but still . . . Julius had been my friend.

Tennyson continued, "Your authorities are quite angry, however. They have quietly detained my people and moved them to a nearby high school gymnasium until this can be sorted. The trailer park residents have been set free."

Thank Iblis. The one thing I'd set out to do since our relationship began was get those vampires the hell out of Myrtle's Acres. I hadn't counted on every-thing else that had come about because of one simple phone call, including a tentative friendship with a Master vampire. After everything we'd gone through in the last few days, I definitely counted him among my allies. Maybe even a friend.

One of the few I had left.

"You were quite clever in deducing the necro-mancer's identity," Tennyson said. "Brighid will not be happy to learn Adelay was alive these past few centuries."

"At least he's really dead this time."

"Too true."

"Did you find the rest of the vampires? The wolves?" I asked.

"The vampires, yes, and they have been released. I will face repercussions for the deaths of Azuriah's people, but that is something to be handled later."

I was way too tired to make him explain further.

"As for the wolves," he said, "they are not on the premises. Kathleen says she was never privy to Weller's plans regarding the wolves, nor their current location."

Fantastic. So much for that vacation with fruity drinks and umbrellas. "Vincent," I said. "He was unconscious. How is he?"

"He is shaken and confused, but alive. He'll suffer no lasting effects from his blood loss, as it was Kathleen who drained him. She said she was careful."

Vincent was alive, which was amazing news, but he was also unlikely to want to have anything to do with me now, after all of this. His last phone message to me suggested deepening our relationship. Most likely, he'd delete me from his cell phone and suggest I take a flying leap off the nearest bridge. I wouldn't begrudge him such a thing. He was safer with a girlfriend who didn't get him kidnapped by crazy, power-hungry US Para-Marshals and their necromancers.

Nine months had been a pretty good run.

"He was quite concerned for your well-being," Tennyson said. My feelings must have been telegraphing across my face. Or he was reading my mind again. Awesome.

"Is he still here?"

"Outside drinking orange juice and overseeing the deconstruction, I believe. I would help, as well, but the sun is up. Would you like me to fetch him?"

"No, it can wait." All I really wanted was my bed at home. Home in my apartment, where it was safe and quiet and no one tried to stab me with a silver melon baller. I couldn't go back to those great nights Vincent and I had spent together, enjoying each other's bodies, but I could climb into bed with the memories. It was likely all I'd bed with for a good long while.

Tennyson grunted. His mouth was pulled tight, his eyes narrow.

I blinked. "What?"

"Your thoughts are distracting."

I blushed scarlet, my cheeks heating enough to catch the sofa on fire. "Then quit listening."

"You took my blood barely two hours ago, Shiloh. The effects are fresh and difficult to block, but they will diminish."

"You said that last time."

"It has only been a few days. More time is obviously

required. You are of a peculiar nature, and magic is not an exact science."

The oddity of his statement made me grin. "My peculiar nature, huh? Is that my human half or my djinn half?"

"I was going to say it was your insufferable sarcasm, but that's beginning to grow on me, too."

"Duly noted." I turned my hand palm up, and after a moment's hesitation, he pressed his palm to mine. Our fingers threaded. My pulse thrummed beneath his touch. "Thank you for saving me. Again."

"You are very welcome. Again. And thank you for saving me."

"I can't say I did all that much."

"You did more than you realize." He smiled. "You made my wish come true."

Ugh—corny. Yet I couldn't help but blush a little more at the intensity behind his words.

Metal clanged outside, and then a brief cheer rose. I grinned at their victory over the necromancer's construct. So much time and energy and blood put into one man's greed, and we'd taken it down with a crash and a cheer. Not just a man, though—a three-hundred-year-old necromancer and the marshal pulling his strings.

What a weird job I have.

Dozens of other questions remained to be answered, but my exhausted mind wouldn't let me focus enough to ask them. I needed another nap, that was all. Another nap and I'd be fine, ready and capable of running my team again.

Such as it was. Kathleen wasn't truly mine. Julius was dead. Novak would need time off until his hands healed. Something sad was coming from Tennyson, and I wasn't sure why. "What else?" I asked.

"Shiloh," Tennyson said, hesitation in his voice. "Do you recall the bargain you made with—" His phone rang, cutting off his question. I stared, unsure which bargain he meant, and waited for him to give the phone a clipped, "I'll let her know," before hanging up.

"Your mother," he reported. "She wanted me to tell you she's holding down the fort and fielding several inquiries into recent events."

"I don't doubt it." Mom was still safe and at the compound. Great news. Which didn't explain the pensive look on his face. "What?"

"You remember her?"

I stared. "Of course I remember my mother, why shouldn't I?"

"And your father?"

"Is there a reason I should have forgotten about my parents?" I was becoming genuinely annoyed at his questions. What the hell kind of reason would I have for forgetting my parents? "What, Tennyson?"

"Nothing," he said, shaking his head. "I suppose my belief was mistaken. Your mother also reports

Jaxon is up and about and demanding to know everything that is happening. He is recovering well."

I frowned and tilted my head to the side, which was hard to do lying down. "Who's Jaxon?"

He closed his eyes, jaw tightening, and when he looked at me again, sadness and understanding warred for attention in their depths. He leaned closer and touched my cheek with the knuckle of one finger. His gentleness was alarming. "Never mind, child," Tennyson said softly. "Get some rest now. You'll meet him again shortly."

Again. I wanted to ask, but fatigue stole my words. So I let myself drift awhile, hoping the pain would be gone when I finally woke to face the tasks yet left to complete, and a little curious to meet this mysterious man named Jaxon.

ACKNOWLEDGMENTS

Shiloh Harrison came to me many years ago, while I was busy writing other urban fantasy stories, and she very stubbornly stayed put. Her entire story was actually birthed after a Friday night movie binge with my best friend, while drinking homemade sangria (fun times!), so I wrote it and then put it away. Then an opportunity came along to write a short story for the Carniepunk anthology, and I had great fun exploring Shiloh's backstory. So thank you to all the readers who've asked for more of Shiloh, Julius, and friends over the years. This one's for you!

Thank you to my agent, Jonathan Lyons, for continuing to believe in me these past ten (TEN!) years. It's been a long and winding road, my friend. Thank you to my editor, David Pomerico, for taking a chance on this series. You were there for the start of my publishing journey, and I've very much enjoyed working with you again.

And a huge thank you to my loyal and patient readers. It's been a while since I've gone old-school urban fantasy, and I think Dreg City fans will find a lot to love in Shiloh's world of the Strays.

Shi and the Para-Marshals may have prevented the necromancer from enslaving the vampires, but there's still the issue of the missing werewolves they are no closer to solving. And the Alphas are only going to sit idly by for so long before they do what needs to be done to ensure their Packs are safe. No matter what the cost.

Read

STRAY MOON

On-sale from Harper Voyager
Impulse Summer 2019!

ABOUT THE AUTHOR

Born and raised in Southern Delaware, **KELLY MEDING** survived five years in the hustle and bustle of Northern Virginia, only to retreat back to the peace and sanity of the Eastern Shore. An avid reader and film buff, she discovered Freddy Krueger at a very young age, and has since had a lifelong obsession with horror, science fiction, and fantasy, on which she blames her interest in vampires, psychic powers, superheroes, and all things paranormal.